SHADOWS OF THE CHILDREN

* * * * * *

BOOK NINE

* * * * * *

D.W. Neuman

ALSO BY D.W. NEUMAN

FICTION

Shadow Series
Shadows of the Mind – Book One
Shadows of the Soul – Book Two
Shadows of the Service – Book Three
Shadows of the Past – Book Four
Shadows of the Heart – Book Five
Shadows of the Sand – Book Six
Shadows of the Serpent – Book Seven
Shadows of the Future – Book Eight
Shadows of the Children – Book Nine

ISBN (978-0-9907247-6-6)

Carol.
Your love of these characters transcends
time and space itself. Thank you for
your continued support! One more ☺.

Connie.
Your love is endless, just like your
cuddles. Every day is a constant
reminder on how lucky I really am.
I love you.

The true sign of intelligence is not knowledge
but imagination.

Albert Einstein

1
Sat Nov 3, 2001

Robert Duncan, the Director of the Central Intelligence Agency, slowly opened his eyes and winced.

Ouch, my head.

He attempted to touch his throbbing head but realized his hands were restrained.

Why can't I move?

He blinked a few times, clearing the haze from his eyes and focused on the man who stood in front of the chair he was secured to. Confusion swept through him.

"Carl?" he managed to say. "What the hell's going on?" Robert looked down and tried to move his arms and legs again to no avail. "Why do you have me strapped down?"

Carl smiled.

"Release me right now," Robert demanded.

"I don't think so," Carl replied. "You have to realize that I went to great lengths to setup your abduction, and within a matter of hours no less, so why would I just let you go?"

Robert continued to struggle. "What's this all about?"

"You might as well save your energy, Director; you're going to need it. Besides, we have much to discuss."

"Like what? Have you forgotten that you're a member of the CIA's Special Activities Division? You answer to me!"

Carl chuckled, walked over and put his face inches away from the DCI's. "Not anymore." He stood up and made his way behind Robert. "Just so you know, I have an array of instruments back here I wish you could see."

"What do you want!? What are you after!?"

"Information of course."

"Go to hell Carl," the Director spat out. "You're fucking with the wrong person."

"It's funny, Director. You keep calling me Carl, but Carl isn't here."

Robert suddenly remembered what Thomas had told him over the phone. *Carl and Eliot aren't who they used to be.*

"I think you may know me by another name."

Carl came around, stared the DCI in the face and sneered.

"I'm Nikolay Dmitriev, and trust me when I say we have all the time in the world to get acquainted."

"What you're saying is impossible. I know for a fact that Nikolay Dmitriev was killed four years ago."

"Actually I can't argue with that because you're absolutely right. I was killed on that beach in Cuba when Sam Paige put a bullet in my head."

The DCI's face reflected his confusion. "What? How could you possibly know that?"

Nikolay stepped away, pulled another chair over and sat down facing his prisoner. "Tell me Robert, can you honestly believe that what I'm telling you is out of the realm of possibility, especially after what I know you've been involved in as of late?"

The DCI closed his mouth.

"This body I inhabit was captured and held by Hamid Emal Habibi, along with Sam, Bill and Eliot, the last three survivors of the six-man team you green-lighted into Afghanistan. But when Thomas Clark, and his son, came to our rescue and took us to the other world, well, this body's previous owner experienced a coordinated attack. And after that assault I emerged from the portal, as healthy and alive as ever. I mean, look at me. I'm young, healthy and most importantly, alive."

2

If he is who he says he is then shit, this is bad. "If you are indeed Nikolay, then what do you want?"

Nikolay smiled. "I'm glad to see you've come around to my way of thinking Robert."

"I said, what do you want?"

"Fair enough. The truth is I haven't fully adjusted to this new body or completely thought through what really I want to do with my new found freedom. However, from the short time I've spent back in the land of the living I know I want the one thing I had before; power. And I'm going to use you to get it."

"What the hell are you talking about?" Robert spat back at his captor.

"I know about Thomas and the powers that he and his family have. I've experienced them first hand, and truth be told, it's absolutely amazing what I learned about that family during the time I was dead."

The DCI stared back at him, unblinking. "So what?"

"I want his power and you're going to help me get it."

"That's what this is all about Nikolay? You want power?" The DCI chuckled. "Even though you've taken over a younger body I'm afraid your brain is as decrepit as ever. You must know that I'm never going to help you."

"Of course," Nikolay responded. "I understand that betraying the ones you made an oath to won't be easy, but you will betray them nonetheless."

The DCI was unimpressed. "Just because you're holding me against my will doesn't mean I'll cooperate with you."

"You're right, which is why I secured leverage to sway your way of thinking."

Nikolay snapped his fingers and a door to the room opened. In the doorway a struggling figure appeared, bound at the wrists with a gag in her mouth. Robert's eyes shot open.

"Emma!"

Robert's wife struggled against the man who held her in the doorway, her face white with terror. She screamed through her gag but all that Nikolay and Robert could hear were her muffled cries for help.

"You sonofabitch!" Robert violently thrashed against his bonds. "I'll kill you!"

"Temper temper," Nikolay told him as he motioned for Emma to be brought in. "You keep that up and you might pop a blood vessel."

Emma was forcibly pushed into another chair and secured to it. She squirmed as the Russian sleeper, who had brought her in, departed and closed the door behind him.

"You bastard. Don't touch her."

"Everyone just calm down. Take a deep breath and relax."

Robert looked his wife in the eyes. "Emma, are you okay?"

She nodded and tried to speak. Nikolay walked over and loosened her gag.

"Y..yes," she was able to tell her husband.

"I'm right here and we're going to get out of this."

Nikolay suddenly drew back his hand and backhanded Emma with an audible crack that echoed throughout the room. She cried out in both shock and pain as a trickle of blood ran out of the corner of her mouth and down her white chin.

"STOP IT!" Robert bellowed. "I'LL FUCKING KILL YOU!"

Nikolay struck Emma again and her entire body shuddered from the blow. Emma slumped to one side, stunned.

"FUCK YOU!"

Nikolay turned around and looked at the DCI. "Tell me how to get Thomas' power or I swear this is just the beginning."

"Go to hell Nikolay, you sick fuck."

"Have it your way."

Nikolay turned back towards Emma and raised his hand once more.

"Doc...doctor...," she mumbled.

Nikolay paused. "What did you say?"

"Ther...there's a doctor..."

"What doctor, Mrs. Duncan?" Nikolay pressed.

"Doc...doctor Mat...Matsushita," she managed to say as bits of blood spat out of her mouth.

"Emma, no," Robert pleaded. "Don't."

I wonder if it's the same doctor that Victor used to brag about? "Tell me more Emma or perhaps I should cut open your husband in front of you?"

She slowly shook her head back and forth. "Don't...hurt...him..."

"Then speak. I know of this Dr. Matsushita? Where can I find him?"

"I...don't...know. He...found...me..."

"Where?"

"Coffee...shop..."

"And what does he have to do with Thomas Clark?"

Robert spoke up again. "Emma, not another word."

Nikolay slowly unsheathed a long combat blade that was attached to his tactical vest and twisted it in front of Emma's face. Her eyes widened and she knew this man was serious about his intentions.

"What does he have to do with Thomas Clark?"

She collected herself. "He needed Thomas' blood."

5

"Why?"

"To create the serum."

Nikolay straightened up and lowered his knife. "Well, isn't that interesting and how are you involved in all this?"

"I gave him the blood."

Nikolay looked at her funny. "And why would you do something like that?"

"I didn't have a choice. He made me."

"How? Did he just ask you nicely?"

"This doctor has an ability. He can control people."

"It sounds like I need to meet this doctor. But first I want control of what he'll ultimately need, and that's Thomas and his blood." He turned back towards Robert. "I doubt they're still at the bunker so you're going to tell me exactly where I can find them."

"No," replied Robert.

In a flash Nikolay had his blade hard against Robert's throat. A thin cut appeared and blood began to pool on the blade's edge.

"Tell me where I can find Thomas and his family."

Robert refused to open his mouth and as Nikolay leaned in Emma broke the silence.

"I'll tell you! Just leave him alone!"

Nikolay didn't take his eyes away from Robert as the cut deepened, their gaze locked on each other.

"They're in a house, not far from the bunker. I can show you on a map."

"All of them?"

"Yes. All three families live there together."

"What about any defenses they might have?"

"They have a panic room, that's all I know. Now leave my husband alone!"

Nikolay slowly backed away and let the blood from Robert's cut seep down his neck and into his collar. Nikolay smiled at Robert, wiped his blade on his sleeve to clean off the blood and sheathed it.

"Thank you. That wasn't so hard now, was it? Thank you for your cooperation." He snapped his fingers and the same sleeper agent reentered the room. "Prep twelve men."

"Rules of engagement, sir?"

"Alive if possible, but dead if you're left with no choice."

"Yes, sir."

2
Sat Nov 3, 2001

Thomas, Laura, Rebecca, Sam, Julie, Bill and Kim had all gathered in the kitchen and sat around the table. They were in the middle of discussing the events that had recently affected each of them, including the school fire, the rescue and the undeniable fact that Rebecca was now in a man's body when Thomas' phone rang. He got up, walked away and answered it. Laura noticed a confused look appear on her husband's face as he walked back over to them.

"What happened?" Laura asked as he thumbed the end button.

"I don't know, but it sounded like the DCI was involved in some sort of accident. He was on his way here."

"So he knows about me?" Rebecca asked.

Thomas shook his head. "No, I didn't want to say a damn thing over the phone."

"Probably better that you didn't," Laura stated, "especially since we don't know who we can trust now."

Thomas sat back down. "Listen everyone. I know we're all in this predicament because of me."

"That's not true," Sam said.

"Come on, bro," Bill added, "what are you talking about?"

Thomas held up his hand before anyone else could voice their opinion. "This road we've been on began with me back in third grade. It started with Nigel and continued with his brother Albert decades later. From the moment Laura and I realized that Emily and Gavin were special our lives, collectively, have been significantly altered and that's the truth whether you want to acknowledge it or not."

9

The table remained quiet.

"What are you trying to say?" Laura prodded.

Thomas looked around at all of them, aside from Hobbes and his children that were still asleep. "All of you are my family, and I want to keep you safe, but we're facing some deep shit now. By thinking I could make things better by getting into bed with the CIA, whether it was the right decision or not, weighs heavily on my heart. I vow to make this right and do whatever it takes to make it right with each of you."

The house phone rang and Sam got up to answer it.

"Hello? Yes, this is he." Relief washed over Sam's face. "Are you sure? Okay, so where are they then? I understand you don't know but they're my kids and I want them found!"

All eyes at the table focused on Sam.

"Yes sir, I'll leave you to your job. I appreciate your call."

Sam slowly hung up the phone as Julie stood up, tears in her eyes.

"Tell me," she pleaded.

Bill and Kim's lives hung on Sam's next words.

"They're not dead."

Julie rushed to his side and they held each other. Bill put his arms around Kim as well.

"What else was said?" Laura asked.

Sam continued. "All of the bodies from the school have been identified, but of the five children that are unaccounted for, four of them are ours."

"What do you mean they're missing?" Kim pressed, her anxiety rising. "What does that mean?"

Sam shook his head. "It means they haven't been found yet."

"Well, where are they then? I mean, if they had run off into the woods why haven't they come back?"

10

Laura got up and moved over to Kim to console her as Julie shook in Sam's arms, emotionally distraught.

"I don't understand. WHERE ARE MY CHILDREN!?" Kim screamed.

"The only thing the detective, who's investigating our children's boarding school fire, told me was that they're missing. It means they're out there somewhere."

"But where?" Bill asked with clenched fists. "It's been a day and they still haven't shown up on anyone's radar. That doesn't make any sense so what the hell is going on?"

Kim sobbed on Laura's shoulder. "Where…where are my children?"

Laura stroked Kim's hair in an effort to calm her down. Rebecca, sitting at the table in another man's body, felt distress for the anguished parents. What seemed like an obvious idea hadn't been brought up yet so she opened her mouth.

"What's stopping us from going to Harrisburg, where the school is located, and look for them? Maybe we can track them down ourselves."

Julie and Kim's eyes widened with hope at Rebecca's brilliant idea.

"Yes," Julie instantly agreed. "That's exactly what we're going to do."

"Damn straight it is," Kim added.

Sam put his hand up. "Hold up."

Julie pointed her finger at her husband's face. "Don't try and stop us."

"Not in a million years," he retorted. "I think going up there to find our kids is exactly what we need to do, but…"

"But what?" Julie pressed.

All eyes turned to Sam.

"But we have other issues to discuss."

Julie didn't budge. "Nothing's more important than finding our children."

"I agree wholeheartedly," Sam replied. "But I don't think it's a good idea for us to split up right now."

"Sam's right," Thomas said. "Look what happened at the bunker. Carl, or whoever Carl is now, killed two guards as he fled. We don't know what he's up to, where he went or what he's planning." Thomas looked at Laura. "We absolutely should stay together and, along those lines, should consider abandoning this house."

"Why?" Kim asked.

"We don't know if we're safe here anymore, for one. And two, where you guys go we all go, unless you think you're better off without us around. And believe me when I say that Laura and I would understand if you want to part ways. My family, and our abilities, make us targets and will place you in danger."

Thomas' words hung over the table and Bill took the pause in the conversation to speak.

"I for one am not going to abandon my friend, and his family, especially when I need him right now. Our kids are out there, as we speak, without us and we don't know where they are. We've been through too much together to walk away from you now. Please, help us find our children, together, as a family."

"My sentiments exactly," Sam added. "We need to do this as a cohesive unit." He turned to Julie. "Jules?"

Julie sighed. "I know I've been overly critical of you both lately," she said as she spoke to Thomas and Laura. "I've felt so alone; useless and unneeded. I blamed you for our troubles and that was wrong of me and I…"

Thomas held his hand up to stop her. "It all started with me Julie and I own that. Instead of talking about it why don't we go find your children?"

Alarms abruptly began to sound off throughout the house.

"What the hell?" Bill questioned.

"Shit," Sam said. "I know what those are."

Sam, Bill and Thomas all looked at each other.

"Get the kids, and Hobbes," Thomas told Laura, "and bring them downstairs."

"I'll help," Rebecca said.

"What's going on?" Kim asked as she instinctively moved towards her husband.

Before any of them could leave the kitchen Hobbes rushed in. "The perimeter alarms have been tripped. Somebody's coming for us."

3
Sat Nov 3, 2001

Emily and Gavin rushed down the staircase with Laura hot on their heels.

"Everyone," Sam told the group, "into the Media Room right now."

As they piled in Bill had just pulled a book and a section of the bookcase swung inwards. A spiral set of steps wound downwards and it wasn't long before Julie, Kim, Emily, Gavin, Hobbes, Laura, Thomas and Rebecca went down them to the Panic Room. Sam and Bill closed the bookcase behind them and then joined them.

"What've we got?" Sam asked as he entered the room and Hobbes scrutinized the camera monitors.

"Eight….nine…ten," Hobbes replied. He watched the monitors for a few more seconds. "Twelve. I count twelve men, armed with assault rifles and handguns."

"Oh shit," Bill exclaimed.

Sam grimaced. "We're in for a fight. It's time to arm ourselves."

Thomas was already in motion and pushed the specific brick along the back wall. It silently sunk in and a portion of the wall swung open to reveal the hidden Panic Room. Thomas immediately made his way to the caged armory, unlocked it and began to hand MP5's off to Sam, Bill and Rebecca along with two extra magazines. As they cleared the front of the armory Laura swooped in and picked up a Glock 17 off the shelf as Hobbes, Julie, Kim, Emily and Gavin retreated to the far corner of the Panic Room for protection.

15

"What's going on?" Julie demanded in a panicked voice. "What's going to happen?"

Sam went to his wife's side. "I need you to calm yourself, okay? We need to deal with this situation."

"Situation?" Kim scoffed. "There are men with guns coming to kill us. Why are you so calm?"

"Honey," Bill said from across the room, "we got this. Now let us do what we do best."

Sam and Bill rejoined Thomas and Rebecca.

"Who are they?" Rebecca asked as she inserted a magazine into her MP5 and engaged the charging handle. They all headed back to the monitors in the other room and turned off the light behind them.

"No idea," Sam replied. "None of them are wearing uniforms so maybe that works in our favor."

"They have to be here for me and my family," Thomas stated.

"You don't know that," Rebecca said.

"Let's not pretend otherwise," Thomas replied. "Once again I've placed everyone I love in danger."

Bill put his free hand on Thomas' shoulder. "Ease up brother. We need to deal with this first so we're going to need you're A game."

Thomas looked in their eyes, nodded and buried his insecurities in the back of his head. They collectively turned their attention back to the monitors as the four of them watched twelve invaders breached their house. Two minutes later, after the intruders had cleared each room of the house, the twelve men gathered in the Media Room just outside the bookcase.

"What the hell?" Sam uttered.

"How do they know we're here?" Rebecca inquired.

"That's a good question," Bill whispered, "but regardless of how we're about to have company and it's going to get bloody."

"Hit the lights," Sam ordered.

Rebecca turned off the lights while Thomas shut off the monitors. Then the four of them took up positions throughout the room and brought their MP5's to bear on the only entrance, the spiral staircase. Light appeared at the top of the staircase, out of view, as the bookcase swung open. Each of them unconsciously gripped their weapons tighter in preparation for the upcoming assault.

The first man cautiously entered the alcove at the top of the stairs and slowly circled down the staircase, his handgun out in front of him. In the darkness below he couldn't see the defenders pointing their weapons at him. He took another cautious step down as his eyes started to adjust.

"I can't see anything," he yelled.

"Then flush them out the hard way," a voice called back.

Sam didn't wait for the man to spray the room with bullets and put a round in his head from twenty feet away. The man toppled over on the staircase and his weapon clattered down a few steps before it came to a rest.

Silence.

Three seconds later half a dozen objects were tossed down the stairs. A second later the light from the open bookcase shrouded the room in darkness as it was pulled shut.

"Grenades!" Sam yelled to the others in the pitch black.

Thomas, Bill, Rebecca and Sam instantly retreated towards the other room as six distinctive pops were heard.

"It's gas!" Bill yelled. "They're gassing us!"

"Hit the lights!" Sam ordered.

"I'm trying!" Rebecca answered.

17

The concentrated cloud of vapor quickly expanded and pressed into the adjoining room where they were all gathered. A few of them began to cough.

"I don't like this," Emily said from her mother's arms and coughed.

"I can't breathe," Gavin complained.

Sam could smell the gas all around him. "Everyone on the floor! Stay low!"

As they began to hunker down Rebecca finally located the switch and the room filled with light. She coughed as the gas began to take effect on her and looked over at Thomas.

"Can...can't you use your...your power?"

Thomas felt woozy and he looked down at the weapon he held in his hands. It pulled at his fingers. *It's so heavy.* He fell to his knees and the gun slipped out of his weakened grip. *Use my powers.* He tried to concentrate but the gas in his system had already dulled his senses. Thomas looked back and saw Laura and his children lying face down, struggling to breathe. Next to them Julie and Kim were on their backs, heads tilted to the side and eyes closed. Hobbes was out as well. *Must...save...my...family...*

Sam and Bill desperately tried to cover their nose and mouth with their shirts but with the overwhelming amount of gas their fight was short lived. As Thomas watched his friends toppled over and lay still. He slowly turned and looked over at Rebecca. Her back was against the wall, unconscious, weapon in her lap.

Thomas couldn't fight the urge to sleep anymore as his body gave in. He collapsed to one side, eyes towards the staircase. As his eyelids forced themselves closed he saw one blurry figure after another spiral down the stairs in the distance. With one last effort he screamed even though it barely registered as a whisper.

"Nooooooo."

"I for one am not going to abandon my friend, and his family, especially when I need him right now. Our kids are out there, as we speak, without us and we don't know where they are. We've been through too much together to walk away from you now. Please, help us find our children, together, as family."

Thomas violently jerked in his seat as Bill finished talking and everyone jumped. Laura rushed to his side.

"Are you okay?"

Thomas just stared at her.

"What's wrong?" she insisted.

"Brother, what is it?" Bill pressed.

Thomas stood and looked out the kitchen window. "They're coming."

"Who's coming?" Sam immediately queried.

"Twelve men. Armed. Right now. For us."

Sam and Bill didn't question Thomas. They'd been saved by his premonition before and had heard about how it had saved both Gabbi and Gavin's lives when the bunker's control booth experienced an electrical surge. Whether it was a new ability that Thomas had developed or not this was certainly not the time to question it.

"Head to the armory," Sam ordered.

"I'll grab the kids," Rebecca told Laura as she rushed out of the kitchen.

Alarms abruptly began to sound off throughout the house.

Sam, Bill, Laura, Julie, Kim and Thomas ran past the main staircase as Rebecca took the stairs two at a time. She passed Hobbes who was on the way down in a panic.

"The perimeter alarms have been tripped. We're under attack."

"No shit," Bill countered. "Let's go."

The group entered the Media Room, pulled back on the proper book and the bookcase swung inwards. Thomas stayed while everyone else began to head down. Sam pulled him by the shoulder but Thomas resisted.

"I'll come down once Rebecca and my kids are safe."

Sam nodded and left Thomas in the Media Room. Twenty seconds later Emily and Gavin appeared around the corner with Rebecca.

"What's going on dad?" Gavin asked.

"Intruders."

"And they're coming for us?" his daughter asked.

Thomas nodded. "Rebecca. Take Emily with you."

"Wait, what?"

"Gavin and I will handle this up here."

"But…"

Thomas glared at her. "We're not safe down there together. Now move and keep everyone calm!"

Hobbes' voice wafted up through the opening. "Twelve. I count twelve men, armed with assault rifles and handguns."

"Go," Thomas said again.

Rebecca nodded, took Emily's hand and the two disappeared through the bookcase. A second later it closed leaving Gavin and Thomas alone in front of the huge media screen.

"You up for this again, son?"

* * *

20

"What've we got?" Sam asked as he entered the room and saw Hobbes scrutinizing the camera monitors.

"Eight….nine…ten," Hobbes replied. He watched the monitors for a few more seconds. "Twelve. I count twelve men, armed with assault rifles and handguns."

"Oh shit," Bill exclaimed as he opened the hidden Panic Room for everyone.

Sam grimaced. "We're in for a fight. It's time to arm ourselves."

Sam and Bill entered the Panic Room to arm themselves just as Rebecca and Emily came down the winding staircase.

"Where are Thomas and Gavin?" Laura asked as she grabbed onto Rebecca's arm. "Why aren't they with you?"

"He told me we weren't going to be safe here together."

"So they're up there, alone, against twelve armed men? Is he crazy!? Sam! Bill! Thomas is still up there with Gavin!"

"Fuck!" Sam yelled from the other room as he and Bill inserted magazines into their MP5's.

"Why the hell would he do that?" Bill roared.

Julie and Kim sat on one of the bunk beds and watched as their husbands prepped for battle. Hobbes hadn't moved an inch from the monitors and oversaw the impending incursion.

"They're inside the house," he called out.

Sam and Bill finished prepping their weapons as Rebecca and Laura took their turn at what the armory had to offer.

"We're going up to help them," Sam told the group. "Stay down here."

"Everything's going to be okay," Bill assured them. "Love you sweetie."

Sam stopped and looked at his wife. "Love you Jules. We'll be back for you."

"Be safe!" the two sisters yelled back.

21

As the two men rushed towards the spiral staircase Hobbes called out to them.

"Take these!" he said and tossed an earpiece to both of them.

Without missing a beat Sam and Bill pushed the communication devices into their ears, charged their weapons and headed back upstairs.

*　*　*

Gavin nodded at his father.

"Good. Now we're going to hide behind that couch," he said as he pointed to the one farthest away from the hidden bookcase, "and wait for them to come to us. When they do I'll signal you and you let Stir do his thing, okay?"

Gavin nodded again and the two of them ran over to the couch and ducked down. Twenty seconds later four of the intruders entered the tiered level Media Room, scanned it for threats and stopped.

"He said they'd be in here."

"No, he said this room had a secret door to an underground panic room."

"Great. So they'll be armed and waiting for us to come down to pick us off one at a time."

One of the other men patted the bag that was slung over his shoulder. "Not if these things have anything to say about it."

"What's in there?"

"Gas grenades. It'll put them right out."

Six more men appeared in the doorway and joined the other four. Their leader spoke up.

"The last two are sweeping the rest of the house but they won't find anyone. The people we're after have to be in the safe room just like he said they'd be."

"And where is this hidden room?"

"Stay on me. He told me where it was and how to open it."

Ten men, weapons up, advanced towards the bookcase. The leader inspected the book names and eventually found the one he was looking for. He placed his hand on it and tilted it back. A section of the bookcase swiveled inwards and all ten men aimed their weapons at the new doorway. Light emanated from below the darkened stairwell.

"They're in…"

A burst of gunfire erupted out of the darkness and perforated the man leading the attack. His body toppled over, eyes wide in surprise, as the nine other men opened fire into the hidden doorway, bullets pinging and ricocheting off the metal staircase.

One of the attackers caught some movement off to his left. As the bookcase door snapped shut in their faces, and their bullets shredded them, a large couch sailed through the air and crashed into the nine men. Screams of agony filled the room as multiple limbs cracked when the heavy couch crushed them. Four unscathed men traversed their rifles towards the far corner of the room and saw a man, a child and a small animal standing there.

"Give up," one of the men yelled at Thomas, "or die!"

In a blur Stir accelerated from where he stood, eyes glowing and decapitated one of the men. An instant later Thomas yanked the four men's rifles from their hands then sent them soaring across the room where they hit the wall and tumbled to the floor. The three remaining men, confused but

23

determined, instantly pulled their sidearms. It was at that moment when the bookcase swiveled back open and Sam and Bill came out firing. The three men were cut down where they stood.

Hobbes' voice sprang to life in their ears. "Two more coming at you."

Sam and Bill aimed at the exit to the Media Room and waited while Stir made his way back to Gavin's side. Thomas moved himself and his son behind another couch as he saw his friends aim at the doorway.

"Wait," Hobbes said. "They stopped outside. One of them is pulling out…shit! He's pulling out what looks like grenades!"

Sam and Bill instantly began to pepper the doorway with concentrated fire in the hopes of preventing the attacker from tossing any grenades inside. Unfortunately two bounced off the inside doorway and into the room, spinning in place as they came to a rest on the second tiered level.

"Grenades!" Bill yelled.

Sam and Bill dived over the couch together towards the open bookcase doorway as Thomas stood up. As Sam and Bill crashed to the floor, amidst the carnage, they caught a glimpse of Thomas flinging his hands in the air. Moments later both grenades detonated in the hallway outside the Media Room, splashing the white walls with the blood of the two intruders who had been out there.

"Ohhhh gross," Hobbes said over comms. "The hallway's clear now. But yuck."

Thomas turned and surveyed the scene as Sam and Bill pulled themselves to their feet.

"Hobbes. We're clearing the area. No one comes up yet, understood?"

"Got it."

"Are you fucking insane?" Bill asked his friend.

Thomas stared back at his friend. "You're welcome."

"Okay. You're right. Thank you, of course, but still, what the fuck? Taking on twelve armed men on your own? What were you thinking?"

"He wasn't alone," Gavin told his uncle as he joined his father.

Before the conversation could continue they heard sounds emanating from underneath the couch. Sam and Bill brought their weapons to bear as Thomas used his powers to manipulate the couch out of the way. Two of their attackers were still alive and not in the best of condition. Bill handed his MP5 over to Thomas and pulled one of the men off the floor, relieving him of his sidearm in the process as Sam continued to cover the second one.

"I'll be direct and I'll expect a direct and forthcoming answer asshole," Bill told the man. "Who sent you?"

"Go…go fuck yourself," the man spat back as blood trickled down from the wound in his head.

"Not the answer I was looking for." He turned towards Sam. "So what do you think the rules of engagement should be in this situation?"

He shrugged. "They attacked us. I think defending ourselves was the only thing we could do."

"Soooo, no prisoners?"

"Yeah, no prisoners."

Bill dragged him out of the other survivor's view, threw him down on the floor, picked up a loose sidearm and fired a round into the floor next to the man's head. Bill then bent down and hit the man, knocking him out.

"Yeah, he's dead. Who's next?"

The remaining survivor had a broken arm and Sam stepped on it with his foot.

"Arrgghhhh," the man managed to exclaim between clenched teeth.

"Do you want to die like your friend there? Who are you? Who sent you?"

"My name…my name is not important."

"And why's that?" Sam probed.

"I…I am just one of the many. One of the many who were forgotten."

"Forgotten?"

Sam looked over at Bill, then at Thomas and finally back at the man.

"What are you talking about? Talk!"

"We are the forgotten. We've been in this country for years…as sleepers."

Realization hit Sam. *Oh shit.* "Sleepers for which government?"

The man closed his mouth so Sam pressed down harder.

"Okay…okay," he said as he relented.

Sam let up a little. "Which government?"

"The Soviet Union. Russia."

"So who sent you here, today then?"

"A man we had all thought was dead. We hadn't been called on in years which is why we thought we'd been forgotten."

"Who? What's this man's name?"

"Nik…Nikolay Dmitriev."

"Bullshit. I was the man that killed Nikolay. Try again."

"I swear. He doesn't look like Nikolay, or even sound like him. But he's back…., I swear that Nikolay is back from the dead."

"Shit," Bill said out loud. "Are you thinking what I'm thinking?"

Sam continued. "What's this new Nikolay look like?"

When the man was done talking it was clear that Carl Abney, one of Sam and Bill's teammates that had been captured, and then rescued with them had been taken over by Nikolay, the same way Eliot had been replaced by Rebecca.

"Oh crap," Bill said.

"Anything else?" Sam advised the man.

"There was another man there, tied up, older. Nikolay referred to him as Robert. That's all I know."

"And this shitty interrogation keeps getting worse for us," Bill added.

"Thank you," Sam said and knocked the man out. "Hobbes?"

"Yes?"

"Are the house and grounds clear?"

"I see nothing else out there."

"Okay, we're coming down."

* * *

Laura immediately approached Thomas, anger in each step. "What the hell was that?"

"I know, I'm sorry."

"I hear a 'but' coming."

Thomas nodded. "But I had a premonition. If we had all stayed down here they would have gassed us out and captured us. I had to do something to protect everyone and there wasn't time to explain."

Laura knew he was telling the truth but that didn't mean she liked hearing what he had to say. "Is this going to get any easier?" she whispered as she put her arms around his neck.

"I hope so," he replied as he held her tight.

Julie and Kim rushed over and hugged Sam and Bill as well. It took a minute or two before the adrenaline in their systems dissipated.

"We need to get out of here," Hobbes told everyone.

"Are there any more out there?" Sam instantly asked.

"No, but we all know he'll send more men."

"Who will?" Laura asked.

"Nikolay is the other one who made it through the portal and took over Carl's body," Thomas announced. "He's the one that orchestrated the attack and we're fairly certain he's taken the DCI prisoner, which would explain how he knew about this location and the entrance to the Panic Room. So Hobbes is right, we need to get out of here."

"And go where?" Kim asked. "And what about our children?"

Sam spoke up. "Thomas and Hobbes are right. But first thing's first. We need to get out of here and out of harm's way before we can do anything."

"Hobbes, anything on the police band?"

"Negative. No reports."

"We got lucky. Alright everyone, pack light because we're out of here in ten minutes."

* * *

Eleven minutes later, two Suburbans full of family members, belongings, weapons and Stickers the cat, departed.

28

They had decided to head to a motel outside D.C. to come up with a game plan.

"Okay, how much cash do we have on us?" Laura asked.

"I pulled all forty grand from the safe," Thomas replied.

"I think between the rest of us we have a total of forty-five thousand on us," Sam said, "and that's got to last us for a while because we have to assume we're going to be tracked now."

"God, I don't like any of this," Julie said.

"It's going to be okay," Sam told her.

"Really? Our children are missing and once again our house was targeted. I'm beginning to see a pattern," she stated sarcastically.

"Alright, enough already Jules. We need to work together, not come apart at the seams. We'll fucking figure this out."

Kim spoke up. "This might be a dumb question, but can't we go to the CIA for protection?"

"Interesting idea. What'ya think Thomas?" Bill asked.

"Maybe. When we get to the hotel I'll call Russell and fill him in. Good idea Kim."

* * *

"Thomas? What the hell is going on?" Russell asked.

"It's a long story and not something I can be completely candid with over a public telephone."

"Tell me what you can then and we'll go from there," Russell replied.

For the next minute or so Thomas explained, in coded terms, what had happened at the bunker, at home, the missing children and what they had learned about Nikolay, especially the fact that he might be holding the DCI as a hostage.

"Holy crap, that's a lot to take in. No wonder the DCI hasn't been answering my calls. Fuck."

"No shit. We're swinging in the wind here and I have my family depending on me to keep them safe."

"Okay, right. You're right. Um, head to the airport and I'll get you to a safe house out of the country."

"And leave four missing children out in the wild?"

"Tell me then, what do you want me to do, Thomas?"

"Fuck. I don't know. Setup the chartered flight and we'll go from there, okay?"

"I can do that. Trust me."

"Russell, you're the only one we can trust right now."

"What about Gabbi?" Russell asked.

"What do you mean? Oh shit, she's still out here and could be targeted."

"My thoughts exactly."

"Okay. Charter for eleven plus one cat."

"You got it."

"Thanks Russell. I owe you."

"Be safe Thomas."

The line went dead so Thomas hung up the phone and walked back to the hourly motel they'd paid for in cash.

"What'd he say?" Sam asked.

"He's going to set up a private jet to get us out of the country and into a safehouse."

Julie and Kim's eyes widened. "But what about our children? We can't just leave them out here while we save ourselves."

Thomas put his hands up. "I know and I don't expect you too. I wouldn't stop searching for my children either. But right now we need to make our way to the airport and plan our next move from there, alright? Also, along the way we're stopping to pick up Gabbi. She's in as much danger as we are and if Nikolay went after the DCI, and us, then it's only a matter of time before he targets her."

4
The Other Place

The Caretaker watched from a distance as Gavin's boat, along with his father and the four men they had rescued, surged towards the boy's tiny island. The dark cloud raced in behind them, blotting out the sun as it bore down on the small craft cruising just above the ocean's waters.

They're not going to make it.

"Prepare to jump out!" Thomas yelled at everyone. "Get to the island as fast as you can and then wait for the portal! Once it appears don't hesitate, just go through it!"

Thomas caught Sam and Bill's eyes.

"This is bad, isn't it?" Sam verified.

Thomas nodded. "The kind nightmares are made of. Get ready."

Fifty feet out the boat stopped. Everyone jumped or dove into the water as quickly as possible and began to make their way to the shore. Thomas helped Gavin and as soon as he could put his feet down he picked his son up and trudged through the water towards the sand, along with everyone else. Eliot and Carl reached the beach first. They turned around and pointed up just as two shapes sped out of the sky and tackled them. They began to struggle on the sand.

"What the fuck!" Bill cried out as he rushed forward to help.

Sam was on his heels as Thomas, Gavin and Stir finally emerged from the water.

Bill was then knocked over from his right, and before Sam could react he was catapulted off his feet from the left.

A battle broke out on the beach as each man wrestled for his life.

Thomas looked over his shoulder and two feet collided with his body, spinning him around and down to the ground. Gavin cried out and Thomas watched as Anna Garland wrapped her arm securely around his son's neck. Stir immediately attacked Anna but he passed right through her which made her laugh.

What? What the hell is going on?

"Hello Thomas. I've missed you."

Thomas knew that voice all too well and whipped his head around. He came face to face with Victor Bannon.

"Victor. What are you doing here?"

"Payback."

Thomas was confused and looked over at Anna and his son again. "Let him go!" he screamed at her.

"Awww Gavin," Anna taunted. "Is daddy afraid of what I'll do to you?"

"Look at me Thomas," Victor ordered.

"What do you want?" Thomas heard the fighting rage on behind him. The dark cloud of hatred was no more than ten seconds away. "What do you want?"

"We're taking your lives, it's that simple."

Then, out of nowhere, new shapes ripped the evil off Sam, Bill, Carl and Eliot. A fifth smashed Anna directly in the face and sent her sprawling as a baffled look appeared on Victor' face.

Nine.

Thomas didn't know what had happened but wasted no time as he pushed Victor off balance and grabbed Gavin.

Eight.

34

Sam and the others recovered and got their feet under them.

"DON'T LET ANY OF THEM ESCAPE!" Raven screamed.

Seven.

"THOMAS!" Victor screamed behind him.

Thomas knew there wouldn't be a second opportunity. "Gavin! Portal!"

Six.

The portal formed. Thomas flung his son through it and Stir bounded in behind.

Five.

"GO! GO! GO!" Thomas hollered.

Four.

Sam, Bill, Carl and Eliot raced towards the gateway.

Three.

It was then that Thomas recognized who helped him fight against the evil forces of Yuri, Raven, Nikolay and Alexei. It was his parents, Michael and Betsy; and his grandparents, Ed and Claire. *Dad? Mom?* Nikolay broke free and barreled towards him like a runaway train.

Two.

Sam and Bill plunged through the portal and disappeared with Carl and Eliot right behind them. Thomas looked back and saw Victor walk out of the water just as Rebecca punched Anna in the face.

"THOMAS!" Victor yelled again.

One.

Thomas caught Rebecca's smile as he turned around to leave the island.

Zero.

The dark wave of hatred crushed Thomas and sent him tumbling through the portal. The dark energy, sensing a way to leave this realm, entered the portal in a frenzy; but seconds later the portal snapped shut and cut off their escape.

"What the hell just happened!?" Raven screamed as he looked around at the remaining members of his evil six. Anna, Yuri, Victor and he were the only ones that remained.

"Isn't it obvious, Raven," Victor spat back, "we failed."

"NO! I do not accept that!"

"You should," a new voice said.

Anna, Yuri, Victor and Raven looked towards the voice as they gathered together. Four others walked up to them.

"Michael," Victor said. "We have to stop meeting like this."

"Hello Victor, and to you as well, Yuri. It's been awhile."

Michael and Betsy stood side by side with Ed and Claire.

Raven spoke up. "You're Thomas' parents and grandparents, aren't you? I have to admit that even I didn't see this coming. Well played." He paced back and forth before speaking again. "But you know, I've noticed we're both short on people. If my numbers are correct we had six and you had five, but now we both have four."

"What's your point?" Michael said with a challenge. "We stopped your plan cold."

"But did you really?" Raven taunted. "I mean, where could our people have gone other than through the boy's portal?"

Michael and Betsy shuffled their feet uneasily.

"That's right," Raven beamed, "apparently the game's not over. I mean, look around us. This island is the center of interest now, surrounded by concentrated dark energy that's just waiting for a taste of freedom. The same freedom I

36

imagine Alexis and Nikolay are experiencing right now, along with your precious Rebecca."

"Alexis never made it," Betsy said with a certainty that made the smiles on the evil four fade.

"What? What are you saying?"

"Alexis wasn't able to inhabit a host before the portal closed. He no longer exists in any realm."

Raven rubbed his jaw. "Well shit. That's too bad, but at least Nikolay is back in play and I know he can't wait to cause some havoc. I hear he has quite the history with your family, and certainly none of its positive, isn't that right Michael?"

Michael clenched his teeth and stared Raven down.

Betsy spoke up again. "But you're forgetting that Rebecca made it through as well. Whatever Nikolay can dish out we know Rebecca will be there to stop him."

Raven laughed. "You keep thinking that. In the meantime, we have places to be. Good luck to all of you, you'll need it."

Victor, Yuri, Anna and Raven flew up into the sky and away from the island. The dark energy continued to flow around the island. Grotesque figures sporting talons scrutinized the four that remained on the beach while they maintained their endless wait for freedom to present itself once again.

"Pompous asshole," Claire said under her breath. "So what do we do now?"

"We've done all we can," Ed told his wife. "It's up to Thomas and his friends now."

"However, we should be proud of ourselves," Betsy told them.

"Indeed you should," the Caretaker said as he landed on the warm sand near them.

The dark forms avoided the Caretaker, sneering at their jailor as they perpetually circled the island.

"Thank you. Your efforts have not gone unnoticed."

"So why didn't you stop them?" barked Michael. "You're the one with all the power."

"My roll here is fluid, and I must confess that I was taken by surprise."

"So what are you going to do about it?"

"There's nothing I can do."

"Can't or won't?" Michael replied with a strong edge to his voice. "At least the five of us had the guts to do something, speaking for Rebecca who got sucked into that portal without her consent. How many innocent people are going to get hurt because of your inactions Caretaker?"

"Your point is well taken Michael Clark. I will continue to monitor this situation."

"Just monitor?"

"In the meantime," the Caretaker continued, "I have released you from your Membranes."

"What?" Betsy asked. "Why?"

"You acted when you did not have to and stemmed off a chronicle of history that would have devastated both our worlds. All of you are free to go, or stay, if you so desire."

Ed, Claire, Michael and Betsy were stunned. They had been prevented from moving on due to their constant violations of interference, but now in the sweep of a hand, their bonds had been removed. The Caretaker took another look around him, frowned and rose into the air, leaving them behind.

"So what do we do now?" Betsy asked.

"Yeah," Michael said, "what indeed."

High in the air the Caretaker watched as the seemingly endless concentration of dark energy continued to gather around Gavin's island.

What has now occurred will trickle throughout time and change everything.

5
Sat Nov 3, 2001

It didn't take much to convince Gabbi, after they arrived at her apartment, that she'd be safer off with the family especially after the obvious newcomer to the group, Eliot, was introduced to her as Rebecca Cross. Gabbi, with her purple hair, fumbled for a second but then extended her hand.

"Rebecca. Wow. It's a real pleasure to meet you even though…, well…"

"That I'm dead," Rebecca stated as she finished Gabbi's sentence and ended the handshake.

"Yeah, exactly that actually. Sorry, I hope that wasn't too weird of me to say out loud?"

Rebecca smiled. "No Gabbi, your candor is quite refreshing. I think we're going to get along just fine."

"Hey Gabbi," Hobbes said.

Gabbi smiled awkwardly. "Hey Hobbes. Soooo, it's great to see everyone, and I'm happy to see that Sam and Bill are safe. But wait. Weren't you guests of Hamid in Afghanistan like…now? How did you guys get out of there?"

Sam opened his mouth but Gabbi cut him off as she continued her train of thought.

"You must have used Gavin's portal…"

"That we did," Thomas confirmed.

"But that means the dark stuff was out there. How did you out run it?"

Thomas spoke up. "We didn't so I'll get right to the point. We're being hunted."

"Hunted?"

"There was an incident…"

Gabbi's eyes lit up as she put the pieces together. "Something came through with you, didn't it?" Then she caught Rebecca's eyes. "I mean, not something of course...sorry, my bad."

"Yes. Rebecca somehow came through from the other side and merged with Eliot's body."

"But Hamid had Sam, Bill and two others..."

Thomas nodded.

"And three of those four are now here, standing in my apartment,...so where's your fourth?"

"Something dark came through and took over Carl's body."

Gabbi understood. "And that's the person who's hunting you, and well, maybe me now?"

Thomas nodded. "That's correct. His name is Nikolay Dmitriev and he's an old enemy of my family."

"Shit," Gabbi exclaimed. "What you're telling me doesn't sound good. What happened?"

"Long story short," Sam stepped in and said, "Nikolay sent twelve Russian sleepers to our house to capture us. Let's just say it didn't work out for them."

Gabbi smiled. "No, I wouldn't have expected a different outcome going up against all of you."

"There's more," Thomas said. "He took the DCI prisoner and that's the only person that knew where we lived, so we have to assume he's been compromised. And, to top it all off, Dr. Matsushita is alive and now has samples of my blood. You could be the next target which is why we're here."

"I'm in," she replied. "What's the plan?"

"Russell's chartering us a flight out of the country. We're heading to the airport right now."

42

"Now? Wow, okay, hmmm." She quickly scanned her small apartment. "I guess I'll pack light."

* * *

The group, now eleven in total, arrived at the airport and walked up to the check in counter. Russell had been busy since they'd talked and the chartered flight to London had already been arranged. They were directed down an offshoot corridor, to the outer perimeter of the concourse, scanned themselves through security and then found themselves alone as they waited. Two televisions hung from the ceiling at varied angles that jumped back and forth between the news and airport security tips.

"How long until we can board?" Laura asked as they all settled in.

"Thirty minutes," Thomas replied.

"Are you okay?" she whispered to her husband, but Julie overheard it.

"I will be once we put some distance between ourselves and Nikolay."

Julie spoke up, clearly distressed. "What do you mean 'is he okay' Laura?" Her voice rose in pitch and fervor. "Amanda and Craig are out there somewhere, alone and scared, and here we are escaping to another fucking country to get away from some madman intent on killing us without them!"

"I have to agree with my sister," Kim added. "Too much has happened lately and I can't stop thinking about Sarah and Edward."

"Sweetie," Bill said as he tried to console his wife, "everything's going to be alright."

43

"What!?" Kim yelled, startling everyone. "How is that even possible!? You'd rather run away to London and leave our flesh and blood to somehow fend for themselves?"

"No…no, " Bill stammered.

"And what are you going to say to smooth this situation out?" Julie said as she glared at Sam. "What the hell are we doing here, seriously?"

"Listen, I…," were the only words Sam could get out.

"Save it. Whatever you're going to say just don't. Just don't Sam." She stood up and turned away. As Sam stood she whipped back around. "I should have gone through with the divorce, you gutless piece of shit."

"Woah woah woah," Laura exclaimed as she bounded out of her seat. "I know you're upset but…"

"Oh go to hell, Laura."

"Take it easy," Sam insisted and placed a hand on Julie's shoulder.

She swatted it away. "How dare you! Get your hand off me. By us being here, right now, you're expressing that your friends are more important; that their lives matter more than our two children. You should be ashamed." Julie swung her finger around at everyone. "All of you should be ashamed."

Kim moved over by her sister to create a unified front, defiant, while Rebecca, Hobbes and Gabbi looked down and shuffled their feet. Emily and Gavin, on the other hand, walked past the adults and stood with their two aunts.

"We're not leaving without them," Emily insisted.

"They're family," Gavin added. "They're our family."

Bill stood up. "You're right and I never planned on leaving without them Kim."

"Me either," said Sam.

"But…"

Sam held up his hand and Julie stopped. "Bill and I already discussed this."

"But why are we here at the airport then?"

"Because we needed to make sure everyone else was out of danger first. Look around. We're past security and the plane is going to take them to London. Once they're off the ground the four of us are absolutely going to go find our kids."

Julie and Kim burst past Emily and Gavin and hugged their men as hard as they could.

"I…I thought…" Julie began, tears streaming down her cheeks.

"I know," Sam replied. "It's okay."

"Me too," Kim said through sobs.

"It's going to be alright," Bill told her.

Out of the corner of his eye Thomas saw a familiar scene on the television behind them.

"What the…?"

"What?" Laura said as she caught the seriousness of his tone.

"The news."

They all swiveled their heads towards the screen as Thomas used his ability to turn the volume up.

"In breaking news, a video of the daring rescue of American Special Forces has just been released. The footage it contains is difficult to comprehend because it appears to be footage straight out of a movie. However, the video aside, what's even more shocking is the identity of the man who released it, Hamid Emal Habibi."

6
Sat Nov 3, 2001

"No indication you were heard," Hobbes informed him.

Fucking go!

Thomas vaulted the wall and ran to the now unguarded door with Gavin on his heels. Stir bounded over and joined them just as Thomas opened the door. When he did five Taliban, including Hamid, turned and stared, open mouthed at Thomas' bold entrance. Thomas instantly ascertained that Sam, Bill, Carl and Eliot were lined up on the left wall, bloody and bruised, but alive. On the opposite side of the room was the video camera that had been used to film the execution the world had witnessed on television.

"Thomas?" Sam barely managed to utter through his cracked and bloodied lips.

The Taliban raised their weapons to shoot the American intruder but before they could their AK's were ripped from their arms and sailed across the room, clattering to the floor in a heap. A few of the men cried out in anguish with bent and broken fingers. One Taliban rushed Thomas and managed to take two steps before his body toppled over. His head rolled and came to a rest at Hamid's feet while Stir stood his ground in the middle of the room next to the man's corpse. Thomas closed the door behind him, without taking his eyes off Hamid, as the other three backed up towards their leader.

"I could cry out and you would be swarmed in a matter of seconds," Hamid boasted from across the room, clearly uncertain of the situation but needing to show strength in front of his men.

"You could try," Thomas told him, "but you'll end up just like him," as he motioned towards the headless guard. "Now Hamid, before I change my mind and decide to kill all of you, please secure your men and do it quickly."

Hamid hesitated as his mind tried to wrap itself around what he'd just witnessed. "Who are you?"

"Don't talk. Don't think. Just do it, right now."

Hamid's men, who didn't speak English, looked to their leader for guidance. With a wary eye on the red-eyed creature in the middle of the room Hamid motioned to his three remaining men in the room to get on their knees. Afterwards he proceeded to zip tie both their hands and feet. When he was done he tapped their mouths closed.

"Untie my friends," Thomas commanded.

A yell emanated from outside and Thomas knew they were short on time. Hamid smiled and refused to comply.

"Whoever you are, you're not leaving here alive, and neither are your friends."

"You'll be the first to die, Hamid."

"I've already made my peace with my god. Have you?"

Thomas raised his arm and Hamid flew across the room like a rag doll. He hit the far wall and collapsed, dazed. His men began to struggle against their bonds as Thomas used his ability to effortlessly push their bodies against the two doors, temporarily blocking them from being opened from the outside. Thomas then turned his attention to the hostages, turning each one around and stripping off their restraints with just a thought. The men were weak from being tortured and Thomas knew there was no way they could help him fight back.

"Stir. Guard. Gavin. Portal."

Men from the outside began to pound their fists on the doors and push them open.

Gavin formed his portal and then moved next to his father.

Hamid shook his head to clear it, pushed himself up on his hands and knees, gazed at the shimmering gateway in amazement and began to crawl.

Thomas wasted no time and picked up Sam and literally tossed him through the portal.

One of the doors opened wider.

Bill flew into the portal.

Hamid reached the camera that had fallen over and turned it on.

Stir rushed the opening door and disappeared outside. Screams and bursts of automatic gunfire followed.

Carl disappeared as Hamid recorded what was happening in the room.

Stir reappeared inside, blood dripping from his jowls, and Hamid turned and captured that as well.

The second door opened and a swarm of AK wielding Taliban pushed through.

Thomas pulled a flashbang from his vest and tossed it in their general direction just as he pushed Eliot into the portal.

One of the Taliban fired his AK at Thomas and missed.

Thomas picked up his son, protecting him from the gunfire, and rushed the portal.

"Stir!" Gavin yelled.

The flashbang exploded just as the Taliban readjusted his aim and fired a second time. He got off three rounds before his senses were crushed by the deafening and blinding explosion, along with everyone else in the room.

It took a full ten seconds before Hamid's senses began to equalize. He struggled to his feet, the video camera clutched in his left hand was still recording. He pushed a button and it stopped but he couldn't take his eyes off the device. Ever so slowly he lifted his head and gazed around the room, the room that not a minute before had contained his four American prisoners before the unexplainable had occurred.

What in the name of Allah just happened?

One of his men, pushed his way in from the outside, stepped over a few bodies and rushed over to Hamid. Others came inside and began to untie the other three Taliban.

"Hamid? Are you okay?"

When he didn't reply the man repeated the question.

"Hamid? Hamid?"

Their eyes met.

"What happened in here?"

Hamid's brain was filled with images and eventually he opened his mouth. "Madness."

"What? What are you saying? Where are your prisoners? What were the men shooting at?"

Hamid didn't have an answer nor did he feel like being interrogated by one of his own men. He stood fully upright, shoved the fear he felt out of his head and took charge.

"The Americans know we're here and they still have a drone overhead. Get our men to vacate immediately!"

"But what…"

"Now!" Hamid ordered.

"Yes, sir."

After his man reluctantly ran off to order the evacuation Hamid once again looked around the room. His eyes came to rest on the beheaded soldier's body. He walked over to it, knelt down and rolled the corpse over to get a better look.

How is this possible?

As he scrutinized the body he realized his eyes were roaming the floor for the man's head.

And there it is. His death happened so quickly. What was that creature?

Hamid cocked his head to the side and scanned the air where the bright and supernatural light had been. He stood and then entered that same space, turning around within its boundaries.

One by one they disappeared...vanished into it...

"Hamid!"

Hamid turned towards the door.

"We're ready to get you out of here."

Hamid took one last look at the room and left it behind. Outside multiple vehicles had been hastily prepared to leave the village in multiple directions. Hamid climbed aboard one of them and as it accelerated away from the village all he could do was look down at the camcorder he held firmly in his hand.

* * *

Hamid finished watching the video of the encounter, as brief as it was, for the twelfth time. He still couldn't believe what he'd seen, let alone what the camera continued to display with each viewing.

Impossible. What I saw was impossible; yet clearly and undeniably every second of it must have occurred.

Hamid breathed in deeply, held it and then exhaled slowly.

Whoever this 'Thomas' person is he knew Sam and Bill and vice versa. I wonder. Decades ago, when Sam and Bill were training me and my men, they often talked about their childhood friend called Tom. Could this be the same person? And if so who is he? He closed his eyes and thought back to the encounter, before he had started recording. *What did he call the little boy, who I can only assume is his son? Garrett? Galvanized? No. No, he called him Gavin. And the small creature's name he yelled out was Stir.*

Hamid opened his laptop, connected the cable from the camera to the usb port, and then initiated the data transfer. As his video uploaded to his laptop he opened a browser window and navigated to SANDBOX's now defunct website. On the top was a disclaimer that told any visitor that SANDBOX was no longer in business, by order of the U.S. Government. However, for the time being the rest of the website was still intact. Hamid clicked on the Photos link and waited as the page filled with pictures. He scrolled down through numerous snapshots until he spotted one in particular that caught his eye. It was of three men, smiling, with SANDBOX's indoor range in the background.

Hello.

Hamid click on it to enlarge it. Sam and Bill flanked a familiar face and he read the caption with renewed interest.

Sam Paige, Thomas Clark and Bill Nicholson keeping sharp at the range.

Thomas Clark, so that's your name. Who are you Thomas Clark?

Hamid created a new tab in his browser, went to Google.com and did a search for Thomas Clark. After sifting through some erroneous results he found what he was looking for, but it was something that Hamid never expected.

He' a children's book writer with a wife and two children, named Emily and Gavin? What the hell is going on? How does an everyday author have so much power at his disposal? Did something happen to him?

Hamid closed his eyes and shook his head to try and clear it.

It's pointless to ask questions that I'll never get the answers to. What I need to be concentrating on is how I can use this information to my benefit.

He put the laptop to the side, stood up and paced the room.

The four American soldiers, they were my leverage and the world knew that I had them. But they're gone now, stripped away in an instant. Hamid stopped. *The real question I should be asking is does anyone else know about this?* He smiled. *And that answer has to be a resounding no.*

Hamid went back to his laptop and began to create a new video.

"Let's see how you like it when the world suddenly knows both who you are and what you are capable of."

7
Sat Nov 3, 2001

Russell Washington, the DCI's right-hand man for the PsyOps project, called the White House and requested an emergency sit down with the President in regards to Robert Duncan's sudden disappearance. He was granted the meeting and arrived at the White House thirty minutes later, was ushered through security and then escorted to the Oval office.

"Mr. Washington, please come in and sit down," the President said as he turned off the television that hung on the wall.

"Thank you for seeing me on such short notice, Mr. President."

The President and Russell sat down in unison on the couches, facing each other.

"I've been told you're here to tell me something about the DCI, is that correct?"

"Yes, sir. He's been abducted."

"By whom?"

"Nikolay Dmitriev."

"And this has been confirmed in some way?"

"No, sir, but my source tells me that Nikolay is the man responsible."

"I see. And I'm just supposed to believe what you have to say?"

Russell was taken aback. "Sir?"

The President leaned in. "You work directly for the DCI, and have for the past four years, in an unknown capacity."

Russell sat there and stared back at the President, unwavering.

The President studied Russell's face for a few more seconds before he continued. "Mr. Washington, what leads you to believe that Nikolay Dmitriev is behind the DCI's abduction?"

"I can't be more specific than I have, sir."

"That's interesting. As your commander-in-chief I demand you tell me what's going on."

"Sir, the DCI is missing and we're wasting precious time arguing…"

"You're the one wasting my time, Mr. Washington. Tell me what's going on."

"Sir, I answer to the DCI."

"Wrong!" the President snapped. "You answer to me. Furthermore, you came here today to tell me Robert's been kidnapped by Nikolay, but I know for a FACT that he was shot dead on a Cuban beach years ago."

"That's correct, sir, but there's more to it than that. I assure you Nikolay is alive and behind this."

"Then fill me in. Convince me."

"I can't."

The President stood up, walked over to his desk and picked up the remote. "Then I'll try another tack."

He pushed a button and the television on the wall turned back on. He pressed another and Hamid's video began to play. When it was over the President turned the television off.

"What do you make of that, Mr. Washington, because you don't seem overly surprised at its contents?"

Russell cleared his throat but didn't answer. The President continued.

"I know exactly who two of the men in that video are. One is Sam Paige and the other is Bill Nicholson, the co-founders, slash owners of SANDBOX which was recently shut down by our government. The DCI told me, to my face, that they were going on a mission to capture Hamid Emal Habibi. But, as we all know, the mission turned sour and the team was captured."

Russell still didn't comment.

"You're the DCI's right-hand man, involved in who knows what, but I suspect you must know who that man and child who rescued this team are. As for the manner in which they were rescued, well, that's an entirely different conversation, isn't it?"

Russell shifted in his seat. "Yes, sir."

"Good." He put the remote down, walked back over to the couch and sat down. "What I'm trying to wrap my mind around, just like the rest of the world, is what the hell we're dealing with. It's like watching a movie's special effects department throwing everything they have at the audience. Personally I thought it was bullshit at first, but the more I watched it I saw it for what it truly was, a threat."

"They're not a threat, sir."

The President smiled. "So you do know what I'm talking about but you're keeping quiet out of loyalty. Alright, I can admire that, but this demonstration of power has to be reined in, controlled."

"But sir…"

"I have people working on facial recognition as we speak Mr. Washington. It's only a matter of time before I know who this man and child really are."

"But they saved our men, our soldiers."

"That's true, and I commend whoever they are for their heroic deed. But, if we don't harness their powers then you know somebody else will want to. So save me some time and tell me who they are."

"I can't speak for the DCI, sir. That's a question you'll have to ask him yourself."

"Very well, then we'd better find Robert, don't you think?" The President stood up and Russell followed suit. "You're dismissed."

"Sir?"

"This meeting is over."

Russell left the President behind and closed the door to the Oval office behind him. *What the hell just happened?*

The President watched him go. *What has the DCI been keeping from me?* Just then one of his private phones rang and he immediately picked it up.

"What do you have?"

"Sir, facial recognition identifies the man in the video as Thomas Clark. He's a children's book writer and has been lifelong friends with both Mr. Paige and Mr. Nicholson."

"Clark. Clark. That name sounds familiar."

"It should sir. His father was Michael Clark and he worked for the CIA. Our records indicate he even prevented JFK from being assassinated at one point, amongst other recognitions."

"Understood. I want arrest warrants issued for Thomas Clark, Sam Paige and Bill Nicholson to go out immediately with a national security classification. They are now our nation's top priority."

"Yes, sir."

"And, while you're at it, leak to the press that the Russians might be involved in the abduction of the DCI."

"In breaking news, a video of the daring rescue of American Special Forces has just been released. The footage it contains is difficult to comprehend because it appears to be footage straight out of a movie. However, the video aside, what's even more shocking is the identity of the man who released it, Hamid Emal Habibi."

The video began to play as Thomas and his extended family members gazed at the airport television.

Thomas watched the events unfold in front of his eyes, reliving the experience from a new perspective. The recording began as he tossed Carl through Gavin's portal. Right afterwards the shaky footage captured Stir reentering the room, blood dripping from the small creature's mouth. The camera swung around as more armed Taliban finally pushed themselves into the room. Thomas watched himself pull a flashbang from his vest and toss it towards the doorway, push Eliot through the portal and then pick up his son, twisting to protect Gavin from the incoming gunfire.

"Stir!" Gavin cried out on the television.

The same Taliban opened fire again as Thomas' flashbang exploded. The camera fell to the ground and clattered out of Hamid's hand. It came to a rest on its side, capturing Thomas as he was propelled through the portal. As it closed the room was suddenly devoid of all hostile activity and the video faded to black.

The news anchor spoke up again. "Hamid Emal Habibi claims the United States has developed a new weapon and that the man you see in the video, rescuing American soldiers, name is Thomas Clark. We haven't confirmed his identity ourselves yet, but if what we've seen is true, well, the world is about to change. We'll have more on this breaking story in our next segment."

Thomas used his ability, depressed the power button and the television they were watching turned off. Laura wrapped her arms around him as Emily and Gavin came over to make it a group hug. The rest of the family remained silent, contemplating what they and the rest of the world, had just seen.

"I had no idea," Julie finally managed to articulate to Thomas. "I had no idea the danger you and Gavin put yourselves in to bring my Sam back home. I apologize Thomas, and to you Laura, for sounding and being so selfish."

"Me too," Kim added. "Hearing what you can do has been one thing, but damn, seeing it with my own eyes has given me an entirely different perspective. I'm terribly sorry."

"You're all my family," Thomas told them, "and I'd do anything for you, just as I know you'd do anything for me. But now," as he motioned towards the television, "this secret my family and I have been holding on to, and protecting for years, is out there."

"So what does that mean?" Julie asked.

Sam spoke up. "It means we can't leave the country."

"Why not?"

"Because they know who Thomas is and they're going to come after him, if they're not already."

"Who is?" inquired Kim.

"Everyone," Bill told them. "Thomas represents a threat to some and an opportunity to others. I can only imagine the financial gains harnessing his powers would bring if one country was able to isolate them for themselves."

"Cheerful thinking but," Thomas said as broke away from his family, "we can't escape to London anymore. The flight will be flagged and there will be people waiting for us at the other end."

"You could always change the flight plan in midair," Hobbes offered.

"True, but with the world on alert how far do you really think we're going to make it? No, the smart thing to do would be to keep moving and that's what we're going to do."

"Okay," Sam said. "Where are you thinking?"

"We're staying with you; with all of you. Your kids are out there and we've proven that we're stronger together. We need to find them, and along the way we'll look out for each other, like we always have."

Sam stepped up, put his hand on Thomas' shoulder and smiled. "Damn right we will." He turned and addressed everyone. "Pick up your luggage because we're leaving the airport. We'll head back to the Suburbans, drive north to Harrisburg and together we're going to track down our children."

"And evade the entire world tracking us down at the same time," Bill joked.

Thomas smiled. "One step at a time my friend, one step at a time."

9
Sat Nov 3, 2001

"What do you mean they're gone?" Nikolay pressed Khrebtov, his right hand man.

"Like I was trying to tell you, the follow-up team entered the grounds thirty minutes later and discovered the bodies of our men, or what was left of some of them. We recovered two survivors, but the other ten were dead."

"You mean MY men, don't you?"

"Yes sir," Khrebtov replied and lowered his eyes.

Khrebtov had been living in the United States for decades as a Russian sleeper, used by Nikolay throughout the Cold War era and beyond. In the years that followed Nikolay's split from the Soviet Union, due to his being disavowed for embezzlement, he continued to manage a significant number of sleeper agents throughout the world. However, Nikolay concentrated his efforts in the United States and had barely begun his reign of terror, using sleepers to successfully execute public bombings throughout the country, when Sam and Bill infiltrated his Cuban villa and executed him, thwarting his plan to assassinate the President while he was aboard Marine One.

It was at that point that Khrebtov, and the countless other sleepers in the US, went dark and never heard from their puppet master until early this morning. At first Khrebtov doubted the validity of who the unknown voice over the phone claimed to be. But all doubt was quickly removed once Nikolay revealed details to him that only he could have known. But when Khrebtov pulled up, after their early morning phone call and saw the young American soldier that stood in front of him, he knew by his mannerisms that Nikolay had somehow come back from the dead. Khrebtov also knew that he needed to be wary because Nikolay had always been dangerous and capable of many things. But now, in his new body, he seemed even more deadly than Khrebtov remembered. *I'm too old for this shit.*

"So what are you really here for?" the DCI called to Nikolay from across the room, still secured to the chair.

"I'll be with you shortly," Nikolay replied over his shoulder.

"Maybe you shouldn't antagonize him," Emma whispered to her husband from the chair next to him.

Robert twisted his head and looked at his wife. "I vowed to protect the Clark's and I failed because he was able to use the love I have for you against me. I had to make a choice and I chose you over them and now I have to live with that. We're not getting out of here alive so there's nothing to lose by antagonizing this sonofabitch."

That thought hadn't occurred to Emma yet. He watched as her face contorted, grasping the idea of death and how helpless their situation really was. Nikolay finally finished up with Khrebtov and made his way back over to his two captives.

"You were saying something Robert?"

"I asked you what you're really doing here? I mean, what's your plan now that you're back from the dead?"

"My plan is not terribly originally I must admit."

"Which is?"

"Revenge, plain and simple."

The DCI scoffed. "I'm guessing, by your demeanor, that hasn't started off as well as you wanted it to. They thwarted your attack, didn't they?"

Nikolay smiled. "Indeed. But no matter. I will get another opportunity."

"And how do you intend to come out as the conqueror? Their abilities can't be discounted."

"On that point you're clearly not mistaken Robert. I underestimated them and that will not happen again."

Khrebtov walked over and interrupted them.

"Sir?"

"What is it?" Nikolay responded without looking.

"There's something on the television you need to see."

"What could possibly…"

"It's about them, sir. The ones that you're after."

Nikolay abruptly turned to face Khrebtov. "Show me."

* * *

Nikolay replayed Hamid's video over and over, rewinding the VCR time and time again. *No wonder my men failed. His power, and his child's power, are incredible.* Nikolay paused the playback and leaned back in his chair. *But now the world knows about Thomas which means everyone is going to go after him in the hopes of taking his power and trying to make it their own. I need to find a way to capitalize on this and quickly.*

"Khrebtov."

"Yes, sir."

"Has the private number of the Russian President changed?"

"I don't believe so."

"Good."

Nikolay picked up the phone and dialed another number from memory. The connection took a few seconds to establish and he heard it ring. On the fourth it was answered.

"Da?" *Yes?*

"Mr. President," Nikolay said in Russian, "I have an opportunity for you."

"Who is this? How did you get this number?"

"You are Demian Anatolievich, the Russian President, and I am Nikolay Dmitriev, a patriot long forgotten."

"Nikolay....Dmitriev?"

"That's right, Mr. President."

The President sneered. "I don't know who you think you are but Nikolay is dead, in life and to my country."

"What was once true is no longer the case, Mr. President. Yes, I was killed on a Cuban beach four years ago after instigating a series of bombings throughout the United States. And my plan to kill the American President nearly succeeded, and that would have made me the first man in history to have killed two sitting American Presidents."

The line was quiet for a few moments. "How do you come to know this information?"

"Because, Mr. President, I am Nikolay Dmitriev and I've come back from the dead."

"Ridiculous."

"Is it? Everyone's reality has suddenly shifted, has it not?"

"What are you referring to?"

"I take it you've seen the video that Hamid Emal Habibi released earlier today?"

"I have. I believe it to be rubbish; a fake."

Nikolay shook his head as he held the phone to his ear. "It's not, I assure you. What you saw was absolutely real."

"And why should I believe you, the man who calls himself Nikolay?"

"The man in the videos name is Thomas Clark. He and his son are not the only ones with abilities. His wife and daughter possess their own power as well. I'm calling you, Demian Anatolievich, because these people are going to change the world. But more importantly, whoever controls these people will find themselves in a position to change the world."

"What are you saying?"

"The Clark's are being hunted by me, and the rest of the world may or may not decide to join in; but I'm guessing some will. Harnessing their power will bring about the next evolution of mankind, and whichever country facilitates that will immediately see a dramatic shift in global dominance."

"I'm listening."

"In the video you saw Thomas throw the American soldiers into the portal where they disappeared?"

"If I'm to believe what I saw, then yes, I saw him do that."

"The boy's portal leads to another plane of existence, one where all souls go to. I was dead and I was able to come back, through the boy's portal, and take over one of those American soldier's bodies you saw Thomas toss into the portal."

"Even if I were to believe you, how can you prove any of this?" asked the Russian President.

"I have detailed files during my time in the Politburo. I leached millions from the sales of our weapons and was eventually exiled from the country I love. Would you care for me to go through a portion of this information now or should we dispense with the pleasantries and get down to business?"

The President chuckled. "Alright, I believe you because that's the Nikolay I remember. However, I'm having a difficult time wrapping my head around both the video and what it ultimately means. What are you proposing?"

Nikolay sat up straight. "I want to be reinstated back into the ranks of the Russian government."

"You realize that Russia is not the Soviet Union. The Cold War is over Nikolay."

"With all due respect, Mr. President, the war between the United States and Mother Russia will never be over. The moment either country relaxes, thinking the world is a better place, is when their belly gets slit open. You still need people like me, sir; people who know how to get things done."

"What you're asking, Nikolay, is out of the question. Even if I were to reinstate you the world knows you as a killer of innocents. The bombings, they've irrevocably tainted your name in the history books. Bringing you back into the fold would only disrupt what I've accomplished for Russia."

"True. But my face is no longer my own. I can now emulate anyone I want to be on the outside. However, the window of opportunity is short and I will act with or without making a deal with you. There are plenty of other countries that will take me in once I have the Clark's, and their powers, as bargaining chips. They will throw more money at me than even I could count just to own the new medical technologies and military super solider programs that will be developed. And that's just the tip of the iceberg. The world is going to change so you have to ask yourself, what side do you want to be on when it does?"

The line went quiet and Nikolay pressed it further into his ear.

"Demian Anatolievich, are you still there?"

"Yes, Nikolay," he reluctantly replied. "You've given me quite a lot to think about, and to overcome in a short amount of time. However, your terms are accepted and will be honored once you deliver these 'people' to us. But, you must prevent any other country from securing them in the process. Is this understood?"

"It is. I'll be in touch Mr. President."

Nikolay slowly hung up the phone. *Reinstated within the Russian hierarchy. Excellent.* His thoughts were interrupted by the DCI.

"I don't speak Russian but it sounds like you just made some sort of arrangement in exchange for the Clarks."

Nikolay walked over as the DCI continued.

"But I see it in your face. You don't trust the Russian President, do you?"

"No. No, I don't. He'll double cross me as soon as he gets what he wants. But the fact is, even if I do capture the Clarks I might not even need them."

"What?"

Nikolay shifted his gaze from Robert to Emma. "You said this Dr. Matsushita controlled your actions and used you to spy on your husband, all without your knowledge."

Emma clenched her jaw in response.

"Perhaps he'll want to do it again."

Nikolay beckoned Khrebtov over to his side. "Take our good friend Emma here back to her favorite coffee shop, along with a few men."

"I won't help you," Emma said with defiance.

Nikolay leaned down and took firm hold of her jaw with one hand. "Are you sure about that? Your husband is still my guest and I know you'd hate for anything to happen to him while you were out on this errand for me." He produced his knife and placed the blade over one of Robert's fingers. "He has ten of them right now. Defy me and I won't be able to guarantee how many he'll have left."

"You're a monster," she said between clenched teeth.

Nikolay put away the knife. "I am what I am, liberated, free and doing everything I can with this second chance."

10
Sat Nov 3. 2001

Dr. Yamato Takuma Matsushita turned off the television, after taking in Hamid's video, and sat back.

"Well well well, this certainly puts a wrench in things." He thought about it a little longer. "Sonofabitch, it actually completely interferes with my plans."

Yamato slammed his fist down on the nearest table then stood up and swept everything off of it, hurtling its contents to the floor.

"Dammit! With Thomas exposed the governments of the world will want what he can do for themselves. I have to locate him before they do."

Dr. Matsushita left the mess he'd made behind as he entered an adjoining room. He stopped a few feet inside and looked around, smiling eerily as he admired his handiwork. Spread out before him were five children, each of them strapped down and secured to individual beds.

"Hello children. How are you feeling?"

An IV solution was stationed at each child's bed with clear plastic tubing that meandered down from each bag. On the back of each of the children's hands were needles that were attached to the slow drip, the liquid kept at a trickle to keep his young creations sedated. He moved into the room farther and closely inspected each connection until he was satisfied that his equipment was still operational.

"Sleep my little beauties. Sleep as my serum binds to you, changes you. Sleep until I choose to unleash you."

He stopped at the last bed on his way out and squatted down next to Amanda, Sam and Julie's thirteen year old.

"I'm going to need you most of all, especially if your ability develops the way I engineered it to be."

Matsushita stood back up and left the children behind. He walked over the mess on the floor and paused when he caught his reflection in the television screen, thinking back to the video.

Thomas must be on the run by now, desperate for sanctuary. He looked over his shoulder at the room he just left. *My specialized serum hasn't fully metastasized in their systems, so all I can do is continue to wait. Perhaps I should take this time and treat myself to a coffee, and see what new information Emma Roberts might contain in her pretty little head of hers.*

* * *

It was early evening when Dr. Matsushita stepped out of his car, and then closed and locked its door. After pocketing his keys he made his way to the front of the coffee shop and headed inside. H felt lucky as, moments later, he picked Emma out of the crowd as she sat by the windows in a far corner. Yamato waited his turn in line and eventually ordered a coffee and a bagel. As he took his food to an open table he realized he was salivating.

How strange. I don't remember the last time I ate.

He sat down, took a bite and glanced over at Emma once again.

She seems distracted by something. I wonder what it is? Oh right, I'll just find out.

Dr. Matsushita took control of Emma and her demeanor instantly changed.

I want you to stand up, come over and sit down by me.

72

Emma did as she was commanded and ten seconds later she was sitting across from him.

Tell me everything you know about the location of Thomas Clark.

"I don't know where he is."

Then what has your husband, the DCI, told you as of late?

"He hasn't. Can't."

What do you mean he can't?

"He's tied up. Captured."

What the hell are you talking about? Who has him tied up?

"Russian men."

Dr. Matsushita abruptly leaned towards her, a look of confusion on his face. *What?*

The huge fist, meant to connect with the side of Yamato's head, sailed painlessly through the space where his head used to reside. Yamato twisted his neck and saw the large man behind him. He forcibly lifted his chair and brought it down on his attacker's foot. The audible crack resounded throughout the room as patrons began to move out of the way, unsure of exactly what was happening, as the enormous man bellowed in pain. Emma shook her head and looked around as if she'd been in a fog.

As two others immediately advanced on Yamato he backed away, knocking his coffee and bagel to the floor. The sixty-five year was not a fighter, but he was a survivor, and instinct kicked in.

Attack your friend!

The large Russian cradled his broken foot while one of the two new attackers, the one Yamato had subjugated, produced a handgun from beneath his jacket and pointed it towards the other, a confused look on his face. People panicked and began to run out while others ducked behind the barista's counter for cover.

"Back off or I'll have your partner kill you where you stand," Yamato boldly stated as he regained his composure.

"How…are you doing this?" the sleeper asked.

Yamato smiled. "Haven't you watched the news lately? The reality you're used to is changing and I intend to…"

Dr. Matsushita collapsed to the ground unconscious as the man with the gun suddenly was unsure what he'd been doing. He lowered it as Emma dropped the metal napkin holder she held in her hand, dented from its impact with the doctor's head.

"Grab her," one said to the other who already had his gun out. He then turned to the bulky sleeper with the broken foot. "And pick him up and get him in the car. We need to vacate the premises before the police arrive."

* * *

Dr. Matsushita groaned.

Ouch. My head.

He was lying on his back and slowly rolled over before h realized he was on a cot. He swiveled his hips, got his legs over the side and planted his feet on the floor. His head still hurt.

"Where am I?"

"And that is the question of the hour," an unknown voice replied.

Yamato reluctantly cracked his eyes open and tried to focus on the young man who sat in front of him. The man's face seemed familiar somehow.

"Welcome back," the man said.

"Where am I?" Yamato repeated, gaining his strength back.

"Where is not important, but rather, who you're currently sharing your company with is."

Yamato squinted and saw the DCI and his wife secured to chairs in the middle of the large room. He also noticed ten men with weapons pointed at him. Yamato hastily turned back towards the stranger who quickly held up his hand.

"Before you take control of me, or one or more of my men, let me assure you that I just want to have a pleasant conversation with you."

Yamato sat up straight, unafraid and it showed. "With so many armed men you'll understand why that's difficult for me to believe."

"You're right." He waved and the men lowered their guns and dispersed. "My apologies for being overly cautious. I'd also like to apologize for the method in which you were brought here. Would you care for some water or something else to drink?"

Yamato was intrigued by the man's calm demeanor and ignored his offer. "Who are you?"

The man smiled. "You've caught me on an off day Dr. Matsushita. I wasn't prepared for diplomacy and manners. My name is Nikolay Dmitriev."

"You don't sound Russian."

"No, in this body I definitely do not."

Yamato cocked his head to one side. "What do you mean 'in this body'?"

"We'll get to that in a moment. But first, Emma over there has experienced firsthand what you can do and so did one of my men at the coffee house. You can control people by thought alone, instilling suggestions and bending them to your

75

will. Now, the reason I mention this is to illustrate that my mind is open to such phenomenon."

"And why is that?"

"Because before the sun rose this morning I was dead."

A confused look passed over Yamato's face. "Explain."

"Let me ask you this first. Did you happen to watch the video that Hamid Emal Habibi released to the news media?"

"Yes." Then it hit him. "I thought you looked familiar. You're one of those soldiers that Thomas rescued."

Nikolay nodded. "The portal, that you saw, leads to a different plane of existence."

"You're telling me the afterlife is real?"

"In a manner of speaking. In my case it was purgatory."

"Okay. So you're not the American soldier anymore because your soul, or essence, took over the body?"

"Something like that."

Yamato shifted on the cot and looked around the room at all the men. "It's time for full disclosure then. Who were you before you died, Nikolay?"

"I rose up through the ranks of the Russian Politburo after I assassinated my father and took his place. Over the decades I've been a part of more operations and projects than I can remember, from drugs to weapons, before I was exiled from the Soviet Union when the wall fell in the late eighties."

"And why's that?"

"The main reason is because I skimmed millions off the top for myself."

Yamato grinned. "If not you then someone else."

"Indeed."

"So what's with all the men? They don't seem Russian either."

"Some of them used to be, while others were brought to the United States when they were young."

"Sleepers? They're sleepers?"

"Yes. I have a vast network. You might recall the bombings that occurred throughout the US a few years ago. That was my handiwork."

Yamato looked at the young man in front of him. His body was young but his eyes were filled with both history and experience.

"So what's your game Nikolay? You're leading up to something."

"Fair enough, so I'll get right to the point. I believe you and I have a common enemy."

"Which is?"

"The United States, for one."

"So you're implying that we have more than one enemy in common?"

"More than you know," Nikolay replied. "The world's tapestry ebbs and flows as history and circumstances continue to overlap each other. Over three decades ago a portion of the money I stole was taken from me."

"Alright, I'll bite. By who?"

"Michael Clark, Thomas' father. He worked for the CIA and took it upon himself to thwart me while he worked for the agency."

"So you want revenge on Thomas?"

"No. But along the way I do want to kill Sam Paige and Bill Nicholson for murdering me."

Yamato chuckled. "Small world. But why would you think your needs concern me?"

Nikolay pointed at Yamato's right arm. "That's Thomas' handy work, if I'm not mistaken."

Yamato glared. "What do you think you know about that?"

"Nothing specific. But I do know the DCI and Thomas are working together. I also know that you spent some time playing doctor with Thomas and his daughter, Emily."

"What of it?"

"Victor Bannon was very forthcoming about your involvement."

"You couldn't have known Victor. By your own admission you were…"

"Dead?" Nikolay nodded. "Perhaps, but I got to know Victor sometime later, shall we say."

"He's dead?"

"Yes."

"How did he die?"

"That's not for me to say. What I will say to get back to my point, however, is that you obviously tinkered with Thomas while he was under your, shall we say, protection. The fact that Thomas developed his own ability, after being injected with a serum that you not only created but injected him with, means you have mastered the engineering process of it. Case in point; your power of suggestion. It's very specific and very impressive."

"Thank you. But I still fail to see your point."

"I want access to your serum. In return I will provide the manpower and resources to help you capture Thomas." *Not that I won't take him away from you later on.*

"And that's what you think I want, Thomas?"

Nikolay leaned in. "I can sense that's exactly what you want." He leaned back. "And besides, what do you have to lose? This partnership is a win-win for both of us."

Yamato thought about it. *He wants my serum because he wants the power that comes with it, that much is certain. It's a risk but I'll still hold all the cards when this is said and done. What Nikolay is bringing to the table is muscle, and locating and detaining Thomas will move along much faster with his help. What Nikolay isn't aware of is that I'll use him to disburse my mutated smallpox throughout the world, and then watch it burn around me.*

Dr. Matsushita smiled and stood up along with Nikolay. He extended his hand and shook Nikolay's.

"It's a deal. Thomas for the serum."

"Excellent. And perhaps along the way we'll both be able to enact our revenge."

"Absolutely. Oh, and by the way, I have something to show you that I'm sure you'll be very interested in."

"Which is?"

"My latest and greatest achievements."

11
Sun Nov 4, 2001

"Good morning and welcome to Sunday's edition of 'Straight Talk'. I'm your host, Beth Cohen. This morning I will discuss the controversial video that has captivated this planet's attention. Joining me are two renowned scientists, Dr. Raymond Perry, who specializes in biochemistry; and Dr. Kristina Murphy, who specializes in neuroscience."

On screen the camera pulled back as the two doctors walked on stage, greeted Beth and sat down on the couch next to the host's chair.

"Dr. Perry, would you please tell our audience the definition of biochemistry?"

"Certainly Beth, and let me take this moment to thank you for having me on your show. Now biochemistry, in layman terms, is a branch of science that's concerned with the chemical and physiochemical process that occur with living organisms. In this case we're talking about humans."

"Thank you Dr. Perry. Now, Dr. Murphy, will you describe neuroscience to our viewers?"

"Of course, Beth. Neuroscience encompasses other fields like neurochemistry and experimental psychology that both deal with the structure and function of the nervous system and the brain."

"Thank you," Beth said. "Now, in case anyone hasn't seen this very unique and disturbing video that was released to the public yesterday, I'd like to take a moment and show it to you."

The lights dimmed as the large screen behind them came to life. Thomas, Gavin, Stir and the ensuing chaos of the rescue appeared and played until it concluded. The screen went to black and the lights in the studio came back up.

Beth spoke up. "Dr. Perry and Dr. Murphy, how would you classify your reaction to the events you just witnessed?"

"I'm skeptical," Dr. Perry replied, "and let me tell you why. For one thing, the validity of this video has yet to be ascertained. And second, this could easily be an elaborate hoax meant to derail the war in Afghanistan."

"To our audience at home I believe Dr. Perry is referring to Hamid Emal Habibi, the man who released the video. He is also one of the men responsible for masterminding the nine-eleven attack." She turned to Kristina. "And you, Dr. Murphy. What are your thoughts?"

"I'm torn."

"Please explain," Beth inquired.

"As we all know the world is abuzz about the video's authenticity, as Dr. Perry mentioned. In the past twenty-four hours it seems that countless consortiums have voiced their opinion about it; from religious groups, to scientists to conspiracy theorists. Every one of them has either believed what they saw, cast their doubts or openly denied the contents of the video to be real. However, with that said, I'd like to take a different tact if I could."

"And that is?"

Dr. Murphy grinned ever so slightly. "For the sake of argument why don't we accept what we saw, in its entirety, as real. Using that as our foundation we can break down the video to its core components, even though it's obvious the recording started sometime during the chaotic rescue. One, an unknown man came to the aid of American soldiers, the same soldiers that were on Hamid's first video. Second, we are shown some kind of portal, for lack of better words, and one of the soldiers is propelled through it without any assistance of any kind. Third, there's a young American boy in the room, and from the expression on his face he doesn't appear to be afraid. Fourth, a small animal with red eyes appears from outside the room and shakes its head back and forth, dispersing the blood on its mouth over the walls. And fifth, the unknown man grabs the boy, protecting him from gunfire, and the two rushed the portal as the boy screams out the word 'Stir'. The explosion that followed, clearly from the device the man tossed, white washed the camera; and when it finally focuses we see that the portal, and they, are no longer in the room.

"Now," as Kristina continued, "I find this all extremely fascinating."

"Please continue, Dr. Murphy," Beth prodded.

"Once again, taking what we saw as real, my first question is who are those people? And that's quickly followed by how did they get their abilities?"

"My colleague makes a valid point," Dr. Perry said. "If we consider that the video is unaltered in any way, the questions instantly begin to pile up. And the reason Dr. Murphy and I are so enthralled is obviously because of our scientific backgrounds."

Beth took over again. "Let's talk about that for a minute. What are the ramifications if what we've seen happens to be real?"

Dr. Murphy's face lit up. "Amazement, for one."

"And fear is another," Dr. Perry quickly added.

"It's true that people fear what they don't know," Kristina said as she continued, "but all we've seen is a man, and apparently his son, rescuing men that the world understood were going to be killed. To me he performed a heroic act."

Dr. Perry took up the reins. "And the fear comes from not knowing who they are and what they can do. Besides, if this man was heroic and did indeed save those soldiers, where are they and why haven't they come forward?"

"Both interesting elements," Beth said. "But I think Dr. Perry has a point. What happened to these soldiers?"

"I don't know," Dr. Murphy answered, "but that's not the focus of why you asked us on your show, now is it?"

Beth smiled. "No, it's not. The fact remains that the world is looking for answers. You're here because I want to peel back the layers and talk about what all this could really mean."

"Scientifically speaking," Dr. Murphy said, "the abilities we briefly saw are probably only the beginning."

"The beginning?" Beth asked.

Dr. Perry continued. "Yes. From a biochemistry point of view I'm more than intrigued. I need to know, see and experience more. If you actually stop and think about it we're talking about human evolution, and that part of me desperately wants to study this man."

"And that's where things get really complicated," Dr. Murphy said.

"Go on."

"That man. His son. They're both human beings. I'll say that again. They're human beings."

"With abilities that the world has only seen in the movies," Beth told her.

Dr. Murphy nodded. "I agree. But that doesn't mean we can write their humanity off. Now, truth be told, I would love to study this unknown man in depth; figure out how he does what he does. However, that's a deadly precipice to stand upon."

"Why, just because you want to decipher how he does what he does?"

"Yes. Scientific curiosity, in this instance I believe, is going to win out over rational thought and action."

"I'm afraid Dr. Murphy is correct," Dr. Perry said. "Extrapolating what we saw in the video I can only assume that the portal was some sort of transportation conduit. Now, using that assumption, think of the scientific and technological breakthroughs the world could both see and benefit from. Taking that train of thought even further one could argue that one man's life pales in comparison to the lives of everyone on this planet."

Beth flipped through a few notes and then looked up at her guests. "Speaking of one man's life, or creature in this instance, what are your thoughts of the recent attack on downtown D.C.? The world saw that creature, larger than life, struggle for its life during the firefight with the police. During that encounter we saw an enormous and deformed monster toss and smash vehicles until the police finally brought it down. My question is, do you think these events could somehow be related?"

Dr. Murphy answered. "The fact that these two events happened within a week or so of each other can't be coincidental. Once again the scientist in me is desperately curious about how the creature came to be, as well as how it constantly healed itself during the shootout."

"I noticed that as well," Dr. Perry acknowledged. "And yet the scientific community, and the world, don't have an answer to that question because the government came in and confiscated the body."

"And you know this for a fact?" Beth asked.

Dr. Perry smiled. "Seriously? Who else would have the resources to take it?"

"Dr. Perry is right," Kristina said. "We've been left with an endless string of questions, both from the D.C. incident and from the recent events recorded in Afghanistan. I want answers but I fear we might never get them."

"And why's that?"

"Because if the abilities the world has witnessed are genuine, and the people who have these powers are real, then this man and his family are no longer safe. Right or wrong, I believe any government would do whatever it takes to obtain this man just so they can harness his power."

12
Sun Nov 4, 2001

The direct line from the White House rang in the hallway outside Building 42's main underground laboratory, located in the Nevada desert some eighty-three miles north-west of Las Vegas. Initially the immense facility had been constructed during world war two and utilized as an air base. In the years that followed the base had expanded; its primary function transforming to research and development. During July, 1947 the base was put through its paces when a flying saucer, or UFO, crash landed in Roswell, New Mexico. Using the cover of a faulty weather balloon the military transported the partially destroyed craft, and its occupants, to the secret Nevada installation now popularly known as Area 51.

"Groom Lake," the armed guard said as he picked up the phone, its line heavily encrypted.

"Get me Dr. Glover," a demanding voice told the guard.

"Yes, sir. Hold one."

The guard withdrew a keycard from his vest pocket, swiped it through the reader and gained access to the first of three consecutive cleanrooms that eventually lead to the laboratory itself. He walked over to the intercom on the wall and pressed a button.

"Dr. Glover?"

"Yes?" a muffled voice replied through the device.

"Sir, the President is on the line."

"Now?"

"Yes, sir."

"Very well. I'm coming out."

The guard waited as Dr. Glover methodically went through two stages of decontamination before he appeared in the same room as the guard he'd talked to. The doctor was older, in his seventies, with a somewhat gruff exterior which translated to those he worked with that he wasn't going to take any of their shit; mainly because he'd worked at Area 51 for the past fifty years and had been a witness to everything.

"Just outside, sir."

The two exited the cleanroom and Dr. Glover lifted the receiver.

"This is Doctor Glover."

"I'll get right to the point," the President told him. "I want an update."

"Mr. President, always a pleasure," he replied with a hint of dissent. "The creature, classified as Specimen R, has been dissected and it's a marvelous example of anthropological mutation. Just amazing."

"And?"

"And nothing sir. We're still running tests."

"Doctor, by this point you must have some preliminary findings. What are they?"

It never changes. "I located a concentration of an unknown chemical in Specimen R's liver. It's very advanced and it's something I haven't seen before, which says a lot based on what I've been privy to over the decades. In any case I'm analyzing the chemical."

"How much time before you can report something definitive and tangible?"

"I don't have an answer for that, sir. At this stage I'd have to guess weeks, but I'd put my money on months."

"Doctor. Your work on the creature is of the utmost priority and is considered a National Security issue."

"Thank you for reminding me of that, Mr. President."

"Listen Dr. Glover, I only put up with your shit because you've consistently proven yourself as an innovator to the United States government. I need you to figure out what this creature is and how it came to exist."

As Dr. Glover smiled his face cracked. "I understand."

"Good."

"Mr. President, there's something else."

"What is it?"

"I've seen the news, sir. When will I be getting my hands on them?"

"That's undetermined at the moment."

"But I will be getting the first crack, will I not?"

"Dr. Glover," the President said, "when we have them, you'll have them."

"Thank you, sir. Now, if you don't mind, I'd like to get back to work so I can produce these answers for you."

13
Sun Nov 4, 2001

The family, after collectively leaving the airport, drove north to Harrisburg, Pennsylvania. It was late afternoon when they arrived, too late to head to the boarding school, so they found an off the beaten path motel that would take cash and paid for three rooms. They were exhausted and after a meal of takeout food they all collapsed into bed, worn-out. However, everyone spent the night tossing and turning, their sleep interrupted by unfamiliar sounds and tremendous anxiety.

In the morning they ate at the adjoining diner, sequestered towards the back in connected booths. They were tired, each of them robotically eating as they pondered whether they'd find their missing offspring as well as how the day was going to turn out now that the world was well aware of Thomas and Gavin's faces.

"So what's the game plan?" Gabbi asked.

"We need information," Sam replied, "so our first stop is Culver boarding school."

"And then?"

"And then we'll figure it out from there," Bill told her.

Gabbi gave them an odd look.

"We're making this up as we go," Sam said, "while trying to stay under the radar."

"Sorry," she said. "I'm not used to the whole 'running for our lives' thing."

"It's an acquired taste," Thomas commented, trying to lighten the mood.

Gabbi nodded. "I'll bet. Have you ever gotten used to it?"

Laura spoke up. "Let's just say it hasn't been our favorite thing to do over the years. We hid who we were and what we could do. But now…, well, now it's an entirely new playing field we have to contend with."

* * *

After breakfast Gabbi, Hobbes and Rebecca remained at the motel while Sam, Bill, Thomas, Laura, Julie, Kim and Emily drove over to Culver. As they drove up everyone, aside from Julie and Kim who had already been here, finally took in the devastating damage the school had been subjected to. The fire had ravaged some of the older buildings, and had consumed the wood and left the stone behind. The area had been cordoned off, the investigators choosing not to work on a Sunday, but the family saw a lone vehicle parked off to one side.

"Holy shit," Bill said as he took in the scene for the first time.

"You can say that again," Sam added. "Wow."

Julie and Kim, with the thoughts of their children forefront in their heads, grimaced.

Laura gently placed her hand on Julie's shoulder in support. "We'll find them."

Sam parked the Suburban next to the other vehicle and they all got out. Yellow 'caution' and 'do not cross' ribbons crisscrossed the affected buildings and added to the landscape's ominous tone. Bill caught some movement in the distance as the door to the main office fluttered.

"Over there," Bill pointed. "My guess is that the owner of this car is in there."

"It's a start," Sam said.

The group cautiously walked over towards the main building, their handguns tucked underneath jackets in the small of their backs. Sam and Bill took the lead and quickly entered what was left of the structure through the open and unlocked front door.

"Who are you?" a woman's voice cried out. "What's the meaning of this?"

A few seconds later Sam and Bill opened the front door and exited with an older woman. She stopped struggling when she saw Emily with the other adults and realized the two men weren't with the police.

"Ms. Jones," Julie said with some surprise. "What are you doing here?"

"I could ask you the same thing," she retorted. "This area is off limits."

"And yet you're here," Kim said. "Why?"

"That's none of your concern. Why are you here?"

"Amanda, Craig, Sarah and Edward are missing," Julie began. "We need to know where they are and why they haven't been found. Do you know anything?"

Ms. Jones looked around at the faces that intently stared at her. "No. I don't know anything."

"She's lying," Laura said matter-of-factly.

That rattled the headmaster. "How dare you."

"What do you know?" Kim pressed. "What aren't you telling us?"

"There's nothing to tell," Ms. Jones insisted.

Laura had had enough. "We don't have time for this. Em, if you would please."

Emily stepped forward and locked eyes with Ms. Jones.

"What's goi…?"

Before Ms. Jones could complete her sentence Emily reached out and grabbed the headmaster's hand. Ms. Jones' face instantly relaxed.

"What happened before and after the fire?" Emily probed.

"I was in my office having a chat with Tad, one of the school's bullies who believes he can do whatever he pleases. The next thing I know there was an explosion and it knocked us to the floor. The ensuing fire spread and smoke began to fill the building. I ran for my life. I ran and left Tad behind in my office."

"That explains her hesitation," Bill said. "No wonder she doesn't want to talk about it. Her reputation would be ruined if this became public. She abandoned children and her staff just to save herself."

Emily continued. "What do you know about Amanda, Craig, Sarah and Edward?"

"They had been called to the office for a telephone call."

Kim stifled her emotional response as she recalled being on the phone with her daughter when the explosion occurred.

Ms. Jones kept talking. "The next time I saw the four of them they were getting inside a van."

"Wait. What?" Julie pressed. "What does she mean?"

"What van?" Emily asked.

"I saw a white van that didn't belong to the school after I ran outside to escape the fire." Her forehead contorted. "There was a man and the five children were walking towards him. I don't know how or why but when he opened the back of the van they willingly climbed inside."

Julie and Kim gravitated towards each other in support. Their children were alive.

"Who the fuck is this guy and why did he take our kids?" Sam demanded.

Emily followed Sam's queue. "What did this man look like?"

"He was Japanese," Ms. Jones replied. "An older gentleman."

Thomas shook his head back and forth as he walked away. "Fuck fuck fuck."

Laura caught the implication, bent down and whispered in her daughter's ear. Emily nodded.

"You will forget this conversation or that we were ever here. Go back inside."

Emily released the headmaster's hand. Ms. Jones turned on her heels and disappeared back inside the building. Collectively the group turned and made their way over to Thomas who had walked back to the Suburban.

"Talk to us," Bill said.

"All I have is my own speculation," Thomas replied.

"Please," Kim begged.

Thomas looked at them and finally nodded. "Okay, alright. I think Dr. Matsushita took your kids. We already know he's still alive because he used Emma to bring my blood to him. And, on top of that, we know he can control people by thought alone. What Ms. Jones just told us leads me to believe he's behind their kidnapping. I'm sorry."

"But…but what does that mean?" Julie probed.

"Nothing yet," Sam replied. "Let's head back to the motel and talk about it there before someone else drives up and happens to see us."

* * *

Gavin watched his parents and sister drive away with the others.

95

"You okay, kiddo?" Rebecca asked him.

Gavin nodded. Together they walked into the motel room and joined Gabbi and Hobbes. Rebecca closed the door behind them as Gavin made a beeline for Stickers' carrier and opened it. Stickers cautiously exited, stretched and curled up in Gavin's lap.

"Do you think they'll find anything at the school?" Gabbi asked.

"I hope so," Rebecca answered. "I can only imagine what they're going through."

"Absolutely," Hobbes said. "I wish there was more I could do to help. I feel useless without a computer in front of me."

Gabbi nodded. "I understand. I'm not that much help at the moment either."

"The important thing to remember," Rebecca reminded them, "is that we're safe."

"Sure," Hobbes said. "But for how long?"

"I get that this isn't easy for either of you," Rebecca told them. "Our future is uncertain, at best, right now and that's scary as hell. Even I don't know what to expect and I'm trapped in an entirely different body. But, if I may point out, look at Gavin over there. I think he's the bravest one in the room and that's saying something."

Both Gabbi and Hobbes nodded.

"Yeah, he's one special kid, that's for sure," Gabbi said.

"So what can we do to help out while they're gone then?" Hobbes asked.

"Why don't we scan the television for anything new?" Gabbi offered.

"Good idea," Rebecca said as she hit the television's power button.

A few minutes later they caught the opening sequence to a talk show.

"Good morning and welcome to Sunday's edition of 'Straight Talk'."

* * *

The ten minute ride back to the motel was silent. When they pulled in Hobbes, Gabbi and Rebecca met and joined them in one room together.

"What happened?" Rebecca asked right away as she sensed the significant mood shift in everyone's demeanor.

"We're pretty sure Dr. Matsushita is behind the kidnappings," Laura replied.

"Shit."

"What does this mean?" Kim implored as she looked around the room. "Where are my kids?"

"He's going to be wherever they are," Thomas told her.

"But why did he take them?"

Bill spoke up. "My guess is that he's using them as leverage to get to us."

"Then why haven't we heard from him already?" Sam said. "None of this makes any sense."

Julie didn't like it. "Then why take them? What does he want with them?"

Julie's question hung in the air but Thomas had had his suspicions ever since Emily manipulated the truth out of Ms. Jones. Sam noticed his friend's facial expression change.

"What are you thinking?"

Thomas just shook his head side to side. "It's my fault. I thought he was using your kids to get to me but I think it's much, much worse."

97

Julie and Kim didn't like where the conversation was heading.

"You're scaring me," Julie stated. "What the hell are you talking about?"

Thomas couldn't bring himself to answer her question right away.

"Thomas," Kim insisted, "Answer us. What does he want with our kids?"

He finally looked up and met their gaze. "Guinea pigs. I think he wants to use them as guinea pigs."

Julie and Kim, emotionally drained already, merely sat down on one of the beds in silent contemplation.

"I'm sorry," Thomas said. "This is all on me."

Rebecca took the break in the conversation to speak up. "I'm afraid this isn't the only obstacle we have to figure out a solution for."

They turned their attention to her, waiting for Rebecca to continue.

"While you were gone Gabbi, Hobbes and I scanned the morning news on the television. It's worse than we thought."

"Tell us," Laura said.

"We watched a portion of a show called 'Straight Talk'. The host had two guest scientists on that were empathetic to your plight Thomas, but ultimately said they would love to discover how you tick."

"Lovely," Thomas said.

Hobbes took his turn. "And the majority of other news stations were filled with question after question about who you are and what you can do. Your face is out there and people are talking about you. Some people want you to be caught, locked up; while others want you to be left alone. It's scary stuff and the momentum is building."

98

Laura pulled Gavin and Emily close to her side and put her arms around them.

"Are they coming for us?" Gavin asked.

"I don't know," his mother replied.

"We're not safe anymore," Emily stated. "They're going to hunt us down and torture me like they did before."

"I'm not going to let that happen," Thomas told her. "We're going to be okay."

Laura knew that Thomas didn't believe what he'd just said but she let it go. Sam and Bill took that moment to pull Thomas to the other side of the room.

"What are we going to do?" Bill asked. "We have to come up with a plan."

"We don't know where Matsushita has our kids," Sam replied, "and that's a huge problem. On top of that it's just a matter of time before we're recognized and then targeted."

"So we just run and hide then?" Bill said.

"No," Sam told him, "but we need to come up with a plan that doesn't put us out in the open where we will get caught. The fact is if we do get captured we won't be able to do a damn thing to save our kids."

Thomas and Bill nodded.

"We all need to get some rest and think this through," Sam said. "Until then I propose we stay right where we are. If we stay inside we'll reduce the chance that any of us are identified until we figure out our next course of action."

14
Sun Nov 4, 2001

Dr. Matsushita chose to take Nikolay to his secret research laboratory for one purpose only; to establish trust with his new partner. Yamato knew it was only a matter of time before Nikolay betrayed and backstabbed him, fearing his ability to control people. Dr. Matsushita believed that once Nikolay got his hands on his serum, and the process he used to make it, his life would become forfeit.

And I won't let that happen. However, in the meantime, the first step is to locate Thomas and I'll graciously allow Nikolay to fetch him for me.

Dr. Matsushita gave Nikolay the nickel tour of his underground lab ending it just outside the door where he held the five children.

"Very impressive doctor."

"Thank you."

"And you had this place built after you recovered from your burns that Thomas subjected you to?"

With Nikolay looking on Yamato realized his left hand was tracing the scars on his right arm.

"Yes. And during that time, in the last two years, I completely broke down Thomas' genetic sequence. And in doing so I'm now able to modify my serum to obtain a predictable outcome."

"That's amazing. Just amazing. You and your work are going to change the world. But I have a question."

"Yes?"

"So far, unless I'm mistaken, your ability to control people has been your only success story."

Dr. Matsushita tried to read Nikolay's face to see if he was mocking him. *I should just take control of you right now and make you eat a bullet from your own gun.* Instead he smiled back at Nikolay. *All in good time.*

"It's true. I'm sure you've heard of the creature that attacked downtown Washington D.C."

"I have," Nikolay responded.

"Well, that batch I created turned out to be tainted."

"Tainted?"

Yamato nodded. "It was Thomas' blood, but it wasn't pure. It had been collected and delivered to me on a towel. I moved ahead with my experiments and injected the new batch of serum into some homeless man I picked up off the street. Needless to say the only survivor was a man called Peter. The tainted serum made his body grow in strength and size; expanding it. But it grotesquely changed him; altering who he'd been."

"And then he escaped?"

"Hardly. I released him on purpose so he would express his newly discovered fury upon the city."

"Thus opening Pandora's box for the world to see."

"Something like that."

"So what are you working on now?" Nikolay asked.

"I'm glad you asked because it's the reason I brought you here in the first place."

Dr. Matsushita unlocked the door and the two of them walked in. Nikolay immediately saw that five children were strapped down, each in their own bed with IV lines protruding from the backs of their hands.

"Who are they?"

Dr. Matsushita smiled. "I believe you of all people will enjoy this irony. Four of them are Sam and Bill's children."

Nikolay turned and looked at Yamato's face, a grin appearing. "How?"

"I started a fire at their boarding school. In the confusion I took them, willingly of course," he said as he tapped the side of his head to remind Nikolay of his power.

"If Sam and Bill didn't hate you before, they certainly will now."

"They don't know I have their children."

"No?"

"Well, not yet at least. But that's going to change right now."

Dr. Matsushita moved past Nikolay and began to disconnect the IV lines from each child.

"What are you doing?"

"I'm waking them up. They're going to help locate Thomas and his family for us."

"How? I don't understand."

"I used the two vials of Thomas' blood, two clean vials I might add, and created specialized traits for all five of these children. I injected that individualized serum into each of them, and now it's time to verify that it actually works."

"But why use children?"

"Because they're easier to control, mentally speaking, and their bodies metastasize the serum faster than adults do. Now stand back and give me some room. This should make your jaw drop."

As the children started to stir Dr. Matsushita took control of all five of them at once. They stopped moving and lay back down in their beds; all except one.

"Tad," Yamato said, "please stand up."

The thirteen year old bully immediately stood up.

The doctor glanced over to Nikolay. "I'm speaking out loud for this one so you don't feel excluded."

"Of course. But I'm curious, what power did you give him? He doesn't look different or changed in any way. In fact, none of them do."

"That's called progress." Yamato adjusted his attention back to the teenager. "Tad, grab hold of the IV pole."

Tad extended his arm out and wrapped the five fingers of his right hand around the cold metal.

"Squeeze."

With Nikolay looking on Tad clenched. The metal pole snapped in two as if made of balsa wood and the IV bag crashed to the floor.

"Huynya!" Nikolay exclaimed in Russian. *Shit!*

Dr. Matsushita smiled at his success. "Lay down Tad."

The young boy, with enhanced strength, released the broken IV pole and stretched out on the bed.

"Remarkable." Nikolay looked around the room. "What about the others?"

"Let's see if Edward, Bill's nine-year-old, is ready for take-off."

"Take off? What do you mean?"

As Yamato concentrated, Edward stood up next to his bed. A few seconds later the boy's feet lifted a few inches off the ground. Nikolay was enthralled as he watched Edward float down the aisle and back to his bed again.

"Levitation?" Nikolay inquired.

"Flying actually, but this room is too small for a real test. Still, pretty incredible, isn't it?"

"You can say that again," clearly impressed.

"Let's continue."

Yamato turned his attention to Sarah, Bill's thirteen-year-old, next. She got up from her bed, under his control, and suddenly vanished from sight.

"What?" Nikolay exclaimed. "Where'd she go?"

Yamato pointed at him. "Behind you."

Nikolay turned and there she was. "Teleportation?"

Yamato shook his head. "No. This one can turn invisible and I'm very happy to see how successful it is. I wasn't able to see her at all."

"Neither could I."

"Okay Sarah, back to bed."

Yamato moved on to the next demonstration, Craig, Sam's nine-year-old. The boy stood up, turned to face Nikolay and suddenly ran straight at him full force.

"Wha…"

Nikolay barely had time to react as Craig barreled into him head first. But the boy's impact never came as Craig phased through Nikolay and ended up in the adjoining room. Craig knocked on the glass behind Nikolay and made him jump. Nikolay's reaction, and the look on his face, was priceless and Yamato enjoyed every second of it.

"Gotcha," Yamato said.

Nikolay looked down at his midsection. "He went through me."

"Yes. He phased through you and the wall."

Nikolay was astounded. "The applications that his power could be used for are absolutely mind boggling."

"One more to go, although the ability she possesses is somewhat unique."

"What do you mean?"

"I'll show you."

Yamato made Amanda, Sam's thirteen-year-old, get out of bed and walk over to him. Nikolay waited for her to do something spectacular but all she did was raise her arm and point.

"How far?" Yamato asked her.

"One hundred and twenty miles, give or take," Amanda replied.

Nikolay was confused. "What is she talking about? What does she do?"

"Thank you Amanda. Back to bed." He turned to Nikolay. "I gave her the greatest ability of all."

"She didn't do anything other than point."

Yamato nodded. "That's true. But it's not where she pointed that we're interested in."

"Why not?"

"Because she wasn't pointing to a where, but to a whom. I gave her a homing ability, and the individual she's attuned to is no other than our favorite target, Thomas Clark."

Nikolay grinned. "Outstanding. I'll gather my men." Nikolay turned, stopped and looked back at Yamato. "I have to say doc, you've accomplished something great here."

"I know. But it took a lot of effort, and time, to perfect my serum."

"And do you have any more of it left?"

"Unfortunately, no. I can't make any more until I have access to Thomas and the blood that runs through his veins."

"Well then, I should get the two of you together sooner than later."

15
Mon Nov 5, 2001

In the Oval Office the President of the United States sat back and closed his eyes. Almost immediately makeup was applied to his face to nullify the camera lights that would reflect during his upcoming speech.

"All done, Mr. President."

"Thank you Susan," he told her.

"Two minutes, Mr. President," an aide said from behind him.

The President got up from the makeup chair and bee-lined across his Oval Office, stepped over the cables strewn over the floor, crossed in front of the cameras and finally sat down behind his desk. He twisted it around to look out the window, his back facing the cameras.

I can't believe I'm making this speech. The world is changing, becoming darker and bleak. Our soldiers are dying in endless wars in campaigns I don't anticipate culminating during my lifetime. This world, torn apart by religion, beliefs and politics, will never unite together as one because of our incompatible ideologies. On top of that the world's technological advances continue to push the envelope of how quickly humans receive and digest information. And now, amongst everything else, the world has been slapped in the face with the reality that we are no longer on top of the food chain. They're scared, anxious, disbelieving and intrigued at the same time. But the reality, whether I believe what I saw or not, is that it's my responsibility to help bring order and peace to this world. Sometimes that means starting a war and other times it means doing what's necessary, right now, so in the long run people can sleep without fear. Now is one of those moments.

"Twenty seconds, Mr. President."

He swiveled his chair back around and faced the lights and the cameras. His speech was ready to go on the teleprompter. He cleared his throat and adjusted his tie one last time.

"Ten seconds."

The low murmur within the Oval Office ceased and all eyes focused on the task at hand.

"Five seconds."

The President focused.

"Three."

The man went silent and used his hand for the remainder of the countdown.

Two fingers.

One finger.

And finally the 'go' sign.

"Good morning. Over the past week our country has been subjected to two subjective and unexplainable incidents. The first was the downtown D.C. attack, covered heavily by the media, by an unknown humanoid creature of incredible strength and resilience. The second, although not carried out on U.S. soil, was the video that included the rescue of American soldiers. However, that rescue paled in comparison to the events in Afghanistan that undeniably captured the world's attention.

"I am taking the time to speak to you today, my fellow Americans, about that event. Is the man we saw rescuing American service men a hero? Absolutely. But the power this individual displayed, and the portal he used to escape, are straight out of a science fiction movie. This man represents the next step in the human evolution, for better or worse.

"With that said I come to you this morning with a concern for the safety of you and your families. This man must be detained and I come to you this morning because he has been identified.

"His name is Thomas Clark and he's a children's book writer. His wife's name is Laura. They have two children, Emily, age ten, and Gavin, age eight."

Pictures appeared on the screen of all of them.

"I am issuing warrants for their arrest, as well as the following individuals we'd also like to question. Sam Paige, Julie Paige, Bill Nicholson and Kim Nicholson."

Four more pictures appeared on the screen.

"A reward of five-hundred thousand dollars will be given to anyone with information that leads to their apprehension. Let me be clear about this situation. This is a national security issue and will be handled with the intensity it demands.

"Now, I've been in contact with other countries and they share their concerns that abilities, that we've all seen Mr. Clark perform, will dramatically alter the balance of power throughout the world. I would like to take this moment to clarify that any country caught operating within the boundaries of the United States, in an effort to apprehend Mr. Clark, will be held responsible; and the act alone will be considered a prelude to war."

He paused.

"Mr. Clark, if you're watching this broadcast I suggest you and your family do yourself a favor and turn yourselves in.

"Thank you America."

The President held his gaze until the lights and cameras switched off.

"We're clear, Mr. President."

He stood up, pushed his chair back and waved for everyone to immediately leave his office. Ten seconds later he had it to himself and picked up his phone.

"I want a full dossier on the locations Thomas Clark has lived at since childhood. Task men, drones and satellites to locate him. I want you to contact the NSA and get them involved immediately. Have them tap phones and use whatever tricks they have up their sleeves.

"Yes, sir."

"We're on the clock and I can guarantee we're not going to be the only ones hunting him down. Find him and find him now."

16

Mon Nov 5, 2001

The family's second night at the motel had been just as
restless and uneasy. The new revelation that Dr. Matsushita,
the same man who tortured and experimented on Thomas and
Emily four years prior, was responsible for their missing
children didn't come as a comfort to any of them. And even
though they knew this they were no closer to finding them then
they had been before, which only added to the mounting
tension.

Rebecca and Hobbes walked across the street, in the
morning, and ordered takeout breakfast. They brought it back
and everyone dug in as they gathered around the television.
Halfway during their meal the news was interrupted by a
special announcement by the President of the United States.

* * *

Thomas switched off the television. He, much like the
others, had been stunned into silence as the President outed
them.

"Shit," Bill managed to finally articulate. "We have to get
out of here. The whole country is going to come after us for
that reward money."

"And go where?" Sam argued.

"I don't know, but I know it's only a matter of time before
the front desk remembers our faces."

Thomas and Laura gathered Emily and Gavin on the bed
and held them close. They were still at a loss for words.

"Why don't we just turn ourselves in?" Julie said out loud.

"Jules, you can't be serious?" Sam probed.

"But why not?" she continued. "They don't want us."

"Enough!" he snapped. "I get that you're scared and that our children are still out there, but don't think for a second that we're turning ourselves over to the government. So next time, before you open your mouth and say something incredibly stupid, think about the consequences. You're talking about giving up on your family and trying to save yourself."

"No, I…"

Sam wasn't listening. "That's exactly what you just said. Don't you get it yet? We're in this together till the end. It's always been that way because it's the right thing to do."

Silence filled the room as Kim moved next to her sister to comfort her after Sam's tongue lashing.

"So what are we supposed to do?" Kim asked. "Our kids are still out there and you can't expect us, their mothers, to just abandon them because we're worth half a million dollars to every other American out there."

"We don't even know where to begin searching for Dr. Matsushita," Thomas said as he broke his silence. "Maybe Julie's right. Maybe you should go your own way and get as far away from us as you can."

"Come on bro," Bill said, "don't be like that. Our pictures were up on that television screen just like yours."

"We're stronger if we stay together," Sam repeated, "so get that nonsense out of your head."

"I don't know if…"

Emily interrupted her father with two simple words. "I'm scared."

Gavin tried to console his sister. "Everything's going to be alright."

"No. No it's not."

112

Laura pulled her daughter close and began to rock her back and forth. Hobbes took the brief lull in the conversation to open his mouth.

"You know, the President didn't mention Gabbi, Rebecca or me during his speech."

All eyes shifted to Hobbes.

"What are you saying?" Thomas asked him.

"Well, it's not much of a plan but the three of us could get out of here and head back to the bunker."

"The bunker?" Rebecca probed. "Why?"

"Well, it's someplace safe, to begin with, and only a few people actually know about it."

Bill voiced his opinion. "You mean like Nikolay, who in case anyone forgot, has taken the DCI hostage."

Hobbes continued. "I'm saying I want to be proactive. The bunker's servers, my servers, have information in them about you and your powers. I need to delete that data before Nikolay thinks about accessing them."

"And what makes you think the bunker hasn't already been compromised?" Sam asked.

"I don't know, but if we access the bunker through the farmhouse entrance, which exits out into the breakroom, we'll bypass any outside security and know for sure if the bunker has been taken."

"I can't let you do that," Thomas told him. "It's too dangerous."

"With all due respect, Thomas, I'm part of this family and I'll do whatever it takes to keep you guys safe. If we can reclaim the bunker I can change out the access codes and then provide you with intelligence to keep you guys off the grid and out of harm's way. My point is, I'm doing this and you can't stop me."

Hobbes stood there defiantly as Thomas rose to his feet, walked over and embraced him.

"You're a good man Hobbes. Thank you."

"Yeah he is," Gabbi added, "and I think his plan makes sense. I'm going too."

"It could give us the edge we need," Rebecca told everyone, "even though I don't like the idea of splitting up. However, I plan on staying with the family to protect them."

Hobbes nodded. "I understand. They need you more than Gabbi or I do."

Sam, Bill, Julie and Kim had stayed on the sidelines during this entire conversation and had finally cooled off somewhat.

"I'm sorry," Julie said. "I'm scared too. I just want this nightmare to be over."

"It's okay," Laura told her. "Trust me, we're all scared."

Sam regained his composure. "Okay, so that's half a plan. But where are the rest of us going to go while the entire world hunts us down?"

17
Mon Nov 5, 2001

"Mr. President?"

The Oval Office, and the equipment that had been in it, had been cleared away shortly after the President had finished his speech. He'd remained in his office, alone, contemplating Thomas Clark and what he ultimately meant to the human race when his intercom buzzed.

"Yes?" he replied.

"Sir, I have the Russian President on line two for you."

And it begins. "Thank you." He picked up the secure line. "Mr. President, a pleasure as always to speak with you," he said halfheartedly.

"And to you," replied Demian Anatolievich with an equal amount of veiled contempt.

"What can I do for you?"

"I'll get right to the point," Demian said. "We are concerned about the speech that you made earlier today."

"We?"

"Russia and our leaders."

"And what concerns you specifically, Anatolievich?"

"We are…troubled…by your statement that when you find these people you intend to keep them all to yourself, much like the creature that attacked D.C. At this point, no doubt, you're dissecting its body to acquire its knowledge."

"Now Anatolievich…"

"We demand access to the creature and any scientific advances you happen to gleam from it."

I despise this guy. "Mr. President, let me assure you that we have no intention of…"

The Russian President immediately interrupted him. "You want to assure me? Russian will not be placated in this matter. It is inevitable that the balance of power will dramatically shift to the United States' favor in the foreseeable future if this new technology, for lack of better words, is not shared with the rest of the world. Russia will not stand for such a blatant power grab and neither will other nations, some of which you consider your allies."

"What are you trying to say, Anatolievich?"

"Don't be naïve, Mr. President. You know exactly what I'm saying, but in case you have any doubts I'll take the time to make myself crystal clear. We will be searching for Thomas Clark, and the other individuals, with or without your consent."

The President bristled. *Sonofabitch.* "Any overt action conducted on American soil will be taken as an act of provocation."

"You can take it any way you'd like, Mr. President. The bottom line is that the future of our country, yours or mine, will become stronger based on who ends up with Thomas Clark. The power of teleportation alone, as we've seen in the video, is breathtaking and if harnessed would bring about a new era of commerce, technological advances and military potency to the world. I intend that future belong to Russia."

Shit. "Anatolievich, let me be forthcoming and direct. Your words ring hollow and are spoken from a position of weakness. I will not be dictated to nor coerced in this endeavor."

The Russian President was unphased. "Have it your way, Mr. President, but who's to say I don't have boots on the ground already?"

116

The President immediately drifted back to the conversation he had with Russell earlier. *Let's see how he handles this.* "Anatolievich, I've heard reports that Nikolay Dmitriev is alive and has taken our DCI hostage."

The Russian President chuckled. "I've read that you believe we are behind his abduction. Your 'leaked' story made me laugh and I'll tell you why. How would Nikolay Dmitriev kidnap one of your top ranking men, on American soil no less, when he's dead?" He chuckled again. "What a strange and magnificent age this world is embarking on when a dead man can come back to life. As to your 'rumor' of your Director of Central Intelligence being held hostage by a walking corpse, well, that sounds ludicrous, wouldn't you agree?"

The President remained silent as Anatolievich continued.

"However if what you're saying is true, and we happen to locate your man, I'll be sure to let you know where he can be picked up safe and sound. Good day, Mr. President."

Demian Anatolievich disconnected the line before the American President could respond. He dialed a new extension and the phone rang twice before it was answered.

"Send Tatiana Danilovna to my office immediately."

Two minutes later a curt knock came at his door.

"Come."

The door opened and a woman in her mid-thirties, with black hair and stunning features, entered his office. She approached and saluted. Tatiana Danilovna was a high ranking member of the SVR, the Foreign Intelligence Service of the Russian Federation. The SVR was responsible for intelligence and espionage 'activities' outside the Russian Federation, the counterpart to the CIA.

"Sit."

She did as she was told and for the next five minutes he read her in on Nikolay and his mission to capture the Clarks.

"You would reinstate Nikolay?" she inquired.

"No. He's far too dangerous, and if I'm to believe what he's told me, he's currently inhabiting an American soldier's body. But I need what he proposes he can obtain and that's where you come in."

"Sir?"

"Tatiana, I need you to leave for America within the hour, rendezvous with Nikolay and coordinate the Clark's successful extraction."

"Yes, sir."

"There's more. Nikolay didn't mention this to me but there's a chance that he has taken the American DCI prisoner. I need this verified firsthand because it complicates the delicate mission that's underway already. In any case, convince Nikolay to move quickly."

"Yes, sir."

"Good. Remember, there's a large number of moving pieces on a chess board and some of them have to be sacrificed along the way. Do you understand?"

She stood up. "Absolutely."

Demian smiled. "Dismissed."

Tatiana left his office and closed the door behind her. As she did Anatolievich picked up his phone and dialed yet another extension.

"Yes, Mr. President."

"Retask our submarines in the Atlantic and Pacific. I want them parked off the American coastlines."

"Yes, sir. I'll relay the orders immediately."

"Also. I want the fleet deployed within twenty-four hours and headed to the same location."

"By your command, sir."

Demian Anatolievich hung up and leaned back in his chair.

This is Russia's chance to reclaim our dominance in the eyes of the world. I will be known as the man who brought Russia back from the depression my country has wallowed in since the Cold War ended.

18
Mon Nov 5, 2001

The President of the United States stared at the phone in his hand.

That bastard hung up on me.

He replaced the receiver back on the cradle and thought about the conversation he'd just had for a few minutes. The President then picked up the phone and dialed a well-known number.

"Yes, sir?" a man with a stern military edge to his voice said on the other end.

"General, we've got a problem. It's come to my attention that we have Russian sleepers, on American soil, actively searching for Thomas Clark and the others. They are being led by Nikolay Dmitriev, a veteran of the Cold War and an enemy of the United States. If he finds and extract Thomas before we can contain him then the Russians will have a distinct advantage over us and the rest of the free world."

"The NSA has begun satellite coverage and is running facial recognition through traffic cameras nationwide. There's been zero activity on any of these individuals' credit cards or cell phones. It's just a matter of time sir, we'll find them."

"Hope that we do, General. As tough as it is to wrap my head around what Thomas Clark did on the video, well, I can only imagine the things he's capable of that we don't know about. So do our country and the people in it a favor, and find him."

19
Mon Nov 5, 2001

"It's okay," Laura told Julie. "Trust me, we're all scared."

Sam regained his composure. "Okay, so that's half a plan. But where are the rest of us going to go where we'll be safe while the entire world hunts us down?"

"Well figure that out as soon as Hobbes and Gabbi get out of here," Thomas said. He turned to them. "Good luck you two."

"Thanks," Hobbes replied.

"Be careful Gabbi," Gavin said and gave her a hug.

"I will cutie. We'll see you soon."

Gavin went back and sat down next to Stickers' cat carrier and comforted his pet.

Bill peeked through the curtains and checked the outside. "It's clear."

Sam cracked open the door, did another sweep with his eyes, then let Hobbes and Gabbi out. They quickly bee-lined to one of the Suburbans, got in and drove away. Sam eased the door closed and Bill let the curtains fall back together once again, blocking out the sun.

"Now what?" Sam asked.

"We need to discuss what our next steps are," Thomas replied.

"Find the children," Laura said, "and we need to locate a safe place to hole up."

"But where do we think Matsushita has our kids?" Bill asked.

"Good question," Rebecca countered. "But, if you think about it, he has to be close to the bunker. I mean, Thomas, your blood was handed off to him right around there, right?"

Thomas liked her reasoning. "Good thinking and yes, that makes sense."

Bill sighed. "And we just sent Hobbes and Gabbi back to that area. Their plan might not be as thought out as we..."

Three hard knocks on the motel door reverberated throughout the room. Worried looks flashed between everyone for a split second before they jumped into action. Sam, Bill and Rebecca pulled out their handguns and looked towards the door.

"Get down behind the beds," Thomas whispered as he simulated what he wanted with his hands. Rebecca moved back and made sure the rest of the family was protected.

"Maybe it's Hobbes and Gabbi. Maybe they forgot something?"

The hard rap on the door repeated. With the family ducked down Sam peered through the peephole while Bill covered the window which was covered by heavy shades.

"What the hell?" Sam muttered softly. "It's just some teenager."

"What? You mean some kid?"

Sam nodded and spoke through the door. "Yes?"

"I have some information about your missing children, all four of them," the teen said loud enough that everyone heard.

"What!?" Julie exclaimed and abruptly stood up beside the bed.

Sam and Bill barely registered their surprise when the door to their room was torn outwards. The teenager, with hands on either side of the door, turned and tossed it into the parking lot as if it weighed nothing. The boy stared at Sam, grinned, took three steps forward and reached out. Thomas acted on instinct and forcibly propelled the teen backward, who landed in the middle of the parking lot and rolled over a few times. It was then that Thomas, Sam and Bill registered that a dozen men, with weapons up, had the entrance to their room covered.

"Shit," Sam said as backpedaled farther into the room. "Get back."

Bill remained in the space between the window and the front door as Sam relocated behind the television for cover. Laura pulled Julie down next to her and held her there.

"Thomas," a familiar voice bellowed outside. "I know you're in there. You need to surrender."

Oh shit, no. Thomas knew exactly who was out there. He'd never forget the man behind that voice and what he had done to him and his daughter. *Matsushita.*

"Go fuck yourself Matsushita!" Thomas yelled back.

"That's Dr. Matsushita and may I say it's good to hear your voice again. It's been far too long since we last shared each other's company."

"You're a sick sonofabitch."

Bill popped his head out and took a quick peek, but he wasn't prepared for what he saw. As he pulled his head back his facial expression and reaction reverberated throughout the room.

"Oh shit."

"What?" Kim pressed. "What is it?"

Bill shook his head. "It's bad. They have a shitload of guys, but the worst thing is that Craig and Amanda are out there with them."

"WHAT!?" Kim and Julie cried out in unison.

The two sisters tried to get up and it took Laura, Rebecca, Hobbes and Gabbi to restrain them.

"LET ME GO DAMMIT!"

"I WANT MY CHILDREN!"

They started crying, tears flowing as they fought against the hands that held them back.

"Thomas, it sounds like you have your hands full in there."

"Go to hell!"

"Our patience is running thin. Why don't you come out and end this peacefully?"

"Peacefully? You have a warped sense of reality. Besides, why would I come out and show you my face? You'd just take control of me," Thomas shouted back.

Dr. Matsushita chuckled. "So you know about that? Good. But you also need to know that it took me a long time to perfect my serum, to augment your blood into something spectacular. And with all that work, and the pain you put me through, why shouldn't have I rewarded myself?"

"I put you through pain?" Thomas ridiculed. "You fucking tortured me and my daughter, poking and prodding us for your own advancement and amusement you asshole. I should have killed you when I had the chance."

"I hear the regret in your voice Thomas. You poor thing. Why don't you come out and give me a hug."

Thomas gritted his teeth. *Fucking psycho.*

"What are we going to do?" Bill whispered.

Before Sam or Thomas could answer a new voice took over the conversation.

"Enough! I want you alive Mr. Clark."

"And who are you?" Thomas shouted.

"And old friend of the family that's back from the dead, unlike your father."

Shit. Nikolay and Matsushita are working together?

126

"Nothing Thomas?" Nikolay taunted. "No quippy retort? Well, maybe Sam will want to talk to me instead, isn't that right Sam?"

That's Carl's voice but that isn't Carl anymore. Sam looked over at Rebecca who inhabited Eliot's body.

"How do you like the new body, Nikolay?" Sam asked.

"I feel young again Sam, thanks for asking. But I'm afraid we're getting off topic. I have a gun Sam. I have a gun and I'm pointing it at Edward's head."

Bill stiffened and Kim cried out.

"NO!"

Nikolay continued. "I will shoot Edward if you don't surrender."

"OH GOD NOOOO!" Kim screamed.

"NONONONONO!" Julie shrieked.

"You should listen to your wives before this situation turns in to a tragedy. I'll give you thirty seconds to come out with your hands up."

"What's going on Matsushita?" Thomas goaded. "Are you scraping the bottom of the barrel for people to work with again? Nikolay doesn't give a shit about you."

"We have a mutually beneficial relationship Thomas. I get you and he gets the serum. It's simplistic actually."

"But why? Why go down this path?"

"Seriously Thomas? Didn't you enjoy watching my creation tear downtown D.C. to shreds?"

"That was you? Why?"

"Because I could, and because I enjoyed it!" Yamato sneered.

"Fifteen seconds," Nikolay reminded them.

Thomas tried a new tact. "What did you do to the children? Why did you take them?"

127

"I took them to save them, of course."

"Bastard," Sam breathed out.

"Motherfucker," Bill quietly added.

"Where are the others?" Thomas asked. "Why are Amanda and Edward the only ones with you?"

"I imagine you'll know the answer to that question any second now," Dr. Matsushita replied.

"Five seconds," Nikolay stated.

Thomas looked around the room at his extended family and saw both fear and sadness in their eyes.

"Four"

Is this how it's supposed to end?

"Three."

Sam and Bill nodded to Thomas and readied their weapons. No way in hell they were going to surrender.

"Two."

Without warning Gavin cried out. Thomas and the others turned and saw Sarah, her arms wrapped tightly around Gavin's body, holding him in place. She had appeared out of nowhere.

"Sarah!" Kim cried out to her daughter. "Sarah, what are you doing!?"

In the next instant Craig appeared halfway through the adjoining room wall, spotted Emily and began to sprint through everyone's bodies to get to her. No one had time to react as he rematerialized in front of Emily and tackled her to the ground.

"CRAIG!" Julie screamed. "WHAT THE HELL IS GOING ON!?"

"Sarah?" Kim asked again, but her daughter's eyes were dead. "SARAH!"

"Watch the front!" Thomas bellowed to Sam and Bill.

Outside Dr. Matsushita put his hand on Nikolay's handgun and lowered it.

"There's no need for that now Nikolay, and I'd appreciate you not threatening my creations in the future. Understood?"

Nikolay grunted and then gave an order to his men. "Quiet them down."

Four gas canisters tore into the motel room; two flew through the front door and the other two shattered the large plate window as they penetrated the motel's interior. Gas immediately filled the room.

One of the canisters slammed into Thomas' head and his blood sprayed the bedspread. He collapsed to his knees and then fell on his side.

"Thomas!" Laura yelled. "Help." She then began to cough, her eyelids half closing as the gas began to take effect.

"I can't breathe!" Julie cried out, her hands around her throat.

Sam and Bill held their breath and looked helplessly at each other. They knew there was nowhere to run. If they went outside they'd be cut down in seconds and there was no possible way they were going to leave their family behind. It was only a matter of time before they had to inhale, and when they did the gas made their legs wobble.

Laura and the others, their screams subsiding as the gas invaded their systems, fell against each other in a haphazard pile; eyes wide and filled with terror.

Sam and Bill's handguns slipped from their hands, hit the carpet and skipped away. As they fought against the gas their legs gave way; their knees hit the floor. They both toppled over shortly after a final gasp for air, their lungs not finding any.

On the floor, between the two motel beds, Thomas coughed. Blood ran down the side of his face and oozed into the carpet.

Not like this. Not like this.

"Noooooo!"

Bill sighed. "And we just sent Hobbes and Gabbi back to that area. Their plan might not be as thought out as we..."

Three hard knocks on the motel door suddenly reverberated throughout the room. Worried looks flashed between everyone for a split second before they jumped into action. Sam, Bill and Rebecca pulled out their handguns and looked towards the door.

Thomas's head hurt.

"Maybe it's Hobbes and Gabbi. Maybe they forgot something?"

The hard rap on the door repeated. With the family ducking down Sam peered through the peephole while Bill covered the window that was covered by heavy shades.

"What the hell?" Sam muttered softly. "It's just some teenager."

"What? You mean some kid?"

"Don't open it," Thomas told Sam. "The doctor, Nikolay and about twelve men are out there. They've come to capture us and they'll use gas."

"What?" Bill exclaimed. "How could you know any of that?"

"Because," Thomas replied solemnly, "it worked before on us just a moment ago right here in this room. Trust me and remember the sabotage on the plane. If we don't get out of here right now they're going to take us, all of us."

Another series of powerful knocks made the door shake.

Sam was convinced. "How?"

"Gavin's portal," Thomas replied.

"Oh hell no," Bill instantly declared.

"No," Gavin said. "We'll die if we go back there."

Rebecca shook her head. "I have no idea what will happen to me if I go back there."

"You're not going to get a yes from me either Thomas," Sam told him. "It'd be suicide. If we go back there you know those horrific creatures will tear us apart. Are you fucking insane?"

"What other choice do we have?" Laura asked the group.

"With all due respect, Laura, you don't have the first clu…"

Craig phased through the adjoining wall and tackled Emily to the ground just as Tad ripped off the motel door and tossed it away. Thomas, using his power, tossed Tad away from them and back into the parking lot.

"Do it son!" he yelled as he beseeched Sam and Bill with his eyes.

In the back of the motel room Gavin gulped, formed his portal and placed a death grip around Stickers' carrier handle.

"GOOO!" Thomas roared. "GO NOW!"

Outside Thomas saw the Russian sleepers begin to rush towards the room. As Sam and Bill reluctantly subjected their family to the perils of certain death, on another realm of existence, Thomas held off the armed men.

Multiple gas canisters crashed through window and dispersed their contents into the enclosed space.

Thomas ran towards the rear of the room, helped Laura picked up Craig, his arms still firmly clasped around Emily, and together they were the last ones that passed through the portal.

20
The Other Place

Julie lost her footing, as she came through the portal, and fell to her knees on the warm, soft sand. She was knocked over as Kim appeared, which sent them both sprawling. Afterwards Gavin and Rebecca arrived on the small island, and quickly added to the pile up, falling over and onto the sand. Gavin lost his grip on Stickers' carrier and it plummeted to the sand, toppling over on its side. Sam and Bill, right behind them, somehow managed to say on their feet until they were knocked down from behind as Thomas, Laura, Emily and Craig materialized. The portal snapped shut behind them as gruesome and horrifying creatures began to dive at them.

The island was surrounded in a thick, black fog that consisted of the evil that inhabited this realm. Upon sensing new prey the inhabitants of the fog surged towards the family like predators. Mutilated and disfigured faces formed out of the blackness around them. Shadowy claws, jagged and obscure, swiped and cut the air, as if taunting their upcoming meal. Shrill screeching filled the air and intensified to earsplitting levels within seconds.

As the family disengaged themselves from each other Julie and Kim's senses became overloaded. They weren't prepared for the horrors the Other Place consisted of.

"MAKE IT STOP!"

"I CAN'T TAKE THIS!"

"WE'RE ALL GOING TO DIE!"

Laura pulled Emily, Gavin and Craig close to her in an attempt to shield them from the incoming danger. Sam, who had righted himself, yelled.

"WEAPON'S UP! DEFEND!"

Almost in unison Sam, Bill, Rebecca and Thomas extracted their side arms, brought them up to bear, and began to fire into the dark shapes that dove at them. Round after round tore through the apparitions, but the dark phantoms sluffed off the bullets like they were nothing.

A billowy arm reached out from the swirling mist and grabbed hold of Kim's arm. The smokey hand clenched tight around her wrist and sadistically jerked her body sideways.

"No no no no no no!" Kim screamed, her eyes closed as she tried to pull away.

"GET OFF HER!" Bill yelled as he shifted his weapon's sights and fired into his wife's assailant.

Discovering his gun had no effect Bill dropped it, dove for Kim and wrapped his arms around her waist. The specter laughed at him and Bill caught a glimpse of its rotting teeth inside the churning obscurity of its body.

"Don't let go!" Thomas screamed and moved to help.

"HELP ME!" Kim shrieked, panic dripping from her throat.

Another formless creature, sensing weakness, rocketed in and wrapped its hands around one of Kim's legs. The struggle abruptly ended as Kim's body wrenched free of Bill's grasp, was swiftly dragged across the sand and disappeared into the surrounding darkness.

"NOOOOOOOOOO!" Bill cried out, as his arms reached out in desperation. "NOOOOOOOOOO!"

Sensing victory another shade zipped in, followed by yet another and another. The family had no choice but to hunker down as claws sliced through the air inches away from them. The dark cloud's screeching intensified and they were left with no choice but to place their hands over their ears to alleviate the unbearable pain that had filled the air.

"BEGONE!" a deep voice commanded.

The dense black fog, surrounding the family, suddenly dispersed up into the sky and sped away from the island. As the darkness shrank into the distance the sun was able to cascade down to the sandy beach.

Bill was already up and running, as the rest of them started to recover, towards Kim's inert body that floated face down in the shallow ocean water.

"KIM!" Bill pleaded as he hastily slogged through the water. "KIM!"

A few seconds later Thomas, Sam, Julie and Rebecca took off after Bill, grasping the dire situation. Bill reached his wife, dropped to his knees in the calm, shallow water and rolled her over. Her eyes were closed and water dribbled out of her mouth.

"Kim?" he asked with desperation. "Kim?"

No response. Trying to contain his fear Bill quickly checked the pulse on her throat as the other four arrived. Nothing.

"She's not breathing and doesn't have a pulse either," he told them.

"Kim?" Julie probed with fear as she took in her sister's dismal state. "Kim? Please, talk to me. Please Kim. PLEASE! WAKE UP!"

"Get her to the beach right now," Thomas instructed.

Nodding, Sam and Rebecca immediately picked Kim's unresponsive form out of the water and moved with purpose back to the beach as Bill slumped down, Thomas at his side.

"She's dead...and I couldn't help her..."

Kim's arms flopped from side to side, of their own accord, as they carried her lifeless body. Julie, clearly in shock, followed aimlessly behind them. Thomas yelled over his shoulder as he placed a reassuring hand on his friend's shoulder.

"GAVIN! GET READY!"

Thomas then put his arm under Bill's armpit and lifted him to his feet.

"I've got you brother."

Bill's eyes were someplace else, someplace far away as Thomas helped him back towards the shore.

Gavin, when he heard his father yell, pulled himself away from Laura, stood up and saw his aunt's inert form being brought towards him. He met Sam and Rebecca as they reached the beach and waited for them to lay her gently down on the sand.

"Kim!?" Julie said again as she got closer. "Wake up!"

Julie tried to go to her sister's side but Sam forcibly restrained her.

"Kim!? No! Let me go! Kim!? KIM!? WAKE UP!"

Gavin plopped down next to Kim and placed his hands on her forehead. With everyone looking on he closed his eyes and concentrated. The tension in his face was palpable as he strained to heal her. Thomas and Bill barely made it to shore just as Kim's body arched upwards. Her hips extended and a fountain of water erupted out of her mouth. She turned to one side and vomited another torrent of water out of her lungs before she was able to take in a tremendously loud and deep breath.

"UUUUHHHHHHHHHH!"

"KIM!" Julie screamed and squirmed out of her husband's grasp.

Bill, upon hearing his wife take a lungful of air, pulled himself back from the brink and managed to refocus on her. He pushed away from Thomas and joined Julie in the sand next to his wife. Kim took a second breath, then a third and finally opened her eyes. Tears were running down everyone's faces as Bill took her into his arms and held her.

"I thought I had lost you," he barely managed to say. "I thought I had lost you."

"Kim?" Laura asked gently. "How…how do you feel?"

She tried to look around but the sun was in her eyes. "A little blind I guess. Could you help me sit up?"

Bill and Julie assisted Kim to a sitting position.

"Are you okay?" he asked.

Kim slowly nodded her head. "Yeah. Better." She took her time and glanced around at everyone and their wet faces. "Did something happen?"

The fact that Kim was alive and had made an unintentional joke helped to alleviate the horror they had all just been subjected to. Bill even managed a half chuckle.

"Fucking hell, sweetie, are you serious? You died."

"I did? I don't remember anything after coming though the portal."

"Nothing?" Bill asked.

She shook her head and wiped her mouth off. "How could I have died? What happened?"

"The creatures…, the creatures ripped you away from me. I thought…"

Kim put a reassuring hand on Bill's face. "I'm okay. I'm right here."

He hugged her again and then the two of them got to their feet.

"Don't die on me again, you hear me?" he said half-jokingly.

Julie pulled her sister close and hugged her fiercely. "You bitch," she said softly. "You had me worried for nothing."

"I guess you're not the only one who's died and come back to life, right sis?"

Julie hugged her tighter. "You scared the crap out of me."

"I only wish I could have seen your face. Priceless."

Julie laughed as she wiped away a tear. "I hate you."

"I hate you too."

"Truly amazing," a deep voice said behind them.

Sam instinctively whirled around, pulled out his handgun and pointed it at the unknown man who now stood on the island with them. Everyone else turned to face the unknown visitor.

"Who are you?" Sam demanded.

"He's the Caretaker," Rebecca told everyone. "You can put your gun down now Sam."

Sam's weapon didn't waver. "Are you here to hurt us?"

"I was the one that sent the demons, for lack of better words, away. But, on the contrary," the Caretaker replied, "I was going to ask you a similar question."

"What are you talking about?" Thomas asked.

The Caretaker sauntered across the sand, past Sam and straight up to Thomas.

"Thomas Clark, you've upset the balance."

"What? What do you mean?"

The Caretaker backed away and leaned on the lone palm tree as Sam holstered his weapon. Laura continued to hold Emily and Craig's hands firmly in her own.

"Are you all alright?" the Caretaker asked as he looked over at Kim.

"I am now," she replied.

He addressed Gavin. "And you, Gavin Clark. I'm very impressed. You and your powers have come a long way."

"Thanks, I guess."

The Caretaker walked over, bent down, righted the cat carrier and then opened its door. Stickers, orange fluff and all, exited the carrier and sniffed the Caretaker's hand. With his curiosity satisfied Stickers rubbed against his hand and purred.

"Apparently I didn't arrive in time, but the truth is I wasn't expecting any of you to come back here ever again." He stopped for a second. "I apologize. We have plenty of time to chat. For the time being, first thing's first," as he gestured towards Craig.

It was then that Sam and Julie's heads cleared enough to realize that their son, Craig, was there with them. It didn't take long before they rushed over and pulled him close.

"I missed you sooo much," Julie said as she gushed and lavished her son with attention.

"Are you okay?" Sam asked as he took his turn to hug his son.

Craig nodded of his own volition, free of Matsushita's control. "Yes."

"What happened to you?"

Craig didn't answer right away. "He…he did something to me." He paused and then said. "To us."

"What are you talking about?" Julie asked.

"Craig's no longer under Matsushita's control," Thomas said as he spoke out of turn. "At least we have that going for us."

Craig turned to face Emily. "Sorry for tackling you. I couldn't stop myself."

"I know," Emily replied and smiled. "It's okay."

139

"Would someone please tell me what's going on?" Julie asked again.

Laura bent down and looked into Craig's eyes. "I'm glad you're safe, we all are. We're very interested in what you've been through. Can you walk us through what you remember? Do you recall the fire at your school?"

He reluctantly nodded and his mother picked up on it.

"Can't you see that he doesn't want to talk about it?" Julie said. "He's been through enough already."

Sam sighed. "It's more complicated than that, Jules, and you know it. We need answers and that means we need to know what our son knows."

Bill and Kim waited anxiously on the sidelines because she knew that Dr. Matsushita still had her children.

Laura looked at Julie until she finally relented. She then turned her attention back to Craig as everyone looked on.

"What's the first thing you remember?"

"Sarah was talking with her mom, I think, and then there was an explosion. We were all knocked to the floor."

Kim's face contorted as she recalled the helplessness and panic she'd felt in the restaurant, days earlier, after she'd heard the loud boom over the phone.

"Go on," Laura urged.

"There was a lot of confusion. I remember screaming as the fire neared us, but then someone appeared. The next thing I know I'm walking outside, across the grass, and I got in a van."

Laura nodded. "Who else is in there with you?"

"My sister, Edward. Sarah…and Tad. He and I don't get along. I had to kick him in the balls one time when he was bullying me."

Sam tried to suppress his grin, but Julie caught it and elbowed him in his side.

"Did the van have any windows?"

Craig shook his head. "No. He made us keep our eyes closed the entire ride back to where he took us."

"Do you have any idea where that place is?"

He shook his head again. "No. I'm sorry." He looked dejected.

Laura smiled to reassure him. "It's okay Craig, you're doing great." She cast a quick glance over at Julie and then settled back in on the young boy again. "Then what happened?"

"The man with the scars on his arm made us lie down in beds. After that I don't know what happened until he woke us up. And when he did we were all...different."

"What do you mean different, sweetheart?" Julie asked her son.

"The man did something to us."

Thomas took the opportunity to speak up. "He injected them with modified serum, tailored to each child. That's what he used the two stolen vials of my blood for."

"What?" Julie exclaimed. "He experimented on my son!?"

Craig looked down and away from his mother.

"It's okay," Emily told Craig. "Why don't you show them?"

"Show us what?" Julie uttered with a hint of alarm.

Craig looked around, a little apprehensive.

"Go ahead," Gavin said as he voiced his support. "We're all family here."

"Okay. Here goes."

Craig activated his ability, turned and ran straight at the trunk of the palm tree the Caretaker stood under. Julie's hesitation quickly turned to concern when she saw her son was on a head-on collision with the tree.

"Sto…"

Craig phased right through the tree and appeared on the other side, unscathed. He walked back and when he couldn't take his eyes off the Caretaker he tripped over something but caught himself. Craig's demeanor changed when he saw what he'd stumbled over and he backpedaled.

"That's a skeleton!" he exclaimed, finger extended towards the bones on the beach.

"Sorry," Gavin told Craig. "He can't hurt you."

"He? Why are there some guy's remains on your island, Gav?"

"You know the story already," Gavin reminded him. "That's Victor Bannon, remember?"

Craig took another look and shrugged. "Oh yeah. Serves him right." He then turned and rejoined his parents.

Sam smiled. "Son, that was pretty cool."

"Yeah, it was," Bill added.

Thomas came over and squatted down by Craig. "Show me. Phase out."

Craig nodded. "Okay."

Thomas slowly extended his hand towards the boy's chest. As he reached it his hand passed through. Thomas pulled it back.

"Nice trick," and smiled. "How do you feel?"

Craig smiled back. "Good."

Julie touched her son's arm and found it solid. "What did you just do? How…"

"Craig now has an ability, like me and the rest of my family, which means that Dr. Matsushita has perfected his serum based on my DNA."

142

Julie was still trying to wrap her head around everything. "But…but what does that mean?"

"It means," Thomas said, "that he's going to be sought after as well."

"Shit," Bill said. "Thomas is right. But what about Edward and Sarah? And what about Amanda? What happened to them?"

Thomas readdressed Craig. "We know that Tad was given strength, especially since he ripped that door right off its hinges. But do you happen to know what abilities the other three received?"

He nodded. "Edward can fly."

Bill interjected. "Did you just say he can fly?"

"Yeah."

"Okay. Okay. That's something I didn't see coming. Just the number one thing I've always wanted to be able to do, dammit."

"Go on," Laura told him.

Craig picked up where he left off. "Sarah can turn invisible."

Bill interrupted again. "Are you kidding me right now? Those are any kid's top two wants, flying and invisibility."

"And Amanda?" Sam asked. "What can she do?"

Laura motioned Craig to continue. "It's not good."

"What's not good?" Julie probed anxiously. "What the hell did that psychopath of a doctor do to our daughter?"

Craig didn't want to tell them.

"It's okay Craig," Laura said with a soothing tone.

He mulled it over, looked at Thomas and finally spit it out. "She can track you."

Thomas was taken aback. "What?"

"Her ability is to know both where and how far away you are. Sorry."

"No wonder they knew we were in that motel," Bill stated.

"Shit," Thomas breathed out. "And it's not your fault Craig, none of this is. It's mine."

Laura put an arm around Thomas as he absorbed the new information.

"It's not your fault," she told him.

"But it is. None of this would have ever happened if it wasn't for me."

"Thomas is correct," the Caretaker said as he left the shade of the palm tree and walked over. "As I said, he's upset the balance."

"Listen, Caretaker," Sam said, "or whatever your name is. I don't know who or what you are but putting this all on Thomas is bullshit."

"Perhaps, Sam Paige, but certain lines have been crossed; barriers broken and torn open. No matter how you dissect it the fact remains that your reality, your entire world, has begun to change…and it all started with you, Thomas."

"Back off," Sam told the Caretaker. "Whether you think you're God or not I will not stand here and listen to your accusations against my friend."

The Caretaker turned and addressed Sam. "While your mind won't comprehend the totality of what I'm about to tell you I'm going to try to explain it to you anyway. There are no gods, nor have there ever been. All that's out there, past your insignificant speck of a planet, is the will of the universe. Your history is filled with the notion of gods and lording over mankind throughout the ages, but religion and gods all came from the same place, from the imagination of men."

"If that's true," Sam replied, "what's religion's purpose, whether someone is a Christian, Jew, Muslim or whatever then?"

"Religion, and all gods for that matter, have always been created and used by man as instruments for control and power."

"Control?"

The Caretaker nodded. "Unfortunately, yes. Mankind, as a whole, is notoriously greedy and selfish. What better way to control millions of people than to tell them how to think and what to believe. And then, if they don't, make them believe they'll end up in Hell."

"That can't be right. People have believed in God for thousands of years."

"True. Traditions are valued amongst your people, and those believers gain comfort, in exchange for the shackles they unknowingly, but willingly, place around their own necks."

"And the bible?"

"It was written by men, who are human, and that by definition means it's fallible by nature. Of course, if it had been written by women your history would have turned out very differently. In any case, the bible and other religious texts your world considers sacred, were created, once again, as a means of creating and maintaining control."

"How?"

"By using fear that preaches that 'the gods' will smite you down if you do anything bad. And these beliefs still continue to this day, which consistently amazes me."

"And why's that?"

"Because people have evolved, Sam. They're smarter, more educated and have finally begun to think for themselves. When all's said and done I'm surprised organized religion is still as strong as it is. I guess people are still afraid to take responsibility for their own actions. They seem perfectly happy using the bible and 'the gods in the sky' as shields, living within a man-made prison, content as slaves. Religion, as a whole, has taken humanity and torn it apart over the centuries. In the Middle East entire regions hate each other, and over what, land? And that holy land is based on stories that were, once again, created by men. It's a never ending cycle of hate, distrust and violence. But the funniest thing about it is that all sides believe their god fights on their side, and that they're the good guys.

"But I digress." The Caretaker turned back to Thomas. "As I said, the balance has been upset."

"I didn't ask for any of this," Thomas finally said.

"No, you didn't, but that is irrelevant now."

"Why?"

"Because Thomas, time is irrelevant and I'm going to show you exactly what I mean."

Before Thomas or anyone else could react, the Caretaker touched Thomas's face and accessed his history. The island transformed into a stage that consisted of Thomas' history for everyone to see. Thousands upon thousands of pictures had appeared, like photographs, and floated in the air all around them.

"Holy crap," Thomas exclaimed. "What are these?"

"Look closer."

It took a moment. "These are me. They're mine."

The images filled the space but no one felt crowded by them. It was an amazing display and they were awestruck. Shortly after the initial shock wore off each of them began to examine the snapshots that had made Thomas the man he was today.

"This is incredible," Laura said wide-eyed.

"Wow," Sam said as he reached out and touched one in front of him. "I remember that day."

"Hey," Bill smiled, "this one's the day at the park when you bankrolled SANDBOX."

"Our first time together," Laura said as her own memories flooded back.

"And this one is from our wedding," Kim announced.

The Caretaker quickly sifted through the floating images, found what he was looking for and touched it. The island, and the beach they were standing on, disappeared and had been replaced by a hospital room. Everyone looked down at their feet and saw that they no longer stood on sand because it had been replaced with a solid floor. The room seemed tangible and authentic because in fact it was.

"Where are we?" Laura asked.

"Is this real?" Julie added.

"I'm taking you all on a trip through time," the Caretaker explained.

Against the wall, on a hospital bed they saw Betsy, Thomas' mother. His father, Michael, stood by her side with her hand in his. A nurse dabbed her forehead with a washcloth while a doctor sat between her legs and coaxed Betsy along.

"What's going on?" Thomas began to say. "I don't remem…"

"Just watch," the Caretaker told him.

Laura, Sam, Julie, Bill, Kim, Rebecca, Emily and Gavin watched as Thomas was brought into the world, then placed on his mother's chest. Tears of joy and relief washed down Betsy's face, as did Michael's. They were proud parents and it showed.

Thomas smiled and asked the Caretaker a question. "This isn't my memory, is it?"

"No, but I'll get to that. But for now, it's time to take you down the path that led you here, for better or for worse."

"What does that mean?"

Before Thomas' question could be answered the hospital vanished and was replaced with a children's birthday party. Young kids were running around and presents were stacked in the corner of the living room.

"Wait," Thomas said. "This is the house I grew up in."

Pin-the-tail on the donkey was finishing up just as the clown arrived. Soon afterwards the children were laughing as the clown continued to find money behind everyone's ears. He tied balloon animals for some of them and then left.

"No," Thomas muttered.

Happy Birthday started up in the kitchen and the group moved from the living room to the dining room as Betsy pushed through the swinging door with a birthday cake. There were five candles and written in frosting were the words 'Happy 5th Birthday Tommy."

"No," he said again.

The song ended and Tommy blew them all out. Cheers erupted from the other children as his mother handed him a cake knife. Betsy couldn't locate the paper plates and went back to the kitchen to find them, and when she couldn't she spoke to Michael.

"I spaced on the plates. I'll be right back. Start getting people back in the living room for presents and we'll save the cake until afterward."

As the kids were ushered back to the other room Betsy grabbed her purse and headed to the garage. She backed out of the driveway and continued down the street, heading into town.

Thomas was disturbed as he relived the sequence of events. "No. Don't go."

Laura, knowing this story all too well, moved to Thomas' side and put her arms around him.

As Tommy continued to open gift after gift the phone rang in the kitchen. Michael left the room to go answer it.

"Hello?"

"Mr. Clark?"

"Yes?"

"Men like us never get back the things we love."

"Excuse me?"

"Your wife's dead. I just had her killed in the intersection of Miner Road and Camino Pablo."

Michael's demeanor changed. "I don't believe you."

"Well that's not really my problem. I'll just tell you one more thing then."

"And what's that you sick asshole."

"She's dead because of Yuri, Michael. Have a good day."

Michael threw the phone against the wall, out of control. He found something else with his hands, threw it and it crashed through one of the kitchen windows.

"NO!" he screamed. "NO! NO! NOOOOOOOO!!!!"

"Oh my god," Kim said.

The family cringed as the memory played out. Thomas absentmindedly commented.

"I heard the crash from the kitchen, but I never knew what had happened in there."

Before he could continue the scene transformed once again and everyone found themselves in a morgue. Michael was arguing with someone and locked the morgue door. He walked back over to the table which contained a white sheet that was draped over a human figure. Thomas's father gently pulled back the sheet and exposed Betsy's face. A lump caught in Michael's throat and his eyes welled up.

"Oh baby...oh baby I'm so sorry."

Tears spilled down Michael's cheeks. Thomas cried as well as he watched his father's interactions.

Michael brushed Betsy's matted hair back and looked into her cold, dead eyes.

"I don't want to remember you like this. I love you. It's only been two days but I miss you so much."

His tears ran freely down his face.

"I don't know what to do without you. I don't know what to tell our son. I promise you this Betsy, I'm going to find whoever did this to you and I'm going to kill them. I swear it."

Thomas' heart sank as he heard the desperation in his father's voice.

"Why are you showing me this?" he asked the Caretaker, a distinct sadness in his voice.

The Caretaker didn't respond as the moment in time continued to play out. The morgue assistant came back into the room.

"Sorry about all that, but there's one other thing I believe you should know about."

"What are you talking about?" Michael asked.

"I hate to be the one to tell you all this, but I think it's better it comes from me than him." The assistant jerked his thumb over his shoulder at his boss. Michael waited.

"Mr. Clark. Your wife was two months pregnant. I'm sorry sir."

Thomas knew that revelation was coming but it still hit him hard in the gut when he heard it again.

"Stop it," Thomas begged the Caretaker.

"Why are you doing this?" Laura inquired. "What is there to gain by putting my husband through this?"

The scenery whirled around and changed once again. When it was done everyone now found themselves standing in a large grass field attached to a school.

"Holy cow. We're back at Wagner Ranch," Sam said.

"It's been forever since we set foot in this place," Bill added.

"Who're they?" Kim asked as she pointed to two boys playing with a baseball and bat off in the distance.

Sam's mouth dropped open. "No way."

The Caretaker zoomed in abruptly until the group stood only feet away from the boys.

"Is that you dad?" Gavin asked.

"Yeah," Thomas barely managed to say. "It's been a long time since I was that young."

"And that's you dad," Craig said to Sam," isn't it?"

Sam nodded. "But this is weird. I remember this day."

"So do I Sam," Thomas replied, "and it's about to start all over again."

"Hey, momma's boy!" a large boy around five foot five with black hair spat out as he approached Sammy and Tommy.

"Who is that?" Emily asked.

"Shit," replied Bill. "That's Nigel. Nigel Clemmings."

Tommy and Sammy inched together as Nigel got closer.

"Hey, buttheads."

Nigel loomed even closer.

"Hey Tommy. Let me see that bat." It hadn't been a question.

Tommy didn't respond as Nigel approached, only ten feet away at this point.

"You move and you die," Nigel commanded as he read their body language.

Neither of them moved an inch as he stopped in front of them.

"I said, give me that bat!" he screamed.

Gripped in fear Nigel snatched the bat from Tommy's clenched hands. Both Tommy and Thomas let out a groan.

"Thanks, you little shit." Nigel examined the bat. "Nice Tommy, it even has your name on it," he mocked.

Nigel began to take practice swings and his smile became more pronounced with each one. He then began to take steps towards the two boys, swinging back and forth as he approached. Finally one of his swings barely missed the top of Sammy's head and both of them snapped out of their fear.

"Run Sammy!" Tommy cried out.

The two sprinted towards the school buildings with Nigel after them.

"Hurry Sammy, we can lose him by the dumpsters!"

With Nigel forty feet behind they turned a corner and Tommy slipped on some loose gravel which sent him sprawling on to the asphalt. Nigel was on them in seconds.

"You're dead Tommy," Nigel growled.

Sammy, about twenty feet away, had stopped running after Tommy took his spill, and now he stood there not knowing what to do.

"Get back here or I'll crack his head open!" Nigel promised as he looked at Sammy and raised the bat.

"Run Sammy! Get some help!" Tommy cried.

A moment later Sammy bolted and disappeared. Tommy was left all alone with Nigel.

"Bad move. Now I'm going to teach you a lesson. You will worship the ground I walk on, won't you Tommy?"

The sinister smile Nigel had on his face filled Tommy with horror. He suddenly realized that Nigel was out for blood. Tommy pushed himself off the ground and leaned against the school wall. Nigel watched his prey, grinning the entire time.

"I'm going to do what my father does to me, only worse," Nigel said as he raised the bat over his head and prepared to swing it down.

Suddenly Nigel cried out and fell to the ground sceaming. "OOUUUUCCHHHH!"

A large rock lay next to him and blood oozed from a wound in his head. Tommy saw Sammy with another rock, ready to do battle and didn't hesitate too long before he picked up his fallen bat and hightailed it out of there with Sammy.

"I don't like Nigel," Gavin said matter-of-factly.

"Neither did we," Sam replied.

The scene zoomed forward and started again at Sammy's house.

"Holy crap. Holy crap. Holy crap," said Tommy. "You totally saved me Sammy. Thanks!"

The moment in time faded away.

"So that's what Nigel looked like as a kid," Laura said. "Pathetic."

"Jesus. How old were you when that happened?" Julie asked.

"Ten," Sam replied. "Well, nearly ten."

"And was Nigel always like this?"

"Yes. And it got worse, much worse."

Thomas tried again to get the Caretaker to explain the purpose of reliving his life. "Why are you doing this?"

The Caretaker chose another snapshot, amidst the hundreds of thousands that floated in the air and when he did they found themselves in a bedroom.

"Oh shit," Thomas said. "Not this. Not this night."

"This is after Nigel tossed you into traffic and hospitalized you, isn't it?" Bill asked gently.

Thomas nodded. "This is THAT Christmas."

Laura squeezed his arm in support knowing full well what was coming.

Tommy was in bed when his father walked in and sat down.

"Tommy. Are you going to do anything?"

"What do you mean dad?"

"About Nigel."

"No."

"He's lying," Laura voiced absentmindedly.

"Your friend's parents and I are suing Nigel's father. I want you to know that we're doing everything we can to make this right. Nigel won't be coming to school anymore. He's on house arrest."

"What exactly is house arrest?"

"Basically it means he can't leave his house. He really should be in jail for what he did. Anyway, I don't want you or your friends to worry about him anymore."

"Okay dad."

"I love you Tommy Clark, I really love you."

"I love you too dad."

"Goodnight son."

"Goodnight dad."

As Michael closed the door, Tommy looked over to the other side of his room. His bat was still there.

The moment in time followed Michael out of his son's room and then skipped ahead two hours. Michael reopened Tommy's door and made sure he was sleeping. He tiptoed inside and grabbed his son's bat, then made his way back to the door and closed it behind him.

The scene changed and they found themselves standing in the driveway of an unknown house.

"What are we doing here?" Gavin asked.

Before Thomas could answer a car pulled to a stop down the road and Michael got out with his son's bat. They watched him walk up the driveway, in the middle of the night, and head for the front door. He tested it and found it to be open. Michael pushed it inward ever so slowly, entered the house and closed it behind him.

The Caretaker changed the perspective so they were inside the house.

Harold Clemmings lay on the couch, drunk and passed out. Michael gave the man a sour look and then headed down the hallway towards the bedrooms. He entered the first open door and disappeared.

The scene changed to the bedroom.

Michael stood over the bed and looked down at the bully who had nearly killed his son. He raised the bat over his head and froze as he argued with his conscience. Eventually he lowered the bat and let it slip through his fingers where it clattered to the floor. As Nigel stirred in his bed Michael fled the house.

But the scene didn't change. They all remained in the room.

"What's going on? Kim asked. "Why are we still here?"

Just then another boy, who looked identical to Nigel, emerged from the closet where he'd been hiding.

155

"Who's that?"

"That's Albert," Thomas explained. "He's Nigel's twin brother that was kept in the basement."

Albert walked over, picked up the fallen bat and inspected it. A grin appeared on his face and moments later he began to repeatedly crush his brother's skull with it. Blood and brains flew everywhere.

Julie and Kim turned away from the messy murder, forgetting that they were just observing and couldn't be seen by Albert or even hit by the flying brain matter.

"That's insane," Rebecca said. "Are you sure you want Em and Gav to see any of this?"

"We're way too far down the rabbit hole at this point," Thomas replied. "They've seen worse."

Albert finished and went to take a shower. When he was done he dressed in Nigel's clothing, packed a backpack, took money from his father's room and left the house with the bat.

The scene changed and they found themselves outside Tommy's house.

Albert appeared out of the darkness, slipped into the open garage and into the house, bat in hand.

The scene changed to Michael's bedroom.

They saw Albert sneak into the master bedroom and then notice Michael in his study. Albert entered the closet and waited. As Michael walked by Albert stepped out and cracked him over the head with the bat.

"Fucking Albert," Bill whispered.

Thomas shuddered and Laura gripped him even tighter.

Albert found the shotgun, above the safe in the study, and pulled it off the wall. After figuring out how it worked he dragged Michael's unconscious body along the rug. He then propped him up against the bed and the nightstand and placed the shotgun barrel under Michael's chin.

Thomas turned away as Albert used Michael's finger to pull the trigger.

BLAM!

Blood and brains splattered all over the wall.

Nobody moved a muscle or said a thing as the horrific scene unfolded.

Albert smiled, took the bat and left the house.

"Dad?" they all heard young Tommy say from down the hall.

"Dad?"

Seconds later Tommy wandered down the hallway towards the master bedroom. As he entered the room, and saw what remained of his father, Tommy's face contorted. His eyes fluttered in the back of his head and he collapsed at his father's feet.

The scene fast forwarded until first responders burst into the room, saw the carnage and the unconscious boy lying on the floor.

"Get the kid out of here!"

"Someone grab the kid!"

Emily walked over to her father, took her hand in his and said, "I'm sorry he had to die like that. It wasn't right."

Thomas wiped away a tear. "Me too sweetie, me too."

"This is beyond caustic," Kim declared. "Who do you think you are dragging us through this? What kind of monster are you?"

"The point I'm trying to make," the Caretaker replied, "will become evident in time."

A new moment was plucked out of the air and the scenery around them transformed once again. They were outside

157

Miramonte High School that Thomas, Sam and Bill attended. Sam and Bill looked around and took in the old sights.

"It's graduation day."

"Yeah it is," Bill said.

The scene moved in closer as the conversation between Tom, Sam and Bill was already underway.

"But seriously," Tom said, "I didn't think you guys were going to go through with it."

"Why not?" Sam and Bill asked in unison.

"Well, I guess because the Vietnam War ended two years ago."

"Tom," Bill stated, "it's not all about going to war in some other country."

"No?"

"No. It's more than that, and this is going to sound cheesy, but we want to help people. There are a lot of bad guys out there, and Tom, we want a crack at them."

Sam jumped in. "Remember back when we were Freshmen and we had that altercation on the field?"

"Altercation. Nice big word for you Sam," Tom said as he poked fun.

"Fuck you too. My point is that we didn't get fucked with from that day forward." Sam looked at Bill and then back at Tom. "We're just going to take the ass kicking from local to global." Sam and Bill smiled.

"You guys are hilarious but I wish you both well. Don't quote me on this but, if this shit is real, I'll fucking miss you both."

"You'll be fine Kemosabe," said Bill.

"High School is about to be behind us and the world is our oyster," Sam added. "Speaking of, how's the USC process?

We know you got in but when are you taking off to find a place to live?"

"I don't know. I need to talk to my grandparent's about that. The paperwork from school says the sooner the better or I could get stuck pretty far from campus."

"So, can I ask a favor?"

"Sure Bill," Tom replied.

"Can I pwease have a bedtime story now?" Sam and Bill died laughing.

Tom grabbed Bill's graduation cap and tossed it away. Bill ran after it still laughing.

"Listen Tom, you're the smart one out of our trio," Sam told him.

"What? Shut up," Tom replied." Bill returned with his cap.

"No seriously, listen. Go out in the world and kick its ass. Leave the other shit behind you. We're going to be friends forever and you know we'll always have your back. Just make us proud at USC, okay?"

"What he said," Bill added and then got really serious. "I may give you a ton of shit brother but it's only because I love you. That day, at the sandbox, you guys could have turned me away, but you didn't. We've been through more shit than I want to remember, and if it wasn't for you two I don't know if I would have survived."

Tom was speechless. They all looked at each other, and without speaking took the moment to hug each other.

Julie spoke up. "Well this helps me understand why you're always looking out for each other."

The scene dissolved and everyone found themselves standing in Loard's Ice Cream. The front door opened and Tom and Ed, his grandfather, walked in.

"Good afternoon and welcome to Loard's," a young woman said.

"Thank you."

"What can I get the two of you?"

"Tom, what would you like?" his grandfather asked.

Tom smiled. "Like you don't know." He turned to the young woman behind the counter. "I'll have a double scoop of Rocky Road on a sugar cone please."

"Coming right up. And for you, sir?"

"That sounds good, but just make it a single for me."

"You got it."

Soon afterward the two of them were sitting at one of the tables and began to work on their cones.

"Your ceremony was nice."

"It was okay I guess."

Ed raised an eyebrow. "Is there something on your mind Tom?"

Tom sighed. "Yeah. I just found out that Sam and Bill are joining the Army."

"Voluntarily?"

Tom nodded. "I know. It seems bizarre."

"And you're worried about their decision?"

Tom looked his grandfather in the eye. "That's partially it. The other part is that I'm starting to feel isolated."

"What do you mean?"

"Well, there are a lot of changes that are right around the corner for me. There's college, a new city to get used to, new people to meet and my two best friends that I won't see for a long time. I'm having a hard time processing everything."

Ed nodded. "And add to that list that your grandmother and I are moving to a new house. That's a lot to take on in such a short amount of time."

"It feels that way, kind of."

"Only kind of?"

Tom shifted in his seat. "Yeah. I'm excited and nervous about all these changes at the same time."

"Good. That's a great way to look at your future. Speaking of, you must be curious why I asked you here?"

"I figured it was to celebrate graduating high school."

Ed shook his head. "No Tom. It's time to share something that your father left for you."

A puzzled look appeared on Tom's face. "What do you mean? I don't understand."

"To tell you the truth, your grandmother and I didn't understand either."

"What does that mean?"

Ed extracted an envelope from his coat, paused for a few seconds in contemplation and then handed it over to his grandson. Tom gently took it.

"What's in it?"

"You'll have to open it to find out."

Tom could sense that this was a very unusual experience and his grandfather appeared somewhat nervous as he'd handed him the envelope. *What the hell is going on?* Tom looked down at the envelope and then carefully slit it open along the top. He slowly removed the official document within and read it. *Wait. What?* Tom reread it just to make sure and then looked at his grandfather. The document shook slightly in his hands.

"Is…is this for real?"

Ed nodded. "It is. That statement you're holding is current as of a week ago."

"But…but I don't understand. This isn't a joke?"

A new customer walked in to Loard's and up to the counter. Ed leaned forward and lowered his voice. "Your father gave your grandmother and I money as well. He wanted you to be taken care of, to be provided for, so you could live your life and pursue your talents."

"But this statement says the trust he setup for me has twenty-two point seven million dollars in it. Million." Tom pressed his hand against his forehead before speaking again. "This is insane. What did my father do for a living? How did he get so much money? What the hell is going on?"

Ed didn't respond immediately.

"What?" probed Tom. "What is it? What aren't you telling me?"

"Tom, when your father was alive…well, let me back up. That Christmas morning, before he passed, your father gave me some envelopes. Inside were the trusts he'd created for us. You can imagine my surprise was similar to yours. I asked him the exact same question Tom, about what he did for a living. And do you know what he told me?"

"What?"

"Nothing. He didn't tell me what he did or where he got the money."

"Why not?"

Ed shook his head. "To this day I still don't know. However, what I do know is that the money he gifted your grandmother and I has changed our lives for the better. Your father intended the same for you, Tom."

"But why now? Why not eight years ago?"

"You know the answer to that. You were too young but now you're mature. You're an adult and you're headed off to college. You have your entire life ahead of you."

"But what am I supposed to do with all this money?"

Ed put his hand back on his grandson's shoulder. "That's for you to figure out. I do have a couple of suggestions while you're going down that particular road, if you'd like to hear them."

"I'm all ears."

"Keep this information to yourself, like your grandmother and I have from the people we know. Its human nature to want what you don't have and if nobody knows you have money then no one will be able to take it away from you. Do you understand what I'm saying?"

Tom slowly nodded. "I think so. What about Sam and Bill? Can I tell them?"

His grandfather looked him square in the eyes. "You can do whatever you feel is right Tom. This is your money now and you can do whatever you'd like with it, or tell anyone about it. Just be careful. People with money are typically treated and looked at differently, even by close friends. I'm sorry to say, but money changes the status quo."

"I get it. Wow, I...I don't know what to say. This is more than I can take in right now. I'm positively overwhelmed."

Ed smiled. "Good. You weren't supposed to be instantly okay with this." He paused for a few seconds. "Listen. You have a good head on your shoulders, Tom. Your father would be proud. Now, let's go home so we can talk about USC and try to alleviate some of your nervousness about heading off to college."

Bill spoke up. "I don't know how you managed to keep that secret for so many years."

"It wasn't easy," Thomas replied. "I wanted to tell you and Sam but I knew my grandfather was right. It would have changed our friendship and I didn't want to take that chance."

163

The ice cream parlor dissolved and was replaced by an office located somewhere in downtown Los Angeles. Thomas sat across from Nick Raynes, his book agent.

"I'm excited to see what you have for me today," Nick said.

Thomas smiled. "I hope you like it," he said as he handed over his latest work.

"Well Thomas, if it's anything like your first book then I can't wait."

Nick opened the binder and read the title. *The World to Tom.* He looked up at this new friend and client. "What's it all about?"

"I don't want to spoil it for you. Give it a read and then we can talk about it."

"Before I start I wanted to ask how you're enjoying your new home in Running Springs."

"It's been great. I still need to make a run up to my grandparent's house and retrieve my things, but aside from that it's just what I need. It's quiet, secluded and since the snow's gone I've been riding my new bike around the mountain quite a bit."

"I'll have to come up and visit sometime."

"You should. There's this great waffle house that sits right on Lake Arrowhead. Its views will blow you away."

The world around them morphed again and they found themselves looking down at Thomas, in his bedroom, who was asleep at his house in Running Springs. Thomas was restless and continuously clutched at the sheets. The sheen of sweat was evident all over his body.

"Stop it," he whispered. "Stop it."

164

The scene rapidly altered and they now stood in another office. It was Laura's office and she was guiding Thomas through a session of hypnotherapy.

Laura was concerned. She had anticipated how Thomas might react but he had gone beyond her safety zone. Thomas had pulled his legs up and was sitting in an upright fetal position in the chair. His head thrashed back and forth. The only thing she had asked Thomas was about his father and their relationship. He had quickly started to panic. It took Laura almost two minutes to calm him down. She continued.

"Thomas. Do you like the meadow?"

"It's beautiful. What are all these scary trees doing here?"

"What trees Thomas? Describe them to me."

"They're surrounding me. I can't leave the meadow unless I go through them. Why do they surround me?"

"What do they look like Thomas?"

"They are black with huge trunks. The tree branches look like arms that want to reach out and get me. I'm safe in the meadow. I can't ever leave."

"Just stay where you are Thomas. Don't go towards the trees. I'll protect you. Trust me."

Thomas tried to curl up tighter on the chair. Laura noticed, "What are your greatest fears?"

He started to shake again. "Relax Thomas. Calm down. Nothing's going to happen to you."

He responded faster this time. "What are your fears?"

"I don't want to be alone."

"Who left you alone Thomas?"

"Where are you Mommy? I need you Mommy. Please come back. Mommmmmy!!" The painful scream filled her office. His cries hurt her ears. Thomas was in real pain.

"Easy Thomas. Slow down. Breath. You'll be okay. I'm right here for you."

He continued to tremble but they were only from the pent up years of not letting his feelings out about his mother and her death. Tears streaked down his face. She waited for them to subside before continuing. She was getting somewhere.

"Now listen to me Thomas. You're back at school when you were a child. Billy and Sammy are there. You're in the sandbox."

"Is Nigel there? I'm scared."

"No, Nigel is nowhere around. He can't get you," Laura said.

"I know he can't."

"What do you mean that he can't get you?"

"He can't get me. He's not around."

"That's right, he's not around." Thomas' voice had lowered and he had a devilish grin on his face.

"What do you see Thomas?"

"I see Billy. I see Sammy. I don't see Nigel. He can't get me. I don't want him to."

The scene fast forwarded to when Laura was bringing him out of his trance.

"Three. Two. One." Laura looked at Thomas and smiled. Curled up in the chair, Thomas looked like an innocent little child. Too bad he had to go through so much pain. *How the heck did he survive?*

Thomas stirred in his seat and his eyes fluttered and then opened. "That was a great sleep. This chair is so comfortable. Did it work again?" Laura got up and turned off the video camera.

Laura sat back down. "I asked about your mother, father, Billy, Sammy and Nigel. I got mixed reactions across the board. You have some really scary issues to deal with. It's going to take some time but we'll get through it."

"My life isn't my own right now. I need it back Laura. If these memories are holding me back then I have to keep moving forward."

"I'll do my best Thomas. These walls that you have built up inside you, your defenses, are substantial. It's going to take some time breaking through them."

"I'm aware of my normal defenses. Are you saying that I have defenses I'm not even aware of? Would that explain my memory loss?" asked Thomas.

"You bet it would. There are different explanations but in a nutshell you blocked out whatever the event or events were. Your mind was unable to cope with the reality. Your conscious mind does not remember but your subconscious certainly does. As I continue to dig through your subconscious I'll eventually locate the trigger. However, once that happens you might consciously remember whatever it was. The plan is to lead you up to that point and not trigger a surprise recall."

Thomas sat back in his chair.

"That's actually pretty scary and upsetting to think about Laura. Waking up with blood on my hands wasn't exactly my best day. And, like you said, I don't remember it. What else in my life don't I remember?" Thomas suddenly wanted to go home. "Is it wrong to say that I'm afraid to remember?"

"No Thomas, it's okay. You're also not alone. We'll get through this together."

Emily squeezed her mother's hand. "I'm glad you helped dad through it."

Laura smiled. "Me too honey, me too."

The office disappeared as the Caretaker pulled another moment in time out of the air, activated it and they found themselves in some sort of laboratory. Sam and Bill were strapped down to tables and a man had just injected Thomas with something.

Albert backed away from Thomas and said, "Can a condemned man at least have his last words?" Albert was clearly unafraid as he smiled. "Yes? No? Tell you what, I'll just go ahead with my speech then." They heard Albert clear his throat and then say, "Cry Tommy."

Sam and Bill saw Thomas stiffen and stop. His face relaxed; snarl gone. His arms dropped to their sides. His entire body remained stiff, but he was suddenly non-threatening. Albert approached Thomas.

"Well boys," Albert said speaking to Sam and Bill, "how do you like my creation?"

"What have you done to him?" asked Sam.

"When I get out of these restraints you're going to pay for what you've done to him," Bill promised.

Albert was deliriously happy. "You have no idea how happy I am right now. Billy. Sammy. I'd like to introduce you to Tommy. He's the last thing you're going to see before you die."

Sam started yelling. "Thomas! Wake up Thomas!"

"Oh, he can't hear you Sammy boy, he's off in his own world, having a nightmare. It was fun implanting those beatings in his head. Oh, how he must be suffering. What fun!"

"You sick fuck!" hollered Bill.

Albert looked at Bill and Sam. "It's too bad really. All good things must come to an end at some point." He walked back towards the front and picked up the bat. "Tommy." Thomas turned to face Albert. "Take this bat and smash these

168

two in to oblivion." Albert handed Thomas the bat who took it without hesitation.

"Don't listen to him Thomas! Snap out of it!" Sam screamed.

"Stop it Thomas. Don't let it end like this!" Bill added.

Albert just grinned madly and clapped his hands together in anticipation. "Do it."

Thomas calmly walked over to Sam and looked down at him without any expression on his face whatsoever. Sam couldn't believe what was happening.

"WAKE THE FUCK UP!!"

Thomas slowly raised his old bloodied bat. Sam's eyes widened in fear; he knew this could be the end.

"COME ON THOMAS. STOP IT!!" Bill yelled from the other table.

The bat slipped from Thomas's hands and clattered to the floor. Thomas fell to his knees.

"Nooo!" Albert yelled. "Get the fuck up. Finish them!"

Thomas didn't move. His head was lowered; shoulders slumped over. Albert came over to Thomas and smacked his head with his hand. "Get up and kill them!" He hit Thomas again and still didn't get a reaction. Albert grabbed Thomas by both shoulders, twisted Thomas so he faced him and then picked up the bat. Albert held the bat in both hands and thrust it at Thomas. "Take this bat and you will kill them Tommy. You will do as I command. You will worship the ground that I walk on."

Thomas stirred. He tilted his head up and saw the bat being offered to him.

"Good Tommy. Now take it and finish them off," Albert commanded.

Thomas grabbed the middle of the bat with his left hand. Albert still had both of his hands on the bat, tightly gripped. Thomas looked up into Albert's face.

"Do it Tommy. Do it!" Albert was beyond himself with anticipation.

Thomas smiled and sharply pulled the bat towards him. Albert crashed in to Thomas and they both sprawled on to the floor. Albert jumped up holding the bat.

"What the fuck are you doing? Kill them with this bat goddamnit!" He was frothing at the mouth.

Thomas slowly stood up and looked at Albert. "I'd rather use this." Thomas raised his right arm.

Albert tracked Thomas' arm and sudden realization set in. "MR. PETERSON!" Albert screamed.

Thomas rapidly discharged three rounds into Albert's chest. The sound deafened everyone in the enclosed room. The bat slipped from Albert's hands and joined in the sweet sound of expended brass casings 'tinging' on the floor. A red spot spread on the front of Albert's chest. He gasped; his eyes wide.

"No…fair…" Albert said as he fell to the floor.

"I don't think I'll ever get tired of reliving how that encounter ended," Sam stated.

Bill nodded. "Oh yeah. Albert definitely got what he deserved."

It changed again and everyone looked down at Thomas and Laura snuggling in bed.

"I love you Laura," Thomas said a few minutes later.

Laura turned and looked at him, smiling. "I love you too."

"I know things seem to be moving pretty quickly but I want you to know that I trust you. What we have makes me feel really good inside. Thanks for taking a risk on me."

Laura caressed his face. "I should be the one thanking you Thomas. We ended up saving each other." Laura kissed Thomas deeply.

Thomas broke the kiss and sat up.

"What is it?" Laura asked.

"I have something else to tell you and I'm not sure you're going to like it."

Laura sat up and looked at Thomas. He was nervous.

"Laura."

"Yes?"

"Will you marry me?" Thomas smiled.

Laura beat on his chest with her fists. "You bastard! You had me going." She was laughing. "And yes, yes you silly man, I'll marry you."

The scene changed again and they now stood on a beach, but it wasn't from Gavin's island.

"I now pronounce you man and wife. You may kiss the bride."

"I love you," Thomas whispered.

"I love you too," Laura whispered back. They both had huge smiles on their face.

"Congratulations Thomas." Sam stepped in and gave each of them a big hug.

"I second that notion," Bill added and followed suit.

"Laura. You are so radiant," commented Kim. Susan and Julie both nodded their heads in agreement. "And what an amazing backdrop. I could move here in a second."

"Thanks Laura," Bill joked. "No pressure on us, right Sam?"

"None at all. What do you think sweetie?"

Julie didn't hesitate. "My sister's right, in a damn second."

Sam and Bill could only roll their eyes.

Thomas jumped in and saved them. "That's it for the ceremony. Thank you all for coming. We'll see you at TAO at seven o'clock."

The group finished congratulating them and then moved off down the beach towards the resort. The weather had been perfect. The sun had begun to set during the ceremony as planned. The backdrop to their wedding couldn't have been more beautiful. They slowly walked hand in hand up the beach as man and wife.

"I love you Dr. Laura Clark."

Laura smiled and tilted her head. "Say it again."

Thomas turned and smiled at Laura. She returned it as the world shifted around them and they found themselves in a hospital delivery room. Laura was on the bed and Thomas was by her side.

"Doctor Harper is on her way," said one nurse.

"Thank you," replied Thomas.

Laura had just reached full dilation and her contractions were much closer to each other now.

"You're doing great sweetie."

"Then you get in this bed and give birth."

He smiled. "I would do just about anything else. You seem like you have this covered. I'm just going to step out into the hall." He pretended to get up.

"Don't you even think about it mister!" She smiled back at him before her face contorted again. She squeezed his hand hard. Another contraction had hit. "Yeah, you owe me big time for this."

Doctor Anna Harper glided into the room. She had just scrubbed up and checked the machine's readouts.

"Laura. How are the contractions?"

"They're more frequent Anna."

"Thomas, good to see you haven't passed out yet." He could see her smile behind her mask.

"Give it time doc."

"We have a pool going."

"Swell." He smiled at their banter.

"Hello? Mother giving birth here," said Laura.

"And we're back," said Anna.

Anna checked Laura's dilation, pulse rate and both heartbeats. The machines beeped in the background. "I think we're ready to kick this off Laura. What do you say?"

"Get this kid out of me."

"That's the spirit." She turned to Thomas. "Now for the hard question. From what angle are you going to experience the miracle of birth?"

"I'm okay right where I am doc. No need to traumatize me from your end. But really, thanks for the invite."

Anna smiled. She was definitely having fun at his expense.

"Okay Laura. This is all you now. We're going to get you through this just fine. When the next contraction hits I want you to push."

Laura's nails bit in to Thomas's hand as the next wave hit. He gritted his teeth and bore the pain silently as his wife started giving birth to their first child.

"That was great Laura. A few more of those and you're going to have the easiest birth on record." She kept watch on Laura's pulse and both heartbeats. Both were nominal. She noticed that Thomas was a little pale but he was holding his own.

A different beep started up on the heartbeat monitor. Anna glanced over at it and froze. A third heartbeat had appeared.

"What the hell?" she breathed.

"Is everything alright doc?" Thomas asked.

She looked over at him. "Everything's fine." She glanced back at the monitor again and only two heartbeats were displayed. She shrugged it off and continued with the birth.

Twenty minutes later Laura gave birth to a healthy baby girl. The cord was cut and then the nurse took her, cleaned her and brought her back. She placed the newborn in Laura's arms; who was crying. Anna noticed that Thomas's face wasn't dry either.

"Congratulations you two."

"Thank you Anna."

"My pleasure. Do you have a name for her yet?"

Thomas and Laura looked at each other. "Emily," said Laura. "Her name is Emily."

"That's a beautiful name."

"Awww," Emily said on the beach. "By the way, what's with the third heartbeat?"

"We still don't know," Laura told her.

The hospital room changed to an entirely new one.

Doctor Harper came in and met them in the delivery room.

"You two certainly know how to ruin a good night's sleep." She smiled.

"Exactly as planned…mhuahahaha," replied Thomas.

"Cute honey," said Laura. "Why don't you let the women work now?"

"Ouch." He grabbed her hand and made sure her nails couldn't dig in this time around.

Laura's contractions had peaked and the process began just like before. Anna kept one eye on the monitors.

"Breath sweetie."

The machine beeped regularly and then made a distinctive new sound. Anna's eyes grew wider and Thomas caught it.

"Is everything okay?"

She caught herself. "Everything's fine. Push for me Laura."

The regular interval of machine beeps returned.

Seven minutes later a healthy baby boy was delivered and placed in Laura's arms.

"Congratulations again you two."

"Thanks doc."

"You have a name for this little monster?"

Thomas spoke up this time. "Gavin. His name is Gavin."

"And a third heartbeat occurred when I was born too," Gavin said. "That's weird."

The Caretaker stopped, lowered his arms and they all found themselves back on Gavin's island. Thomas fell to his knees, emotionally overcome by the myriad of memories he'd just been put through again, both good and bad. Laura followed him down to the sand and held him as he wept.

"Why did you do that to him?" Sam asked as he took a step towards the Caretaker.

"What you all saw is nothing he hasn't experienced before. I merely showed him some of the choices that were made, either for or by him, that got him where he is today."

"But that was sick and over the top," Bill said. "Why torture him? Don't you think Thomas feels enough pressure already? We all know he blames himself for our circumstances."

"Thomas is unique," the Caretaker replied, "and his history is unique. He both intrigues and troubles me at the same time."

"Explain what you mean by that," Sam demanded.

"You are being hunted. Your world has begun to change with breathtaking but frightening new possibilities. But the people of your world are not ready for those possibilities because there are those that only want to harness your abilities for their own gain. They will harm anyone in their way, stepping on the corpses left in their wake without so much as batting an eye."

"That's not an explanation," Sam pressed.

"And I'm under no obligation to give you one. However, I do require something that I believe only you can bring me, and for that I will help you."

Sam and Bill shared a look. "What are you proposing?" Sam asked.

"The balance needs to be restored."

"The balance here or the balance on Earth?" Bill questioned.

"Here," the Caretaker replied. "The history of your world has proven, time and time again, that balance can never be achieved on the planet you call home. For eons your race has proved that you'd rather kill each other than work together to make your planet a better place for everyone. Perhaps in time that mentality will change. No, now I require balance, here, in my realm and I will have it."

Thomas picked himself up off the sand and wiped his face off.

"How?"

"Bring me Nikolay Dmitriev."

"I don't understand. Why should we help you?"

"Because we want the same thing Thomas. Nikolay and Rebecca are the only souls that have returned from whence they came."

Rebecca shifted uncomfortably in her new body as the Caretaker turned towards her.

"I should detain you, but instead I will allow you to work with you to retrieve Nikolay rather than remove you from your new body."

Gavin stepped up defiantly as Stir appeared next to his side. "Don't you dare touch Becca!"

"Gavin," Laura cautioned, "don't."

The Caretaker looked down at the small creature that had red eyes and was made up of tangible smoke. "Hello Stir."

"How do you know his name?" Gavin asked in surprise.

"Perhaps I spoke too soon when I stated that Nikolay and Rebecca were the only souls that ever made it out of here. But, to be honest, where do you think Stir disappears to when he's not by your side?"

"I don't know. Here?"

The Caretaker nodded as he bent down and petted the creature. Stir's tail thumbed against the sand.

"Yes. Stir was the first to depart this realm and that warranted my attention. Then, young Gavin, as you began to visit this island I watched you. You, like your father, intrigued me."

"Maybe you're just lonely," Emily said offhandedly.

The Caretaker stood up and smiled. "I do get lonely from time to time, but that pales in comparison to the purpose this realm provides to the universe."

"And that is?" Thomas asked.

"Trust me when I tell you that you're not prepared for that particular conversation; and it does not relate to the present task I've asked you to accomplish."

"So that's it?" Julie pressed. "You get what you want we're left to fend for ourselves?"

"Humans," the Caretaker said as he shook his head back and forth. "Your race always wants something in return."

"Are you kidding me? Our entire world is after us and you're asking us to bring you one person. Please explain to us how that's ever going to work out in our favor. Why not let us stay here?"

"No, you can't stay here. The events that are transpiring in your world are a product of your own devising. Perhaps you weren't paying attention during the abbreviated history lesson."

"You have to give us something," Sam told the Caretaker. "If we agree to get you Nikolay you can't expect us to go back through the portal and end up in the motel room seconds after we left it. We'll be captured and neither one of us gets what we want."

The Caretaker mulled Sam's words over. "I will allow you safe passage this one time, to any location of your choice. However, from there you must figure out your own destiny and a way to return Nikolay to me. Agreed?"

"We don't have any other choice," Thomas said as he picked the backpack up off the sand, the same one he'd dropped after the portal escape from Hamid in Afghanistan. Thomas stripped the kevlar vest, with three bullet holes in the back, of flashbangs and put them inside the pack that contained five Glocks and extra magazines. "I have an idea of where we can go."

"Very well."

The Caretaker, along with Gavin, walked over to the water's edge and he dipped his toe into the vast Ocean of Time.

"Listen to me closely. I will not help you again if you come back here so I hope you understand the point I was trying to make."

"We understand," Thomas told him.

"I hope you do Thomas Clark, because if you do come back here you will die." The Caretaker reached out and put his hand on Gavin's shoulder. "Please, I am ready for you to make your portal now."

21
Mon Nov 5, 2001

While Nikolay's men anxiously waited for the knockout gas in the motel room to dissipate Dr. Matsushita pulled a device from his pocket. As the vapor cleared out two men, wearing gas masks, made entry into the room where the motel's door used to reside. They swept the room looking for bodies, came up empty and exited.

"There's nothing sir. It's empty."

"No one?" Nikolay responded irritably and turned to Matsushita. "I can't believe they took the portal. They were foolish to go back there."

"Wouldn't have you," Dr. Matsushita asked Nikolay, "made the same choice rather than subject yourself to yours truly?"

"You don't understand. It was suicide to go back there. If they somehow made it out I need to know where they ended up. Send your child to find them again before someone else stumbles upon them."

"I can do better than that."

"What are you talking about?" Nikolay asked.

Dr. Matsushita tapped the device he held in his hand. "I implanted trackers in all five of my test subjects. And now we can assume that one of them, Craig to be exact, has reunited with his parents."

Nikolay smiled. "You're one devious bastard. Show me."

Yamato stared at the screen but only four blips appeared.

"That's odd. It shows the others but not Craig. Maybe his tracker malfunctioned. In any case, Nikolay, you still need to track down the family so we can both get what we want out of this arrangement."

Nikolay bristled at the way the doctor spoke to him. But he kept his anger locked away. "And where would you propose I start, doctor? The child led us here in the first place."

"I'll leave her with you so you can find Thomas again. And, if Craig's tracker comes back online, I'll call you with a location."

"Leave her? Where do you think you're going?"

"I need to prepare for your return with Thomas and the rest of his family of course."

"Why?"

Dr. Matsushita smiled. "Nikolay. You want my serum, don't you? Of course you do, and to make that happen I need to prepare my lab. Besides, I'm surprised the police haven't shown up yet."

Nikolay looked around and then signaled to his men. They withdrew and piled back into their vehicles.

"Very well, doctor. Go and prepare 'our' lab."

Dr. Matsushita turned to Amanda. "Find Thomas."

Amanda slowly rotated her body in a full circle and ended up facing Yamato when she was done.

"Something wrong with your new toy?" Nikolay mocked.

Yamato ignored him. "I said, find Thomas."

Amanda made another slow circle and never raised her arm to point in a specific direction.

"That's fantastic, doc. We're dead in the water now, aren't we?"

Nikolay's phone rang and he answered it.

"Good," he said into his phone. "It was only a matter of time before someone came back there. Detain them, we're two hours away." He put his phone away and looked back over at Matsushita. "Get in doc."

"But I need to get back to my lab."

"I'll drop you off on the way because we're all headed back to your neighborhood."

22
Mon Nov 5, 2001

Hobbes and Gabbi arrived in Falls Church, Virginia, two hours after they'd left the family at the motel in Harrisburg, Pennsylvania. As they drove through town their level of nervousness began to rise.

"Do you think we did the right thing by leaving them?" Gabbi asked.

"I honestly don't know," Hobbes replied. "To a certain degree I feel like we abandoned them when they needed us the most."

Gabbi nodded. "That's the word I was searching for; abandoned."

"But, if we can utilize the bunker's equipment to help them avoid capture then it justifies our decision, don't you think?"

Gabbi smiled at Hobbes. "You're a good person and you have a kind heart."

"Maybe. I'm just trying to make up for my past mistakes."

"What are you talking about?"

Hobbes glanced over at her from behind the wheel and then turned his attention back to the road. "That's right, you don't know."

"Know what?"

Hobbes sighed. "Four years ago, or so, I worked for the CIA in the Information Technology department, or IT. Victor Bannon, the DCI at the time, formed a special group to track down Nikolay Dmitriev, the man responsible for the mass bombings throughout the United States. To keep it covert and off the books he hired Sam and Bill as his 'boots on the ground', while behind the scenes Thomas, Emily and Michael worked with me and another IT tech to locate Nikolay."

"And Michael is Thomas' father?"

"Correct."

"But Michael wasn't alive. So how did Thomas and Emily get away with fooling everyone? I mean, Emily used her powers to pull Michael out of the other realm, but that must have put a serious strain on her."

Hobbes nodded. "It was, but that's just the beginning because Victor figured it all out, and when he did his entire demeanor changed. He took Thomas and Emily hostage and sent a team to recover the rest of the family who had escaped from Hawaii in a yacht. That team killed their bodyguards and seized the family because Victor's obsession with power had overtaken him. During that time Victor had Dr. Matsushita delving into Thomas and Emily with a fine tooth comb employing torture and experiments to find his answers."

"Shit."

"Yeah."

"And you said you were a part of all this?"

"I was. At first it was just a well-paid job with long hours. But then it turned ugly. The DCI, Victor, threatened me and the other tech and I admit I valued my life above theirs when it came down to it."

"Wait. Who was the other IT guy, the one that you worked with?"

"He went by the handle of Calvin, and he was my friend. We lived and worked together."

"I get it now. Calvin and Hobbes. Clever."

"Not as clever towards the end of this story I'm afraid," Hobbes told her.

"What do you mean?"

"Well, long story short, Rebecca helped Thomas and Emily escape. After that Thomas, Sam and Bill took down Victor and tossed him through the portal, never to be heard of again."

"But when did Nikolay die throughout all of this?"

"Sam and Bill took a team and parachuted into Cuba. They took out his guards and were extracting Nikolay when the family was attacked in Hawaii by Nikolay's men."

Hobbes shook his head at the memory.

"What?" Gabbi asked. "Are you okay? What is it?"

"We were watching the firefight via satellite and we saw Julie get shot in the chest. But Gavin, Gavin opened a portal and walked through it. We'd never seen that before. But what was even more amazing is that Gavin appeared a moment later with something."

"Something?"

"It was a person, but transparent. It lay down over Julie's body and she came back to life. It was surreal."

"I think I would have shit myself as well."

"Anyway, when Sam heard that his wife was dead he cut off communication to Victor, who wanted Nikolay alive. We learned later that Sam put a bullet into Nikolay's head right there on the Cuban beach."

Gabbi thought for a few moments. "So with Victor effectively silenced the only two people that were left with any knowledge of Thomas, and his family's abilities, were you and Calvin?"

"For the most part. But what you don't know is that Calvin turned during all of this. He embraced the dark side while I eventually turned against it and decided to work with Rebecca and Thomas to find and recover everyone else who had been taken hostage off the boat. In the end Emily wiped

187

Calvin's mind and wiped some of my memories as well, as it turns out."

"Seriously?"

"Yeah. But they saw the good in me and gave me a second chance, so I went to work for SANDBOX."

"And yet here you are and you know all about them."

"Well, that's another story. Remind me to tell you about a guy named Serpent and his psychopath of a son named Raven some other time."

"I might just do that."

With the entrance to the farm around the bend Hobbes began to slow the Suburban.

"Don't slow down. Drive past and let me see if I can see anything."

"Okay."

As they passed the road that led up to the farm Gabbi looked for anything out of the ordinary.

"Did you see anything?" Hobbes asked as they left the turn-off in the rear view mirror.

She shook her head. "Nothing. Turn around."

Hobbes found a place to swing the Suburban around and headed back. Gabbi craned her neck but still didn't see anything.

"The way I see it we have two options," she said.

"Which are?"

"We can park on the side of the road and hike in, or we can drive up to the farm like we own the place. Thoughts?"

"Hell, I don't know. I'm just the resident geek."

"And a cute geek at that," Gabbi told him. "Pull over as far as you can and we'll go on foot."

"You got it."

Hobbes parked the Suburban between some trees about twenty feet from the road. They got out, ran across the road, hopped the wooden fence and looked back.

"Not bad," she said. "Someone might see it but you hid it pretty well." She turned and continued on towards the farm house and barn. "Time's a wasting. Come on."

Fifteen minutes later the two were hunkered down in the tall grass within eyeshot of the two buildings. They slowly scanned the area.

"You see anything?" she whispered.

"Nothing. It's weird. If Nikolay broke out of here I can see why he wouldn't come back. But, since he's abducted the DCI why wouldn't he decide to use this place as his base of operations?"

"Maybe Nikolay thinks it's too risky or maybe he has a different hideout."

"Perhaps. But if I were him wouldn't I keep this place under surveillance just in case?"

Gabbi agreed. "I know I would, especially knowing how priceless Thomas is to him and the rest of the world."

"Okay then. We'll take this nice and slow as we approach the rear of the farmhouse, make entry and use the secondary tunnel to make entrance into the breakroom."

"And then?"

"I'm figuring this out as I go. If we make it that far then we make a bee-line to my tech area so I can start purging the data you've been collecting on Thomas and his family's abilities."

"Okay," she replied. "That sounds like a plan."

They took another look around and then withdrew into the grass. Five minutes later they had made their way around to

189

the back of the farmhouse and peeked out of their concealed location.

"Looks clear to me," she whispered.

"Me too."

They hurried out of the grass, across the open backyard and planted their backs against the rear wall of the farmhouse. Gabbi pointed towards the back door and a few seconds later they had opened it and slunk inside. They listened for any sounds and after a minute decided they were alone.

"That was easier than I thought," she said.

"Well, the armed guards used to watch over the property, so I can see why they left everything unlocked. Look around, there's nothing of value to steal in this house anyway." He started moving towards the front hallway. "Let's go."

They tiptoed through the house, turned to the right when they reached the front door and looked into the large floor to ceiling mirror attached to the wall. Hobbes removed his identification card out of his pocket, inserted it in a small indentation in the side of the mirror and swiped downwards. Something behind the mirror clicked and it silently swung inwards.

"Nice," Gabbi commented as they stepped through and closed it behind them.

Ahead of them a set of stairs led down, followed by a long unlit corridor. Hobbes looked around and then pulled two rechargeable flashlights out of a wall mount.

"No need to alert anyone that we're coming by turning on the overhead lights," as he handed her one.

She smiled and accepted it, her hands slightly shaking.

"You nervous?" he asked.

"No. Terrified."

Hobbes nodded. "Me too."

They turned on their lights, made their way down the concrete steps and entered the corridor that would take them to the bunker.

* * *

The computer, located in the guard shack directly outside the underground bunker, beeped as a new keycard entry was logged. Two men, heavily armed, looked at each other afterwards.

"Call it in," one of them said.

The other used his cell and dialed a number.

"Sir, a user with the identity of Hobbes, just logged in. I'm looking at the cameras now and they are two people, a man and a woman, who just entered into the bunker through the backdoor."

Nikolay responded on the other end. "Good. It was only a matter of time before someone came back there. Detain them, we're two hours away."

"What'd he say?" the first one asked.

"Just to detain them."

"Excellent. I was getting bored anyway so this will be enjoyable."

* * *

Hobbes and Gabbi shined their lights on the backside of the breakroom door and breathed a sigh of relief.

"So far so good," he said.

"Yeah, no shit."

"If there's anyone on the other side just turn around and run."

"What about you?"

"I'll close the door and be right behind you."

"Kay."

Hobbes was nervous. "Ready?"

Gabbi nodded. Hobbes put his flashlight down, to free up a hand, and then pressed the button that released the lock. The Break Room door swung towards them and they hesitantly looked inside. It was quiet.

"So what'ya say, ladies first?"

"Not a chance."

Hobbes stepped into the room and looked around. Nothing. He ventured into the adjoining room where the bunks were. Nothing. He then made his way back to her.

"It's clear."

Gabbi put her flashlight down, stepped in from the tunnel and pulled the door shut behind them. Without talking the two exited the Break Room, found themselves in the large circular passageway and turned right. Less than a minute later they entered Hobbes' Tech room.

"Home sweet home," he breathed. He immediately went to his desk, sat down and began to type away.

Gabbi walked over and stood behind him. "What do you want me to do?"

They both jumped when a new voice answered her question.

"How about step away from the computer and put your hands up?"

Two men stepped out of the shadows with their guns pointed at them.

"Oh shit," Gabbi muttered.

23
Mon Nov 5, 2001

The President of the United States entered the room and sat down at the head of the table.

"Sit," he told the rest in attendance.

Around the table were a number of his top ranking officials including the Secretary of Defense, Kirk Nash; the Director of National Intelligence, David Cook; the FBI Director, Alan Holmes; and the assistant DCI, Timothy Peterson who was standing in for the missing Robert Duncan.

"Gentlemen," the President began, "in fear of sounding redundant, where are we with locating Thomas Clark and his family?"

"We haven't found them, sir," Alan Holmes informed him. "We have discovered that Mr. Clark booked a flight from San Francisco to Washington D.C. a month ago. Extrapolating from that we scanned the airport video cameras and discovered that Russell Washington met the family at the airport."

The President leaned back in his chair. "I've talked with Russell. He's been extremely closed lipped about his work with Robert Duncan, our missing DCI. What else have you got for me Alan?"

The FBI Director continued. "We tracked down where Mr. Clark has been living since he arrived in town. Sir, the house is located in Falls Church but my agents were unprepared for what they found inside."

The President leaned forward.

"Sir, inside the house they discovered a blood bath. They found ten bodies and the place looked like a war zone. None of them belonged to the family."

"I see. So we're not the only ones after them. The Russian President has threatened that he has men on American soil looking for the Clarks. Have you figured out the identities of these dead men?"

"We're running fingerprint and facial recognition on the ones we can, sir. I'm still waiting for those results."

"So where are the Clark's now?"

Alan shook his head. "I don't know, sir. It's as if they've disappeared off the face of the Earth. We've been tracking credit cards, cell phones and email usage and so far we've come up empty handed. The best lead we have right now is that they were booked on a chartered flight bound for London. Airport surveillance video shows them entering and then, later, exiting. It appeared as if they were headed north."

"This is our top priority. Stay on this and find them."

"Yes, sir," the FBI Director replied.

"Moving on," the President said as he turned to the Secretary of Defense. "What's the status of the Russian fleet?"

"Sir," Kirk replied, "their ships are steaming across the Pacific and Atlantic oceans towards the United States. We predict they'll take positions off both our coasts within days which would give them optimal first strike capabilities. Our sonar nets have also picked up a number of submarine contacts rapidly approaching as well. They'll be in range within twenty four hours."

The President sighed. "It's hard for me to fathom that Demian Anatolievich would escalate this issue with the severity he's chosen. If he doesn't back down we could very well be at war with Russia in the near future." He paused for a few seconds. "What about the rest of the world?"

"Sir, it appears they're watching from a distance to see how this pans out. So far Britain, Germany, China, Japan and the rest are all on the sidelines."

"Fantastic. Options?"

"To protect our nation I believe there's only one response, sir," the Secretary of Defense said. "Deploy our fleet."

"I agree," the President replied. "If we don't then we'll appear weak." He turned to an aide. "I want to make another public announcement in forty-five minutes."

"Yes, sir," the aide replied and departed.

The President turned back to the table. "Gentlemen, we are teetering on a precipice and it won't take much to push us into it. Find me Thomas Clark."

* * *

"Good afternoon my fellow Americans. This morning I spoke to you about Thomas Clark and the national security issue he represents. I'm afraid we're facing an additional threat that's looming on the horizon, and that threat is Russia. President Demian Anatolievich has informed me that he wants Thomas, and the powers he possess, for his country. To back up his threat he's deployed his fleet which will arrive within two days. I am now left with no other choice but to deploy our own fleet in response.

"My fellow Americans, I will not lie to you, tensions are high. But the truth of the matter is if Russia doesn't back down there's a chance our two great nations could end up at war with each other.

"With that said I am ordering the National Guard into service. Regular military leaves of absence have been

195

cancelled and all military personnel will report back to your command structures immediately.

"We must all pray for a peaceful resolution, but we have been provoked and that means we will defend ourselves.

"Thank you and God bless."

24
Mon Nov 5, 2001

Dr. Stuart Glover, at his underground lab at Area 51, quickly injected six rats with the chemical he discovered in Peter's liver. He, along with the other scientists, stepped back and watched the results unfold.

"I'll bet twenty that none of them survive," one of the scientists boasted.

"I'll take that bet," Dr. Glover said.

Two minutes later all six rats started to convulse, their bodies bulging and expanding in hideous and painful ways. Within seconds each rat's body exploded within their separate cages.

Dr. Glover, the main scientist, reluctantly pulled out his wallet and paid off the bet.

"Double or nothing?" the other scientist said as he took the money.

"Not yet, but I might hold you to that in the future once I perfect this sequence."

"You realize it's going to take months, maybe even years to develop something tangible."

Dr. Glover nodded. "Indeed. But just think, our timeline will be shortened once we get our hands on Thomas Clark and figure out what he's made of. Just think of the possibilities."

"I don't disagree, doctor," the man said as he folded the twenty and stuffed it into his pocket, "but the President asked for preliminary results and I'm afraid we've just seen that failure in action."

Dr. Glover nodded. "Yes. We're fighting an uphill battle. Without live specimens our hands are effectively tied." He smiled. "But hopefully that will change in the near future."

25
Mon Nov 5, 2001

"Funny running into the two of you. What did the two of you think you were going to accomplish by sneaking back in here?"

Hobbes and Gabbi, secured to chairs and under guard, looked over at Nikolay as he entered the room.

"Oh shit," Hobbes said.

"Don't be rude," Nikolay continued as he looked down at them. "I asked you a question and I expect an answer."

The two remained silent.

"Very well. Allow me to clarify the situation you two find yourselves in. You are my prisoners and your value is directly equated to the information and or expertise you can offer me."

"I…I don't understand," Gabbi said. "What do you want from us?"

"Alright, we can play this game. I'll start with an easy one." He looked back and forth between Hobbes and Gabbi. "Where is Thomas?"

"How could we know that?" Hobbes said with defiance. "He ditched us two days ago."

Nikolay smiled. "Oh, is that so."

"It is."

"Well in that case, my apologies. Since you don't know anything then perhaps I should just let you go?"

Nikolay's smile instantly faded. He shot a hand out and grabbed Hobbes' throat in one fluid motion. He began to squeeze which blocked Hobbes' airflow.

"Let him go!" Gabbi screamed. "Let him go!"

Since Hobbes was tied up he was powerless to fight against the intense force Nikolay was applying. His eyes bulged and he gasped for breath.

"Stop it!"

Nikolay turned his head and looked straight into Gabbi's eyes. "Tell me something useful and this ends. If you don't, well…, then he dies right here in front of you."

Gabbi frantically watched the life begin to drain out of Hobbes' face. "We came back to purge the database! Now please, let him go!"

Nikolay released his grip and stepped back. Hobbes immediately inhaled one deep breath after another, his eyes retreating back from the far away gaze they'd held moments before. Gabbi watched him slowly recover.

"Tell me more," Nikolay pressured. "What's in this database?"

"Go to hell," she told him.

"Defiant. I can respect that. However, in this particular instance, I don't have time to play around." He motioned to one of his men. "Bring in our other guests."

The man disappeared around the corner as Nikolay turned his attention back to Gabbi.

"I must apologize. I'm really a nice person, but I feel so free in this new body of mine. I have energy and stamina. But the biggest change I've noticed is that I lack any patience." He shook his head side to side. "It's terrible really. I find myself impulsive and often quick to action."

"You're insane," Gabbi said.

From the corridor two armed men marched five people into the room. They had blindfolds over their eyes, their mouths were gagged and their hands were tied behind their backs. Gabbi and Hobbes' eyes lit up as they recognized Dr. Sung, Dr. Brown, Russell, Robert and his wife Emma.

"Put them against that wall," Nikolay ordered as he extracted a gun from his waistline.

The five were pushed against the wall at gunpoint. Nikolay swung back around to Hobbes and Gabbi in delight.

"Now, it's decision time. Where can I find Thomas?"

"I don't know," Gabbi pleaded.

Hobbes tried to speak and it came out as a whisper. "She...she doesn't know. Leave her alone."

"That's very gallant of you, but alas, that doesn't answer my question."

Nikolay twisted, extended his handgun and fired. The bullet entered Dr. Brown's temple and promptly sprayed blood and brain matter on the wall behind him. His body lurched to one side and toppled over as the remaining four began to struggle as they tried to cry out from behind their gags.

"You motherfucker! You monster!" Gabbi shrieked as tears flowed down her face. "Why did you do that!? You didn't have to do that!"

Nikolay wasted no time and placed the barrel of his gun under her chin. She stiffened.

"Now that you know the rules of this game I'll ask you again. Where can I find Thomas?"

"Don't...," Hobbes wheezed.

"Don't worry," Nikolay told him, "your turn is coming." He concentrated on Gabbi. "Where is Thomas?"

"Fuck you, I don't know."

Nikolay withdrew his weapon. "Loyalty. I'm impressed, but not that impressed."

He turned and fired. This time his bullet entered Dr. Sung's chest and pierced her heart. Her body collapsed and landed on the floor next to Dr. Brown's. Russell, the DCI and Emma knew exactly what had happened even though they were blindfolded. Hobbes and Gabbi could only stare at the two people Nikolay had just murdered in cold blood.

"Who's next!?" Nikolay cried out in delight. "Tell me because the stakes have never been higher!"

"You should have stayed dead," Hobbes whispered.

"What?" Nikolay asked as he came closer. "What did you say?"

Hobbes' throat throbbed and it was painful for him to talk. "I said…, you should have stayed dead."

Nikolay smiled. "And yet here I am. But I'll entertain your comment. Why should I have stayed dead?"

"Because…, because Sam's going to enjoy killing you a second time you sick sonofabitch."

"Then let's give Sam that chance. Tell me, where can I find Sam and the rest?"

"You'll never find them."

Nikolay nodded. "I tend to agree with you. But the good news is that I won't have to now. I have a feeling they're going to come for you. And, as you can see, I have a few more hostages to negotiate with. In fact, aside from Thomas and the others, everyone who knows about this underground facility is here, so I'm pretty sure we won't be disturbed anytime soon."

Dr. Matsushita entered the room and pulled up short when he saw the blood splattered wall, the two bodies on the floor and a gun in Nikolay's hand.

"Messy Nikolay, but it looks like you've been productive. Did I miss anything?"

Nikolay smiled. "Indeed. Doctor, I don't think you've met Hobbes and Gabbi. And there," Nikolay said as he pointed to the three standing against the wall, "are Russell, Robert and your old friend Emma."

"And the two on the floor?"

"I didn't get their names. A pity." He turned back to Matsushita. "But since you're here shall I assume you miraculously have my serum?"

"Keep dreaming Nikolay. I'll have it for you once you hand over Thomas." He looked around. "That's strange, I don't see him."

"Not at the moment, but the tracker isn't working and neither is the child's power to locate Thomas."

"So you're telling me that your men can't locate an entire family?" Dr. Matsushita said sarcastically. "I can only assume that your government will be extremely unhappy with that bit of news, won't they?"

Nikolay resented this man and desperately wanted to use the gun he held in his hand.

"Do yourself a favor, doctor, and don't disrespect me."

"Perhaps it is you who should be careful Nikolay. Our relationship is based on the fact that we need something from each other. I need you to bring me Thomas and you need me to manufacture the serum that your country so desperately desires."

"I might just settle for what I already have," Nikolay countered.

"Perhaps. You have the DCI and some data. But are you willing to take the chance that America replicates my serum before your country does? I doubt it. What I'm offering is a game changer and you know it. Besides, don't forget that I could order you to kill yourself in a heartbeat, so do us both a favor and get over yourself before you actually piss me off."

It had been ages since Nikolay had been talked to in such a manner, and he didn't like it. He stuffed his instinctual need to kill Dr. Matsushita and changed the subject.

"What are you doing here?"

"I understand your confusion. I'm moving my lab to this bunker."

"Why?" Nikolay tried to ascertain.

"Because with it here we'll be able to work more efficiently together. The last thing either one of us needs is to draw attention to our end game, and being under the same roof eliminates that, don't you think? Now, why don't you take me on a tour of this facility."

Nikolay turned to his men. "Get them locked in cells and clean this mess up."

* * *

An hour later Nikolay was on the phone with the Russian President, Demian Anatolievich.

"Dr. Matsushita is going to be a problem."

You're the problem Nikolay. "He's the least of my concerns right now Nikolay. Have you found Thomas Clark yet?"

"We had him but they used the portal to escape."

"And why haven't you reacquired him yet?" Anatolievich demanded.

"It's a fluid situation here, sir."

"You're running out of time. The American President has launched his fleet to counter ours. This situation needs to be resolved immediately. Call me tomorrow with an update Nikolay and prepare for Tatiana's arrival. She's with the SVR."

"I don't see the need for the SVR to be involved, sir."

"You don't have to Nikolay. This has become bigger than you and if you don't succeed then your future in Russia will never come to pass."

The President terminated the call which left Nikolay with a sinking feeling.

Where could they be hiding? I need to think this through because both my reputation and future are at stake.

Nikolay called one of his men in. "I want you to activate sleepers in all cities where Thomas Clark has lived before."

"Do you have a list with addresses, sir?"

"Here."

Nikolay handed over a sheet of paper that contained last known addresses in Orinda, Running Springs, Los Angeles, Marin and Hawaii.

You can run Thomas, but only for so long. I'm coming for you.

26
Mon Nov 5, 2001

Late Monday evening the President of the United States met once again with the Secretary of Defense, the DNI, the assistant DCI and the FBI Director.

"Gentlemen, where do we stand?"

"Mr. President, the Russian fleet hasn't altered or slowed down since we've deployed our own. Our estimates indicate they'll be off our coastline in two days. We also have confirmed sightings of additional submarines in the area."

"How many submarines?"

"As of this moment I can't commit to an actual number."

"Best estimate then."

The Secretary of Defense wasn't happy. "The Russians have pulled out all the stops, sir. My guess is that they've left their own shores undefended to concentrate on ours."

The President leaned back. "Wonderful." He rubbed his temples for a few seconds and then asked a follow-up question. "Have the Russian subs or fleet shown any signs of aggressive behavior?"

"No, sir, nothing yet. But that could easily change once our fleet intercepts them."

"Dammit. And all of this over a man that people of the world both fear and envy. What the hell is going on? This is madness."

"Sir?"

"Nevermind," the President told them. "You're all dismissed."

As they filed out and closed the door the President pressed a button and spoke.

"Get me the Russian President on a secure line."

"Right away, Mr. President," came the immediate response.

A minute later the phone rang and he picked it up.

"Hello Mr. President, thank you for taking my call."

"What can I do for you?" Demian Anatolievich replied.

"I was hoping to embark on a straightforward conversation with you before the world watches our two countries collide."

"By all means, Mr. President, I'm all ears."

"We can't go down this path. This conflict could easily transform into World War Three."

"I agree, but you have left my country and the rest of the world, with no other choice. We both know that Thomas Clark represents a new era of military power, espionage and who knows what else. You can understand that I can imagine American troops pouring out of Mr. Clark's portal in the middle of the Kremlin, and I can't have that. The bottom line is that this power can't be left in America's hands alone, nor will I allow it to be."

"And yet you approve of perpetuating acts of violence and kidnapping, on American soil no less, perfectly acceptable?"

"Oh come now, Mr. President, do not talk to me as if I'm naïve. The United States has instigated hundreds of missions on foreign soil without the knowledge or permission of those country's governments. I'm merely going to preserve the balance of power before the scale resoundingly tips in your favor."

"Preserve Demian? You've got to be kidding me. It's clear you want the power all for yourself."

"And so do you, and that's exactly why I'm standing against you. How long do you think it will take before the rest of the world realizes how powerful America will become if you harness these abilities? These powers will astronomically leapfrog the country who owns them ahead of every other nation on this planet."

The President signed. "This conflict won't end well for either of us Demian, but that doesn't mean I can't read between the lines. What are you proposing?"

The Russian President smiled on the other end of the line. "Nothing public, Mr. President, but a secret collaboration would ultimately benefit both of us."

"And if I agreed to such a collaboration, would that mean you'd stop steaming your fleet towards the American coast?"

"Absolutely not. You and I need to keep up appearances, do we not?"

"So by putting our soldiers in close proximity you're willing to risk a potential war?"

"The power gained will be worth that risk," Demian said matter-of-factly.

The President of the United States was silent for a few seconds. "I know you don't have him."

"And neither do you. Mr. President. But this is a race either of us can win individually or we can win it together."

"And what will that entail?"

"Trust between you and I, and a show of faith. The alternative is we go to war."

"I don't take threats very well."

The Russian President continued. "And I don't issue them lightly either. This is a new world. We either decide to work together and share the benefits, or we hang up as enemies and let this game play out naturally. Now, to show I'm a man of my word, tell me something you require?"

"I want my Director of Central Intelligence, Robert Duncan, released."

"Consider it done," Demian replied.

"So you did abduct him you sonofabitch. This isn't the Cold War anymore."

"Mr. President, I admit that our new relationship hasn't gotten off on the best of terms, but I told you the stakes were high and that I'd do whatever it takes to capture Thomas Clark. Robert Duncan knew what Thomas Clark could do and has worked with him in secret behind your back."

"And how do you know this?"

The Russian President didn't reply.

"You tortured Robert to get that information, didn't you?"

"What's done is done, Mr. President. But need I remind you that there is a much bigger picture to remain focused on. Robert Duncan is just one man compared to what Thomas Clark can offer our two countries, provided we work together of course."

"And how am I supposed to trust you through all this Demian?"

"My men have Robert Duncan and Russell Washington."

"You have Russell as well?"

"Yes, Mr. President. I also have a SVR agent arriving tomorrow to help facilitate everything. What I propose is that my SVR agent and your DCI, Robert Duncan, work together on American soil."

"And why would I agree to that?"

"Because our cooperation on this matter depends on constant oversight, and that can be easily maintained by the individuals in play we already have confidence and trust in."

"Perhaps."

"Do we have an understanding, Mr. President?"

POTUS thought about it and decided that making a deal with Demian Anatolievich would be better than going to war with him.

"We do, but we need to talk particulars."

"Agreed. In the meantime, and to show my commitment, I'll even give you the name of the doctor that originally created the serum that gave Thomas Clark his power. It's Dr. Yamato Takuma Matsushita. Now, Mr. President, I've been very forthcoming with you so this is what I require as your show of faith to me."

The President of the United States grimaced as Demian Anatolievich explained what he wanted. When they were done talking he hung up the phone and he punched an extension.

"Yes, sir?"

"Give me everything we have on a Dr. Yamato Takuma Matsushita."

"Right away, sir."

He hung up and leaned back in his chair. *Shit, what have I agreed to?*

27
Tuesday November 6, 2001

Tuesday morning Nikolay walked around the underground bunker's large circular hallway by himself. He had just received a report that Thomas had not been located at any of the previous addresses he'd lived at in his lifetime.

Thomas, where the hell have you disappeared to? I can't move ahead with my own plans until the doctor, as insane as he is, gets his hands on you. So where have you gone?

Nikolay was interrupted by one of his men. "Sir?"

Nikolay stopped and focused. "What is it?"

"Sir, President Anatolievich is on the phone and demands to speak with you."

Shit. "Very well."

The man handed the phone over and departed.

"Yes, Mr. President?"

"Tell me you have something," Demian told Nikolay with a harsh edge in his voice. "Tell me I just didn't make a deal with the President of the United States that I might actually have to live up to."

"Thomas has disappeared off the grid completely."

"So you're saying that you've failed me, is that it Nikolay?"

"No, sir. I just need more time."

"DAMMIT NIKOLAY," Demian thundered through the phone, "THAT IS COMPLETELY UNACCEPTABLE!"

Asshole. "With respect, sir, I was the one that brought you this opportunity in the first place, so don't lecture me on failure. I've done more for Mother Russia than you ever have, or will ever do."

Insolent shit. "Don't ever presume to think you can address me that way Nikolay. Your life and future I hold in my hands. If you fail in this endeavor, well, that's on you. Now explain to me why you can't just bring Dr. Matsushita to Russia?"

Idiot. "Dr. Matsushita cannot replicate his serum without Thomas' blood. Also, and how I hate to point this out, the doctor's power of control hinders your request on every level."

You will die even if you do succeed. "Very well. SVR agent, Tatiana Danilovna, will be arriving in the United States in a few hours. She will immediately make her way to your location to assist in any way possible. Extend her every courtesy."

Like hell I will. "I understand. Is that all, sir?"

Find me Thomas so I can finally have you executed. "Yes, Nikolay, for now."

28
Tuesday November 6, 2001

The original plan for the bunker's holding cells was to house high value prisoners, that would enable Laura and Emily direct access to them for interrogations, in private and out of sight from Langley or any other government agency's overseeing eyes. But now the reason the underground facility had been constructed in the first place was just a fleeting memory because Thomas and his family were being hunted down. However, that didn't stop the small holding cells from being broken in because three of those cells now contained guests for the very first time. Robert Duncan and his wife Emma inhabited one. Russell Washington took up a second. And in the third resided Gabbi and Hobbes.

"We're sooo screwed," Gabbi said as she clenched the cells bars.

"We're all going to be fine," Robert assured her from the adjoining cell.

"How can you be so sure? A maniac is holding us prisoner and, if you haven't noticed, he doesn't seem to have an issue with killing. In fact he seems to get off on it."

"That's enough."

Emma started to cry again. "Dammit Robert, I'm scared. I'm really scared."

Robert pulled her close to him and she put her head on his shoulder.

"I don't know if I can handle any more of this," she sobbed.

He stroked her hair. "Shhhh. It's okay. We'll figure a way out of this, I promise."

"How?" Russell interrupted. "No one knows that we're here."

"Thomas, Sam and Bill will come for us," Hobbes said with confidence.

"But didn't Nikolay mention that there's no sign of him, that the child and the tracker are broken, or something like that?"

"That's good news because it means they're still out there. We know that Dr. Matsushita moved his lab here so if they had captured Thomas already we'd know about it."

"So what are we going to do?" Gabbi asked.

"Russell?" said Robert.

"Yes?"

"Does the President know I'm missing?"

"Yes. I met with him."

"What did the two of you talk about?"

Russell thought. "Well, the President wanted to know why I suspected Nikolay Dmitriev was behind your abduction. I told him that was a question he'd have to ask you. Of course he demanded that I tell him what was going on, especially since he had knowledge that Nikolay had been killed in Cuba by Sam and Bill years before."

"And how did you reply?"

"I informed the President that I only report to you. Needless to say he wasn't happy with my stonewall routine, but I believe he took the information I gave him seriously."

"So that means you never gave up the bunker's location?"

Russell paused. "Shit. No, sir, I'm afraid I didn't. At the time I was protecting both the people and our work. Dammit."

"It's okay," Robert replied. "It's okay. Your loyalty has never been in question and for you to stand up to the President in order to safeguard what Thomas and his family can do, and

216

the location we were conducting our research at, is commendable."

Hobbes spoke up. "So that brings us right back to the same question, what are we going to do?"

"Well," Robert replied, "the President may suspect that Russia is involved with my abduction if he believes that Nikolay is behind it. If he does then he's already put pressure on the Russian President to release me."

"I don't see how that's going to help," Russell said.

"It helps because we're Nikolay's leverage."

"Tell that to the two doctors he shot right in front of us," Gabbi reminded them. "After witnessing that I can tell you I don't feel like leverage. Expendable, yes. Leverage, no."

"We need to stay positive," Robert told everyone. "We're in this together and we have to look out for each other."

"Then how did Nikolay's men know where the house was?" Hobbes spat out. "Twelve men came in shooting and if it wasn't for Thomas we'd all be dead or captured right now. So explain to me how you're looking out for us when it's obvious you gave us up."

"It's my fault," Emma said. "That man used me to make Robert talk."

"Is that true?" Gabbi asked.

Robert nodded even though they couldn't see him. "Yes. Nikolay tortured Emma and I, but that's not an excuse. I broke and I gave Thomas up to save us."

"Shit," Hobbes said. "That's cold, sir."

"Yes, and I'm not proud of it, but you all escaped, right?"

"Yes. After picking up Gabbi we headed north to Harrisburg to look for Sam and Bill's kids at their boarding school. They told us they ran into the headmistress and that

217

Emily persuaded her to talk. As it turns out Dr. Matsushita coerced the children into a van."

"Dear God."

"Exactly."

"So then what did you do?"

Gabbi took over. "They came back to the motel and told us about it. They assumed that Dr. Matsushita was going to experiment on the children; to use them as guinea pigs. It was then that we saw the President's speech on television as he offered five-hundred thousand dollars for Thomas' capture. Hobbes came up with the idea for the two of us to leave, since we hadn't been mentioned, and come back to the bunker to help the family remotely. And you can see how well that worked out."

Robert mulled over the new information. "Did Dr. Matsushita succeed?"

"What?"

"We heard Nikolay say earlier that the child was broken along with the tracker. What do you think he meant by that? Maybe he did use them as guinea pigs…, and was successful."

"Maybe," Hobbes said. "The tracker Nikolay mentioned could either be a physical device and or something else."

"I understand the physical device. But something else?" Russell asked. "What do you mean, like what?"

"At this point anything's possible," Gabbi said. "We've seen some incredible and breathtaking displays of their abilities. It's not a very far leap to think that the Dr. Matsushita, who engineered his own ability for thought control, wouldn't be able to customize specific abilities for others. So, taking that logic a step further, it could be possible that one of the children was turned into a human tracking device, for lack of better words."

"Do you think it's possible he made a human tracker," Robert said, "in order to find Thomas?"

"That's just a theory," Gabbi reminded the DCI.

"But if it's true then why are they broken, both the child and the device?"

Gabbi and Hobbes looked at each other.

"Maybe they took the portal," Hobbes said with hesitation. "But then the only reason they can't be found is because they're still there. And that means they're…"

"Dead," Gabbi said as she finished his sentence.

"Crap," Robert said. "We saw what came out of Gavin's portal last time. If they decided to go back there then it must have been for one hell of a reason."

"This is all still theoretical," Gabbi reminded them. "We're just shooting ideas in the dark here. I don't want to think about what it could really mean."

The five of them were silent for a while.

Emma finally broke the quiet. "If they are out there, and alive, do you think they'll still come for us?"

"I want to say yes," Robert told his wife, "but we can't rely on anyone else to save us. We need to come up with our own plan of escape."

29
Tuesday November 6, 2001

"Sir!" one of Nikolay's men frantically uttered over the radio. "We have incoming!"

Just outside the bunker's barn doors three vehicles pulled to a stop, opened their doors and nine individuals got out. Eight of them were men dressed in matching suits while the ninth was a striking woman, mid-thirties with black hair. From various vantage points Nikolay's men stepped out of hiding with their weapons extended.

"Don't move!"

The eight suits reacted, pulling out handguns. A standoff immediately ensued.

"Drop your weapons!"

The female smiled and casually spoke. "It appears we're in the right location." As tensions mounted she walked with authority up to the individual with the radio.

"Stop where you are or I'll shoot," the man told her.

"Your English is excellent," she replied. "I can only imagine how long you've been living in the country."

The man was unfazed by her statement, his handgun pointed at her chest. "I won't repeat myself again. Stop and drop your weapons or we'll open fire."

She came to a halt right in front of him. "Okay, I'm not moving anymore. But how are you going to shoot me when you don't have a weapon?"

The man barely registered her comment before she swiftly pivoted, lashed out with her foot and knocked his gun from his hand. She continued to move in a blur as she stepped forward and punched his throat. A split second later she swung her body around and elbowed him in his temple. He crumbled to the ground, unconscious.

"Hold!" she commanded everyone as she slowly picked up the fallen radio and stood back up. She thumbed the send button. "My name is Tatiana Daniovna. I am with the SVR and I was sent here by Demian Anotolievich, the Russian President, escorted by eight American Secret Service agents. Knock, knock Nikolay."

* * *

Nikolay met the motley mix of Russian sleepers, Secret Service and Tatiana as the elevator finished its descent into the depths of the underground bunker.

Tatiana stepped forward. "I've seen pictures from your dossier Nikolay and they don't do you justice. I approve of your new look."

"Flattery Tatiana, really?" he said as they greeted, kissing each other's cheek. "And what brings the Foreign Intelligence Service of the Russian Federation all the way to my doorstep with the Secret Service no less?"

"Oh Nikolay, don't act surprised. You're well aware that Demian informed you of my impending arrival. What he might have neglected to mention was the deal he made with the President of the United States."

Nikolay's face faltered. "What the hell are you talking about?"

She smiled. "Why don't we all step inside so we can talk about that?"

Nikolay reluctantly acquiesced and led the large group into the bunker as the Russians and the Secret Service continuously eyeballed each other. Inside, as they walked along the circular corridor towards the Tech wing, they ran into Dr. Matsushita. The doctor's eyes widened when he saw the procession coming in his direction, Nikolay leading the way.

"What's going on?"

"I'm about to find out. Why don't you join us," Nikolay told him as he pointed to his head and whispered, "because this situation might require your unique skill."

Tatiana took it all in as they made their way through the facility. "Amazing. And to think this was all built to accommodate Thomas Clark and his family."

When they reached the Tech wing Nikolay and Dr. Matsushita stopped and turned around.

"Who are you?" Dr. Matsushita demanded.

"Doctor, it's a pleasure to meet you. My name is Tatiana Danilovna. I'm a SVR agent sent here by Demian Anatolievich with orders to immediately take over this operation."

Nikolay bristled as she continued.

"As you may or may not have ascertained already," as she glanced back at the Secret Service agents, "the US and Russian Presidents are working in secret to resolve this Thomas Clark issue before World War Three erupts."

"Impossible," Nikolay told her. "They would never work together."

"And yet," Tatiana said, "here I stand with a compliment of Secret Service agents Nikolay. How else can you begin to explain how I ended up here? It certainly wasn't by chance. You told Demian where this facility was located and he passed that information off to me. The President of the United States, in turn, granted me safe passage on arrival and detailed me these men."

223

"Why would POTUS even consider working with Anatolievich?" Nikolay asked.

"Because harnessing the power that Thomas Clark possesses has become greater than you or I ever imagined. And, more to the point, you Nikolay have failed to acquire Mr. Clark in a timely manner which has greatly agitated Demian."

"I'm in control here," Nikolay boldly stated, "not you Tatiana."

"Not any longer," she countered, her eyes never wavering from his.

"Kill them!" Nikolay ordered as he stepped back.

Weapons, throughout the room, were leveled at each other in a tense standoff.

"I said kill them!" Nikolay repeated.

Tatiana opened her mouth. "I now speak to the men who follow Nikolay Dmitriev. Your President has transferred authority of this operation from Nikolay to me. The respect you hold for Nikolay is not in question; however, he is no longer in command. Stand down."

One by one the Russian sleepers lowered their weapons. The Secret Service agents followed suit once the threat had dissipated.

Nikolay turned to Dr. Matsushita. "Do something."

The doctor shook his head as Tatiana turned towards him. "No Nikolay, I don't think so."

"You backstabbing sonofabitch."

Tatiana introduced herself. "Dr. Matsushita. A pleasure to meet you."

"Likewise. Although I can't say I'm happy I wasn't involved in the decision to have you crash our little party. But, truth be told, I haven't seen any positive results from Nikolay in locating Thomas Clark, so I understand why you're here."

"You bastard," Nikolay said. "We have a deal."

"And what deal is that doctor?" Tatiana asked him.

"A simple exchange. My serum for Thomas Clark."

"For what purpose?" she inquired.

"The most uncomplicated reason of them all. Revenge."

"I see. However, once we've obtained Mr. Clark and you've extracted enough blood to create the serum we need, what do you plan on doing with him?"

"Kill him," the doctor said without hesitation.

"And that's it?"

"Yes."

"Then perhaps I'd be inclined to offer you the same deal. Do you accept?"

"I do," he told her.

"Good. Once we have the serum you may kill Mr. Clark."

"This is bullshit Tatiana," Nikolay said. "From the sound of it only Russia will be getting the serum. Why would the President of the United States agree to that? It makes no sense."

Tatiana turned to face Nikolay. "First thing's first Nikolay. If you want your deal with Demian to stand then you'll acknowledge, right here right now, that I'm in control. Otherwise I'll offer my new friend, Dr. Matsushita, the chance to do with you as he wishes. It's your choice but I suggest you choose wisely."

A few seconds ticked by before Nikolay swallowed enough of his pride to speak. "You're running this operation."

"Thank you Nikolay," she replied. "Now to answer your other question. The President of the United States and the Russian President have agreed to share the doctor's serum. To ensure that happens both me, a member of the SVR, and an American who can also be trusted will oversee this endeavor."

225

"And who might that be?" Nikolay tested.

"Robert Duncan, the DCI, who I believe you currently have residing here as a guest."

Nikolay wasn't convinced. "He'd never agree to help."

"We'll see," Tatiana replied. She turned to one of Nikolay's men. "Bring me all the prisoners."

"Yes, ma'am."

Two minutes later Robert, Emma, Russell, Gabbi and Hobbes were led into the room. Tatiana strode up to the DCI and introduced herself.

"Mr. Duncan, my name is Tatiana Danilovna. On behalf of the Russian President I extend my apologies."

Robert looked around the room, recognized some of the Secret Service agents as well as Nikolay standing off to one side. He focused his attention back on her.

"What's going on here exactly, Ms. Danilovna?"

She smiled. "A change in leadership. You have been freed so that you and I can work in tandem."

"Work together?" He shook his head. "I don't think so."

"Then perhaps you'd like to talk with your President?"

"And why would you let me talk to him after everything Nikolay has put my wife and I through? That doesn't make any sense."

"That's not for me to decide, Mr. Duncan," Tatiana told him. "But this is part of the arrangement that was made."

"Fine, but it's your funeral."

"I doubt it," she replied.

A minute later the President was on the line with the DCI.

"Robert, is that you?"

Sonofabitch. She wasn't lying. It is the President. "Yes, sir, it's me."

"Are you alright? Did Nikolay hurt you or your wife?"

226

"I'd rather not talk about that, sir."

"Very well Robert, I understand. You've been missing since Saturday, four days ago. You've had us all very worried."

"I'm not the only one who was taken, sir. Russell is here along with two of my people. If I may be so bold, what the hell is going on? I've got a SVR agent telling me she and I are now working together to rundown Thomas Clark."

"That's correct Robert. Demian Anatolievich and I have reached an understanding."

"I don't understand, sir."

"You're not required to understand, Robert. However, you are required to follow my orders."

Robert clenched the phone till his hand turned white. "What the hell is this all about Mr. President?"

"It's about the preservation of human life."

"Really? Because it sounds like the two of you want to control how humans evolve, or more to the point, make sure only American and Russians gain access to this evolution."

"Don't be naïve. The world is shifting. I'm just ensuring our country remains at the top."

"I didn't sign on for this, sir."

"No Robert. Apparently you decided on your own to build an underground facility and work in secret with Thomas Clark. I can only imagine what your plans for the future were going to be. I'm sure they were very similar."

"No, sir, not at all. What I chose to do was to learn from Thomas, slowly and over time. You, on the other hand, want to exploit what he has to offer this world."

"Enough Robert. I'm done debating this with you. I'm ordering you to work alongside Tatiana to capture Thomas Clark, is that understood?"

227

"And if I refuse, sir?"

"Put me on speaker," the President demanded.

Robert punched a button and stepped back.

"Ms. Danilovna, can you hear me?" the President asked.

"Yes, sir," she replied.

"Very good. Hold one."

The line muted for thirty seconds and then came back on.

"President Anatolievich, we're on together," POTUS said over the speaker.

"Tatiana, are you there?" Demian asked.

"Yes, Mr. President."

"Excellent. How were you treated when you landed?"

"Like royalty, for lack of better words, sir. I'm in the bunker now along with Robert Duncan, the DCI and Nikolay. I have taken over the operation."

"Very good," Demian replied. "Nikolay, this is business and I want to assure you that our deal is still valid."

Nikolay tried to protest. "Sir, you can't…"

"Enough Nikolay!" Demian thundered over the speaker. "Know your place and accept it or face the consequences."

"Speaking of consequences," POTUS said, "I'm still waiting on an answer Robert. Will you work with Tatiana?"

"You're giving me a choice, sir?" Robert inquired.

"Yes and no."

"What does that mean, sir?"

The President sighed over the speaker. "It means the time has come to prove that I'm a man of my word, just as Demian Anatolievich did for me."

Robert was confused. "I don't understand."

"I'm sorry Robert. Just remember that this is for the greater good."

"What are you talking about?"

Behind them two of the Secret Service agents forcibly pulled Russell out of the group.

"What! What!" Russell said as he struggled.

"Hey!" Gabbi exclaimed.

"What the hell!?" Hobbes added.

The agents pushed Russell up against the bloodstained wall. One of them produced a handgun and placed it against Russell's head.

"What the fuck is going on!?" Gabbi screamed as she backed away.

"Oh shit! Oh shit!" Hobbes managed to say.

"Oh no no no no no," Emma sobbed.

"On your orders, Mr. President," the agent said towards the phone.

"Do it," POTUS ordered.

Russell's eyes opened wide as he realized what was about to happen. A split second later the bullet entered his brain and killed him instantly. His body went slack and collapsed to the floor.

"NOOOOOO!" Gabbi shrieked hysterically. "WHY DID YOU DO THAT!?"

The color drained out of Robert's face as he held on to Emma, his eyes staring at Russell's body.

"Satisfied?" POTUS asked.

"Tatiana," the Russian President said. "What just happened?"

She replied immediately. "A member of the Secret Service shot and killed Russell Washington, the DCI's right hand man for this project."

"Yes, Mr. President," Demian said, "I am satisfied. I believe we understand and can trust each other now."

Robert couldn't believe what had just happened and forcefully picked up the phone.

"Why the fuck did you just do that? He was an innocent man who was just doing his job."

"Robert," the President replied. "I took no pleasure in issuing that command. What you obviously fail to realize is that all of this is bigger than you can imagine. I will sacrifice whoever I need to in order for us to win."

"To win? To win? Have you completely lost your mind, sir? This isn't a game."

"And you be sure to remember that Robert. You're part of this now and I need you onboard. If not, well…"

"Are you threatening me, sir?"

"I am the President of the United States. I don't threaten, I act. Join or perhaps you'd like to see Emma join Russell?"

"You sonofabitch. You wouldn't dare."

"I would. And here I thought you would have learned the lesson with Russell's departure. Am I wrong?"

A part of Robert broke inside as it all came tumbling down. *Oh shit. The President's gone off the deep end, so help us.* He looked over at his wife. *What have I done?*

"Robert, I require an answer."

I have to stay a part of this so I can help Thomas sometime in the future.

"Robert. Tell me what I need to hear."

"Yes, sir. I'll work with Tatiana."

"Excellent. I knew you'd come around. Now find us Thomas Clark so we can move past all this ugliness."

Fuck you, sir. Fuck you.

* * *

Tensions grew as both the Russian and American fleets squared off, the Russian President publically boasting that he'd start a war if America didn't turn over Thomas Clark. The world's anxiety rose, day after day.

Satellites searched the ground as the NSA worked its digital magic.

The FBI tirelessly combed the country looking for any leads to follow up on as hundreds of sightings of Thomas were called in daily.

The reluctant DCI, and Tatiana, waited for any information to come in that would lead to Thomas' whereabouts.

Dr. Matsushita, and his anticipation of acquiring Thomas' blood never wavered. He knew it was only a matter of time.

But for the next week Thomas Clark never resurfaced. He and his family could not be located.

30

Monday November 12, 2001

Gavin's portal materialized on Earth and out of it the family members emerged. After the portal snapped shut behind them it took their eyes some time to adjust to the dimly lit room. The enclosure was devoid of any furniture or objects of any kind.

"Where are we?" Sam asked as they all looked around.

"Good question," Bill said. "Thomas, where did you ask the Caretaker to send us?"

Laura found the light switch and flicked it on, but nothing happened. "Wherever we are there isn't any power."

Thomas opened his mouth. "Laura, you and I haven't been back here for eleven years. Sam and Bill, the last time you set foot in this house was during our senior year of high school."

"Seriously?" Bill said. "You took us here. Wow."

Rebecca shuffled past Laura, opened a door that led to a short hallway and light spilled into the room.

"What is this place?" Emily asked her father.

Thomas looked down at his daughter. "This is the house I grew up in sweetie."

"Cool," Gavin replied. "Can we look around?"

"Sure. Just be careful and don't go outside."

"I'll look after them," Rebecca said.

Craig, Emily, Gavin and Rebecca headed off to explore as Thomas slowly examined the master bedroom. Afterwards he walked to the attached sunroom and turned to his left. There, as it always had been, was his father's large safe. A small smile cracked open on his face as Laura came up behind him and took his hand in hers.

"I remember when we were here," she said. "Your father's letter was in the safe."

He nodded solemnly and squeezed her hand in return. "I remember it too." He reached out and touched the cold steel. He glanced up at the ominous hooks in the wall where his father's shotgun used to rest and pulled his hand back. "What bothers me the most is that I miss my parents. I miss what my life could have been like with them in it. I miss the fact that I grew up without them and without a baby brother or sister. They were all taken away from me."

Julie, Kim, Sam and Bill stood there respectfully as Thomas reminisced, not that the Caretaker had just bombarded Thomas with memories, forcing him to relive some of the most painful instances of his life. Julie chose to break the silence.

"Thomas?"

Laura and Thomas came back into the room.

"Yes?"

"Why here? Why choose to come back to this house?"

"I don't know exactly. But what I can tell you is that it's familiar ground and we're now clear across the country from where we used to be."

Sam understood. "What Thomas is saying is that deciding to reemerge in Orinda is unexpected and may give us an advantage."

"Like what?" Kim asked.

"Time," answered Bill. "And we're going to need every second. Speaking of time and no disrespect intended, but we shouldn't waste any more of it just standing around."

Thomas nodded. "We need to come up with a game plan and fast."

Thomas led the adults out of the master bedroom, down the hall and into the family room. The kids, along with Rebecca, were just coming down the hallway from his old bedroom.

"Pretty neat room dad," Gavin told his father.

Thomas smiled. "I thought so too."

"Yeah," Emily added, "I like it."

Craig made his way back to Julie and she pulled her son close to her side, protecting and comforting him.

"The house is clear," Rebecca informed them, "and the dust hasn't been disturbed. If you don't object I want to walk the perimeter."

Thomas pulled the backpack he'd retrieved from the island off his shoulders, put it down on the carpet and opened it. He withdrew the five Glock handguns inside and distributed them to Sam, Bill, Rebecca, Laura and himself along with extra magazines. He left it resting on the floor as he stood up.

"I think it's a good idea," Sam stated. "We need to be aware of our surroundings and start gathering information."

Rebecca nodded as she placed the gun in her waistband and covered it. "I'll be right back."

"Just watch out for the neighbors. The last thing we need is someone calling the police on a strange male they saw prowling around."

Rebecca understood exactly where Thomas was coming from. Even she forgot, from time to time, that her new body was distinctly male.

"Thanks Rebecca," Laura told her as she headed for the front door.

"Okay," Thomas said, "how about we come up with some ideas on what to concentrate on first. Anyone?"

"I'm hungry," Craig said.

"Me too," Emily added.

Kim joined in. "I could eat."

Bill grinned. "It sounds like we have our first course of action."

"The house is empty," Thomas told them.

"And there isn't any power to cook anything," Laura reminded them.

Thomas began to dig in his pocket. "Shit. We left everything back in the motel. How much money do we collectively have on us?"

Each of them turned their pockets out and handed any bills they had over to Laura to count. Thomas extracted a thick wad of hundreds and gave it to her.

"Eleven thousand, five hundred and thirty three dollars."

"It's a start," Thomas said.

"Can't we go to the bank and get some more?" Kim asked.

Bill shook his head. "By now everything's been frozen. If we try to withdraw anything they'll immediately know exactly where we are."

"Bill's right," Sam said. "But this eleven grand isn't going to last."

"We'll figure that out later," Thomas said. "Right now we need food, some rest and a plan."

The sound of the front door opening startled them and they instinctively put their hands on the butt of their weapons nestled in their waistbands. The door closed and Rebecca called out.

"It's just me."

They relaxed as she came around the corner and rejoined them. In her hand she held a newspaper.

"The outside's clear. I noticed some soil disturbance in the back that looks fairly recent. My guess is that someone was checking the house out."

"Great."

Rebecca unfolded the paper and handed it over to Thomas. "Notice anything?"

The group crowded around and began to scan the front page of the San Francisco Chronicle. The main headline read '**Russia Poised to Destroy the United States!**' and depicted a large photo of Russian naval vessels. They scanned the story and it cited that Thomas Clark was the catalyst to the world's impending nuclear holocaust.

"Shit," Thomas breathed out. "This is worse than I ever could have imagined."

Bill was confused. "But how did the Russian fleet cross the ocean so quickly?"

"I was thinking the same thing," said Sam. "It doesn't make any sense."

Rebecca interjected. "I was actually talking about this," as she pointed to the newspaper's date, "and not the story."

They followed her finger. There, as plain as day, was printed the following: **Monday November 12, 2001**.

"Holy shit," Thomas exclaimed.

"Wait," Bill said. "It was just Monday the fifth. How is it suddenly a week later?"

Their confusion spurred a number of questions.

"What?"

"I don't understand."

"How is this possible?"

Thomas settled them down. "We must have travelled through time."

"Through time," Julie scoffed. "Seriously?"

"It's the only explanation."

"There has to be another reason," Kim stated.

"Why?" Thomas declared. "At this point I'm not even shocked. Look at what we've experienced and have come to accept already." Thomas turned to Craig. "Your son can now phase through solid objects and yet somehow time travel is what you're hung up on?"

"I...it's just a lot to take in, that's all," Kim replied.

"It is," Thomas said, "but the Caretaker told us that time is a variable in the universe. It appears he was correct."

Laura took over. "Listen, none of this really matters, okay? All we have to go on is that it's a week later, we're in Orinda and we're still being hunted. However, right now we still need supplies and a plan. I propose Julie, Kim and I go to the closest grocery store..."

"That'd be Safeway," Thomas said.

"...and stock up."

"It's located a couple miles away and we don't have a vehicle."

"Don't you worry about that," Laura told her husband. "The three of us will stop by a neighbor's house and tell them our car broke down and that we need to call a taxi."

"We still need a vehicle," Rebecca stated, "or none of us are going anywhere anytime soon."

Thomas peeled off eight thousand dollars and handed it over to Rebecca. "Go with them and then head out to Walnut Creek using BART. There're a number of used car dealerships out there. See if you can purchase a used RV or something similar."

"And what about the paperwork they're going to want me to fill out?"

"Convince them otherwise," Sam said.

Rebecca smiled. "I can do that."

Thomas handed over a thousand dollars to Laura. "Aside from food we're going to need a few pre-paid phones."

Laura nodded and pocketed the money. She then hugged and kissed Thomas. A second later Sam and Julie along with Bill and Kim followed suit.

"Be careful," Thomas told everyone. "I hate sending you out there alone but..."

"We get it," Laura said as she cut him off. "Your faces have been blasted into every household across the globe. We'll play it safe and be back as soon as we can."

"And so will I," Rebecca added.

The women departed through the front door, walked out to the driveway and down the street.

Sam, Bill, Thomas, Emily and Gavin sat down on the carpet together. Gavin opened the carrier's door and let Stickers out while Craig sat down in his father's lap.

"You guys okay?" Thomas asked his kids.

"This is nothing," Emily indicated.

"Yeah, Dad, this is nothing."

Sam and Bill chuckled a little.

"And what about you?" Sam asked Craig.

"Honestly, I've been better."

"Scared about all of this?"

Craig nodded.

"It's okay. So am I."

Bill took the opportunity to focus them. "The supplies are being taken care of which leaves us to come up with a plan of action."

Sam addressed his son again. "Craig, you said that your sister can track Thomas."

"Yeah."

"Okay. How long did it take her to find us at the motel?"

Craig shrugged. "The doctor asked her and then Amanda pointed in a specific direction. Then she mentioned a distance in miles."

"Hmm," Thomas said. "It doesn't sound terribly precise but who am I to say. They could already be on their way for all we know based on the fact that someone was already here looking for us."

"Maybe," Bill said, "but we're not going anywhere until we're all back together."

"Speaking of back together, I can't stop thinking about Gabbi and Hobbes. I mean, it's been a week since they left us at the motel to head back to the bunker. I hope they're okay."

"There's no way they could have sent us any kind of message during that time and you know it," Sam said. "While it's obvious we don't know anything it's pointless to speculate."

Thomas nodded. "I know, but they're family so I can't help it."

Sam and Bill nodded but then Sam stopped as his hand traversed something odd under Craig's skin.

"Wait, what's this? Turn your head a little to the right, son."

"What?" Bill asked as Craig shifted position.

"I don't know. I think there's something here."

Sam looked more closely and saw a small incision on the back of Craig's neck. The small nodule he felt under his son's skin was next to the sealed cut.

"Check this out," Sam told them.

Bill and Thomas took a look and felt the bump on Craig's neck as well.

"There's definitely something in there," Bill said.

Thomas concurred. "Whatever it is we should cut it out and take a look at it."

Craig abruptly stood up. "You want to cut my neck open?"

Sam shook his head. "No. But we need to open that incision back up and remove whatever's in there, son."

"No. That would hurt."

"Not necessarily," Emily said.

Craig looked at her suspiciously. "What do you mean?"

"I can knock you out so you won't feel a thing."

"And," Gavin added, "I can heal the wound once they're done. Easy peasy."

Craig looked around at each of them. "Okay."

A few minutes later, with the minor procedure completed, Sam, Bill and Thomas stood over the kitchen sink and washed the device they'd removed from Craig's neck under the water.

"What the hell do you think this thing is?" Sam asked.

"Whatever it is we all know Dr. Matsushita implanted it," Bill said.

"Bill's right," Thomas stated. "Destroy it."

Sam dropped the small implant on the kitchen floor and crushed it with the heel of his boot.

"Now that that's over," Emily said, "we should get back to the plan."

Thomas smiled. "You're absolutely right. I think it goes without saying but I'll say it anyway. We won't be able to run forever."

"No," Sam said, "we can't. But we also can't let your family be captured either, now can we? I think we all have an idea of what the government would do to you, let alone Dr. Matsushita and Nikolay if they got their hands on you."

"It's different now though," Bill said.

241

"What do you mean?" Sam asked.

"What I mean is…we're all in the same boat now." Bill motioned towards Craig. "Your son and your daughter both have abilities now. So do my kids. Whether we want to accept it or not, we're all being hunted. The worst part is that this Dr. Matsushita still has Amanda and my children under his control. I want to strangle that sonofabitch."

"I'm sorry," Thomas told them. "This is entirely my fault."

"Forget it," Sam replied. "It's nobody's fault. We've been looking out for each other since we were kids. I don't plan on stopping now."

"What Sam said," Bill added. "We'll figure it out because we have to. Now back to the plan. What were you thinking about when you asked Rebecca to come back with an RV?"

"I'll tell you about that in a minute. But first I want to toss an idea out that you might think is crazy."

Sam leaned in. "And what's that?"

Thomas collected his thoughts. "If the world is after us then why not throw them off the scent."

"I don't understand."

"What's stopping us from telling the world about Dr. Matsushita and his ability?"

Sam and Bill smiled. "That's diabolical."

"I know. Let the world hunt him for a change."

"So what're you thinking?" Bill asked.

"I think it's time I made a public statement."

31
Monday November 12, 2001

"Good evening. I'm Dennis Richmond and thank you for tuning into KTVU for the ten-o'clock news. We begin tonight with continuing coverage of the tensions and mistrust between the United States and Russia that has kept the world in a constant state of anxiety for the past week.

"But what preempted these two countries to escalate to the current level of military readiness? The consensus is that one man is ultimately responsible, and his name is Thomas Clark. Nine days ago the world, as a collective entity, was presented with a video that defied logic. On it we witnessed an unknown individual who rescued American soldiers, soldiers that had been taken hostage by Hamid Emal Habibi, one of the men responsible for the terrorist attacks on September eleventh. Mr. Habibi, the previous day, released a video depicting these same soldiers and demanded the removal of American troops from Afghanistan. Unfortunately, during that video, he killed one of the soldiers to prove his resolve.

"But this unknown individual who rescued these American soldiers, at the time, used abilities the human race has only experienced in the movie theater. What are these powers? How did he come by them? Are they real? The Russian President, Demian Anatolievich, seems to think they're legitimate and is willing to go to war if he isn't presented with this individual.

"So who is this man? Is he a hero? Some say he is. But what's on everyone's mind is how did he get his abilities and how much of a danger is he to society? It didn't take long for one of those questions to get answered when one week ago the

243

President himself revealed the man's identity to be Thomas Clark. The President wasted no time as he placed a half-a-million dollar bounty on Mr. Clark's head and told him to turn himself in under the guise of national security.

"For the past week Thomas Clark and his family have been targeted by both the United States and Russian governments. As global tensions continue to dramatically rise, and the threat of World War Three looms, every effort to locate Mr. Clark has fallen short. Some speculate that perhaps the abilities he possesses have something to do with thwarting the world's bloodhounds. But aside from that one question still remains. Who is Thomas Clark?

"Ladies and gentlemen, in an unprecedented turn of events Thomas Clark reached out and contacted KTVU and offered us an exclusive interview with him. This afternoon I was blindfolded and taken to an unknown location here in the Bay Area. After my camera man and I arrived I was granted the opportunity to interview Mr. Clark with the stipulation that we wouldn't involve the authorities or air the footage until this evening during the ten o'clock news hour. We readily agreed and here is that unedited interview in its entirety."

The screen faded and Dennis' face appeared. He was sitting in a plastic chair outside on a deck. Numerous trees filled the background and the atmosphere seemed calm and inviting.

"My name is Dennis Richmond and I'm here with Thomas Clark, currently the most wanted man on the face of the planet. Thank you Thomas for granting me this opportunity."

The camera switched to Thomas who tried to appear calm and collected, but he was nervous.

"Thank you Dennis for allowing me this platform."

"Mr. Clark, I'll begin with the obvious. Who are you?"

244

Thomas cleared his throat. "That's not an easy answer, at least not anymore. But, as a profession, I'm a published children's book writer."

"And now you're a writer with some pretty impressive abilities, is that accurate?"

Thomas nodded. "Yes, and that's why I reached out. The media, the public and even the President have made me out to be some kind of criminal or danger to the world, and that's just not true."

"I definitely want to delve into your history in a moment Mr. Clark, but I'm curious so I have to ask. How have you successfully avoided capture and where have you been hiding?"

"Dennis, that's a loaded question. All I can say is imagine waking up one day and the secret you've kept inside for so long everyone suddenly knows and is talking about. My life, and the life of my family, changed instantly from a position of safety to one of fear. We are scared. You speak of capture and that we were hiding, but the truth is we've been fleeing from the people whose only goal is to hurt us."

"Mr. Clark, when you mention your family you speak with a passion."

"Wouldn't you? I love my family and it's my job to protect them. I dare anybody out there to tell me they don't feel the same way, that they wouldn't protect their own family."

Dennis nodded. "I understand. But you're not a normal family, are you? You're a family with an incredible secret."

"But that doesn't give the world the right to persecute us because we're different. I understand the world is overly curious about what I can do, but the reason it's been a secret is because the world clearly isn't ready. I have a bounty on my head. But why? Because I chose to save my friends and it was caught on tape? No. I have a bounty on my head because the people that run this world want what I have for themselves, it's that simple. Now, have I always enjoyed looking over my shoulder expecting someone to be there? No. But now that stress and anxiety has multiplied by a factor of five billion because everyone knows who I am, what I look like and what I can do."

Thomas' chest heaved in and out and he had a hard time catching his breath.

Dennis was concerned and it showed. "Are you alright, Mr. Clark?"

Thomas nodded and slowly regained his composure.

"Please continue, Mr. Richmond."

Dennis nodded. "It's obvious to me that your family are very important to you."

"Absolutely."

"But I have to assume, and correct me if I'm wrong, that you haven't always had these powers of yours?"

"That's right."

"Would you mind walking me, and the world, through how you obtained them?"

Thomas swallowed hard. *Here we go with the secret I've guarded with my life…and I'm about to tell everyone about it.* "What nobody knows is that none of this started with me, it began with my children."

"Your children? I don't understand."

"Something happened to me back in nineteen-ninety that led to the mutation of my DNA and blood."

"Something, Mr. Clark?"

Thomas waved his hand as if swatting the question away. "That part of my life is ancient history."

"Of course. Please continue."

"At the time I wasn't aware of these mutations when I married my wife, Laura. In the years that followed we had two children, Emily and Gavin."

"So your son was the one in the video with you?"

"That's correct."

"Why was he there in such a dangerous environment?"

"I'll get to that in a moment. Needless to say my wife and I began to notice some odd occurrences with regards to our children just four years ago."

"What kind of odd occurrences?"

"Little things at first, mind you, but over time they added up."

"I apologize for saying this, Mr. Clark, but you're coming across as a little vague."

Why is this so hard for me to talk about? Because you still want to protect them. "You're right Dennis. This is more difficult than I imagined. I feel like I'm outing my family when all I've ever wanted to do is protect them. And now look what's happened to us."

"Take your time, Mr. Clark."

Thomas fought against the instinct to jump out of his chair, rejoin his family and flee. Instead he looked past the camera and caught Laura's eye. She smiled and mouthed 'I love you'. Thomas took her strength in and used it.

"Our children, Emily and Gavin, have some remarkable abilities. Our daughter can do two things when she comes in contact with someone else. The first is that she can take control of the individual and make them do, disclose or forget anything. The second is that she can summon a relative, who has passed on, back to this world."

A confused look passed over Dennis' face. "Are you serious or are you just pulling my leg?"

"I'll let you decide after the demonstration later."

Dennis shifted in his chair. "Very well. I look forward to having my reality blown. Please continue."

"And you will. But back to my children. My son, Gavin, on the other hand has three abilities."

"Three?" Dennis uttered in astonishment.

Thomas nodded. "He can heal wounds with his bare hands; summon a small creature he calls 'Stir'; and he's the one who controls the portal everyone saw in the video."

"Remarkable. And I know I'm not alone when I ask..., where does that portal go?"

"It's complicated. But the simplest answer I can give you is that it takes you to an entirely different plane of existence."

"You mean like another planet?"

Thomas shook his head. "No. Another realm, perhaps even a different dimension altogether."

"Seriously?"

"Seriously," Thomas replied.

"And you can demonstrate these abilities?"

"We can."

Dennis was unsure how to proceed and it clearly showed. "I'm sorry, both to our viewers and Mr. Clark. What we're discussing is nothing short of science fiction. If it's real, and what Mr. Clark is saying is factual, then you can understand both my level of excitement and apprehension. However, I'll reserve my judgment for later because right now I'm curious on how you, Mr. Clark, obtained your ability. Or do you have more than one ability?"

"I have two. One that I know of and one that's just started to develop."

"What's the first one?"

"Telekinesis."

"That's the ability to move objects with your mind?"

"Yes, it is."

"And your second?"

"I don't have a label for it. I just know that I can jump back in time."

"You're saying that you're a time traveler?"

"No, not like you've seen in the movies. And granted, take this with a grain of salt because I'm still getting used to it, but I have rewound the present back to the past and then rewrote the future that used to be the present."

"I'm sorry. That was a lot to take in. Are you telling the world that you can rewrite history?"

"I don't know actually. At first when it started happening I thought I had dreamt it. But after a couple more occasions I am beginning to understand what it is."

"Scary stuff. What would you say to the people that may believe that leaving you alone, to use your ability to change the present to your liking, would be a mistake?"

Thomas was taken aback. "I...I would never."

"But if I'm not mistaken you just admitted you had on a few occasions."

"Yes...I suppose I did...but those were extreme circumstances."

"Let's go back to the first question I had for you. How did you obtain your powers?"

"Alright. Four years ago my daughter and I were kidnapped by the Director of Central Intelligence at the time, Victor Bannon. My father and I had been working with the DCI to track down Nikolay Dmitriev, the man responsible for the horrific bombings that happened throughout the United States."

"I'm sorry, Mr. Clark. You said you were working with Victor Bannon alongside your father?"

"That's correct."

"But our records indicate that your father passed away in sixty-seven."

"That is also true. What you don't realize is that my father worked for the CIA, during the Cold War, and discovered a mole within the agency. Before he died he uncovered the truth that Nikolay Dmitriev was the individual who ran the mole, not to mention the actual identity of the CIA mole himself. He left this information, along with additional supporting documents, in the form of microfilm."

"But I'm not following. How did you learn about the microfilm?"

"My father told me."

"I don't understand."

"I told you that my daughter, Emily, can bring back dead relatives. She did exactly that and through that process my father was able to not only tell me his story but he was also able to finish the work he had started decades before and flush the mole out of the CIA."

"Once again, Mr. Clark, this is a lot to absorb. So you Thomas, a children's book writer, worked alongside your father and Victor Bannon at the CIA to take down Nikolay Dmitriev?"

"Yes."

"And did you succeed in taking down Nikolay?"

"Yes. He was killed in Cuba."

"I see. So walk us through how this plays a role in you gaining your powers?"

"Victor Bannon eventually caught on to the fact that my father should not be alive and walking around. Long story short, he kidnapped my daughter and I and turned us over to a man by the name of Dr. Yamato Takuma Matsushita. This doctor took samples of our blood, skin and everything else you can think of while he experimented and tortured us. My daughter was only six at the time. Six."

"That's horrible."

"Dr. Matsushita and Victor Bannon wanted the power for themselves, exactly like the Russian and American Presidents do right now. Dr. Matsushita was able to synthesize a serum from my blood."

"A serum?"

"Yes, but before he could perfect it my daughter and I managed to escape, but not before the doctor injected me with his untested serum. A fire ensued and I thought the doctor had perished in it."

"So let me get this straight, Mr. Clark. The DCI, Victor Bannon, took you and your daughter hostage and then subjected you to torture and experiments in order to discover the secrets to your daughter's powers?"

"Yes."

"So what happened to Victor Bannon? The world knows he disappeared four years ago and has never resurfaced. Do you know what happened to him?"

Shit. "What you don't know is that Victor also kidnapped my family and held them at gunpoint. When my friends and I went to rescue them he turned his gun on my wife and fired. It was at that exact moment I discovered I had the power of telekinesis and barely saved her life. We knew, collectively, at that point that Victor was never going to stop."

"What happened, Mr. Clark?"

251

"We decided to banish him."

"Banish? What does that mean? Where is he?"

Thomas paused. "I was protecting my family."

"Where is Victor Bannon?"

"We sent him through the portal."

Dennis couldn't believe his ears. "You killed him?"

"Technically, no."

"But he's dead, isn't he?"

Thomas nodded. "He died in the other realm, yes."

"I see."

Dennis looked back at his notes he'd made and changed the subject.

"So this Dr. Matsushita. You mentioned you thought he'd died during your escape. Do you think differently now?"

"I do." Thomas was happy to not be discussing Victor anymore. "It has come to our attention that Dr. Matsushita is still alive. When the creature, for lack of better words, attacked downtown D.C. the thought crossed my mind. Close-up shots of the creature, as it was shot, clearly indicated it could self-heal."

"So you're claiming that this Dr. Matsushita is the man responsible for that violent act?"

"I am."

"Furthermore, I'm also willing to go on record that Dr. Matsushita and Nikolay Dmitriev are working together and have taken Robert Duncan, the current DCI, hostage."

"But you just explained how Nikolay was killed in Cuba. What am I missing?"

"After the escape through the portal that Hamid captured on video, we entered the other realm. During the process of returning to Earth we were attacked."

Dennis leaned forward. "Attacked? On a different world?"

"That's right. We fought to make it back to Earth and during that fight the soul of Nikolay Dmitriev took control of one of the soldiers my son and I had rescued."

"So you're saying that Nikolay currently inhabits another human body?"

"That's exactly what I'm saying."

"And forgive me Mr. Clark, but you don't think this sounds just a bit farfetched?"

"I know how it sounds and although I can't prove that to you right now, I hopefully will be able to sway your viewers with a demonstration of our powers."

"Very well. Changing gears," Dennis said. "What are your thoughts about the current tension between the United States and Russia? Do you think you're worth going to war over?"

"My family and I just want to be left alone. We've done nothing wrong."

"And what about your own admission that you 'banished' Victor Bannon? Won't people interpret that as murder and a criminal act?"

Thomas shook his head. "I was defending my family from a man who only took what he wanted from me, no matter the cost. We're not criminals, but if you threaten my family I will defend them to my last breath."

"So after this interview is over Mr. Clark, where will you go with the world on your heels?"

"I don't know, and that's the problem. We've run out of places to hide."

"Why not go to this other dimension you've spoken of?"

"Where do you think we've been for the past week? But no, we can never go back there. Anyone who steps through that portal again will wind up dead."

"Dead?"

"Yes. There are other forces at work in this universe that I can't even begin to describe or talk about. However, I can tell the world that we're not the only ones with abilities. Dr. Matsushita, the same man who tortured my daughter and I, injected himself with his own serum. To that end he now has the power to control people with thought alone."

"Mr. Clark, if this is true, why are you outing him?"

"Because Dr. Matsushita is evil and the people of this world need to know who the real enemy is because it's not my family."

"And you say he can control people?"

"That's correct."

"Similar to what you claim your daughter can do?"

"Yes, similar. But in my daughter's case she needs to be in contact. Dr. Matsushita does not."

Dennis looked at his watch and realized he was just about out of time.

"Mr. Clark, while we still have time, would it be possible to demonstrate some of the abilities you mentioned?"

"Of course, Dennis. I don't expect the world to take me at my word alone." He motioned for Gavin to join him. The camera pulled back to give them more room. "Dennis, this is my son Gavin."

"Hello Gavin."

"Hi. What would you like to see?"

"What are my choices again?"

"Healing, my pet or my portal."

Dennis smiled. "If I didn't choose the portal I think I'd be out of a job."

"Kay. You might want to move back a little."

Dennis stood, picked up his chair and gave Gavin some room. The camera man repositioned further back.

"Ready?"

"Whenever you are," Dennis replied.

An instant later the bright portal appeared in the open space. Both Dennis and his camera man jumped.

"Holy shit," Dennis exclaimed as he stared at it in awe. He began to reach his hand out towards it but Gavin shut it down before he could. "Ladies and gentlemen, that was absolutely remarkable. Words don't begin to describe it."

Thomas patted his son on the shoulders. "Thanks Gav."

"You're welcome."

As Dennis fought to wrap his brain around the experience Emily took her turn and came over.

"I'd like you to meet Emily."

Dennis refocused. "Hello Emily."

"What would you like to see?" she asked.

"Well, I don't want you to control me, although anyone watching would argue that point. What's your other ability again?"

"Bringing relatives back so they can talk. Has your mother or father passed on?

Dennis was uncomfortable with how to answer such a direct question, so it stumbled out of his mouth. "My…my father has passed."

Emily boldly approached Dennis and offered him her hand. "If you want to go through with this all you need to do is touch my hand. I won't force you."

With the camera pointed right at him Dennis was unsure if he wanted to proceed. He hesitated.

Thomas spoke up. "It doesn't hurt but I guarantee it will leave a lasting impression on you, Mr. Richmond."

Dennis summoned his courage and reached out for Emily's outstretched hand. He touched it and a moment later his father appeared in front of him. The camera captured everything.

"Hello son," Dennis' father said. "I've missed both you and your mother."

Dennis' legs buckled under him from the shock and he collapsed to the deck. "How? How? But? But?"

Dennis' father bent down, took his son's hands in his and gently helped him back to his feet. Tears flooded down Dennis' cheeks for the entire world to see.

"But…but you're real. You're here. I can touch you. How…how is this possible?"

His father pulled him close, hugged Dennis fiercely and Dennis returned it. "I'm proud of you son. I'm so proud of you. I love you and I miss both of you. Please tell your mother that for me."

"I love you too, Dad. I never got to say goodbye to you. I'm sorry."

"It's okay son. You don't have to hold on to that burden anymore. I'm sorry, but I have to go."

"I don't understand. You just got here."

And with that his father vanished into thin air. Dennis' arms, previously hugging his father, fell slightly as his father disappeared. The look in his eyes convinced everyone that the experience he just went through was completely authentic. He found his chair and sat back down, oblivious to the camera and lost in his own thoughts.

"Mr. Richmond?" Thomas tested.

Dennis slowly turned his face towards Thomas, tears still running down his face. "I don't know how to thank you enough, Mr. Clark. My father passed away suddenly of a heart attack and died before I could get to the hospital. I never forgave myself for not being there for him. So thank you. What I'm feeling right now…the words…I can't express the gratitude…"

"You don't have to Mr. Richmond. Do you want to stop?"

Dennis looked over at the camera, wiped his eyes and stood up. "No. I'm okay. What's next?"

"Thanks Em," Thomas said as his daughter joined the others.

"Yes," Dennis added. "Thank you."

"Well, Mr. Richmond, you may want to sit back down in your chair."

"Okay," Dennis replied as he followed Thomas' suggestion. "Why…"

All of a sudden Dennis, and the chair he was in, lifted off the deck and floated up in the air.

"Holy crap!" Dennis bellowed. He looked at Thomas. "You're doing this?"

"Yes. Do you want me to let you down?"

"Hell no," Dennis replied with a smile. "The feeling…it's amazing…"

"You don't actually need the chair," Thomas told him.

Dennis looked down and realized he was gripping the chair in a death grip. He unclasped his hands and Thomas let the plastic chair fall back down where it bounced off on the deck. As the camera followed Dennis, Thomas flew him over the railing, some twenty feet above the ground.

"Woahhhhh."

Thomas circled Dennis back and gently landed him back on the deck, feet first.

"Convinced?"

Dennis Richmond nodded emphatically and shook Thomas' hand. "Thank you Mr. Clark, and thank you to your family. As a reporter I'm supposed to remain neutral, but in this case I believe how you and your family have been labeled is unjustified. Yes, you have some extraordinary gifts, and I understand that the world is extremely curious, but that doesn't give any government the right to hunt you down."

"Thank you Dennis."

"I only hope this interview gives the people of the world a new perspective about the type of person you really are Thomas."

*   *   *

Dennis gave the sign to cut the camera recording as the rest of the family walked out to join them. Dennis shook each of their hands.

"It's a real pleasure to meet all of you, but as much as I want to sit here and chat I must insist that you leave right away. The more time you put between here and wherever you're going, before this airs this evening, the better." He paused for a few seconds. Listen, I don't want to be responsible for your capture so I'll completely understand if you don't want me to air this."

"Thank you for that," Laura told him, "but we've already decided to take the risk. People need to view us as human beings and drop the preconceived notions they've made."

Dennis grew solemn. "You're right. And I honestly say you've changed my perspective today. I don't know how you do what you do, but thank you again."

"I appreciate your sincerity," Laura replied.

"You're welcome."

Thomas shook Dennis' hand once more and then walked inside.

"We've got to go," Sam said next to him.

"I know. Let's load everyone in the RV and head out. We have some serious miles to cover."

Laura made her way to Thomas' side and whispered. "Why didn't you mention that I can tell when someone is lying?"

He smiled and kissed her on the cheek. "The world doesn't need to know all of our secrets."

32
Tuesday November 13, 2001

Dr. Matsushita, in Virginia, watched the KTVU interview just after 1:30 in the morning. Every news organization in the world immediately began to rebroadcast it on their stations. In a matter of hours it was the most talked about segment and would dominate the networks for days to come.

As the interview came to an end Dr. Matsushita turned off the television in his lab and was enveloped by the dark.

I didn't see that one coming Thomas. Well played. But don't think it will save you.

He swiveled in his chair, located the tracking device and examined it.

Still only four readings. Why isn't Craig's working? Strange though, I wonder where they've been for the past week? Is it possible that they spent all that time in the other realm? Maybe, but how?

In the dark Dr. Matsushita touched his burned right arm with his left hand, slowly tracing the scar tissue. He frowned.

Tatiana and Nikolay think that I'm an idiot and can lie to me. How naïve do they think I am? I have no doubts that they're going to keep Thomas and me prisoners once I give them the serum. Two can play at that game. I think it's time to turn the tables on this little arrangement of ours.

He smiled. Dr. Matsushita got out of his chair, flipped on the lights and began to work. He expected to have Thomas at his mercy within a few days and needed his catalyst prepared, which would be combined with Thomas' blood, ready for his arrival. In earnest he began the final step of his process, to combine the smallpox he'd previously obtained from Thomas' blood, and mutate it so he could add it to the catalyst itself.

* * *

Nikolay sat back in his seat, previously used by Hobbes', and turned off the monitor. He'd just watched the entire interview.

A bold move Thomas but you should have stayed hidden. You're vulnerable now; exposed. Even if the world comes over to your side it'll be too late.

He stood up and walked out of the Tech wing and over to the laboratory. As he opened the door he saw Dr. Matsushita hard at work. The doctor looked up as Nikolay walked in.

"Thomas has resurfaced," Nikolay stated, "and the tracker you implanted in Craig still isn't working."

"I'm aware of both. Quite an interesting choice he made; to expose his family to the world."

"Just as much as he told the world what you can do."

"Just don't forget it," Yamato sneered.

Nikolay looked over at the four children lying on the floor, sleeping on makeshift beds. "Have you used the girl to get a fix on Thomas' location yet?"

"No. That's your job," Dr. Matsushita told him. "My part of the arrangement is to create the serum. If you recall, yours was to secure Thomas for me."

Nikolay didn't like the obvious disrespect. "Mind what you say and how you say it doctor."

"Veiled threats don't do you justice, Nikolay. You're not scary. You're just an old man in a young man's body stretching your muscles. You're lucky Tatiana hasn't killed

262

you already. I mean honestly, what are you really bringing to the table, incompetence and failure?"

Nikolay reached for his handgun. "No one speaks to me like…"

Dr. Matsushita calmly looked on as Nikolay extended his weapon and pointed it at the doctor's head.

"I could kill you right now," Nikolay threatened with a snarl.

"Then pull the trigger, if you can."

Nikolay's eyes darted to his right hand as his muscles stiffened. The demeanor on his face changed as he realized he wasn't in control anymore.

"Problem, Nikolay?" the doctor taunted.

Nikolay didn't answer as his right arm bent at the elbow. His gun swung away from the doctor until its barrel rested snuggly against Nikolay's own temple.

"You can't kill me," Nikolay said with some bravado. "Without me there is no deal. I'm the only one protecting you from Russia."

Dr. Matsushita laughed. "Whatever you need to tell yourself Nikolay. But know this, threaten me again and I won't hesitate to take your current situation that one additional step."

Nikolay's right index finger started to pull on the trigger. But right before the gun would have discharged Nikolay regained control of his motor skills and was able to pull the weapon away.

"You can't kill me either, Nikolay. Without me there is no serum. And without the serum there is no you. Now get out of here, I have work to do and don't forget to take Amanda with you."

Nikolay grimaced and holstered his weapon. As he left he grabbed Amanda and took her back to the Tech wing with him. Once there he asked her to find Thomas. For the first time in a week Amanda pointed and told Nikolay how far away he was. He turned to the computer, typed in the data and smiled at the results. He called out to one of his men who promptly appeared in the room.

"They've gone to ground in California. Find them!"

"Yes, sir."

The man left as Nikolay picked up the phone and dialed the Russian President.

"Da?" Demian Anatolievich said over the private line. "What is it?"

"Thomas Clark is in California. My men will pick up his trail shortly."

"They'd better find him before the Americans do, for your sake, especially now that Mr. Clark has gone public."

"You saw that?" Nikolay asked.

Idiot. "How could I have missed it? This issue is bigger than you Nikolay. Find Thomas and deliver him to me or I won't be able to protect you. Your name is out there now, and if the President of the United States believes you're alive then you're a target, just like Dr. Matsushita has become."

* * *

The President of the United States hadn't been sleeping very well, as of late, and tonight was no exception. As he tossed and turned one of his aides entered his bedroom.

"Mr. President?"

He sat up in bed. "What is it?"

"I'm sorry to disturb you sir, but there's been a development."

"What kind of development?"

"Thomas Clark did an interview with a news station based out of Oakland, California, sir. It's all over the wire."

The President swung his legs out and pushed himself to his feet. He put a robe on and went to the door.

"Show me."

*   *   *

As the interview came to an end the President leaned back in his chair.

Well, at least we know what happened to Victor Bannon and who's responsible for his disappearance and subsequent death. And now, the world knows too. Mr. Clark, that was quite a gamble but it just might come back to bite you.

He dialed a number on the phone next to him.

"Converge on California. I want it torn apart until you find them."

"Yes, sir but we're already on it. We had tasked our satellites to constantly monitor the locations where Mr. Clark used to live."

"And?"

"Well, sir, I'm happy to report that we discerned movement from the house he grew up in Orinda. We've been following an RV that left the property."

"Where' it currently?" the President asked with discernable excitement in his voice.

"Traveling southbound on Interstate-Five, sir."

"Keep me informed on its movement and the moment it reaches its destination."

"Yes, sir."

The President hung up and dialed another number.

"Da?"

"Demian, I have an update for you."

"You have Thomas in custody?"

"Not yet, but he's in California."

"Anyone with a television knows that already, Mr. President," Anatolievich said with slight contempt.

Asshole. "What you don't know is that our satellites are tracking Mr. Clark as we speak."

"That is fantastic news Mr. President. Where is Mr. Clark?"

"I'll be happy to relay that information once we have him in custody, but not before."

"It sounds like you don't trust me," Demian said, as he feigned being offended.

As if you don't have agents on the ground ready to move already. "Be that as it may, Mr. President, I'll wait until I have confirmation. When that happens you'll hear from me and our next steps."

Shit. "Make sure that you do," the Russian President replied. "I'd hate to remind you that we're in this to the bitter end."

"Please, keep testing my resolve Demian and see what happens. In the meantime we have a common goal we need to focus on."

The President hung up. *We have to find Thomas first and not the Russians. If they grab him before we can, and then deny it, I might be forced to declare war.*

33
Tuesday November 13, 2001

With Rebecca at the wheel Thomas, Laura, Gavin, Emily, Sam, Julie, Craig, Bill and Kim had made themselves as comfortable as they could within the confines of the RV. After the interview concluded they'd piled into the large vehicle, which had been parked down the block, and departed Orinda headed east on Highway-24. At the 680 interchange they turned south and then turned east once again on 580. Eventually they took the southern exit to Interstate-5 towards Los Angeles, which lay a few hundred miles away.

The RV was old and beat up, but it ran well and Rebecca had been lucky to locate and purchase it after taking BART to Walnut Creek. In the meantime Laura, Julie and Kim had managed to call a taxi from a neighbor's house. Once it arrived they headed over to Safeway and loaded up on non-perishable supplies. After they were done they took a different taxi back to the house. When Rebecca showed up everyone packed the RV and the pre-paid phones were distributed. By this time, of course, Thomas' interview with KTVU had been set-up. Rebecca dropped off Sam and Bill, at the pre-arranged location, to wait for Dennis Richmond and his camera man to arrive. When they did they were searched and blindfolded. Satisfied that they hadn't been followed or given Thomas up, Sam and Bill drove the news van back to the house.

Outside Bakersfield, California the family turned east on 58 towards Barstow. After a bit they turned south on I-15 which quickly turned into I-215 headed towards San Bernardino. The family decided that it was a better idea to arrive after dark, so they pulled off the freeway and found a motel. Six hours later, and after merging onto the 210, they eventually exited to the 330 and drove up the mountain towards Running Springs.

"Are we there yet?" Emily asked her father as the dark mountains loomed around her, enveloping the RV as they began the arduous trek up the steep mountain road.

"We're getting close," Thomas replied. "There are fifteen miles of twisting and winding roads ahead of us. Keep your eyes peeled."

Rebecca nodded without looking at him from behind the wheel. "Understood."

The adults gathered as closely as they could around the table. Emily sat in the front seat while Craig and Gavin played with Stickers in the rear bedroom.

"So explain this to me again," Sam said to Thomas. "Why Running Springs? Why come back here of all places?"

"It's secluded, for one thing," Thomas replied. "The second is that I had a neighbor that would only stay at his house during the spring and summer, then head to Palm Springs during fall and winter. His house will be empty and I know where he keeps his key. Third, we don't have anywhere else to go right now. All of our accounts have been frozen and we're down to a few thousand dollars and the supplies we have with us. I'm hoping we can hole up, rest and regroup while we collectively decide on our next course of action."

"I still think it's a bit risky," Sam stated.

"We agreed to this before we left Orinda," Laura calmly told the group. "What's done is done."

"You're right Laura," Sam replied. "I think I'm just starting to feel the pressure. I haven't been on this side of things…"

Julie cut him off. "Side of things? The entire WORLD is after us Sam. I don't know if the fact that you're just 'starting to feel the pressure' is a relief to me or not."

Sam shot his wife a look but let her comment drop. They were all tired, irritable and on the verge of losing hope. The interview had actually been the only real positive encounter they'd had and watching Dennis Richmond react when he embraced his father had touched them all. But the long trip from Orinda to Running Springs had taken its toll and the cracks were beginning to appear once again as the hard reality sunk in.

"What do you think about the idea of trying to contact Russell?" Bill asked.

"I like the idea," Sam said, "but the fact is we don't know if he's been compromised."

"I know, but he might not be."

Laura shook her head. "That's one heck of a gamble."

"I don't like saying this," Thomas added, "but we can't trust anyone but each other right now. I hope my interview has informed people and changed their minds, but that's only hope. In time the public will know the truth, but in the meantime we need to face the fact that we're being hunted."

Bill leaned back. "I can't believe our government took SANDBOX away from us and now they want to 'black-site' us too."

"Black-site us?" Kim inquired.

Sam answered. "He means make us disappear."

"Well," she mocked, "when you put it those terms it just seems too appealing. We should just stop the RV and turn ourselves in."

"Sweetie," Bill said as he tried to console his wife. "We're going to be okay."

Kim immediately looked at Laura. "Does he really believe that?"

Laura took a few seconds and then gently shook her head back and forth.

"See," Kim indicated. "Even you don't believe we're going to get through this. And, aside from jumping ahead in time a week to California, might I remind you that our children are still out there. That crazy sonofabitch gave them powers and has turned them against us!"

Bill corrected her. "It's just mind control…"

"Oh shut up!" Kim yelled. "I'm sick of this. I'm sick of all of this. Hell even Rebecca, who we've all known for years, isn't Rebecca anymore. When is all of this madness going to end!?"

The RV went silent.

"It's okay Rebecca," Emily said quietly from the passenger seat. "I know who you are even though you're different on the outside."

Rebecca took it all in stride. She'd been through more than most of them, having died and come back to life, and now trapped in a stranger's body.

"I know you do Em."

Kim tried to make it right. "I'm sorry Rebecca. I didn't mean…"

"Forget about it," Rebecca said. "You're scared and I get that, we all do. I flinch every time I speak or catch my reflection. I know this isn't my body and I know I don't belong here, so listen up. If I get the chance to take down Nikolay then I will take that opportunity. This isn't my life anymore and the balance needs to be corrected."

"We don't want you to leave us," Thomas told her.

"I know. You've become my family and I'd do anything to protect you, but I made a promise to the Caretaker."

"You can't go," Emily whined. "Promise me you'll stay with us."

Rebecca shook her head. "Em, I made a promise and a person's word is the only true currency that holds any value in this world. You don't have to like it but it's important that you keep any promise you make. Do you understand?"

Emily nodded.

"Good."

Laura redirected the topic. "Kim, you know that your children are on our minds, right?"

Kim lowered her head. "I know. I'm sorry. I…I just want them back so badly. But what I really need to know is that they're okay even though they've been…changed."

Julie pulled her sister close. "Look at Craig. He's okay."

"But he's changed."

"Sure," Julie replied, "and knowing me I should be freaking out about that, but I'm not. I could never love my son any less just because he's different, and neither does Thomas or Laura with their kids."

"I miss them."

"We all do sis, we all do. And somehow, through all this, we'll find and get them back."

"How?"

Julie shook her head. "I don't know yet."

The RV continued to wind up the mountain, hugging the corners as the treacherous drop-offs appeared and disappeared throughout their ascent.

"So let's go over our options," Sam announced. "As I see it we can continue running or we can find a place to hide."

"Are there any other choices?" Julie asked.

Sam looked around. "Anyone?"

"Turning ourselves in is a choice," said Thomas, "but it'll never be an option."

"I second that," Bill said. "I'd rather die fighting then be put in a hole for the rest of my life."

"Are they really going to do that to us?" Kim asked.

"Or worse."

"Shit," Kim said with sadness in her voice.

"Can't we just leave the country?" Julie asked. "I know our passports have been invalidated but what about stealing or borrowing a jet?"

"And go where?" Sam told her. "Everyone in the world knows our faces and we haven't solved our cash problem yet."

Julie's shoulders slumped. "Isn't there anything we can do?"

"I think it's only a matter of time before they catch us," Kim said with a clear sound of defeat.

"Don't say that," Bill said. "We'll get through this."

"I'm just verbalizing what you already believe. They're coming for us and you all know it so do me a favor and stop trying to protect me."

Rebecca called out from the front. "Thomas, I need you up here for directions."

Thomas squeezed out from behind the table and headed to the front as Emily moved out of his way. He placed his daughter on his lap as the green Running Springs sign passed by the RV's window.

Home sweet home. Shit. I never thought I'd ever come back here. But now look at us. We're running scared and losing hope. The worst part about it is that it's all my fault.

272

34
Tuesday November 13, 2001

"I'll be right there," the President said as he hung up the phone and headed out of his Oval office.

It was 7 a.m. in Washington D.C. as the President walked through the White House, flanked by two Secret Service agents, to the East Wing on his way to a private and guarded elevator. As he approached the elevator the Marine stationed there snapped to attention and saluted.

"Good morning, Mr. President."

The President returned the salute and then placed his right hand on the biometric scanner panel which was located on the wall adjacent to the thick vault doors.

"Initiating scan," announced a robotic female voice.

Five seconds ticked by as the process completed.

"Stage One authorized."

A new section opened to reveal a new device.

"Stage Two initiated. You have three seconds before retinal scan commences."

The President leaned forward and looked directly into the red iris. The computer scanned his eye and verified his identity.

"Access granted," the voice said. "Have a nice day."

The thick vault doors cracked open, slid to one side and revealed a large elevator door. On both sides of the door were card slots. The President removed a keycard from his vest pocket and looked over at the Marine who readied the secondary card he kept on his person.

"On my mark, Mr. President. Three, two, one, mark."

Both men inserted their cards simultaneously and the elevator doors opened. The President entered alone and pushed one of the two buttons. The door closed and he began to descend the six stories down to the PEOC, the Presidential Emergency Operations Center. Seconds later, after the quick drop, the door opened and the President stepped out. The room was filled with people, both sitting at the multiple computer consoles as well as watching the large monitors on the walls.

"This way, sir."

The chair at the head of the table was open. The President sat down and spoke at the same time.

"Give me the team's current status."

"Yes, sir. SpecOps group Delta was dispatched to the target's location. Since the target's arrival our view of the area by satellite confirms they have not left the premises. Delta has deployed around the enclosure and the team is holding for your authorization."

"Very well. Patch this in to the bunker and as well as Russia. I want the DCI and our new associates in on this endeavor."

"Right away, sir."

Twenty seconds later the DCI, Tatiana, Nikolay, Dr. Matsushita and Demian Anatolievich were on the line.

"Robert," the President asked. "Are you there?"

"Yes, sir," the DCI replied.

"And President Anatolievich?"

"I too can hear you, Mr. President."

"Good. I'll get right to the point. Special Operations group Delta currently has Thomas Clark, and his family, surrounded in a house located in Running Springs, California."

"How many men make up that group?" Demian asked.

An aide whispered in the President's ear.

"Forty men," the President replied.

"I see. Please excuse me for a moment," the Russian President announced.

"I need Thomas alive," a voice said through the speaker.

"Who's this?" the President demanded. "Identify yourself."

"This is Dr. Matsushita and I need Thomas alive."

The aide whispered once again in the President's ear.

"I've been assured that non-lethal munitions are being utilized. Are there any other concerns before I kick this off? Robert?"

"Just that Thomas isn't going to come quietly if you corner him, sir," the DCI replied. "Give him the opportunity to surrender before you have the SpecOps team move in."

"Do you think he'll actually surrender," the President asked, "or will it just give all of them more time to escape through that portal?"

"I don't know."

"I'm not taking that chance." The President turned and gave the order. "Move in."

*   *   *

"Forty men," the President replied.

"I see. Please excuse me for a moment," the Russian President announced.

Demian Anatolievich placed the conference call on hold and resumed his previous phone call with Tatiana in the bunker.

"Inform our Russian sleepers to hold back immediately. They'll be no match against forty highly trained Special Forces

275

operators." He paused and collected his thoughts. "It appears as if I have little choice but to go along with the deal I made with the President, at least for now."

"Yes, sir," Tatiana replied. "Right away."

* * *

After arriving at the neighbor's house Thomas found the front door key in the same location it'd been hidden in for years. In the dead of night the family let themselves inside and quietly unpacked the RV. Although Thomas felt guilty for effectively breaking in to his neighbor's house he couldn't let that distract him. His family needed a desperate respite and he hoped a few days rest in the mountains, away from the world and its prying eyes, would give them just that.

After they were settled in and piles of blankets were pulled out of multiple closets, the children and the adults created a temporary place to sleep together in the family room. It was 2:15 in the morning by the time they had finished and Emily, Gavin and Craig had fallen asleep with Stickers curled up around Gavin's head. Laura, Julie and Kim lay down shortly afterwards as Sam, Bill, Thomas and Rebecca had a quiet discussion in the kitchen.

"Do you think the government knows where we are?" Rebecca asked. "I mean, is there a chance they followed us?"

"Anything's possible," Bill told her. "Hell, they could have a drone circling above us right now and we wouldn't know it."

"That's a pleasant thought," said Thomas.

"It is what it is. But we got this far without an incident so that's something."

"Which is why we can't let our guard down," Sam said.

"Speaking of, I'll take first watch," Rebecca told them.

"Negative," Sam replied. "You've been behind the wheel all day and absolutely need a break. I'll take the first two hour shift, Bill will take the second and then Thomas. Agreed?"

They all nodded.

"Good. Let's check our phones and see if there's a signal."

The four of them extracted their pre-paid phones and verified they each received a cell signal.

"Two bars," Bill said.

"Me too," Thomas said in agreement.

"Ditto." Sam put his back in his pocket. "Put them on vibrate. If there's an issue I'll call. In the meantime I want you three to get some shut eye." Sam checked his Glock and then put it back in his waistband. "I'm going to walk the perimeter. Bill, I'll wake you in two hours."

"Roger that," Bill replied as Sam headed out.

* * *

After Sam had stealthily verified the perimeter was secure, he placed himself in a concealed but strategic overwatch position. Nearly two hours later, just as he was about to head back inside to rouse Bill, he heard a twig snap sixty feet away. Sam froze in place as his senses immediately kicked into high gear.

Could that have been an animal? Maybe, but then why aren't I hearing it anymore? Because you know that sound was made by a human.

He heard another snap from an entirely different direction.

Okay, that's definitely human and it sounds like they're vectoring in on my position. The only way they'd know where

I'm hidden is by thermal satellite imaging or thermal night vision goggles.

Sam's eyes had long ago adjusted to the dim moonlight and he strained to catch any sign of movement. He closed one eye to preserve his night vision and slowly pulled his phone from his pocket. He illuminated it, using his jacket to shield the light, and instantly saw three words on the screen. **No network detected.** He turned it off and stuffed it back in his pocket.

Shit. They're good, real good. They jammed the cell signals in the area and that means they know what they're doing. It's about to get noisy. Time for me to move.

Sam bolted out of his position, pulled out his Glock and sprinted towards the house.

"DON'T MOVE! STAY WHERE YOU ARE OR YOU WILL BE FIRED UPON!"

Sam fired two rounds into the air to warn everyone inside of the danger as he barreled closer to safety.

"TAKE HIM DOWN!"

The trees and branches around Sam exploded as he was promptly targeted with dozens of projectiles. The once peaceful darkness was shattered by gunfire as soldiers discharged round after round at their fast moving target. Flying tree bark cut Sam's exposed face and hands. He reached the back door just as it opened from the inside. He dove forward through the opening and winced as a round finally caught him.

"Oof!" Sam managed to say as he hit the floor.

Thomas quickly closed the door and used his power to move a heavy couch in front of it.

"What the hell is going on!?" Bill demanded without looking back at his friend, his eyes locked on the closed door, his gun at the ready.

"CEASE FIRE!"

Rebecca and Laura also had their handguns out and had formed a protective barrier in front of Julie, Kim, Emily, Gavin and Craig. Stickers tail had fluffed up and he was clearly agitated.

"I'm hit," Sam announced as he rolled over on the floor.

"What?" Julie said as she realized what her husband had just declared. She pushed Rebecca aside and moved towards him.

Gavin heard Sam as well and went with her.

"Everybody stay low and away from the windows and doors," Bill commanded. "Thomas, block the front door too."

"On it," Thomas replied as he ran to the kitchen, levitated the refrigerator off the floor and manipulated it before the front door.

"You okay brother," Bill asked.

Sam put his gun on the floor and winced as he started to remove his jacket.

"Yeah," Sam replied. "I think so. They snuck up close before I even knew they were there and that's saying something."

Julie made it to Sam's side, along with Gavin, and she helped Sam remove his jacket so they could tend to his wound. As they were doing so something came loose, fell to the floor and came to a rest. Gavin picked it up and looked at it.

"How bad is it?" Julie asked.

"I don't know. My left arm is numb but it doesn't feel like I've been shot."

"But there's blood," she announced.

She rolled up his bloodstained sleeve and took a closer look at the entry point. A pronounced welt had formed on his upper left bicep and it was bleeding, but there wasn't an entry wound to speak of.

Bill shot a glance over at Sam's injury and recognized it right away. "That came from a rubber bullet. It's a non-lethal round. Apparently they want to immobilize and not kill us. Hurray for that."

Sam nodded as Gavin held up the bullet for everyone to see. "I'm getting some feeling back in my arm now. Fuck that hurt."

Emily, Craig, Kim and Laura joined the group as Thomas came back from reinforcing the front door, but before anyone else could speak they were interrupted by a man's booming voice from the outside.

"SURRENDER NOW OR WE'LL BE REQUIRED TO TAKE YOU BY FORCE. YOU HAVE TEN SECONDS TO COMPLY."

"Oh my God," Kim fearfully cried out.

Sam, Bill, Thomas and Laura quickly shot glances at each other.

"Is the portal even an option anymore?" Bill asked.

Thomas shook his head. "No, not anymore. We'd be shredded and killed by the dark forces in a matter of seconds."

"Then what are our options?" Julie asked.

Sam picked up his gun from the floor. "We fight."

"Even against our own soldiers?" Bill questioned.

Before Sam could answer the windows shattered and three tear gas canisters entered the house. Thomas didn't hesitate and sent the metal cylinders sailing back where they came from, but not before some of the noxious gas expelled into the room.

"Cover your face with your shirt, close your eyes and try not to breathe," Sam promptly told the women and children. "I want you in the bathroom. Move!"

Kim and Julie began to cough on the vapors as heavy boots were heard on both the front and back porches.

Thomas looked at Laura and their eyes met. "Please go with them and take Emily."

Laura nodded and she and Emily's eyes teared up from the gas.

Gavin pocketed the rubber bullet, ducked down and summoned Stir by his side, Stickers next to him.

Camouflaged faces peaked in through the windows at them wearing gas masks as Julie and Kim rapidly crawled on their knees with Craig towards the bathroom. Laura and Emily were right behind them.

"TARGETS SPOTTED AND THEY'RE ARMED!"

Bill leveled his handgun and fired five rounds through the back door, hitting two of the operators.

The refrigerator against the front door groaned along the floor as the door was forced open. Rebecca, her eyes watering, moved to a new position in the kitchen and fired a few rounds in that direction, keeping the attackers heads down as they backed away from the door.

Six more gas canisters flew through the windows and Thomas expelled them as fast as he could.

Sam's attention turned to the sounds of windows being broken in both bedrooms.

"They're coming in!" he said and started to move in that direction.

Stir's eyes glowed red as he flew through the closest window. The sounds of surprise and agony immediately followed.

281

Thomas was knocked over as he took a rubber bullet to his side from across the room.

"OUCH!" he hollered and started to crawl out of the line of fire. "FUCK!"

More rounds pinged off the floor around him and Gavin. Bill swiveled and emptied his remaining magazine towards the broken windows the rounds were coming from. He dropped the empty magazine and slammed in a new one before the empty ever hit the floor. He then moved away from the back door towards Thomas pulling Gavin with him.

Sam pushed the screaming women and children into the bathroom a moment before the hallway door splintered from a sustained barrage of gunfire. With his back against the doorjamb he poked the barrel of his gun into a newly made hole and emptied his entire eighteen round magazine into the hallway.

Despite Rebecca holding off their attackers from coming through the front door, two flashbangs were tossed through the gap that had already been made. Rebecca ducked and tried to close her eyes and cover her ears, but the grenades detonated. In the small kitchen the concussion blast amplified and Rebecca was thrown against the wall. She struck her head against the wall and slid to the floor unconscious as a fire broke out.

Bill barely caught sight of Rebecca sailing through the air before her body came to a rest.

"Rebecca's down!" he bellowed.

Sam reloaded as more rounds punched holes through the closed hallway door that led to the two bedrooms. Sam watched as his son stood up, against Julie's will, and phased through the bathroom wall towards the bedrooms.

"Craig!" Sam shouted. "No!"

Two men kicked open the back door, pushing the couch aside, and tossed in more flashbangs towards Bill, Thomas and Gavin. As they flew through the air Gavin formed his portal and the flashbangs vanished. Thomas, in agony from his broken rib, extended his arm and pulled the two operators off their feet. They disappeared into the portal, before Gavin disengaged it, which left the back porch temporarily vacant.

Inhuman cries of anguish could be heard from outside as Stir continued to wreak havoc in the dark.

"FINISH THEM OFF!" the outside voice howled.

More canisters could be heard as they were launched and skittered across the kitchen floor out of sight. The gas contained within expanded rapidly and bellowed out into the family room.

Sam kicked open the hallway door and rushed down it, surprising the four men in the two bedrooms. The four operators aimed their rifles at Sam just as Craig appeared behind one of them and kicked him in the groin as hard as he could. As that operator collapsed the hallway filled with rubber bullets as Sam and the three remaining operators engaged each other. Sam's first bullet struck one of the soldiers in the shoulder, spinning him and his weapon away from the engagement. Sam's second round entered another operator's gas mask and snapped his head back. Before he could get off a third seven rubber bullets devastated Sam's torso. He crashed to the floor unconscious, his momentum taking his body right up to the bedroom's doorway.

"Dad!" Craig cried out.

As Craig tried to rush to his father's side the same soldier who had incapacitated Sam swiftly brought the butt of his rifle down on the boy's neck. Craig crumpled to the floor next to his father.

"Uncle Sam!" Gavin screamed as he witnessed Sam go down.

The gas gushed out of the kitchen, into the family room, around the corner past the bathroom and down the hallway towards the bedrooms in a matter of seconds. But this final volley wasn't tear gas; it was fast acting sleeping gas.

Bill breathed it in first and Thomas caught Bill's puzzled look just before he and Gavin also inhaled it. Bill's hand and body relaxed. His weapon slipped from his hand and clattered to the floor as he stared at it, his mind and reflexes not following his commands.

Thomas tried to push the gas away as he tried not to breathe, but it was a lost cause.

Gavin began to stagger, as if he were drunk, as the gas flew into the bathroom and down the hallway. Gavin looked at his father and then stumbled to the floor, comatose.

In the bathroom Thomas heard the panicked cries that emanated from Laura, Emily, Julie and Kim as the gas enveloped them. Their cries faded away shortly thereafter.

Thomas' lungs, as he stared at his son's face, felt like they were on fire. Desperately needing oxygen, and against his wishes, his body breathed in the toxic gas. Immediately his senses and reaction time slowed, as if he'd consumed ten beers. Thomas felt like he was falling down a long, dark hole as his vision began to tunnel, his son appearing further and further away from him.

Nooooooo!

"DON'T MOVE! STAY WHERE YOU ARE OR YOU WILL BE FIRED UPON!"

Thomas and the others were jarred awake when they heard the two rounds from outside. They scrambled for their weapons.

"TAKE HIM DOWN!"

Thomas rushed to the back door as automatic gunfire erupted. He opened it just as Sam dove through.

"Oof!" Sam exclaimed as he hit the floor.

Thomas quickly closed the door behind Sam and used his power to move a heavy couch in front of it as Bill stood guard.

"What the hell is going on!?" Bill demanded without looking back at his friend, his eyes locked on the closed door, his gun at the ready.

"CEASE FIRE!"

Rebecca and Laura also had their handguns out and had formed a protective barrier in front of Julie, Kim, Emily, Gavin and Craig. Stickers tail had fluffed up and he was clearly agitated.

"I'm hit," Sam announced as he rolled over on the floor.

"What?" Julie said as she realized what her husband had just declared. She pushed Rebecca aside as she moved towards him.

Gavin heard Sam as well and went with her.

"Everybody stay low and away from the windows and doors," Bill commanded. "Thomas, block the front door too."

Thomas paused.

"What the hell are you waiting for!?" Bill yelled. "Do it!"

"No. We've done this before."

"Done what before?" Laura asked him.

"This," Thomas said as he swept his arm around the room. "And the last time we lost."

"Fucking hell," Bill said and looked over at Sam. "You okay brother?"

"They used rubber bullets," Thomas stated.

Sam put his gun on the floor and winced as he started to remove his jacket.

"Yeah," Sam replied. "I think so. They snuck up close before I even knew they were there and that's saying something."

Julie made it to Sam's side, along with Gavin, and she helped Sam remove his jacket so they could tend to his wound. As they were doing so something came loose, fell to the floor and came to a rest. Gavin picked it up, looked at it and then held it up. It was a rubber bullet.

"Okay," Sam said, "I'm convinced you can time travel, or whatever you want to call it. So what are we supposed to do this time?"

"I don't know."

"SURRENDER NOW OR WE'LL BE REQUIRED TO TAKE YOU BY FORCE. YOU HAVE TEN SECONDS TO COMPLY."

"Oh my God," Kim fearfully cried out.

Sam, Bill, Thomas and Laura quickly shot glances at each other.

Bill began to ask a question. "Is the portal..."

Thomas shook his head. "No, not anymore. We'd be shredded and killed by the dark forces in a matter of seconds."

"Then what are our options?" Julie asked.

Sam picked up his gun from the floor. "We fight."

The windows shattered as Thomas turned towards them and forced the tear gas canisters back before they even entered the room.

"How the hell..." Bill tried to say

"It happened before," Thomas said as he cut his friend off.

"So let's do it differently this time," Sam stated. "Walk us through this."

They heard heavy boots on both the front and back porches. Gavin pocketed the rubber bullet and summoned Stir by his side right next to Stickers. He reached down and picked his cat up, cradling him in his arms.

"We have to get out of this house because they'll continue to gas us."

Camouflaged faces peaked in through the windows at them wearing gas masks. "TARGETS SPOTTED AND THEY'RE ARMED!"

Bill leveled his handgun and fired five rounds through the back door, hitting two of the operators.

"We take this outside then?" Sam questioned.

Thomas nodded. "I'm afraid so."

Bill fired a few more rounds to keep their attacker's heads down as the family gathered to flee the structure together.

"Ready?"

"As ready as we'll ever be."

Thomas took the couch in front of the back door and propelled it with an incredible amount of force, tearing the door off its hinges and slamming into the soldiers on the other side. With surprise on their side Thomas led the charge outside with Stir by his side.

"WE HAVE A BREACH! MOVE TO INTERCEPT!"

Stir immediately branched off to the left and attacked the nearest group of operators, ferociously tearing into their arms and legs.

Thomas located target after target, picking them up off the ground and slamming them into each other.

Rubber bullets zeroed in on their position much quicker than anticipated as Sam, Bill, Laura and Rebecca continued to fire round after round into targets that emerged out of the darkness.

"I don't like this!" Julie screamed.

"Keep going!" Sam urged.

The group had started to make a dent when Emily caught a rubber bullet in the chest and fell to the ground.

"Em!" Laura cried out.

She stopped moving forward with the group and dropped to her knees by her daughter's side. Gavin saw his sister hit the ground hard and turned back for her.

"Em's down," Rebecca shouted.

"Fuck! Push them back!" Sam ordered. "Make a circle!"

Thomas, Sam and Bill abruptly stopped and hastily took up positions around their family. They continued to fire as rubber bullets struck the ground all around them.

Gavin put Stickers down, placed his hands on his sister's body and concentrated.

"Changing!" Bill yelled as his weapon's slide locked open. He thumbed the release, jammed a fresh magazine in, racked the slide and reacquired targets.

Thomas pulled one operator after another off their feet and tossed them away from the group as fast as he could, but they just kept coming.

"Changing!" Sam shouted.

Laura looked on as Gavin worked on Emily's wound. Before long his sister finally took a breath, her eyes fluttering. But before Gavin could continue a rubber bullet glanced off his skull and he flopped over and landed next to his sister on the cold ground. Stickers panicked and bolted away into the surrounding woods, away from the chaos.

"No no no!" Laura shrieked.

Stir, in mid-flight towards another operator, suddenly vanished.

Thomas was caught off guard by the panic in Laura's voice and turned his head to look at what had happened. By doing so he opened up his vector and the Special Ops men took full advantage of it. A multitude of rounds suddenly peppered the family, hitting Thomas, Sam and Bill at the same time.

As they reared back from the multitude of hits two canisters landed at their feet. Thomas didn't have the chance to send them flying as another non-lethal round struck his temple. He toppled over and landed on the ground unconscious.

"CEASE FIRE!"

The gas quickly engulfed the family and immediately put an end to the engagement.

* * *

"Holy shit," the President said as he experienced the encounter on the monitors.

"Is that good news or not?" Demian Anatolievich asked over the speaker. "Has Thomas Clark been captured or not?"

"He has," the President replied, "but at an unfathomable cost to human life."

The President, along with the staff in the PEOC, could only stare at the battlefield through the eyes of the satellite. A multitude of bodies littered the ground, some inert and others limping or crawling. Of the forty Special Operations men from group Delta, half of them had been killed and another ten incapacitated in one way or another. The soldiers, albeit highly trained, had been completely unprepared for what they had encountered in Running Springs.

The Russian President spoke up again. "Where will you be taking him?"

The President smiled. "Someplace safe, Demian."

"Are you reneging on our arrangement? If that were so I wouldn't have to remind you that I'm fully prepared to go to war."

"Relax. It's still quite intact, of course."

"So where are you taking him then?"

"Like I told you, someplace safe."

"I demand to know where."

"Area Fifty-One."

35
Tuesday November 13, 2001

Two military transport planes took off from Norton Air Force Base, in San Bernardino, four hours after the family had been captured. The two planes lifted up into the sky and headed west towards the Nevada wasteland. The families inside had been secured and divided between the two aircraft, based on Dr. Matsushita's recommendations. The President asked the DCI to confirm the doctor's recommendations and he reluctantly agreed that separating the families would ensure their compliance.

* * *

"Mr. President," the team leader radioed from Running Springs, "this is Delta One. We have them in custody, sir, but most of my men are either injured or down. Requesting immediate backup."

"Delta One," the President said from the underground PEOC, "this is POTUS. I've been informed that additional medical and backup teams are enroute and will arrive shortly. In the meantime your orders are to sedate and secure all ten individuals, utilizing full quarantine measures. Do not touch or interact with them. Do you understand?"

"Yes, sir."

"Good. When your backup arrives I want them transferred to Norton Air Force Base. In the meantime, immediately lock down your current location to the public. We'll coordinate with local and state troopers from here. When the forensics team arrives they'll scrub the site for further intel."

"Understood, sir."

"Congratulations on a job well done."

"Thank you, Mr. President."

"Carry on, Delta One. POTUS out."

* * *

Where...am...I...? What's...going...on...?

Thomas slowly came to and groaned.

"He's waking up," Thomas heard an unknown voice say close by.

"Watch him closely," a second voice told the first.

"Yes, sir."

Watch...me...?

Thomas tried to open his eyes a few times but he wasn't able to.

My eyes...what's going on?

He attempted to move his arms and legs, quickly realizing they were immobilized. Thomas' senses were coming back as the sedation wore off.

What the hell?

"Hello?"

"Be quiet or I'll gag you," the first voice told him.

Thomas persisted. "Where am I? What's going on? Where is my family?"

"I warned you."

"Stand down Lieutenant," the second voice said. "I'll take over here."

"Yes, sir."

Thomas tried to move again but his bonds kept him immobilized. He knew if he could see his restraints he'd be able to use his powers on them. "Who are you?"

"My name is of no importance to you, Mr. Clark."

"Why don't you take this blindfold off so we can have a proper conversation, face to face?"

"So you can use your power? That's never going to happen but I admire your tenacity."

Dammit. "Who do you represent then?"

"I'm the team leader of the SpecOps group that took you down. You killed a lot of good men you sonofabitch."

Shit. "You brought the fight to us and forced us to defend ourselves. You need to take some responsibility for that instead of placing those deaths at my feet."

Thomas' head whipped to the side as the man struck him hard in the face.

"I was following orders."

Thomas spat out some blood. "And you must have been so proud of yourself when you shot and injured my children. What a good soldier you are; a true hero."

Thomas' face was struck again and additional blood dribbled out of his mouth.

"Is that all you've got kid?" Thomas tested.

"For now."

"Then tell me what the plan is. I can tell we're in a plane, military from the sound of it. Where are you taking us?"

"Someplace where no one will ever hear from you again."

"And why's that?" Thomas inquired.

"You'll find out soon enough."

Thomas realized that he hadn't heard Laura, Emily, Gavin or any of the rest of his family make any noise. His agitation abruptly rose.

"Is my daughter alright? Has my family been administered medical treatment?"

"Your wife and children aren't on board this aircraft."

293

Thomas struggled against his bonds. "What!? Where are they!? What have you done with them!?"

"Yeah, that's a real predicament you have there. I'll leave you alone so you can dwell on it."

Thomas heard the man walk away.

"Thomas, is that you?"

Thomas twisted his head to the left towards the voice. "Sam?"

"Yeah, it's me." Thomas heard Sam struggling. "What the hell man, I can't move."

"Me too, brother. Can you see anything?"

Sam shook his head. "Not through whatever they have over my head. Where is everyone else?"

"I don't know. The asshole I was talking to said that my wife and kids aren't on this plane. I don't know about Julie or anyone else."

"Is that you Thomas? Sam?" Bill's sedation had worn off as well.

"Yeah, it's us," Sam told him. "Can you move or see anything?"

Bill didn't answer for a few seconds. "Nope. Nothing. I'm fucking tied down. What the hell is going on?"

Thomas answered. "They're taking us somewhere, somewhere where he said we'd never been seen or heard from again."

"He?" Bill asked. "Who's he?"

"Apparently he's the team leader of the SpecOps group that we had a disagreement with."

"That's one way of putting it," Sam said.

"Where are Kim and the others?" Bill asked.

"No idea," Sam replied. "Thomas said his family aren't even on this plane so who knows what the fuck they're planning."

"So what are we still doing locked up Thomas? Do your thing and break us out of here."

"I've tried but I can't see anything which means I can't manipulate anything."

"Seriously? Your powers are blocked by a blindfold? Somebody came up with a low tech solution to counteract you."

"Yeah, and I bet we all know who that someone is," Thomas replied.

"Matsushita," the three of them said in unison.

"Fuck me," Bill added.

"I'm sorry guys," Thomas told them. "This is all my fa..."

Sam cut him off. "Fault? Don't start with that shit again, okay? I'm sick of it. We all knew what we were getting into."

"Yeah," Bill said. "The three musketeers have always stayed together."

"And now look at us," Thomas said. "Shit, what are we supposed to do now?"

* * *

On the second plane Laura, Julie, Kim, Rebecca, Emily Gavin and Craig were being held. Per the recommendations from Dr. Matsushita, Emily, Gavin and Craig were kept sedated. The four others had recently woken up just like their husbands.

"Can anyone see anything or move?" Rebecca asked the other women.

"No."

"I can't."

"Me either."

"Be quiet," one of the soldiers told them. "No talking."

"Where is my husband?" Laura asked in defiance. "Where is Thomas Clark?"

"Shut up," he repeated. "You killed my teammates like they were nothing. I hope whatever they have planned entails your suffering and unending anguish."

"You sick bastard," Laura spat out. "How dare you put this on us. We had no choice but to defend ourselves. What you're doing to us is wrong and you should be ashamed."

"Ma'am, I'm a professional soldier so I don't feel shame. We do what we're told."

"It must be nice to live in such a black and white world where you can write off your wrong doings so easily. You're pathetic."

"Not as pathetic as you're all going to be when we land and they take you away to some dark hole in the ground. Count yourself lucky if they don't dissect you the very first day." He paused. "I'll give you some time to talk amongst yourselves and let that sink in."

They heard the man walk away.

"What does that mean?" Julie said in panic. "What is he talking about?"

"We're going to die." Kim began to sob. "They're going to kill us."

"You need to keep strong," Rebecca reminded them.

"He's just trying to scare us," Laura told them but she didn't believe her own words, "that's all."

"Our lives are over," Julie expressed with utter defeat.

"Don't say that," Laura told her.

"Why not? It's true and you know it."

"Julie and Kim, you're both panicking," Rebecca said. "Just try and relax."

"We're dead," Kim muttered. "They're going to kill us and our children."

Julie continued. "So just admit that I was right all along and this is all your husband's fault Laura."

Laura opened her mouth to object but then slowly closed it. *We're so fucked.* Laura shuddered. *Where are you Thomas? Where are our children? What are they going to do to us?*

36
Tuesday November 13, 2001

The President, along with the staff in the PEOC, could only stare at the battlefield through the eyes of the satellite. A multitude of bodies littered the ground, some inert and others limping or crawling. Of the forty Special Operations men from group Delta, half of them had been killed and another ten incapacitated in one way or another. The soldiers, albeit highly trained, were unprepared for what they had encountered in Running Springs.

The Russian President spoke up again. "Where will you be taking him?"

The President smiled. "Someplace safe, Demian."

"Are you reneging on our arrangement? If so I shouldn't have to remind you that I'm fully prepared to go to war."

"Relax. It's still quite intact, of course."

"So where are you taking him then?"

"Like I told you, someplace safe."

"I demand to know where."

"Area Fifty-One."

"That's unacceptable."

"And why's that Demian? It's beginning to sound like you had your own plan for them. Nevertheless, at least with the family sequestered at Area Fifty-One I'm assured of their wellbeing and safety."

"You've overstepped the lines of our deal, Mr. President. Correct me if I'm wrong, but to me it sounds as if you're trying to wall Russia out."

"Absolutely not, President Anatolievich. In fact, I'm doing just the opposite. Robert?"

The DCI spoke up. "Yes, Mr. President?"

"I'm ordering you to relocate from your bunker to Area Fifty-One immediately. I need you, Dr. Matsushita, Tatiana, Nikolay and the others wheels up in two hours or less."

"Yes, sir."

"Dr. Matsushita?"

"Yes, Mr. President?"

"Give Robert a list of any equipment you'll need and I'll forward it off. I believe Demian and I would both agree that we'd like you to get to work on the serum as quickly as possible."

"Absolutely," Dr. Matsushita replied.

"Good. President Anatolievich, do you agree that you and your country are being involved in every step of this process?"

"So far," Demian brusquely replied.

"I give you my word that Nikolay and Tatiana will have the same access to the family as my people do. It's in my county's interests, and the world's, that we work together to avoid a global confrontation. Do you agree to these terms?"

"Tatiana?"

"Yes, President Anatolievich?"

"You will continue to report back to me with updates every six hours."

"Yes, sir."

The Russian President continued. "And Mr. President, if she fails to check-in just once, I will be left with no other choice than to believe you have broken your word. Do you agree to THOSE terms?"

"I do. We're partners now Demian so we'll need to start trusting each other."

Demian chuckled. "Your American sense of humor makes me laugh. Tatiana, call me as soon as you land in Nevada."

"Yes, Mr. President."

Demian Anatolievich dropped off the call.

"Is there anything else we can help you with, Mr. President?" asked the DCI.

"Get yourselves to Nevada, Robert, and keep me updated."

"Yes, sir."

The President of the United States hung up as well. The DCI looked over at Dr. Matsushita, Tatiana and Nikolay.

"It looks like we're in this together for the long haul."

"You expected any different?" Tatiana questioned.

Robert shook his head knowing he was in the toughest of spots. "I suppose not." He looked at Dr. Matsushita. "Doc, do you think you'll have your list and what you need from your lab ready to go in under two hours?"

Dr. Matsushita nodded.

"Good. I'll make preparations for Hobbes and Gabbi to be moved while you two," he said as he pointed to Nikolay and Tatiana. "We're heading out of here in an hour and a half so go get ready."

Robert Duncan left the Tech wing and started to walk around the circular corridor towards the cells. When he was out of sight he stopped, leaned against the cold concrete wall and slumped over, hands on his knees. *Fuck. I can't believe the President screwed Thomas and the rest of us over. I knew if Thomas' abilities became public the world would react this way, vying and scrambling for power while crushing anyone and anything in their way.* He paused. *I have to find a way to put a stop to this, but for now I have to play along knowing that they'll kill Emma in a second just to prove a point, just like POTUS killed Russell. Fucking bastard. I need to figure out a way to make him pay."*

301

* * *

Upon landing at Area 51 the DCI, and subsequent entourage, were escorted to Building 42. As the contents of the plane were being unloaded, including Hobbes and Gabbi, the DCI, Nikolay, Tatiana and Dr. Matsushita were asked to submit to a thorough pat down. Satisfied that no weapons were being brought into the facility they stepped into the elevator. As soon as the doors closed the group rapidly descended until, finally, they came to a soothing stop. The doors reopened and before them unfolded a breathtaking and vast underground maze, filled with hordes of rooms and hallways.

"Welcome to Area Fifty-One," Dr. Glover said as he greeted his new guests. He was flanked by two armed security men. Additional armed men were posted throughout the facility. "My name is Dr. Stuart Glover and I head the research and development division here at Groom Lake. Before we continue I believe introductions are in order."

"Robert Duncan, Director of Central Intelligence."

"Dr. Yamato Takuma Matsushita."

"Nikolay Dmitriev."

"Tatiana Danilovna, SVR."

Dr. Glover shook each of their hands. "Very nice to meet each of you, especially you Dr. Matsushita, as you can imagine. I'm anxious to begin working with you."

"You were misled then, Dr. Glover," Dr. Matsushita told him.

"Oh? How so?"

"I work alone. You are not here to learn how I create the serum so you can replicate it. Do I make myself clear?"

Dr. Glover was slightly ruffled but kept his composure. "This is highly irregular but I completely understand your need for secrecy. Perhaps in the meantime, while the final touches to the equipment you requested are pieced together, I may pick your brain on a different project that you're familiar with."

"By all means doctor."

"Excellent. These men," Dr. Glover motioned to, "will take you to your rooms where I suggest you freshen up and get something to eat. We're all going to be busy once Thomas Clark and his family arrive."

"And when will that occur?" Tatiana inquired.

"Within the hour. I imagine you'll want to contact Russia as soon as possible, Ms. Danilovna. Secure and encrypted lines have been placed in each of your rooms. And for transparency sake, please note that they are monitored just as your movements and actions will be." He pointed around at the numerous closed circuit cameras that littered the facility. "Feel free to move about as you see fit but you are restricted to this facility. In other words, don't try to take the elevator to go back up to the surface without permission. That could be a fatal mistake."

"So you're saying we're prisoners," Nikolay stated.

"Hardly, Mr. Dmitriev. You're our guests during this historical occasion, brought to us by Thomas Clark and Dr. Matsushita." Dr. Glover turned to Dr. Matsushita as he dismissed the others. "Shall we doctor?"

"Lead the way."

* * *

In Dr. Glover's lab, in an isolated and hermetically sealed area, lay Peter; or Specimen R as Dr. Glover had labeled him.

303

Dr. Matsushita saw his creation, walked over to the glass partition and stared. It didn't take long before Dr. Glover materialized by his side.

"I see you've been studying my creation."

Dr. Glover nodded. "I have been fascinated by this magnificent creature ever since it was brought to me."

"And you have questions, no doubt."

"Indeed I do. Somehow you've managed to…"

Yamato stared at him. *Stop.*

Dr. Glover interrupted himself in mid-sentence.

Look ahead and point as if you're explaining something to me. Now, tell me what's premeditated in regards to my future here at Area Fifty-One?

The doctor pointed at the creature. "I was informed to give you anything you requested so you could create the serum."

And that's all? Nothing devious?

"No, nothing devious."

Interesting. Very well. You will forget this conversation and continue on before I interrupted you.

The doctor lowered his arm. "…augment this individual's body. Yes, I have many questions but I have a strange suspicion you won't talk about it."

Dr. Matsushita smiled. "You never know. There's a chance my hubris could get the better of me."

Dr. Glover chuckled. "One could only hope."

"May I examine Peter closer?"

"Peter?"

Yamato motioned towards the inert form on the table behind the glass.

"Ahh. I've only known him as Specimen R. And yes, of course you can. There's no need to ask."

Oh, I know, but I have to keep up appearances for all the cameras scrutinizing my every move.

"Thank you."

Dr. Matsushita suited up in the adjoining room in full protective gear before entering the same room as Peter.

Hello old friend. Or shall I say, hello lump of cold, dead flesh. You served your purpose didn't you? He walked around the side of Peter with his back towards Dr. Glover. *But now I have just one more task for you.*

"So what have you gleamed from my creation so far, Dr. Glover?"

"Honestly? That it would take months, and perhaps even years, to replicate anything from Specimen R's tissues and fluids. His body was heavily damaged, as you can tell, but I'm still in awe of its healing abilities. I assume you gave that to him on purpose along with its strength?"

Dr. Matsushita nodded from behind the glass. "You assume correctly."

"I thought as much."

Yamato pealed back Peter's chest cavity and scrutinized his insides.

"How'd your analysis on the liquid you found in his liver turn out?" he asked as he removed a needle from his pocket.

"Somewhat inconclusive."

"Why's that?" Yamato probed.

"The material I salvaged seemed to be teeming with various genetic materials. I began to isolate the strands until I realized it would be a pointless endeavor."

"With nothing to compare or test them against."

"Exactly," Dr. Glover replied.

Yamato leaned over Peter, found the organ he was looking for, inserted the needle and extracted a full syringe of the liquid.

"Is there something I can help you with?" Dr. Glover asked.

"If you don't mind I'd like to run some tests on this sample I just took."

"Absolutely, Dr. Matsushita, anything you need. My lab is your lab."

Oh, there's no doubt about that.

Yamato finished up with Peter, removed the protective gear and brought the syringe to one of the equipment benches.

"What do you hope to find?" Dr. Glover queried.

"I won't know until I run my tests. While I'm doing this would you make sure my equipment I requested is ready to go? Once Thomas arrives I don't think the President of the United States will understand that I had to wait to get started on the serum."

"Of course," Dr. Glover replied, put off by being dismissed so easily. "Do you need anything else?"

"No," Yamato replied curtly.

Dr. Glover departed and left Yamato alone to run his tests. Thirty minutes later he'd refined the fluid into a usable liquid. He filled a new syringe with his new concoction and slid it into his coat pocket.

* * *

The two planes carrying the ten family members landed and immediately taxied off the runway. They came to a halt a hundred feet away from Building 42. The rear doors of the transport planes lowered and the hot desert air rushed in. Area

51 security waited at the bottom of the first plane to take possession.

"Move them out."

From out of the belly of the plane Laura, Julie, Kim, Rebecca were led out under guard. Behind them Emily, Gavin and Craig were carried out, still very much sedated. As their lungs breathed in the hot air the guards finally removed each of the women's blindfolds. They shied back from the sudden bright sunlight and looked around.

"Where are we?" Rebecca asked. "Where are you taking us?"

One of the security men answered her question. "We were instructed to remove your blindfolds so that you could experience and remember the sense of freedom one last time."

Kim didn't want to understand "What?"

"What the hell does that mean?" Julie exclaimed.

Laura looked back and saw her children being carted off towards the nearby building. *Is this really it? Are we really never going to be heard from again?* She hung her head and let the tears fall. Each tear struck the hot concrete and quickly vanished, just like they were about to.

With the first group of family members transported underground the last three prisoners were wheeled out of the transport plane, still bound and blindfolded.

"Where do you think they took us?" Bill asked his friends as the sun bore down on their heads.

"My guess is somewhere in the desert," Sam replied.

"Where's my wife?" Thomas demanded.

"You'll see her soon enough," answered one of the security men. "Now relax and shut up, all of you."

The three of them were wheeled towards the large building, and as they entered the hanger the warmth on their skin instantly dissipated. Thomas shivered slightly as they were carted to the elevator.

The Caretaker said there wasn't a Heaven or a Hell, but this certainly is beginning to feel like Hell.

* * *

The elevator doors opened and Emily, Gavin, Craig, Laura, Julie, Kim and Rebecca were greeted by the two doctors, the DCI, Nikolay, Tatiana and a contingent of security.

"Welcome to Groom Lake," Dr. Glover told them. "I'm Dr. Glover."

"Go to hell you asshole," Laura spat back. "What you're doing to us is both illegal and immoral."

"Those are two words that aren't in my vocabulary, Mrs. Clark." He glanced over at the three sedated children with a look that instantly made Laura's stomach churn. "And with your arrival I believe I'll be adding more to that list."

"You sadistic sonofabitch. These are my children!"

Dr. Matsushita stepped forward. "Hello Laura. I was afraid we've never meet."

Laura disliked the man immediately and she knew why when she caught sight of his burned right hand that protruded out from his lab coat. *Oh shit. Not him.*

"You must be Dr. Matsushita, asshole of the decade."

He looked pleasantly surprised that Laura knew his name. "That's correct."

"Too bad your entire body wasn't disfigured in that fire. The world would have been much better off without you, you sick fuck."

Dr. Matsushita's smile promptly receded. "That may be true, but the world now begs for what only I can provide. And perhaps I'll take this moment to remind you that you're in no position to throw stones. Look around you and get used to it because this is your new home."

Laura looked directly at the DCI. "Why are you allowing this to happen? Why!?"

Robert didn't have a response and just stood there.

Dr. Matsushita turned to the security men. "Take Mrs. Clark away but leave the others behind. I have something to show them as soon as their husbands join us."

"Yes, sir."

"Where are you taking them?" Julie pleaded. "Where?"

"Oh don't worry about Laura," Nikolay told her. "It should be Sam you really should be concerned about."

Julie's eyes went wide. "I don't understand."

"Your husband is the one that killed me. I can't wait to return the favor."

"No. No. Nonononono."

"This isn't happening," Kim murmured. "This isn't happening."

Nikolay smiled and ignored Julie's previous question as Laura was led away, taken around a hallway corner and disappeared.

"While we wait for our main course to arrive I'm going to reacquaint myself with these youngsters."

The DCI, Tatiana and Nikolay watched Dr. Matsushita saunter over to Craig's inert form and checked the IV drip. Satisfied Yamato walked over to Emily next and checked her IV line. He then bent over, looked at her and brushed some of her hair away from her face, the back of his burned hand touched her face.

Hello Emily. It's been a long time since I saw you last. I know you can't wait to get started on our work again. I know I can't.

He leaned down and took ten seconds to whisper something in her ear before he stood up and went to her brother's side.

Hello Gavin. You have an amazing gift but I think it's time you reach your full potential. This might sting but you're drugged at the moment so you won't even remember it.

Dr. Matsushita extracted the syringe from his coat pocket, removed the safety cap and then deftly jabbed it into Gavin's arm through his clothes.

"What did you just do?" Tatiana demanded as Yamato stood back, the empty syringe in his hand.

Dr. Glover was furious. "Yes, what the hell did you just inject him with doctor?"

Dr. Matsushita turned towards them. "So now you're questioning my every move? Perhaps you don't want the serum then? I hardly need to explain my methods, now do I."

"You will be held accountable," Dr. Glover warned.

"You and I know we're well past that point now. Need I remind you that the next evolution of mankind is the prize that you're after? Don't forget that when Thomas Clark, and the blood coursing through his veins, stands before me; the world will forever be changed."

"So you're not going to tell us what you just did?"

Dr. Matsushita shook his head. "I'm not going to talk about any of my processes with you, and you should know that by now. This entire arrangement relies on the one fact that we both get what we want, and that's it, so back off. You mean nothing to me Dr. Glover. You're a hack and not worthy of my attention."

"How dare you," Dr. Glover retorted.

At that moment the elevator dinged and the doors opened. Thomas, Sam and Bill were wheeled out, still completely immobilized into the receiving area.

"Where are we?" Thomas insisted. "Who's there?"

All eyes focused on Thomas except for Nikolay's, who's were on Sam. A grin appeared in the corner of his mouth.

"Sam!" Julie cried out.

Kim was right there with her. "Bill!"

"Jules? How are you? Are you okay?"

"Kim? I'm here now. Everything's going to be okay."

"Enough!" Dr. Matsushita insisted. "Be quiet!"

"I know that voice," Thomas verbalized.

Yamato couldn't' contain himself. "It's been a long time, hasn't it Thomas? I can't tell you how happy I am to see you once more."

"That makes one of us. I'm relieved this blindfold's on, it saves me from having to look at your repugnant face."

Dr. Matsushita strode over to Thomas' side and ripped off the blindfold in one fluid motion. As their eyes locked Thomas immediately used his ability to toss Yamato across the room. He landed on the hard floor and came to a halt as he hit Gavin's stretcher, knocking the needle administering Gavin's IV drip loose just enough so the liquid no longer entered his bloodstream.

As Yamato sailed through the air, and before anyone else could react, Thomas saw the bonds that held him and used his powers. As they popped off his arms and legs three security men rushed towards him. Without missing a beat Thomas shoved them backwards as he quickly bore down on the fallen doctor.

311

"Get that sonofabitch!" Sam yelled, unable to see but understanding what had just occurred.

Yamato, dazed from the fall, looked up just as Thomas' fist connected with his face. Blood splatter, from the doctor's now bleeding nose and lips, sprayed across the white floor. As Thomas pulled his arm back for another strike Yamato intervened.

Stop!

Thomas froze in place, unable to move as Yamato entered his mind and took control. He slowly picked himself off the floor as security and everyone else watched their encounter unfold.

"I should kill you now," Yamato hissed at Thomas, using his sleeve to wipe blood from his face. "You have balls Thomas, I'll give you that, but when I'm done with you this time around you're the one who's going to be begging me to put you out of your misery, I guarantee it."

He commanded Thomas to get back on the table. Security men restrained him and reapplied the blindfold before Yamato released him. Thomas, now under his own control, started to struggle against his bonds.

"Go to hell Yamato! I won't let you touch me or my children ever again!"

"Well then, you'd better get used to another one of your promises being broken."

"Fuck you."

Gavin began to come around as the sedatives wore off and Rebecca noticed. She slightly repositioned herself.

Nikolay walked over to Dr. Matsushita and smiled. "I enjoyed the show, but you have to admit that he got the better of you."

Yamato didn't care or like Nikolay and that still remained true. "Are you sure you want to gloat in my direction, Nikolay? I guess you still haven't realized yet that your presence here is redundant."

Nikolay's smile faltered.

"That's right, think about it. You're no longer needed. Tatiana is just waiting for the chance to kill you. Why would Demian Anatolievich reinstate you now when you have nothing to offer him? You weren't the one that captured Thomas, were you?"

"You lie. Russia needs me."

"Am I lying, Nikolay? Am I? Your time in the history books has already come and gone. As far as Russia is concerned you died on that Cuban beach. I'm sure the Russian government wanted nothing more than to thank Sam for killing you, but they didn't know where to send the gift basket."

Gavin suddenly opened his eyes and Nikolay caught it. He took a step forward and pointed.

"What the hell? The child is awake!"

Rebecca screamed at Gavin as she knocked two of the security men out of the way. "GAVIN! PORTAL!"

Gavin, even though only half awake, recognized Rebecca's voice and in the next instant his portal appeared. Nikolay, having heard Rebecca's shout, twisted his head to the right just as she barreled into him and her momentum carried them both into the portal.

"Wha…"

A split second later the two reappeared on the floor, their clothes cut and tattered as the portal closed behind them. One of the security men punched the alarm panel on the wall and the facility's hallways filled with a loud klaxon as the other men rushed forward to pull Rebecca off of Nikolay.

"Code five! I need immediate backup on level seven!"

As Nikolay was pulled to his feet he came face to face with Dr. Matsushita who wasted no time in telling Nikolay exactly what he was thinking.

"Who's gloating now, Nikolay, you fucking idiot."

Nikolay gave Dr. Matsushita a confused look in response. "Who's Nikolay?"

37
The Other Place

The bodies of Carl Abney and Eliot Marlow, inhabited by Nikolay and Rebecca, sailed out of the portal, landed hard on the soft, warm island sand and came to a rest. The dark and evil beings, that constantly flew and encircled the island, wasted no time to strike at the two human forms, claws fully extended.

"Arggg!" Rebecca screamed as one of the creature's talons gashed her back.

Nikolay rolled away from Rebecca and barely avoided the ragged claw that dug into the sand where his head had just been. As he pushed himself to his knees Nikolay was pummeled from the side, his arms slashed by ghastly and gloomy apparitions.

"Uggghh!"

Rebecca raised her right arm up and fended off another attack and the resulting blow scattered additional blood across the white sand. The portal still stood open next to two other shredded bodies clad in body armor; two of the men that attacked the family in Running Springs.

"BEGONE!"

The black mass reared back, away from the Caretaker, and promptly fluttered away from the small island. Rebecca and Nikolay, their wounds oozing, looked up at the Caretaker as he approached. His expression displayed complete satisfaction.

"Welcome back Nikolay. We all missed you."

"Go fuck yourself," Nikolay uttered in rebuttal.

"Oh, you'll have to do much better than that I'm afraid."

Nikolay groaned as he stood up, blood running down his arms. "And what makes you think I care? There's nothing you can do to me Caretaker." Nikolay grimaced. "At least I was someone important back on Earth. I actually made a difference! But you, you're pathetic and you know it. Face it; you're just an insignificant jailer, a warden with no other purpose than to keep us corralled. You must be so proud."

The Caretaker never flinched, but as Nikolay finished his rant a grin slowly appeared on the Caretaker's face.

"I'm going to enjoy this."

"Enjoy wh…"

The Caretaker plunged his hand deep into Nikolay's chest, closed his fist and pulled back all in one swift motion. In his grip was Nikolay's soul, once trapped in Carl's body, who now tumbled to the sand unconscious. The Caretaker watched Nikolay writhe and squirm within his grasp until he finally released him.

Nikolay looked down at Carl and then sneered at the Caretaker. "You've ruined everything!"

But the Caretaker wasn't listening. "You must be lonely Nikolay. Allow me to rejoin you with your friends."

There was a flash and suddenly General Aleman, Anna Garland, Victor Bannon and Frank Russell appeared on the island.

Raven began to yell. "Nikolay, you backstabbing sonofabitch, you fucked us! We had a plan and you took it upon yourself to do your own thing!"

"Oh shut up," Nikolay retorted. "We all had the same plan, to escape and seek our revenge. You're just upset you never made it out of this place; all of you are."

"Then where's Alexei, Nikolay? He made it out with you. Where did he go?"

"Alexei ceased to exist," the Caretaker interjected, "when he crossed over without securing a vessel to reside in."

"What do you mean he ceased to exist?" Yuri asked.

"If he died wouldn't that mean he'd come right back here?" Victor added.

The Caretaker shook his head. "You misunderstand my point so I'll say it again, Alexei no longer exists." The Caretaker walked over and placed himself in front of the portal and the two humans. "And because of your group's continued contempt, and enthusiasm to insight chaos, I'm left with no other choice than to perpetually abolish your timelines."

"Perpetually abolish our timelines," Anna arrogantly declared. "Whatever does that mean? If you haven't noticed we're already dead."

"It means," the Caretaker continued, "that you still haven't grasped the simple concept that time is a variable."

"So what?" Nikolay spat out.

The Caretaker took his time as he stared at all five of them. "I've decided to delete you from history. From this moment your lives, and the lives you will experience over and over, will be abridged; becoming unimportant and worthless."

Before any of the remaining evil six could open their mouths the Caretaker clapped his hands together in one large motion. The resulting shockwave slammed into them and obliterated their souls. The resulting ash, what little of it remained, floated down and was absorbed into the Ocean of Time that surrounded the small island.

The Caretaker turned around and helped Rebecca to her feet.

"Thank you," he told her, "for keeping your word."

She nodded, still very much in pain. "What now?"

"Nothing. For now the balance has been restored and future iterations have been amended. As for you, Rebecca Cross, I can't let you go back. If I did the balance would once again be in jeopardy."

"I understand." She stood up straighter. "I'm ready."

The Caretaker took her hands in his. Eliot's body fell sideways onto the sand while Rebecca's soul stood upright, her hands clasped in the Caretaker's.

"You're free to depart, if you so desire," he told her.

Rebecca looked over her shoulder and saw that Ed, Claire, Michael and Betsy had silently gathered behind her. She turned back to him.

"I choose to stay with my family."

"Very well. Know that any of you may move on whenever you wish."

"Not until we know Thomas and the rest of his family are safe," Betsy announced.

The Caretaker nodded. "I thought as much."

He watched as the group took Rebecca into their fold and flew away into the distance.

"I'm sure I'll regret my decision at some point."

The Caretaker turned his attention to the unconscious and bleeding forms of Carl and Eliot that lay on the sand. He went to each one, swiped his hand over their wounds, which in turn closed them. He then simultaneously lifted both men and heaved them back through the portal, which then snapped shut. As the Caretaker left the island he watched the dark cloud head back towards it, anxious for more blood and willing to wait an eternity to taste it again.

38
Tuesday November 13, 2001

Immediately following the portal incident Gavin's IV line was restored and he rapidly drifted back to sleep. It didn't take long to realize that Nikolay and Rebecca, who had come back through with sustained injuries, were no longer contained in the bodies of the two Special Activities Division soldiers that were previously part of Sam's six-man team that had been captured in Afghanistan. The two confused men were detained and taken away to individual cells to be dealt with later.

Sam, Bill, Julie, Laura, Emily and Gavin were confined in separate cells that were completely sealed and monitored. The security personnel were given strict orders, as were each of the prisoners, that any overt actions on their part to violate their new enclosures would result in their cells being flooded with gas. Craig, on the other hand, was brought back under Dr. Matsushita's control.

Dr. Matsushita moved Thomas to his lab and made certain he was secured. Once the doctor was ready he inserted a needle into Thomas' arm and began to extract his blood. As instructed, the doctor and Thomas had been left alone, aside from the five children that hovered under his control.

"What's your game, Yamato?" Thomas asked.

"I don't know what you're talking about."

"Like hell you don't. You're always working an angle."

Thomas wasn't able to see Yamato smile from behind his blindfold. "I'm just here to create my serum so I can pass it on to the American and Russian Presidents."

"Bullshit."

"It's true, I assure you."

"So you're planning on just giving your hard work away? I don't buy it for a second."

"And why's that?"

"Because as much as I hate to admit it, I know who you really are. You're a narcissistic, sadistic and selfish prick so I know you don't want to change the world."

"And what makes you think I don't want to change the world, Thomas? The events of the world changed me when I was just a boy, so why not return the favor."

Thomas tried to shake his head but he couldn't move it. "No, that doesn't make any sense. You've always wanted to destroy the world."

"So you're saying that by freely giving my serum to the world that somehow it isn't going to change?"

"You're no humanitarian, Yamato. What's your angle? What could they have possibly promised you in return?"

"You Thomas. They gave me you."

"You're doing all of this because of me, because I left you to burn in that fire?"

"Yes."

"I smell more bullshit. You're way more complicated than that."

"Am I? Who's to say I won't drain you dry when I'm done with you?"

"Oh, I'm sure that exact thought has been more than prevalent in your mind, dominating really. But the truth is you're not that petty. You think grand scale, the big picture and how to get the most out of any situation, much like how you used Peter to attack downtown D.C. and create a news frenzy. No, you're orchestrating something huge and you have from the very beginning, so what is it?"

Dr. Matsushita grinned. "Very astute Thomas, you caught me. But the reality of the situation is that you're the only individual that allows me to bring my plan to fruition."

"What plan? What are you talking about?"

"That's an easy one. Your blood, as we both know, is the catalyst that allows my engineered serum to work. But what you may not be aware of is that your blood also contains a dormant but very deadly virus."

Thomas was unnerved. "Wait, what? What virus?"

"You have Smallpox coursing through your blood, Thomas. When I discovered it I decided to genetically modify it."

"Why? To what end?"

"Well, you said it yourself earlier."

"Said what?"

"That I always wanted to destroy the world."

The realization hit Thomas like a sack of bricks. "Oh shit. You're going to mix the smallpox with your serum. American and Russia won't think twice when they eagerly accept your serum, which you've already proved works, and administer it into their own test subjects. You've modified this virus so that it'll spread like wildfire, haven't you?"

"Very good, Thomas."

"Goddammit! You can't just decide to release this plague on the world! That's insanity!"

"And yet you fail to realize you're in no position to stop me."

"Oh, I'll stop you. I'll tell the first person that comes in here."

Dr. Matsushita chuckled. "Thomas, I allowed my hubris this one indulgence because you had a right to know that you're responsible for the end of mankind. But that time has passed now and I must concentrate on my work. I have people depending on me to finish this."

"It's over Yamato. Everyone will know."

"No, Thomas, they won't."

"And what makes you so sure?"

"Because we never had this conversation, did we?"

Dr. Matsushita concentrated on Thomas. *Forget.*

* * *

Air Force One landed at Groom Lake Tuesday evening. Shortly thereafter POTUS, with a contingent of Secret Service, stepped out of the large elevator and into the bowels of Building 42.

Dr. Glover greeted the President. "It's an honor to finally meet you, sir."

"I don't have a great deal of time because I'm due back in Washington so I can reassure the public on television in the morning, so let's dispense with the pleasantries. Take me to Thomas Clark and Dr. Matsushita immediately."

Dr. Glover's smile faltered. "Of course, sir, right this way."

The President was led through a series of corridors until they entered the lab in which Dr. Matsushita and Thomas resided. Yamato looked over his shoulder as the group entered and he abruptly stood up.

"No. Everyone get out."

"But this is the President," Dr. Glover countered.

Yamato walked towards them. "I don't care who it is. Our arrangement is that no one comes into my lab. You'll contaminate my work."

322

He shooed them out while the Secret Service kept Yamato at arm's length from the President.

"Dr. Matsushita, I presume?" the President said in greeting as they gathered in the hallway.

"Mr. President. Thank you for obtaining Thomas Clark for me."

"You're welcome. Do you have everything you require?"

"I do, aside from the privacy I requested."

"That couldn't be helped," the President responded. "This endeavor has cost our nation time, effort and money, not to mention placing the world at the brink of war."

"You're not used to being threatened I take it?"

"Excuse me?"

"I meant America of course, not you personally. In fact, America has been at war for years for one reason or another. But when the Russians come knocking on your country's doorstep you capitulated, killing innocents to prove your loyalty to them."

The President wasn't used to being lectured and he didn't like it. "I don't expect you, Dr. Matsushita, to understand the nature of politics."

"Perhaps not, Mr. President, but I do know when I have the upper hand. I'm a necessary evil, much like yourself, and you need me for my serum if I'm not mistaken. So you will stand there and take my judgmental tone."

"I most certainly will not."

"I don't think you understand. You're well out of your depth and I'm not giving you a choice."

In a flash one of the Secret Service agents pulled out his handgun, in one smooth motion, and pointed it at the President's head.

"What the…" POTUS exclaimed as he flinched backwards from the barrel.

The other agents reacted and pointed their weapons at the rogue agent. One by one, almost in unison, each of the other agents pivoted and pointed their handguns at the President.

"You see, Mr. President," Yamato explained, "you're out of your depth, but I'll give you points for coming to check on this delicate operation personally."

"I am the President of the United States. I demand that you stand down."

Alarm bells began to sound throughout the complex as security became aware of the situation.

"We don't have much time." Yamato stepped forward as the agents stepped out of his way.

"What are you doing?"

"I just want to whisper something in your ear."

And Yamato did just that before he stepped back. He dropped his control of the agents and smiled. They immediately turned their weapons on him.

"Stubborn till the end," Yamato said. "That's okay, but what about that precious serum you desire? Are you really going to have your men kill me for having just a little fun at your expense, sir?"

The President was angry and embarrassed. "Hold," he ordered.

His men stood their ground, weapons pointed and ready to fire. Yamato and the President stood there and continued to stare at each other, eyes locked.

"Stand down."

"But, sir," one of his agents argued.

"Stand down!" the President ordered.

The agents reluctantly lowered their weapons and put them away.

"How do you propose we should proceed?" the President asked Dr. Matsushita.

Yamato smiled at the game he'd just won with the most powerful man in the world. "I'd like to give you a tour and demonstrate everyone's abilities, if that's something you'd like to see."

The President was now wary of the doctor but determined the power struggle was over. *I'll play along for now.*

"By all means."

"Excellent. Let me introduce you to Thomas Clark first and we'll go from there."

"Won't it be dangerous for them to demonstrate their powers?"

Yamato nodded. "Yes, it is. But I'll control each of them as we go along so there's nothing to worry about."

* * *

The President departed on Air Force One and two hours later, once he returned to his lab, Dr. Matsushita used Thomas' blood to create a large batch of serum. He split the syringes into two groups, one for the Americans and another for the Russians, and wheeled the protective cases out of his lab to the designated hand-off point surrounded by five children. In the enclosed room the DCI and Tatiana stood ready to receive the cases that held the serum filled syringes.

"As promised, this is the first batch," Dr. Matsushita told them. "I assumed that both countries wanted enhanced strength for their test subjects, which will be comprised of soldiers. Further serum customization can be tailored for future deliveries, as desired of course."

Tatiana smiled and opened the case meant for Russia. Inside were twenty syringes, packed in protective foam. The DCI opened his case, verified the contents as well and closed it.

"Excuse me," Tatiana told them. "I need to contact President Anatolievich immediately and then depart for Russia."

"I'll call the President and then make this delivery as well," the DCI said as he departed, the door closing behind him.

Yamato smiled as the two disappeared with their cases.

Well that was easier than I expected. Time to see what move they're going to make now.

He walked to the lab door, pulled on the handle and found it locked. Gas immediately poured out of the ceiling vents and filled his lab.

I knew it!

"Tad, break down the door!" He then called out to the other children. "Get outside!"

Craig ran at the wall and phased through it just as Tad bashed open the closed door with a tremendous kick. Yamato ran through the destroyed doorway as Amanda, Sarah and Edward slumped to the floor, unconscious. Yamato, confident of his abilities strode down the empty hallway with Craig and Tad behind him.

They were smart not to give me anyone else to control.

At the end of the hallway a large steel door slammed down, sealing off that avenue of escape. As he turned around to go the other direction the lights began to flicker so he glanced up at them.

326

What the hell?

Before he could look away, and within a matter of milliseconds, the intensity of the lights grew a thousand fold, much like a flashbang blinding him.

"Arrrghh! Protect me!"

Two doors opened, one on either side of the hallway near him, and a single man appeared out of each one armed with a tranquilizer gun. They wasted no time and shot Yamato before Tad and Craig could reach them. The darts struck Yamato in the chest and took effect. He crashed to the floor, unconscious. The men turned their weapons on the two boys, ready to fire, but stopped. Tad and Craig looked around, clearly confused about what had happened and where they were.

"We're clear!" one of the men yelled into his headset. "The doctor is down."

"Incapacitate the two boys as well."

"Roger that."

The two security men took aim, fired again and the boys dropped.

"I want all five of them sedated and secured in individual cells right away."

"Yes, sir."

* * *

"President Anatolievich, I have the serum."

"Excellent, Tatiana. That is excellent news. How many?"

"Twenty syringes, sir. I'm leaving Area Fifty-One and heading back to Moscow."

"Good, good. Do you have anything else to report?"

"If you're referring to Nikolay, sir, I was unable to personally nullify him. However, he's been taken out of the equation."

"Explain."

"There was an altercation. Dr. Matsushita goaded Nikolay and during that confrontation the other male soldier, the one named Rebecca, called out to the little boy to make his portal. Before anyone could react she tackled Nikolay and they both disappeared, only to reappear moments later. I don't know what transpired, sir, but whoever came back wasn't Nikolay anymore."

"Good riddance. It was very fortunate for us that you didn't have to kill him yourself."

"If you say so, sir."

"Now, make haste Tatiana. You've served Mother Russia with honor and secured our future today."

"Thank you, President Anatolievich."

* * *

The President of the United States hung up with Robert Duncan and placed a new call to President Anatolievich. He was tired but elated that the serum was on its way.

"Yes, Mr. President," Demian said. "I was expecting your call."

"I just received confirmation of the serum handoff."

"As have I. I've also confirmed Tatiana Danilovna is safely in the air and headed to Moscow."

"You have what you want Demian. It's time to back your fleet off."

"Agreed. I look forward to doing business with you in the future."

"I wish I could say the same thing Anatolievich."

Demian chuckled on the other end. "Until next time, Mr. President. Do svidaniya."

39
Wednesday November 14, 2001

"Ladies and gentlemen, I give you the President of the United States."

Dozens upon dozens of reporters were crammed together to hear, first hand, what the President was about to announce to the world. They had been informed that the President would make a statement before taking any questions. As POTUS appeared from the left and approached the podium video cameras tracked his movement while flashes from photographers lit up the stage. The President cleared his throat before he began.

"I am pleased to announce that in a joint venture with Russian President, Demian Anatolievich, Thomas Clark and his family have been apprehended. As part of our arrangement the threat of war is now averted and the Russian fleet has withdrawn from our shores. The world and it's people, once again, are safe."

The reporters couldn't contain themselves.

"Mr. President! Mr. President! Mr. President!"

One voice rose above the others. "Where is Mr. Clark being detained?"

"That is a matter of national security. Mr. Clark's whereabouts are classified."

"Mr. President! Mr. President! Mr. President!"

A new question sifted up above the rest. "We all saw Mr. Clark's demonstration during his interview. What are your plans for him and his family?"

"Mr. Clark, and the threat he represents, have been contained. The safety of the public was naturally my primary concern."

"But, Mr. President, you haven't answered the question. What are you going to do with him now that you have him?"

"Study him."

"Doesn't Mr. Clark have rights as an American citizen?"

"Those rights have been rescinded as soon as he became a threat to our nation and the world as a whole."

"Then how do you respond to the rumors the Mr. Clark and his family's abilities are the keys to the next evolution of mankind, yet the public has been kept in the dark about your actual intentions? Is it safe to assume that the United States and Russia have made an exclusive arrangement to cooperate in the research and development of Mr. Clark's abilities? And if so, how do you think every other country on Earth, and its citizens, will react to this collaboration as America and Russia refuse to let anyone else benefit from this exclusive arrangement?"

The President stepped back from the podium, frustrated, and walked away as an aide took over.

The reporters continued to shout at him as he quickly departed. "Mr. President! Mr. President! Mr. President!"

"The President is no longer taking questions at this time. Thank you."

* * *

After the President's botched speech a crowd of protesters began to gather on the Great lawn within New York's Central Park. In time word quickly spread and more and more people showed up to hear, participate and their share concerns in an open discussion that revolved around Thomas Clark. In no time at all a makeshift stage had been erected and audio equipment installed. Anyone who wanted to speak was asked to stand in line and take their turn. One man was already on a roll and his thoughts mirrored many of those who were there.

"What does this mean for the free world? Can we no longer trust that our government will do the right thing when power, like we've all seen, is now out there? Where does the public go from here? What are we going to do about it!?"

Cheers rose out of the crowd as their combined energy mounted.

"We should take it back for ourselves, that's what we should do!"

The crowd roared and applauded.

"Just think about the possibilities, just even for a moment. Haven't each and every one of you out there," he said as he pointed, "dreamt of flying or having some other ability that your imagination came up with at some point in your life? I know I have. So why should we allow the United States and Russian governments to take that potential away from each one of us? It's not up to them. I say the people of the world should unite. We need to demand answers, and if they're not given then we need to take those answers for ourselves!"

*　*　*

Across the globe countless rallies, gatherings, prayer groups and demonstrations began to take place. Numbers grew as people flocked to become part of the new movement. Coverage of these events exploded and dominated the news channels as the people of the world did everything from demand answers, pray for Thomas Clark so the demons would leave him, accuse the government of targeting its citizens, and more. The movement had started and the voices of the world began to unite as one, for better or worse.

40
Wednesday November 14, 2001

Each of Building 42's cells were hermetically sealed and sound proofed to both segregate the family members from talking to each other and contain their powers. The hermetic seals also permitted gas to be released into any cell, at the push of a button, thereby rendering the occupants unconscious. A few of the adult 'tenants', as Dr. Glover referred to them, were doubled up because they poised zero threat; which included Sam, Julie, Bill, Kim, Carl and Eliot. They were kept in pairs unlike those that had abilities like Laura, Gavin, Emily, Amanda, Craig, Edward, Sarah and Tad. Out of those eight Tad and Craig were the only ones that were continuously sedated, their powers enabling them to potentially escape. Emily and Gavin's powers were deemed manageable and, once isolated, had their IV needles removed. The two had woken up to find themselves locked in a ten by ten cell, alone.

"Mother!" Emily screamed as she pounded her fists on the door. "Father! Can anybody hear me!"

"Calm down," a voice boomed out of the ceiling speaker.

Emily looked up. "Who are you? Where are my parents and my brother?"

"Further outbursts will not be tolerated."

She stepped up onto the bed. "Answer me!"

The voice didn't respond.

"Let me out of here!"

"Calm down or gas will be dispensed."

Emily slowly sat down on the bed, grabbed the pillow and rolled over on her side. She buried her face in the pillow and began to cry.

* * *

Gavin's cell was identical to his sister's except for one small difference; he had company. Stir, after he had been summoned, who proceeded to lick Gavin's face uncontrollably.

"Okay Stir," Gavin said as he pushed Stir away, "okay. I love you too."

Stir jumped down off the bed and began to explore the tiny space. Gavin watched him go and then coughed.

I'm not feeling so good.

Gavin looked around his cell as he felt his forehead; it was hot and clammy.

Where am I?

He coughed again and stood up to inspect his room, but before he could he sat back down.

I don't have any energy.

Stir bounded over, jumped up and cuddled in next to him. Gavin pet Stir.

What's the last thing I remember? We were attacked at the house in Running Springs. I miss Stickers.

A tear formed and rolled down his young cheek.

He's all alone now and it's my fault. I couldn't protect him.

Gavin rubbed his head as a headache began to form.

No, wait. I was tied down and…and I remember Rebecca yelling at me. I made the portal and…and she went through it with Nikolay. And now I'm here. What happened?

"Becca?" Gavin called out. "Becca, are you there?"

Stir thumped his tail on the bed next to Gavin.

"Becca!" Gavin yelled and then was besieged by a fit of coughing.

"Calm down," a voice from the ceiling instructed.

Stir gazed upwards and his tail stopped moving.

"I'm…I'm not feeling very well. I think I'm sick."

No reply.

"Hello?"

Nothing.

"Hello!"

Gavin coughed again and became lightheaded.

"Ugh. What's wrong with me Stir? I feel like crap." He looked around some more. "We have to find a way out of here, but how?"

Gavin shifted and something dug into his leg. He put his hand in his pocket and withdrew the rubber bullet he'd picked up off the floor during the attack. He slowly rotated it in his fingers and gazed at it. It was a stark reminder that the situation he and his family was in was nothing short of dire. He stuffed the rubber bullet back in his pocket and tried to find the strength to focus.

I have the means to escape, but the question is would I survive? I know there are hundreds, if not thousands of creatures waiting on my island for someone to come back. Would the Caretaker protect me if I went there? Gavin shook his head. *No, he said to never come back. So what do I do?*

Gavin coughed.

Well, maybe it wouldn't hurt to open my portal and jump through real quick. If the creatures are still there then I can come back right away before they have a chance to get me.

Gavin stood up and Stir, sensing something was about to happen, stood up beside him.

Here goes.

337

Gavin formed his portal and the small room was immediately illuminated. But as Gavin took his first step to enter a large, dark hand reached out from its center. The ragged fingers, smelling of rotting flesh, stretched out and grabbed hold of Gavin's shirt before he could react.

"No no no no!"

Stir's eyes glowed red and he growled deeply as Gavin was yanked off his feet towards his portal.

"NO!" Gavin screamed and the portal vanished just before he crossed its threshold.

"Calm down," the automated voice announced.

Gavin landed on the cold floor, the dark hand still clutching his chest, severed from the arm of the monster. As he looked down the hand began to dissipate into black vapor until it evaporated completely. Stir sniffed his shirt and did a complete circuit of the room before he was satisfied there were no other threats. Meanwhile Gavin had pushed himself up to a sitting position and scooted away from where he had landed.

What the hell? What just happened? No one's ever been able to come through my portal from this side. It's always been one way. So what's changed? Are my powers growing and changing again? Gavin coughed again. *Oh enough with this sickness already.*

Gavin placed his hands on his head and concentrated. Seconds later he felt a hundred times better and his clammy skin regained its color.

That's better.

Stir came over and jumped in his master's lap as Gavin continued to work through the problem.

Well whatever it is I know I can never form my portal again. He shuddered. *I can only imagine what would have happened to me.* His eyes opened wide as he realized the other

338

very obvious issue. *That creature pulled me towards it, but it emerged first. If it hadn't found me then it would have completely come through and taken me over. Shit, who knows how many more would have followed.*

*   *   *

In another cell Sam held on to Julie and tried to comfort her.

"What are they going to do to us?" she asked. "What are they going to do to Amanda and Craig?"

She wasn't able to see his expression when he grimaced. *Unimaginable things.* "We can't think about things like that. We have to stay strong and figure a way out of here."

"I'm scared but I'll try." She pulled him closer. "But you know that everything as of late hasn't been looking good for our team, don't you?"

Sam didn't have an answer so they just sat there in silence.

*   *   *

"First the government takes away SANDBOX," Bill said as he paced back and forth in front of Kim. "Then our children are kidnapped by a madman and given special abilities. And now the President himself has locked us up so he can further his own agenda."

"You need to try and relax."

"I can't relax. Shit, how can I relax? How can you relax with everything going on? You're usually the one freaking out."

"I don't know anything anymore. It's all become too much for me to handle. I saw my sister dead on the road in

Hawaii, shot through the heart and I lost it. Then she was brought back to life but didn't have any memory of who I or anyone else was. We were hunted down on the boat, your men killed as they tried to protect us. The list goes on and on and now we're locked in a cell." Kim looked up at her husband. "I'm relaxed because I don't think my soul can take any more. I know this is the end."

Bill sat down by her side. "Don't say that. Don't ever say that."

"And you know why I know that? I know it because I see it in your eyes. We're not getting out of here, are we?"

"Not if I have anything to do about it. Everything's going to be okay."

"I don't need your platitude because I already know the truth. We're dead."

41

Wednesday November 14, 2001

SVR agent Tatiana Danilovna's plane landed in Moscow and was met by a contingent of armed security. They escorted her, and her briefcase, to awaiting vehicles and sped off towards a classified military testing facility. Once the group safely arrived Tatiana was once again chaperoned by a protection detail into the building. She was greeted by the woman in charge, Dr. Kalina Krysova.

"Agent Danilovna?"

Tatiana came to a stop. "Yes. And you are Dr. Krysova. President Anatolievich ordered me to hand this case off to you and only you."

Dr. Krysova nodded. "I hereby acknowledge that you have fulfilled your duties Agent Danilovna. I will take possession of the syringes now."

"Very well," Tatiana replied and handed over the briefcase.

"Thank you."

Dr. Kalina Krysova turned and headed deeper into the facility with the briefcase grasped tightly in her hands. After bypassing two security checkpoints she entered her lab, placed the briefcase on a table and gently opened it. Inside, protectively packaged in foam, were twenty syringes. She put on latex gloves and then carefully extracted each one, inspecting them for damage. Satisfied that all twenty were intact she closed the case, removed her gloves and picked up the lab's phone.

"Yes doctor?"

"I've confirmed that all twenty syringes have arrived safe and sound, Mr. President."

"Excellent. Are you ready to proceed with stage two?"

"Yes, sir. I have twenty soldiers in an adjoining room."

"Then proceed. I'll have the Generals there to oversee the subject's process within the hour."

"Sir?"

"What is it, Dr. Krysova?"

"I'd like to run some tests on one of the syringes before stage two is initiated."

"Denied. We're out of time. The Americans were given the same batch and I have no doubt have already commenced with their injections. If there were any complications I would have heard about it by now."

"But, sir…"

"Doctor. You will proceed with stage two immediately or I will have you replaced. Do we understand each other?"

"Yes, Mr. President."

The line went dead and Kalina hung up. Against her wishes she carried the briefcase across the hallway and into another large room. Inside twenty shirtless men, with bulging muscles, stood around talking to one another. Lining the walls were twenty beds, each affixed with leather restraints. As she entered they turned and stared her down. She pressed a button on the wall and two assistants appeared through another doorway. They came over to Dr. Krysova as she placed the briefcase on a counter and opened it. As the assistants went to work preparing the syringes Dr. Krysova turned and addressed the soldiers.

"Each of you has volunteered to be part of this historic endeavor. After you lie down you will be strapped in. Then, in turn, you will be injected with the contents of a syringe.

342

This serum will endow you with superhuman strength. Are there any questions?"

There weren't as twenty pairs of eyes continued to stare at her.

"Very good. Your superiors will be here within the hour to observe your progress. In the meantime please find a bed so my team and I can get started."

* * *

Dr. Eva Lawrence finished injecting the contents of the syringe into the American soldier's arm and then withdrew the needle. He hadn't flinched as he watched the serum empty into his bloodstream.

"How long till I feel something, doc?" he asked her.

"I've been told the results vary, but we should see a change within twenty-four hours."

"Roger that. Thanks."

She smiled. "You're welcome. Good luck."

Dr. Lawrence walked away from the restrained soldier's bed and deposited the spent needle in the appropriate bio-waste disposal container before she stripped off her gloves. She glanced down the room at the other nineteen men who had volunteered and caught herself.

Even though the world is screaming that they're ready for this, I don't think they are. The only reason I agreed to be part of this is because my curiosity got the better of me. I just hope this project is a success because history will judge me for my participation in it, no matter how it turns out.

42
Wednesday November 14, 2001

Dr. Stuart Glover gazed down at Dr. Matsushita who lay strapped to a bed, unconscious with an IV drip protruding from his arm, and smiled.

You're one of the most powerful humans in the world and I was still able to nullify you. Your arrogance led you to where you are now. It's only a matter of time before I'll be able to replicate your work, and when that day comes I'll make sure you're permanently removed from the playing board.

Dr. Glover left the room and headed to the security room that controlled all of the cells. The two men in the room looked up from their monitors as he entered.

"I want to address all the 'tenants' at once," Dr. Glover stated.

"Right here, sir," one of the men replied and pointed to a microphone. The man flipped a few switches. "All cells have been activated. Whenever you're ready."

Dr. Glover repositioned the microphone to his liking. "Hello Tenants, this is Dr. Glover. For those of you who are unaware Dr. Matsushita has manufactured and delivered twenty vials of serum, utilizing Thomas' blood, to both the Russians and Americans yesterday. Thomas' blood level dwindled so he's been sedated while his body produces more. However, what you might not be aware of is that Dr. Matsushita has also been neutralized. He was a direct threat, much like you are, to this nation and to this project. So, if you haven't surmised it yet, I'm in charge moving forward. Do you have any questions?"

The speakers in each cell conveyed Dr. Glover's message. As he concluded Laura spoke up from her cell.

"What are you going to do with us? What you're doing is illegal and you need to let us go. Please, we've done nothing to you."

"You have all been classified as a threat to national security. Don't be naïve. None of you are going anywhere."

"How do you live with yourselves!?" Sam bellowed. "We're human beings. There's nothing to be afraid of from Thomas, his family or our children!"

"The simple truth," Dr. Glover said, "is that you're a threat and you will be studied."

Laura stood up. "You're no better than Matsushita! You're just as much of a monster as he ever was you fucking bastard! Just give me my children and leave us alone! You gutless sonofab…"

Dr. Glover nodded to one of the men and he disabled the speakers. Laura continued to scream but her voice no longer resonated within the control booth.

"Prep Mrs. Clark and then, as soon as I'm finished with Laura, I want to start experimenting on her children."

*   *   *

Over the next few hours Laura and Emily's screams drifted out of Dr. Glover's lab, down the hallway and into the ears of everyone caged in a cell. The women's desperate and pain filled cries tore at the family's heart strings and hope, stripping away the likelihood that they'd ever get out of this place alive. They instantly became aware, once the experiments on Laura and Emily started, that Dr. Glover was just as driven as Dr. Matsushita. It also meant his proclivity for life wasn't high on his list. The family and their abilities were only obstacles for him to overcome and learn from.

With tears running down her face Julie somehow scrapped together the guts to ask Sam a question. "We're never getting out of here, are we?"

Sam didn't turn to face his wife or answer her question. "Sam?"

"I heard you," he said softly. "Trust me, I heard you."

In the next cell over Kim wasn't faring any better.

"I can't believe they're torturing Laura….and now poor Emily. This is crazy!" She faced Bill, panic written all over her face. "They can't hold us here! Make them let us out!"

"You've got to take it easy."

"How can you stand there and say that when you know our children are going to be next. That monster is going to torture Edward and Sarah! Do something!"

"Like what goddammit? Tell me what I can do that I haven't already thought of? You think for a second I want to be in this cage listening to our family members being poked, prodded and who knows what else?"

"They're not our family," Kim stated.

Bill was stunned. "Do you really think that or are you just mouthing off because you're scared?"

"You know it's Thomas' fault we're involved in any of this."

"Un-fucking-believable. I guess you'll think whatever you want to make yourself feel better, won't you Kim? The fact is that even though you got a crash course on Thomas' life you apparently still don't know shit about him. Or maybe you do but you're so selfish that all you really give a shit about is yourself."

"That's not fair!"

Bill pointed his finger at her. "No, you're not thinking straight. Look around Kim. This isn't some dream that's going to end nicely. If you haven't noticed we're in this together whether you're ready to accept it or not. So blaming Thomas, at this point, is a fucking joke." He paused for a few seconds. "I love you babe, but get off your warpath. I need your head straight right now so we can figure this out together."

Gabbi and Hobbes, both in separate cells, lay on their beds, their pillows mashed over their ears as soon as they realized what the atrocious sounds were. They were frightened and all too aware that they'd probably never see the light of day ever again.

43
Wednesday November 14, 2001

Dr. Eva Lawrence continually walked through the lab, stopping at each soldier's bed to check on their condition. After each soldier she stopped and made a notation on her clipboard, then moved on to the next.

"Doc."

Dr. Lawrence swiveled her head towards the closest soldier who'd just spoken.

"Yes? What is it Zero-six?"

This man had been given a coded designation, like the other nineteen, and was secured to his bed with leather straps. She immediately noticed his forehead was glistening with sweat, a condition he hadn't exhibited the minute before.

"I'm…I'm not feeling so good."

She smiled. "You're going to be just fine. I'm going to recheck your vitals."

"Okay."

She placed two of her gloved fingers on his neck and ascertained that his heartbeat was severely elevated. Next she placed the auto-thermometer in his ear and pressed the button. A few seconds later it beeped. She withdrew it and looked at the results but wasn't happy with the numbers.

"Oh shit." Her exclamation got the attention of one of her assistants and he came over. "Get me ice and a chill blanket stat!"

"You got it," he replied and hurried off.

"What…what is it doc? Give it…to me straight."

Dr. Lawrence locked eyes with the soldier. "You're overheating and I need to get your core temperature down immediately before your brain swells up more than it already has."

He smiled weakly. "Oh, is that all. That's nothi…"

Before Dr. Lawrence could do anything the soldier's back violently arched, the leather straps straining to hold him in place.

"What the hell…"

The man's eyes bulged uncharacteristically outwards from their sockets and the soldier finally acknowledged his intense pain.

"ARRRRRGGHHHHHH!"

"I need help over here!" she bellowed.

In a matter of moments the man's arms enlarged and his muscles swelled. These immediate changes rippled downwards to his legs, his pants tearing as the seams popped. There was nothing Dr. Lawrence could do but stand back and watch his transformation take hold, her hand instinctively covering her mouth.

"I'm sorry, I…"

The leather restraints splintered and fell to the side as his body continued to expand. She backed away, putting distance between her and the mutation that was occurring right in front of her eyes.

"IT HUURRRTTTTSSSS! MAKE IT STTTOOOOOPPPP!"

"The same thing is happening over here!" one of the assistants yelled.

"And here too!"

Dr. Lawrence looked around and saw other soldiers begin to struggle in their beds, writhing in pain as their cries of pain filled the room.

"Get out, right now!" she ordered. "Evacuate!"

"But…"

"Do it!" she screamed.

As the assistants dropped what they were doing and scrambled towards the doors Dr. Lawrence's ears were besieged by the sound of buckling metal. She twisted her head back towards the soldier only to see a badly disfigured form standing there, the crushed bed beneath it. She couldn't move; paralyzed from what he had transformed into. As they stared at each other dozens upon dozens of nodules quickly began to appear on his skin. In no time they covered his body.

This isn't right. Run!

Dr. Lawrence turned to follow her assistants but the soldier, now more monster than man, moved with blazing speed and enveloped her throat with one of his hands.

"No!" she yelled and tried to pry his hand loose.

He pulled her close until they were inches apart, face to face. His words came out slow and painful. "What…did…you…do…to…me?"

"Ca..n't…brea…th…"

One of the nodules popped and puss splashed on her face and filled the surrounding air. Other beds in the lab, and the soldiers in them, began to shake as their metamorphosis occurred. Zero-six turned his attention back to the female doctor he held firmly in his hand and scowled.

"You…hurt…me…us…no…more."

The doctor had passed out from lack of oxygen, her limp form dangling from his large hand. He shook her back and forth, like a rag doll, and snapped her neck. He then threw her against the wall, indenting it deeply before her corpse unceremoniously dropped to the floor.

The soldier grunted through his mouth, which now consisted of a mass of twisted and broken teeth. Zero-six started to lumber, each step leaving cracks in the floor as he headed towards the doors. On either side of him the other nineteen volunteers were well into their own mutations as their bodies violently and rapidly grew stronger and less human.

Twenty feet from the doors four armed guards pushed into the lab with their rifles at the ready. They weren't prepared for the creature coming right at them. Zero-six instantly charged.

"What the fuck!?"

"Take it down!"

The four men opened fire on Zero-six but only managed to get a few shots off each before he collided with the four guards. He grabbed a rifle from one and immediately clubbed two others with it, which sent them sprawling. Zero-six dropped the rifle and took hold of the other two's limbs, turned around and tossed them deeper into the lab. Zero-six then barreled through the doors as the four guards were torn apart by the other nineteen. Alarm bells sounded throughout the building as he frantically looked for a way out.

Escape. Run.

* * *

The lab that Dr. Lawrence worked out of was located on the outskirts of Atlanta, Georgia. As thick black smoke billowed into the evening sky twenty severely malformed and strength enhanced creatures gathered together in the parking lot one last time. They heard a multitude of fire engine sirens getting closer and dispersed on instinct in random directions. Some headed towards Atlanta, some to the west towards Alabama, while others went east to South Carolina and south to Florida. They all ran, their augmented strength allowing them to travel swiftly. But what they didn't know, now reduced only to their primal thoughts, was that they were all carriers and that death would follow them wherever they traveled.

Run. Escape.

44
Wednesday November 14, 2001

"Code Red!" Dr. Kalina Krysova screamed as she slammed her fist down on the emergency button. "Code Red!"

Alarms wailed throughout the building located in the heart of Moscow. Lab technicians and personnel, along with a number of high ranking military generals, had just witnessed twenty Russian soldiers morph into grotesque creature's right in front of their eyes; listening to their wails of pain reverberate inside the lab. But all that remained, as each soldier's transformation concluded, was their rage. The lab technicians never stood a chance and their blood was splattered all over the laboratory's walls.

"Run! Evacuate now!"

The Generals, who had observed the process from the second story glass-enclosed observation balcony, exited the room as quickly as they could. Two of the rampaging soldiers, now strength enhanced and sensing movement above, leaped towards the glass partition and exploded through the large windows. Shards of glass, along with puss from torn nodules, showered the men and Dr. Krysova.

Two of the Generals kept running forward, panicked and spooked, towards the exit and away from danger while everyone else became instantly trapped. Dr. Krysova immediately backpedaled the way they'd come as the two beasts grabbed hold of the closet General to them and started a tug-of-war with his arms and legs. She slammed the door closed behind her just as the man's limbs were torn off. Wide-eyed she quickly scanned the room for a place to hide as additional screams emanated on the other side of the door. She barely made it into the cabinet under the sink when the door she'd closed was bashed inwards. It sailed across the room and imbedding itself into the wall. Dr. Krysova closed her eyes, in the tight space, and tried to control her breathing as heavy footsteps entered the room. With each step the floor shuddered and her dread grew. An overhead cabinet was torn off the wall and disintegrated when it was smashed into the floor. She stifled a whimper and placed both hands over her mouth as a precaution.

I'm not going to make it. It's going to kill me.

Another cabinet was ripped off the wall and the sound of breaking glass followed as it was thrown through the balcony window. With blood dripping down her face, from the glass cuts, Dr. Krysova expected any second that her hiding place would be discovered. But the creature's footsteps receded away from her seconds later.

With the alarms still ringing Dr. Krysova waited another ten minutes before she gently pushed the sink door open and peered out. The room had been destroyed as if a localized whirlwind had been trapped in the room. Debris littered the floor and she gasped when she saw the door firmly embedded in the wall. Dr. Krysova extracted herself from the small enclosure and stood up.

How in the hell could this have happened?

She glanced down the hallway, where the door used to reside, and recoiled. Multiple bodies, and body parts, were scattered up and down the hallway. The urge to vomit manifested itself quickly and Dr. Krysova barely had time to turn around and use the sink.

Oh shit oh shit oh shit. They're all dead.

As she stood up to wipe her mouth she caught her reflection in the cracked mirror above the sink.

What? What are those?

On her face she saw that a multitude of vesicles had formed. She reached up and touched one of them. It was soft, malleable and filled with liquid.

No. This is impossible. It just can't be.

She touched another one and it popped, the puss warm to the touch.

No!

She tore off her lab coat and rolled up one of her sleeves. There, on her arm, were more vesicles.

This doesn't make any sense. The incubation period for smallpox is twelve days.

She turned and hurried down the hallway, stepping over arms, legs and bodies while doing the best she could not to slip on the blood saturated floor. She also happened to notice that the bodies were covered in nodules, just like hers. At the end of the hallway the corridor split. She poked her head out and looked both ways before she took off at a run to her office a few corridors away. Dr. Krysova closed her office door behind her and immediately sat down so she could access her computer.

I have to be wrong. It has to be something else.

As she began typing she wiped the sweat off her hot forehead.

Dammit, I'm not feeling good.

She pulled up the webpage she'd been looking for and quickly scanned it, confirming her symptoms. She sat back in her chair, tired and confused. She realized she was having a hard time focusing on her thoughts.

None of my symptoms should have accelerated this quickly...unless...unless...think dammit, think.

She looked around the room and saw her master's degree from Bioscience hanging on the wall. She snapped her fingers.

Of course. Unless it was genetically engineered.

Her head bobbed suddenly and she caught herself.

It's metabolizing within me at an expediential pace. She coughed and spat out blood all over her keyboard. *Fuck.*

* * *

"Dr. Krysova?" Demian Anotolievich said over the private line. "I'm sure you're calling me to tell me that the serum was a resounding success."

"No," Mr. President she replied as she coughed up more blood.

"No?" His ears picked up on the alarms and he stood up. "What's happened?"

"The serum was injected in all twenty men but they turned into monsters, similar to the one that attacked D.C., except…" She coughed again and spat out more blood.

Sonofabitch. "Dr. Krysova, are you there? Except what?"

"Except….except we were tricked."

"Tricked? What are you talking about?"

"The augmented soldiers went crazy and attacked everyone in the building. I barely managed…"

He heard the sound of the phone as it fell from her fingers and hit her desk.

"Dr. Krysova? Dr. Krysova?"

"I'm…I'm here. Losing…it though."

"Tell me what happened!?" he demanded. "What's going on!?"

"Smallpox. The ser…serum contains a mu…mutated strain of smallpox. It's fast acting and spreads like wildfire. I've…I've never seen anything like it before."

She pulled the phone away from her face and had a huge coughing fit. She barely had the energy left to put the phone back up to her ear as she collapsed in her chair.

"Doctor?"

"Sti..ll here."

"What are you telling me?"

She gathered what remaining strength she had. "You have to listen to me, Mr. President. This was engineered on purpose."

"Then contain it."

She shook her head and closed her eyes. "I'm dying. It's too…too…late. They've already escap…"

The phone fell out of her lifeless hand and clattered to the floor.

"Dr. Krysova!? Dr. Krysova!? Dr. Krysova!?"

Nothing.

"Shit!"

He slammed down the phone and immediately dialed an emergency number. It was picked up right away.

"There's been an incident," President Anatolievich said urgently.

* * *

"I have very little time at the moment, Mr. President," POTUS said to Demian Anatolievich. "What is it?"

"You did this to us you sonofabitch!"

"What are you talking about?"

"Stop playing games! The serum you supplied to us was tainted and our test subjects went crazy and have killed everyone. I have an epidemic of unheard of proportions on my hands!"

Shit. "President Anatolievich, I assure you we're in the same boat. I've just been going over preliminary reports that the same thing happened to our people."

"I don't believe you, Mr. President and I will make you pay for your actions! I'm turning my fleet back towards the United States. Your precious country will pay for your deception with their lives!"

45
Thursday November 15, 2001

Early Thursday morning, as the sun came up, twenty-four year old Alecia Jones boarded her United flight bound from Atlanta to Las Vegas, found her assigned seat and rested her head against the window in preparation for the lengthy flight. She was excited to be traveling and looked forward to the long weekend to reconnect with her older sister as they tore up the Vegas strip. Alecia glanced at her watch and saw that the plane was already ten minutes late. Shortly afterward one of the flight attendants made an announcement.

"Ladies and gentlemen. We're experiencing a slight delay in our departure this morning because we're missing one crew member. As soon as they arrive we'll seal the doors and be on our way. Thank you for your patience and understanding, and as always, thank you for flying United."

Five minutes later the tardy male employee showed up. The man appeared haggard and slightly hungover as Alecia watched him apologize to his fellow flight attendants. The outer door was quickly secured and the plane, shortly thereafter, took off into the sky towards Las Vegas. Alecia closed her eyes and drifted off to sleep as visions of cocktails and dancing filled her head.

* * *

"Mayday. Mayday. Mayday. This is flight twelve-zero-three declaring a medical emergency. Requesting priority landing at McCarran along with medical personnel. I repeat, this is flight twelve-zero-three and we are declaring a medical emergency. We've got some kind of virus....I don't know how to describe it. Over."

"Flight twelve-zero-three, this is McCarran tower. Proceed to runway one-four, I repeat runway one-four, for immediate landing. All in and outbound traffic has been diverted. Medical teams will converge on you. Do you copy?"

"Copy tower. Initiating landing procedure."

* * *

A bevy of ambulances and fire trucks were on hand as the airplane rolled to a stop at the end of the runway. A portable stairway was pushed into position as the main cabin door opened from inside. The six-man medical team headed up the stairs but weren't prepared as the Captain emerged from the interior, his face covered in vestibules. He somehow found the strength to stagger towards them, their eyes wide open, and collapsed. As his body hit the metal stairwell the vestibules, on the rest of his body, exploded and instantly mixed the puss into the air that surrounded the medical team.

"Back!" the team leader yelled as he covered his mouth. "Back up now!"

The six-man team retreated down the steps and away from the plane.

"Call the tower and tell them this runway is quarantined. I don't know what happened in that plane but whatever it is we need to stop it before it spreads any further."

"You got it, sir."

But what the team leader didn't know is that all of them had already been infected, and in turn had spread it to the rest of the first responders. A call came in over the radio

362

requesting that one of the firetrucks divert to another issue. Without knowing any better one truck answered the call and drove away.

Hours later Las Vegas became a major epicenter for the contagion, and before long the bodies began to pile up.

* * *

"Thank you for taking my call, Mr. President," said David Harper, the President of the CDC, the Center for Disease Control.

"What the hell is going on David?"

"I wish I knew, sir. Last night, as I'm sure you've heard, a rash of violence broke out in Atlanta and its surrounding areas. Soon after we began to receive calls from multiple hospitals regarding a huge uptick of infected people that needed assistance. However, it didn't take long for the casualties to pile up and panic to kick in. I don't know where this came from, Mr. President, but it's sweeping across this country by the second. I've even heard from our Russian counterparts that they're experiencing similar cases. This is beginning to take on the characteristics of a terrorist attack."

"What's your recommendation?"

"Lock this country down immediately, sir, or we all die."

* * *

Televisions across America transitioned to the Emergency Broadcast System with the following scrolling tagline: **We interrupt your regularly scheduled program for the following breaking news**. Twenty seconds later the President for the CDC, the Center for Disease Control, appeared.

"Reports continue to flood in about thousands of people that have overrun hospitals, in the southeastern states, with a highly contagious disease. Initial diagnoses of these individuals have led us to believe that this is a mutated strain of smallpox, but to be quite honest the CDC has never seen anything quite like this before. This particular strain of smallpox is primarily airborne but can also be transmitted by coming in proximity with an infected party. If you do become infected the incubation time, before you experience external symptoms, is less than an hour and those symptoms include a high fever and external nodules appearing all over your body. I'm sorry to report that the mortality rate is between eighty-five and ninety-five percent, and those that are infected succumb from this smallpox infection anywhere from thirty minutes to three hours after acquiring it.

"What we are experiencing is unprecedented and if we are unable to contain this outbreak the world will be faced with a pandemic, which is why we need your help America. I have conferred with the President and he will be activating the National Guard. In the meantime, to protect you and your families, shelter in place. I repeat. Go home and shelter in place. Do not venture outside for any reason. If you are infected, or have been exposed to the disease, go home. Do not spread this deadly outbreak by traveling to a hospital or care clinic because the only thing you'll be doing is spreading this incredibly infectious disease further.

"I'm also compelled to inform you that we currently don't have a cure, but we will work tirelessly to find a solution. Thank you and good luck."

* * *

News channels across the world presented footage of the urban violence, the disfigured bodies in the streets and the brazen attacks from both Moscow and Atlanta, Georgia taken from any internet sources they could locate. Panic started to spread as information about the severity and seriousness of this contagion rippled all over the world. People, afraid for their lives, scrambled to stores for supplies, food and water. Community retailers, and their shelves, were quickly emptied.

And that's when the riots kicked off.

The National Guard rolled into the outskirts of Atlanta and setup a command post. Eight hours later military engineers had hastily erected a quarantine perimeter that surrounded Atlanta, manned by armed soldiers in hazmat gear. They had been given strict orders, by the President of the United States himself, to fire upon anyone attempting to breach that quarantine zone.

But they were too late. By that time the contagion had already run unchecked throughout the city, spilled into neighboring territories and was traversing throughout the nation in every direction.

46
Thursday November 15, 2001

"Sir, I don't think that's a wise course of action," Dr. Glover cautioned over the phone.

"He's responsible for the shit storm that's ravaging America. Wake him up now doctor," POTUS commanded, "or I'll have you dropped into a contaminated zone."

"I'll need some time to prepare a suitable environment and..."

"NOW!"

Dr. Glover cringed. "Of course, Mr. President. I'll call you back via video in fifteen minutes."

"You have seven minutes."

"Yes, sir."

He ended the call with the President and then dialed an extension.

"I need Dr. Matsushita moved to the 'Majestic Twelve' video conference room immediately. Yes, I'm fully aware of the risks but this order comes directly from the President himself. Drop whatever you're doing and get it done now. I'll meet you there."

Dr. Glover hung up, raced out of his office and down the corridor towards the cells where he kept his 'tenants'. As he rounded the corner two guards had just exited a cell with a sedated Dr. Matsushita strapped to a gurney, a blindfold wrapped tightly around his head. The guards pushed that gurney down the hallway towards Dr. Glover.

Dr. Glover glanced at his watch. "The President is waiting. We have to hurry."

The trio rushed Dr. Matsushita to 'Majestic Twelve' and parked him in front of the video monitor, still strapped down. Dr. Glover checked the IV line and made sure the kill-switch attached to it was ready and enabled.

"Clear the room," Dr. Glover told the guards.

As the two departed Dr. Glover dialed the President. It rang twice before the President's face appeared on the monitor.

"He's here, Mr. President."

"I can see that. Why isn't Dr. Matsushita awake?"

"I didn't want there to be any complications transporting him from his cell to this room, sir. The sedation, once disengaged, wears off very quickly."

"And the blindfold?"

"For everyone's protection, Mr. President. This isn't a man anyone should give an inch to. He's extremely dangerous."

"I recall, Dr. Glover, which is why I took your recommendation to silence him so seriously. But now he's the only one with any answers, even though it's obvious he's the man responsible for this deadly outbreak." The President paused and took a deep breath. "Wake him."

"Yes, sir."

Dr. Glover extracted a remote control device from his lab coat pocket and clicked a button. The electronic IV drip beeped and shut off. He stepped back and away from the gurney.

"He'll be fully alert in thirty seconds, Mr. President. If he does anything out of the ordinary all I have to do is press this button and he'll be knocked out immediately."

"Thank you, doctor."

Twenty seconds later Dr. Matsushita began to tug at his restraints, unable to move or see.

"What's going on?"

The President spoke up. "You sonofabitch. You have a lot to answer for, Dr. Matsushita."

Yamato smiled as he recognized the President's voice. "Why hello, Mr. President. Too bad I can't look you in the eyes. Is there something amiss?"

"What the hell have you done!? People, all over the world, are dying because of you!"

Yamato adjusted a bit on the gurney. "Then it sounds like my plan worked as intended."

"You sick bastard. Why would you do this?"

"I don't need to explain myself to you." Yamato jostled the restraints that held him in place. "And apparently you can't be trusted either, Mr. President, can you?"

The President tried to push his rage aside and focus. "You are going to fix this, Dr. Matsushita."

"Go to hell. I gave you exactly what you wanted and this is how you repaid me. The world will perish before you even get close to discovering a cure. And the best part about it, Mr. President, is that all of this is on you. You killed mankind and the human race because of your need for power."

"So you're not going to help?"

"Absolutely not," Yamato defiantly replied.

"Very well," said the President. "Dr. Glover, press the button, and then I have another task you're going to hate."

* * *

With Dr. Matsushita safely tucked back in his cell Dr. Glover was given the unfortunate responsibility to bring Thomas to the 'Majestic Twelve' conference room to converse with the President.

"Hello, Mr. Clark," the President said in greeting as Thomas entered the room.

Thomas didn't hold back. "How dare you speak to me as if nothing horrific has transpired to me and my family since you captured us. Instead we're being held prisoners and Dr. Glover has taken over where Dr. Matsushita left off, torturing us for his own amusement."

"My apologies..."

"Shut the fuck up!" Thomas yelled, his eyes wild. "Whatever comes out of your mouth doesn't hold any weight! You're just like everyone else who's wanted to take what we have, but I'm done! I'll bring this damn building down on all our heads before I let anyone of your sick doctor's touch us ever again! I'll kill us all if I have to!"

"Before you do that, Mr. Clark, you need to be caught up to speed."

Thomas was caught off guard. "What are you talking about?"

"I need your help," the President stated matter-of-factly.

"Excuse me? Why? What's happened? Is my family..."

"Your family is fine. However, the world as we know it is not. The serum that Dr. Matsushita created was given to us and the Russians."

"What characteristic did he say was in those syringes?"

"Strength and twenty of our soldiers were injected with it."

"And?"

"And, Mr. Clark, something went horrible wrong. Dr. Matsushita hid a mutated and fast acting smallpox strain within the serum. Long story short, everyone in the lab where the soldiers were injected are dead and those enhanced soldiers have been on the loose since last night. They infect everyone they come in contact with and those newly infected hosts, in turn, spread the disease to others before they die one to three hours later."

Thomas pulled out a chair from the conference table and sat down in utter dismay. "Dammit. How bad is it?"

"To be honest, we're past initial containment and even though I've ordered people to stay indoors it's still disseminating across America, as well as Russia and Europe. No one has ever seen anything like this before."

"And you said you need my help?"

"That's correct. The world is in danger and people are dying. We need your help."

"That's strange because I clearly remember watching you on television telling the world my family and I are a national security issue, a threat to each and every person in the world."

"Mr. Clark, now's not the ti…"

"Tell me, why would we help you after what you've done to us?"

"Because you're responsible."

Thomas scoffed. "That's bullshit and you know it, Mr. President. Matsushita is the one who did this, and you're the one who made it possible when you allowed him access to my blood. So do us all a favor and point that political fucking finger back at yourself, you asshole."

The President swallowed his pride. "Very well, Mr. Clark. Help us before there isn't a world left to live in."

"What are you offering?"

"I…I don't know. What do you wa…"

"Our freedom. Let us all go. You pardon each and every one of us immediately, in writing, or I'm just going to sit back and watch the world implode around us as the human race ceases to exist, on your watch I might add, Mr. President."

"Anything else, Mr. Clark?"

"We just want to be left alone. None of this would have happened if you had just left us alone."

"Very well, Mr. Clark, you have a deal. I'll fax the pardons to you and order your family released immediately. And for what it's worth, I'm sorry. I had no idea what I was getting in to."

Thomas stood up. "Know this. If you're lying, Mr. President, or anyone fucks with this deal, well..., we will come for you."

* * *

Laura wrapped her arms around Thomas for the first time since Running Springs.

"I love you," she told him.

"I love you too."

Gavin and Emily joined in on the family reunion. On the other side of the room Sam and Julie couldn't let go of Amanda and Craig, just as much as Bill and Kim couldn't stop holding onto Edward and Sarah. Gabbi, Hobbes and Tad, along with the two SAD men, Carl and Eliot, stood idly by while the families reunited. Carl and Eliot caught continual glances from Gabbi and Hobbes and finally spoke up.

"What is it?" Eliot asked.

Hobbes shrugged. "Sorry. I, well..err...we had gotten used to you being someone else, that's all."

"Who?"

Gabbi and Hobbes looked at other and then back at the two men.

"You don't remember anything?" Gabbi asked. "Either of you?"

Eliot and Carl both shook their heads.

"Remember what?" Carl asked.

"Wow," Gabbi stated. "What do you remember?"

"We were tied up," Carl stated. "Gunfire."

"Yeah," Eliot said, "gunfire. And then all of a sudden we were on some sunny beach."

Eliot nodded. "After that it gets hazy."

"That's brutal," Hobbes told them.

"Yeah it is," Gabbi added.

Eliot and Carl shifted on their feet. "So what happened to us then? It sounds like you might know."

"You wouldn't believe us even if we told you."

"Maybe," Eliot said. "Maybe not. But what I do know is that we're being held at Area Fifty-Two under orders from the President of the United States for reasons of national security. What could be worse?"

"Point taken," Hobbes said. "Gabbi?"

"Here's the short version. You were rescued by Thomas and his son Gavin. They took you to another realm of existence. Once there you were assaulted by dead beings and barely made it back to Earth with your lives. However, in the process of crossing over your bodies were taken over by the other souls. Eliot, Rebecca Cross became you; and Carl, Nikolay Dmitriev became you. After that a shitload of bad stuff ensued including taking Robert Duncan, the DCI, hostage and interrogated him about Thomas and his family."

"I'm sorry," Carl sincerely replied. "I don't remember any of that."

"It's not your fault," Hobbes said. "It's just that we're used to talking with Rebecca..., but she's gone now."

Gabbi found Hobbes' hand down by her side and gripped it in support.

Sam and Bill finally split off and walked over to Thomas.

"What kind of deal did you have to make to set us free?"

"And whatever it is," Bill added, "thank you."

"Yes, thank you," Sam said.

Thomas nodded. "We're not out of the fire yet. In fact, even though we're back together things have gotten a whole lot worse out in the real world. Matsushita somehow developed a deadly strain of smallpox and hid it within the serum he developed for America and Russia. As of last night the disease is rampaging across the world, unchecked, and is leaving bodies in its wake."

"And we're supposed to help stop it?" Bill asked. "How?"

Thomas looked down at his daughter. "The plan is to utilize Emily's powers to force Matsushita to talk. If there's a cure he'll divulge it. However, while we have the chance I suggest we remove Dr. Matsushita's tracking devices from Amanda, Sarah and Edward."

* * *

"He'll be awake in thirty seconds," Dr. Glover told Thomas and Emily.

"Good," Thomas replied. "Now get out of here before I start to dwell on how much I hate you."

Dr. Glover swallowed hard and quickly disappeared out of the room.

"I don't like Dr. Glover," Emily said.

"Neither do I. But right now we have a much larger problem to tackle. Are you ready?"

Emily nodded.

"I'll be right here if you need me."

Ten seconds later Dr. Matsushita began to stir.

"Where…where am I?"

Emily clamped her hand on Dr. Matsushita's arm and he went ridged.

"What is the disease you created?"

"It's a deadly strain of smallpox," he told her.

"How many will die?"

"It will continue to indiscriminately kill every human being, jumping from one host to another, leaving the world devoid of human existence."

"Why did you do this?"

Dr. Matsushita's face grew dark. "The world needs to feel my loss as deeply as I have."

"But they are innocent people. So many innocent people."

"No one is innocent."

Thomas pointed back at the pre-determined questions they'd come up with to get Emily back on track. She nodded and continued.

"How did you create this smallpox strain?"

"From Thomas. It all started with Thomas and his blood."

Thomas' jaw dropped because he knew Yamato couldn't be lying. *Again, it's all because of me.*

"So is there a chance a cure could be manufactured?"

"Yes."

Thomas whispered to his daughter. "Make him sleep for a few minutes so we can talk."

Emily nodded. "You will sleep for one-hundred and twenty seconds."

Yamato's eyes closed and Emily released his arm. She looked over at her father.

"Can you command him to work on the cure?" he inquired gently.

"Yes."

"But that still means he's a threat because of his powers."

Emily shook her head. "I have an idea about that."

"I'm all ears."

"I want to see if I can suppress his ability."

"What? Can you really do that?"

"I think so."

"But will that do anything to you? Will it harm you in some way?"

"I don't think so. When I took memories from Amanda and the others that time it was different."

"Are you sure?"

"I have to try."

Thomas thought about it for a bit and finally relented. "Okay. Do your thing."

Emily placed her hand back on Yamato's arm and waited for him to wake up. As soon as his eyes opened she concentrated and spoke.

"You will generate a cure for the disease you created."

"I will give you the cure," Yamato stated.

"Good," Emily replied. "Now, I have something else to tell you."

*   *   *

"Help! I need help in here!" Thomas yelled.

Laura and Gavin burst into the room followed by Sam and Bill who immediately saw that Thomas cradled Emily's head as she lay on the floor.

"What happened!?" Laura cried out.

"I don't know," Thomas explained. "She suppressed Yamato's ability and then just passed out."

Gavin knelt down by his sister, put his hands on her head and closed his eyes. He focused his healing powers and tried to mend whatever was ailing Emily. Ten seconds ticked by, then twenty. Nothing. Gavin opened his eyes and saw that her condition hadn't changed.

"It's…it's not working."

"We'll find a doctor," Bill told everyone before he and Sam swiftly departed.

Laura and Thomas' eyes locked.

"What's going on? What did she do?"

"She said she could do it and I took her at her word. I'm sorry."

"Then I don't understand why she's unconscious, even after Gavin healed her."

"Neither do I."

The doors to the room opened once again and a gurney was brought in, accompanied by two nurses. Thomas picked Emily up and placed her on it. The nurses reversed their course and raced out with Gavin, Hobbes and Gabbi behind them. As Thomas and Laura turned to follow a familiar voice spoke up behind them.

"I can't work on the cure if I'm tied up, can I Thomas?"

Thomas spun on his heels and went straight for Dr. Matsushita, his fist ready to crack his jaw. "You sonofabitch! What did you do to my daughter?"

"Emily? Nothing. What are you talking about?"

Laura grabbed Thomas' arm to stop him. "He's telling the truth."

Thomas looked back at his wife. "What?"

"He's not lying."

Thomas slowly lowered his fist and looked down at his restrained nemesis. *I should just kill you now, you heartless monster. But apparently the world still values your skills.* Thomas began to unbuckle the leather straps.

"Whoa," Sam said as he took a step forward towards his friend. "What the hell are you doing?"

"I'm making sure Emily did her job, and that whatever condition she's in now wasn't for nothing."

As Thomas finished Yamato swung his legs out over the bed and sat up. He used his free hands to remove his blindfold.

"Hello Thomas. Laura. Sam. Bill. So nice for all of you to be here so I could use you."

Yamato reached out with his mind, as he had done so many times before, to take control of Thomas but nothing happened. A puzzled look washed over his face.

"What the hell?"

"Is there a problem, Yamato?" Thomas asked as he lowered his own hands from a defensive posture.

"I...my...ability. I can't use it. I know I have it but I don't know how to."

"He's not lying," Laura stated for the record.

Thomas smiled and relaxed. "Why don't you go check on Emily while the three of us escort Dr. Matsushita to the lab? I believe he has a cure to work on."

Yamato's confusion dissipated. "Oh, that's right. I have a cure to create."

As Laura rushed out of the room Sam and Bill walked over and violently hoisted Yamato to his feet.

"Let's go," Bill told him.

As they departed out of the room and down the hallway Sam finally questioned his friend.

"So this deal you made with the President."

"What about it?" Thomas asked.

"So we're free, just like that?"

Thomas nodded. "Just like that. And we now have the paperwork to back that up."

"It can't be that easy," Bill said. "If we're free then why don't we just get the hell out of here?"

"Cure first," Thomas told them, "and then we can leave. However, even though we have our freedom again, we just can't leave."

"Why? Because of the disease?"

Thomas nodded. "Yeah. Unfortunately we're located in the safest place possible right now."

"Shit."

"Yeah, what you said. Oh, and by the way Sam."

"What?" Sam asked.

"Happy forty-fourth birthday."

"What? Is it really the fifteenth of November? Shit."

"Yeah, and this is one for the books that we'll look back and hopefully laugh on one day."

"I hope so brother, I hope so."

47
Thursday November 15, 2001

The President turned away from the video monitor to the only other person who was in the PEOC's command center with him, Robert Duncan.

"Robert. Thank you for remaining quiet while I spoke to both Dr. Matsushita and Mr. Clark."

The DCI leaned forward. "Do you now fully comprehend why I went to such great lengths to keep Thomas and his family's abilities a secret?"

The President slowly nodded. "I had no idea such horror could befall the world."

"Maybe not, Mr. President, but you knew who you were getting into bed with from the very beginning. Dr. Matsushita should have never been allowed to become involved."

"He was working with Nikolay dammit. If I hadn't intervened then the Russians would have captured Thomas and Dr. Matsushita would have created the serum anyway."

"You can spin it anyway you'd like, Mr. President, but we both know you wanted the power and were prepared to do anything to obtain it. When you gave up Russell, and had him killed to seal that deal with the Russians, I knew there was no coming back for you. You crossed that moral line in the sand on your own accord."

"I did that to avoid World War Three."

"Oh bullshit, sir. You didn't have to kill an innocent man to prove anything. You did it out of fear, plain and simple."

"How dare you."

Robert stood up. "No, sir, how dare you. If the world survives this extinction level event that you helped create, I'm

381

going to do whatever it takes to make sure you pay for your crimes. In the meantime I suggest you'd better sign those Presidential Pardons and fax them to Groom Lake immediately, especially if you want Thomas to help fix your mess." The DCI started to walk towards the exit.

"Where are you going Robert? I need you to help me through this."

Robert shook his head. "No you don't Mr. President. In a moment you're going to be swarmed by Secret Service agents and they're going to escort you to a secured location. From there you can watch as the world implodes around you even after you ordered the transportation lockdown. Sure, you might survive this apocalypse, or you might not. Either way I can no longer serve a President I don't respect. I tender my resignation and resign as the Director of Central Intelligence, effective immediately."

The President abruptly stood up. "You're an invaluable asset and you know Thomas and his family better than anyone. I don't accept your resignation."

"I don't care," Robert snapped. "Don't you see what's happening out there? Thousands of people are dead and you're worried about my resignation? I don't know how you prioritize, sir, but this is absurd. I'm leaving."

"I understand, Robert. I will accept it on one condition."

The DCI paused. "Which is?"

"I want you to go back to Groom Lake and facilitate any work that needs to be accomplished with Thomas. He trusts you, and I need a man on the ground who will never take his eyes off Dr. Matsushita."

"What are you saying?"

"I need you to oversee the cure's creation and distribution. I'm placing you in charge of saving the world."

* * *

Air Force One touched down outside Colorado Springs, Colorado. The President disembarked and was immediately whisked away to NORAD, the North American Aerospace Defense Command bunker. Each team member was individually inspected for any sign of the deadly smallpox virus before being allowed admittance inside the enormous mountain facility. Once the President entered the mountain was sealed behind them, when the large doors and locks engaged.

In his NORAD office the President's first call was to the Russian President.

The first words out of Demian Anatolievich's mouth were, "You betrayed our deal."

"No, Dr. Matsushita used us both. You know as well as I do that the same plague is ravaging both our countries, but I have him working on a cure as we speak."

"I don't believe you. My people are dying and there's nothing I can do about it."

"And so are ours," POTUS replied. "Neither one of us wants the world to die off. We need to stand united, together and fight."

"You do whatever you want, Mr. President, but I can't let this pass. I've already ordered my fleet to turn back towards your American coastlines."

"Threatening me makes no sense when we're in the exact same predicament. I'll make sure Dr. Matsushita gets what's coming to him when this is all said and done, you have my word. He will pay."

"Bah. Empty words and promises. Know this, Mr. President. If this plague cannot be stopped then I will have no other choice than to launch our nuclear warheads at your country. Perhaps you will do the same to me. Only time will tell."

"I look forward to…"

The line went dead.

"Demian! Demian! Are you there! Fuck!"

He placed the phone back on the receiver. *Get me that cure Robert, get me that cure.*

48
Friday November 16, 2001

The realization that the world was dying, slowly, began to dawn on the people that inhabited it. A handful of people, in the scheme of things, welcomed the impending apocalypse having prepared for years to become self-sufficient. But when it came down to it this plague had simply interrupted the majority of the world's inhabitants that were used to waking up to go to work and follow their daily routine. But now people barricaded themselves inside their apartments and houses, fearful and afraid. Neighbors, once friendly to each other, became potential threats. As panic grew hundreds of disputes broke out that involved fists, knives and firearms.

The news stations relentlessly reported on the endless riots, looting and violence as the death tolls climbed higher and higher, hour after hour. Cities and towns, once safe to navigate, had been desolated by the plague, bodies littering the streets as fires raged out of control.

With boats, trains and airplanes grounded across the world the only option left for people were their vehicles. Without any military presence to stop people from migrating, thousands of citizens attempted to evacuate by car which then led to clogged roads, highways and freeways across America, Europe, Russia, China and other countries. And with nowhere to run to it only took a couple of infected hosts to instigate a massive chain reaction, which rapidly sent the disease rippling throughout the crowds.

Those that sheltered in place weren't faring any better. The threat of death and violence were only a stone's throw away from any of their front doors, aside from the fact that electricity had gone out in most districts. Without any new updates of information many people decided to venture out into the streets only to discover empty shelves, fires and unlawfulness everywhere they turned. Over half of them never returned to their families and were swallowed up into the abyss.

49
The Other Place

Dark energy, consisting of menacing and horrific apparitions, continued to encircle Gavin's island in the vast Ocean of Time. Unwavering, and with eternal patience, these foul creatures waited. Their numbers had doubled quickly after word spread of Nikolay's successful escape, each one of them more than eager to leave this realm. The Caretaker, well aware of the current state of affairs, kept a close eye on the situation. But it was a distraction, and one that he couldn't afford to maintain, because the duties and responsibilities he needed to concentrate on had become marginalized.

The Caretaker hovered close to the island, unseen, and continued to assess the situation.

I told them never to come back here, that if they did I wouldn't be able to help them. But would I step in to help them?

Before he could continue his train of thought the portal appeared, a shining beacon in an otherwise shrouded environment.

No! I warned them!

Instantly the creatures stopped circling and surged towards the portal, drawn to it by the possibility of freedom to inhabit whoever came through. But when no one did one of the large monsters, infuriated and hateful, pushed his long dark arm into the portal, talons extended and searched. The Caretaker barely had a chance to register his own dread, upon witnessing this action, when the portal snapped shut. The creature shrieked as his arm was unceremoniously amputated. It flew off into the sky, away from the island, until eventually its howls diminished off in the distance.

The Caretaker was stunned at what he'd just seen. *That should have never happened. The boy's portal is supposed to only work in one direction.*

His brow furrowed as the dark entities pulled away from the island and encircled it once again.

But I know what I saw. For some reason the portal goes both ways now...but why?

He shook his head as he contemplated this new reality.

Maybe the boy's powers have grown. But whatever the reason Gavin must now realize he can never summon it again.

The Caretaker flew away to resume his duties he'd overlooked.

Thousands of new inhabitants have suddenly arrived, and all because of a man-made contagion that's spreading across Earth's surface. Some will move on, but the Dark District's capacity will be overrun if the volume of incoming souls keeps up its current pace. And I don't have a contingency for that, which doesn't bode well.

50

Friday November 16, 2001

Within Building 42's medical division Emily slowly opened her eyes.

"Hey, she's waking up," Gavin informed everyone.

Thomas, Laura, Gabbi and Hobbes rose out of their chairs and quickly came over to Emily's bedside. Laura took her daughter's hand in hers and smiled warmly.

"How are you feeling?"

"Better."

"I'm so glad you're okay," Gabbi said.

"Me too," Hobbes added.

"You had us worried," Thomas said as he sat down by her side. "I'm sorry I made you do that to Dr. Matsushita."

"It's alright," Emily replied. "There wasn't another option and I knew what had to be done. I wonder who I learned that from?"

Thomas chuckled as the others smiled.

"Cute," Thomas said. "But that still doesn't justify what you went through." He paused before he continued. "Em, what happened?"

"I don't know exactly. I thought I could suppress his ability."

"Oh, you did, and he's not happy about it."

Emily cracked a smile as she sat up. "Good. But, I thought I could handle it. Don't worry, I'll be okay."

Laura spoke up. "Maybe you should rest some more?"

"I feel fine," Emily insisted. *Something else is wrong though, but I don't know what it is.*

Laura gave her a strange look but let it go. "Okay. But stay close to us. They've granted us our freedom but we all doubt its validity."

Emily nodded.

"You sure you're okay?" Thomas asked.

"I'm good, dad."

"Okay. Well, unfortunately I'm going to go check and see how Dr. Matsushita is faring with the cure. Stay with everyone, alright?"

"I will."

"We won't let her out of our sight," Gabbi assured him.

"Thanks." Thomas leaned over and gave Laura a kiss. "Be back in a bit."

"Be careful around the doctor," she warned.

"Always."

Thomas got up and left the room. As he closed the door behind him he was immediately besieged by Sam, Bill, Julie, Kim and their children.

"How is she?" Sam asked.

"Apparently Emily bounced back as if nothing happened, which still begs the question, what actually did happen?"

"Whatever it was it scared me," Julie offered.

"You and me both," Thomas replied.

Julie continued. "Listen, I'm sorry I've been blaming you for all our troubles."

"Me too," Kim added.

Thomas held up his hand to stop both of the sisters from apologizing. "I get where you've been coming from and I appreciate it. But the truth is you've been right all along."

"What?" Bill said. "They have?"

390

"I'm ready to accept that I've been the catalyst that has been responsible for taking our extended family down these very long and dangerous roads."

"Thomas…" Sam began to say before he was cut off.

"No Sam. You and Bill have been my best friends for my entire life. It goes without saying that we share a bond that won't ever be broken. But let's be honest, the majority of shit we've been through together has been due to the powers my children manifested, a direct result of Albert Clemmings chemical tinkering with my body. If anything I should be thanking you for your endless support in helping me protect them over the years."

Sam put his hand on Thomas' shoulder. "We'll always be there for you and your family, just as you've always been there for ours."

"What he said," Bill confirmed. "And to think it all started with Nigel all those decades ago."

Thomas nodded. "But we have other pressing matters to worry about right now." He turned back to Julie and Kim. "Are we good for the moment?"

They both nodded.

"Okay," he said as he readdressed Sam and Bill. "Tell me you guys have been working on a plan to get us the hell out of here in one piece?"

"You think the President is going to go back on his word?" Sam asked.

"I don't know but we have to be prepared for that contingency."

"Agreed," Bill said.

"We'll figure something out," Sam assured him.

"I know you will," Thomas said. "You guys always do. I have to go check in with Dr. Matsushita now."

"You're favorite person in the world," Bill joked.

"Tell me about it. Every time I see his face I just want to punch it."

"And who's going to stop you from doing just that?" Sam proposed.

"Cure first," Thomas said, "and then anything goes. I'll catch up with you later."

"Roger that."

Thomas left them behind as he headed down the hallway towards the lab. On his way he ran into Robert Duncan and came to a stop, a frown on his face.

"Thomas, I need to talk with you."

"What the hell do you want?" Thomas demanded. "You sold us out."

The DCI put his hands up. "Easy. It's not like that."

"So Russell wasn't executed, in front of you, while you did absolutely nothing about it?"

"I had to play along so I could stay close to the project and make sure you and your family were going to be treated right."

"Sure, I understand," Thomas sarcastically replied. "And that worked out so well. Dr. Glover didn't torture me, Gavin or Emily whatsoever you sonofabitch."

"I understand your frustration but the President took over calling the shots once he realized the Russians were hunting you."

"I can't believe I let you talk me into moving to Virginia so you could run tests on us. I must have been an idiot to think I could trust you."

"I never intended for any of this to happen."

Thomas shook his head. "I tell myself the same thing every single day. But look around us now Robert. The world knows exactly who and what we are, aside from the obvious fact the human race is in the process of being wiped out. And you know who's ultimately responsible for that? I am. I should have killed Dr. Matsushita when I had the chance. Instead I made the assumption that the fire would finish him off. So this shit storm is all on me. Now get out of my way before I do something to you."

Thomas pressed on but Robert grabbed his arm.

"Don't!" Thomas warned him.

Robert let Thomas go. "I don't agree with what the President's done, alright? I haven't betrayed you. I came back here to help under the guise of making sure the cure is created."

"Bullshit. You told Nikolay everything about us."

"You're not the only one who was tortured Thomas. I held out until he threatened to cut up my wife right in front of me. I'm sorry but I dare you to say you wouldn't have talked if our roles had been reversed."

Thomas let the DCI's words hang in the air for a few seconds. "You said you came back to help us. How?"

"What do you need?"

"I don't know. The President has pardoned us but who's to say he'll keep his word. Our world, or what's left of it after all of this, still knows who we are so we'll never feel safe anywhere we go."

The DCI nodded. "Assuming that the cure is created, distributed, and you all make it out of here alive, it sounds like you need a sanctuary of sorts, is that it?"

"That'll help, but it's just a start. Everything's different now because Sam and Bill's kids are now part of this."

"One thing at a time but I have an idea you might want to consider."

"I'm all ears."

Robert stepped closer and whispered his plan into Thomas' ear.

* * *

"Hello Thomas," Dr. Matsushita said as Thomas walked past the guards and entered the lab.

Thomas grimaced as he stepped closer to check on the doctor's work.

"How's the cure coming along?"

"I never thought we'd be collaborating together again, Thomas."

"Shut up Yamato."

A smile formed on the doctor's face. "Oh, temper temper."

Thomas didn't waste any time. "Why did you do this? Why kill innocent people?"

"Maybe I did it so you and your family wouldn't have to hide from anyone ever again, well, you know, because they'll be no left alive. Ha!"

"Bullshit."

Yamato shrugged. "You're right, probably not."

"Then why?"

Yamato stopped working. "When the United States dropped those atomic bombs my entire world ceased to exist in the blink of an eye. I vowed revenge and grew older with that ball of hatred inside me. That hatred grew as the years progressed and I continually criticized myself for not having taken any action. But four years ago I was given an opportunity by Victor Bannon, and it was an opportunity I couldn't pass up. Once I broke your genetic code I was flooded with endless possibilities of how I might finally enact my revenge."

"You should have died in that fire," Thomas stated, a strong edge in his voice.

Yamato caressed his burned right arm as the memories danced in his mind.

"Perhaps, but I didn't. And here we are because of that moment in time, talking while the world continues to dissolve into chaos and death above us."

"You're a monster and what happened to your family was during a time of war."

"That's no excuse," Yamato snapped. "My family and I were collateral damage to a war we weren't even involved in."

"Admit it, you hatred has grown so much that even you are blind to the rampant destruction and deaths of millions of people around the world. They don't deserve any of this and I promise you're going to pay for what you have done."

"On the contrary, Thomas, the world is going to die a painful death, but it's on you. You allowed this to happen. Without you I could have never sowed such devastation."

"You can't put this on me. You don't know what you're talking about. You're insane."

"Insane? Dedicated is more like it and remember that I'm the only one that can cure this plague in time. Ironic, isn't it?"

"You're sick and demented."

"Sticks and stones, Thomas, sticks and stones. Besides, I'll let you in on a little secret."

"What?"

"I've always had the cure for the outbreak. The truth is I just wanted to make a point."

Thomas was stunned as Yamato's admission hung in the air.

"You have the cure?"

"Yes. It's right here."

Motherfucker. "You know they're never going to let you leave here alive, right? You must get that."

"We'll see about that," Yamato replied.

"There's nothing you can do about it. Your power is gone."

Yamato grinned which sent a chill down Thomas' spine. "Is it? My mind has only been blocked on how to use my ability. By now, my dear Thomas, we both know how easy it is to manipulate minds."

* * *

Eleven hours later Dr. Matsushita handed off the cure to the DCI who then gave it to a group of scientists. They confirmed its validity after putting it through a battery of tests. Soon afterward additional labs, across the country, began to mass produce the cure while everyone at Building 42 was injected with it. The DCI, pleased with the results, spoke over the phone with the President and filled him in on the successful prognosis.

"Dr. Matsushita had the cure the entire time, sir."

"That sonofabitch," the President angrily replied. "I want him permanently incarcerated so he can be tried and then executed."

"I'll see to it. What about the timing of the cure's dispersal?"

"I've been informed we need two days."

"Two days, sir? Millions more will be dead by then."

"It can't be helped. The plan is to load rockets with the cure and detonate them in the atmosphere over our country, especially populated areas. People will breathe the particles in and become immune."

The DCI nodded. "I understand. That's far more efficient than trying to communicate the cure is available and putting additional personnel at risk."

"Exactly." The President paused. "Listen Robert. You've done a good thing. I hope we can move forward together and put all this behind us. Our country still needs you."

"Thank you, Mr. President, but you know exactly where I stand. You are not fit to hold the office of the Presidency and I will make sure you are held responsible for the murders that you ordered."

"I'm sorry to hear you say that, Robert. I officially accept your resignation and relieve you of your responsibilities as Director of Central Intelligence. Consider yourself confined to the facility. If you attempt to leave I will have you shot."

"You'll pay for this, sir."

"No, I'm the President and I'll sweep this under the carpet like it never happened. Goodbye Robert."

51

Saturday November 17, 2001

A few hours later Robert Duncan, just after midnight, cautiously entered Hobbes and Gabbi's room, with a backpack over his shoulder and eased the door closed behind him. The DCI walked over to Hobbes' bed, knelt down and shook him awake.

"Hobbes," he whispered, "wake up."

Hobbes mumbled something and rolled over. Robert nudged him again and Hobbes' eyes slowly opened.

"What' going on?" he asked sleepily. "Who's there?"

"Hobbes, it's me."

Hobbes shifted and turned on the lamp next to his bed. The low watt bulb did it's best to illuminate the room. Hobbes frowned.

"You'd better have a damn good reason for being here," he growled.

"I'm not here to hurt you," Robert assured him.

"You won't get the chance," Gabbi said behind him.

Robert turned and saw that Gabbi held a desk chair over her head and was prepared to use it on him. He held up his hands.

"Thomas sent me. I come in peace."

"Thomas?" Hobbes questioned. "None of us trust you so tell us why he suddenly does?"

"I resigned as DCI directly to the President after I told him I was going to expose him for the murders he'd sanctioned. I also held him personally responsible for the epidemic the world's currently reeling from. He then informed me that he was going to sweep this entire 'mess' under the carpet and confined me to this facility."

Gabbi lowered the chair back to the floor as Robert continued.

"The President will have me silenced and buried in an unmarked grave. I told this to Thomas and he already suspected as much, as do the others, that even though you've all been pardoned and are free to leave, that none of you ever will. Thomas believes that once the cure is distributed the President will recant and they'll once again become scientific experiments."

"So what is Thomas planning to do about it?" Gabbi asked.

"To fight, when the time comes. But he asked me to get the two of you out of here."

"No way," Hobbes told him. "They need our help."

"I'm with Hobbes on this one," Gabbi said.

Robert shook his head. "I understand your loyalty and the need to stay together, but when the shit hits the fan the fact is you'll only get in the way. Thomas said, and I quote, 'tell them they don't have the power to fight alongside us and the only thing I want is for them to be safe and out of harm's way'."

"If that's true then why didn't Thomas tell us himself?" Gabbi queried.

"Because he knows his movements are being constantly tracked and monitored."

"Alright," Hobbes said, "then why should Gabbi and I trust you? You betrayed everyone."

"My wife and I were tortured into betraying you and I'm sorry for that. And I swear I didn't know Russell was going to be shot in front of you just to prove a point. He was my friend too. I need to make the President, Dr. Glover and Dr. Matsushita pay for what they've done, but now's not the time. We have to leave."

"What? Now?"

Robert nodded and looked at his watch. "In three minutes there's going to be some sort of distraction."

"A distraction?" Gabbi asked.

"Yes. During that time the three of us, and Emma, are going to use that diversion to flee this facility."

"And go where?"

"Initially we'll go south to Las Vegas. Once there we'll figure out our next move." He paused. "Listen, I understand if you don't trust me or if you don't want to go. I have to get my wife and I out of here before sunrise, period."

"Where is she?" Hobbes asked.

"Emma's right outside the door."

"Okay, but what about the state of the country?" Gabbi asked. "Will Las Vegas be safe?"

"I don't know. It was ravaged but you both received your injection of the cure, right?"

"Yes."

"Yes."

"Then all we have to do is defend ourselves until the cure is dispersed two days from now." He checked his watch again. "Two minutes. Are you coming?"

Hobbes and Gabbi shared a glance and then nodded to each other.

"Good," Robert said. He opened his backpack and pulled out two white lab coats. "Get dressed and put these on."

* * *

Fire alarms emanated their shrill wails throughout Building 42. Seconds later an automated voice instructed the facility's inhabitants to evacuate in an orderly manner.

"Let's move," Robert said to his wife, Hobbes and Gabbi. "But stay close."

The four of them hurried down the corridor as doctors, scientists, support staff and off duty guards opened their own room doors and joined them in the hallway as everyone headed towards the large elevator. Once there they stepped inside the elevator and moved to the rear as it filled up. As soon as the elevator reached capacity the doors closed and it shot to the surface, dispensing everyone aboard into the hanger. The doors closed and the elevator descended to retrieve the next group. Armed guards were stationed across the hanger entrance to prevent anyone from leaving.

"Now what?" Emma whispered.

"Follow me," Robert told them, "and look confident."

With Robert in the lead the four approached one of the guards.

"Halt," the man ordered.

"Take it easy Sergeant. I'm the Director of Central Intelligence."

"Yes, sir, I know who you are, but we have orders to keep Building Forty-two on lockdown."

"I'm countermanding those orders, Sergeant. I've been given orders to escort these two scientists, along with my wife, to a top secret location to further develop the cure."

"On whose orders, sir?"

"The President of the United States. Now get out of my way, these two have millions of people to save and every second we stand here arguing means the loss of more innocent lives."

The soldier stood fast, his eyes searching the ex-DCI's face for a hint of deception. After an excruciating long six seconds he finally responded.

"Very good, sir. Be careful out there."

"Thank you Sergeant, we will."

The four strode out of the hanger towards an enclosed aviation fence in the distance.

"Don't look back," Robert told them, "and keep walking. We're almost there."

When they reached the fence Robert scanned his badge. The gate beeped open and they walked through.

"That one," Robert said and pointed at a mid-sized helicopter.

"I didn't know you were a pilot," Hobbes said.

"Neither did I," Gabbi added.

"He's full of surprises," Emma told them as they climbed onboard.

Robert pulled his right door shut and began the startup process as Emma closed the front left door. Hobbes and Gabbi piled into the back seat.

"Get your seatbelts on." Robert looked over and saw a few of the guards pointing at them. "I think this is going to get bumpy."

As the propellers started to spin up six guards began to sprint towards them.

"Oh shit, they're coming," Gabbi informed them.

"I see them," Robert replied. "But I still need twenty more seconds."

"They'll be here before that!" Hobbes exclaimed.

"I know! I know!"

The guards made it to the fence, badged themselves in and raised their weapons at the occupants inside the helicopter thirty feet away.

"Fifteen seconds. Come on you piece of shit."

"Get out of the helicopter!" one of the guards yelled and made a motion with his arm that indicated the same intent. The six men fanned out in a semicircle, their rifles up and ready to fire.

"Ten seconds."

"Exit now or you will be fired upon!"

"Fuck, they're going to kill us," Hobbes uttered.

Emma turned her head towards her husband. "I love you."

Robert never had a chance to reply as Emma disengaged her seatbelt and burst out of the helicopter, her door left wide open.

"NOOO!" he screamed after his wife.

Emma ran straight at one of the guards, screaming at the top of her lungs. The guard depressed his trigger and shot her three times. Blood, from her exit wound, sprayed into the cockpit, across the console and Robert's face. Her body pitched backwards from the bullet impacts and landed on the pavement.

"NOOOOOO!" Robert screamed as a beep sounded from the console that indicated the propellers were at speed.

The other guards turned to reacquire their targets in the helicopter.

"GOGOGOGOGO!" Gabbi shouted. "GETUSINTHEFUCKINGAIR!"

Robert, knowing his wife sacrificed herself for their freedom, pulled hard on the throttle while stomping down hard on the right rudder. The helicopter lifted off the ground and pivoted to the right, bullets impacting its side rather than the windshield. As the rudder spun around the guards had no choice than to dive out of the way or be chewed up. In that moment Robert centered the rudder and pushed forward on the cyclic stick. The craft shot forward, soared over the fence and flew just feet off the ground as they made their escape across the enormous desert complex known as Area-51.

52
Saturday November 17, 2001

Later that same morning the President, from the depths and safety of NORAD, made a televised announcement.

"My fellow Americans, I send this message of hope out to those that are huddled in your houses and afraid to go outside. I send this message to those that have experienced the horror that this plague has bestowed upon our world and have lost all hope. And I send this message out to all other countries we share this planet with. We have the cure.

"We're currently mass-producing this cure and forty-eight hours from now we will distribute it throughout the United States in one fell swoop. The cure will be loaded onto rockets, launched into the atmosphere and detonated. The cure, heavier than air, will float down to the surface to be breathed in. From that moment on you will become immune to this outbreak. Until then, stay indoors and ride this out.

"I know our country was brought to the brink of disaster, and millions of lives have been lost, but we are strong. We will survive and rebuild as a nation, and we will do it together. With that said I need each and every one of you to help me with this endeavor. America isn't the only country that's suffered and unfortunately our planet will continue to suffer for the next two days until the cure is dispersed. Until then stay strong and stay safe."

The President remained fixated on the camera in front of him for a few more seconds until the overhead light dimmed.

"And we're out. Thank you Mr. President."

POTUS stood up from behind the Oval Office desk, a mere production façade to fool anyone watching that he had sent his message from the White House.

"Phone calls are already coming in from heads of state," a staff member said. "They want the cure."

"Of course they do," the President replied. "Send it to all of them, whether they've requested it or not."

"Yes, sir."

One of his aides walked up to him and whispered in his ear. "We have a situation."

The President walked with his aide to a secluded corner of the room. "What is it?"

"Early this morning Robert Duncan, along with three others identified as Emma Duncan, Hobbes and Gabbi, escaped from the confines of Building Forty-two and fled Area Fifty-One in a helicopter under the cover of darkness."

Shit. "What? How could this have happened?"

"Sir, a diversion was used, a fire alarm to be precise. During the evacuation the DCI countermanded your orders and boarded a helicopter."

"So you're telling me that all four of them escaped?"

"No, sir. There was one casualty."

"Who?"

"Emma Duncan, sir. She was shot and killed."

Fuck. If Robert didn't want to hang me out to dry before then he sure as hell does now. "Have there been any reports on their current whereabouts?"

"The helicopter was picked up briefly entering Las Vegas airspace, but it was only for a moment. Nothing since, sir."

Dammit. "I want them found."

"Yes, sir."

"And I want assurances that Thomas, or any of the others, never step foot out of Building Forty-two."

*   *   *

The entire family had gathered together in a single room, as a precaution, once rumors began to circulate that Emma had been shot during the escape.

"Do you think Hobbes, Gabbi and Robert got out?" Julie asked.

"I hope so," Thomas stated. "I can't believe that Emma's dead."

Sam spoke up. "But now we know for certain that they are going to detain us."

"That's just a fancy word for keeping us prisoners," Bill said. "Why are we still sitting here and not fighting for our own freedom?"

"And go where?" Kim told her husband. "We have nothing. No money; no vehicles; and no place where we'd ever be safe. Presidential pardons or not, we're currently holding the short end of the stick."

"Maybe," Bill conceded, "but the longer we stay here willingly the more time the President will realize he's made a mistake."

"Bill's right," Sam said. "They have their cure and we're responsible for taking Dr. Matsushita out of play for them. There's nothing standing in their way from putting you back on that table and letting Dr. Glover continue to work on you."

Laura visibly shuddered and Sam caught it.

"Sorry Laura," Sam told her. "I'm just trying to make a point."

"You definitely made it," she replied, "and I know we're all on the same page, and that means we all need to get out of here."

"And how do we do that?" Julie asked. "There are guards and cameras everywhere, not to mention the only way to the surface is in that one elevator."

"We can try brute force," Sam offered, "but we wouldn't get far."

Bill nodded. "Yeah, not with the entire complex rigged with gas. We'd be out before we made any significant progress, not to mention having to contend with an unknown amount of guards on the surface; gunships; satellites…"

"Okay, okay," Thomas said, "we get it. So we need to create a list of what we need and where it's located."

Sam nodded. "For example, the Armory will have gas masks and small arms."

"Exactly," Thomas said. "But we're going to need much more than that to make it in the real world. We need money, a place to hide, supplies and a method of transportation to get us wherever that is. And we have to definitely figure out some of those answers while we're still guests here at Groom Lake."

53
Monday November 19, 2001

Around the world millions continued to die, ravaged by the plague. However, some were just plain unlucky as people who thought there was nothing left to lose chose to add to the anarchy. Murders, rapes and violence overwhelmed the cities and their streets. Lawlessness abounded and some people took full advantage of it. Bodies cluttered and clogged the roads, strewn haphazardly; their expressions forever etched in pain and anguish.

For those that had been lucky enough to avoid the plague altogether, or had sequestered themselves behind barricaded doors, remained fearful while the world they once knew burned like they'd never experienced before.

Anarchy ruled the streets as the true hearts of men were revealed.

* * *

Two days later, after a whirlwind of mass production and engineering, the United States was ready to disperse the cure into the atmosphere. Five hundred nuclear tipped missiles had had their atomic payloads substituted and were all now in the final phase of prelaunch. Deep within NORAD a multitude of operators worked the consoles as the President looked on.

"Three-three-five through three-four-nine just came online in Nebraska. I'm showing green across the board. Please confirm."

"Roger that. Confirmed."

"I now show that all birds are green and prepared to fly."

"Green confirmed. Stand by." The operator turned to the President. "Sir, awaiting your launch authorization."

The President watched the enormous main screen and absorbed the incredible amount of work that had been accomplished in so little time. Missile trajectories crisscrossed the United States and were overlaid with cure disbursement projections.

We've lost so much in such a short amount of time, but we've also come a long way. I will be the world's savior and will take us into the next era of mankind.

The President swiveled his head and looked at a smaller screen to the right that constantly monitored the status of the Russian fleet and frowned.

If Demian Anatolievich thinks he can continue to threaten the United States then he's sorely mistaken. I'll give him just one more day before I blow his ships out of the water.

"Sir?"

The President refocused on the task at hand and addressed the servicemen and women in the room.

"Each of us here has been tainted by this deadly plague as it indiscriminately decimated one populated area after another across this great country. Its reign of terror ends now and we will take back this country. My authorization is omega-five-niner-sierra-charlie-xray."

The operator punched in the President's code. "Authorization identified and accepted. On your mark, sir."

"Fire."

Across the country silos spewed missiles into the sky and left white trails in their wakes.

"What's the countdown?"

"Two minutes until synchronized detonation, Mr. President."

"Very good. Carry on."

All eyes watched and never wavered from the monitors as the computers tracked each missile's progress and displayed it in real-time. The first minute ticked by at an agonizing slow pace for everyone in the command center.

"Sixty seconds."

I will rebuild this nation and make it stronger than ever before. And to accomplish that I'll need to utilize Thomas Clark and his family of freaks. Their powers, if properly harnessed, will elevate our country to a position of dominance; a position that can never be rivaled. But sacrifices will be made along the way, and those responsible for our current dilemma will pay the ultimate price; isn't that right, Dr. Matsushita?

"Twenty seconds."

The President stared silently at the screen as the seconds ticked down.

"Five seconds."

"Four"

"Three."

"Two."

"One."

"We have detonation."

Satellites, who had been visually tracking hundreds of missiles, captured the exact moment as all five hundred rockets exploded in unison, at the edge of space. The air, above the United States, became chock-full of the cure as it rapidly filled the empty space and began its gradual descent back towards the Earth. Cheers instantly saturated the command center as a multitude of congratulatory hugs and handshakes were exchanged.

An operator took that moment to change the clock to display two hours. He then punched a button and it started to count down.

"Two hours until ground saturation is fully attained, Mr. President."

* * *

Throughout the country the effects of the cure, as it was breathed into lungs, were immediate. Nodules, on hundreds of thousands of infected people, shriveled and fell off their bodies within minutes, their smallpox symptoms annihilated. Chaos still gripped the infected zones as buildings continued to burn and bodies littered the streets. But for the moment a new sense of hope washed over the country.

The President having seen the results, from a variety of video footage, took to the air waves to make a new announcement.

"My fellow Americans, we have prevailed. The cure has been spread and all you need to do is go outside and breathe the air. Look outside and you'll know this to be true. It's time to celebrate!

"And now that this plague has been eradicated we need to come together to rebuild this grand nation of ours. Your government, along with your help, is committed to your survival and long-term prosperity. With that being said I have ordered FEMA into the most heavily affected zones with the assurance that they will have medical and relief teams in place within twelve hours.

"Stay strong and keep your chins up because the worst is now behind us."

The President ended his speech and continued to look at the camera until the lights dimmed.

"And we're out."

He got up from the desk and made a beeline to his underground office where he immediately dialed a well-known number.

"That was a very moving speech, Mr. President. Congratulations on saving humanity. What are your plans now? Going to Disneyland?"

The President wasn't amused. "Move your fleet away from my coastline, President Anatolievich, or I will destroy it."

"Temper, temper, Mr. President. Consider it done. Now, with that bit of unpleasant business behind us, perhaps we should talk about your upcoming plans for Mr. Clark and his family."

"Plans? What plans? Mr. Clark is dead and so is Dr. Matsushita. Whatever future we were going to extract from them is no longer viable."

"Oh come now. You really don't expect me to buy that explanation, do you?"

"I don't care either way."

"Exactly my point, Mr. President. We both know you still have them and just like we both know you're going to keep experimenting on them."

"I can't stop you from thinking that."

"No, of course not. But know this. We'll be watching and waiting. Now, I will commend you on this cure. My people inform me that we'll be ready to spread it ourselves within the next twenty-four hours. Course, can you imagine what the public would think of you if they ever learned that you were the one responsible for the outbreak? It boggles the mind."

The President gripped the phone tightly as Demian Anatolievich continued.

"But that doesn't matter for the moment. I'll just hold that bit of information in my back pocket for a rainy day because right now we're both going to be extremely busy rebuilding our country's infrastructure. Take care, Mr. President, and good luck."

The line went dead. *That smug sonofabitch.* He put the phone down. *It's time to move Thomas to a new location and deal with Dr. Matsushita once and for all.*

54
Tuesday November 20, 2001

The day after the rockets flew and FEMA began administering aid across the country the President, back in his real Oval Office, made a video call to Groom Lake's Building 42. When Thomas, and the rest of the family, were brought to the large room they instantly discerned that Dr. Matsushita and Dr. Glover were already in attendance. But what was more disconcerting was the excessive number of armed guards, and they all noticed that right away.

"Are you seeing this shit?" Bill whispered.

"Yeah," Sam replied. "I don't like it."

"Do you think they know about our plan?"

"I don't know. Anything's possible but we need to play along and see why they brought us here. You good, Thomas?"

Thomas hadn't taken his eyes of the two doctors since they'd entered the room and his mind was awash with murderous intent.

"Thomas?" Sam asked as he nudged his friend. "You good?"

"Yeah, I'm good."

Thomas looked back at Dr. Matsushita. *What's stopping me from snapping your neck right here, right now? The world would be much better off without you in it. But there's a chance that these guards would then open fire on my family so I can't take that risk. Not yet anyway. Count yourself lucky doctor, you sonofabitch. Your time is coming.*

The huge overhead monitor on the wall blinked on, the President's face appeared and everyone turned their attention towards it.

"Good morning everyone. I wanted to take this opportunity to thank you. The cure is a success and in time our country, and the world, will be back to normal. However, I can't stress enough how many millions of lives were lost to this plague, but I'll address Dr. Matsushita and his role in that shortly."

The President locked eyes with Thomas. "Mr. Clark, what am I going to do with you now that the former DCI, Hobbes and Gabbi have vanished and are nowhere to be found?"

"I don't see why that is any of your concern," Thomas replied. "If I'm not mistaken, we all have our pardons and are free to leave."

"This is true."

"Good. Then we're leaving right now, Mr. President."

The family took a few steps towards the exit before the President spoke up.

"Stop them. Don't let them leave."

The armed guards instantly raised their weapons. The family froze as Thomas addressed the President.

"You're a liar."

"I'm a politician, Mr. Clark. The truth is that when I issued you those pardons I actually meant it, at the time. But you need to look at this fluid situation from my point of view. Look at the impact the world has incurred as a direct result of your abilities."

"That's bullshit," Thomas spat out. "You and I both know that Dr. Matsushita was the one behind the genocidal attack on humanity."

"I don't disagree with you," the President said. "But the fact remains you have much to offer the world."

418

"You can twist your words anyway you'd like, sir, but we all know you're not one of the good guys, certainly not after sanctioning murder and then trying to justify it."

"I did what had to be done and I don't expect you to understand."

"The truth of the matter is that it was your desire, much like Dr. Matsushita's, to take from us. All you want is power, and you don't give a damn about who you step on to attain it."

The President ignored his comment. "The world has drastically changed, Mr. Clark, and we're going to need your help, whether you give it willingly or not, as we move forward."

"So you're saying our pardons are worthless?"

"No. What I'm saying is that you're new home is now Building Forty-Two. You can fight this change or you can embrace it. That's entirely up to you. In either case, welcome home."

Thomas gritted his teeth and clenched his hands as the President migrated to Dr. Matsushita.

"Yamato Takuma Matsushita."

"That's Doctor Matsushita to you."

"Perhaps, doctor, you'd like to clarify why you murdered millions of innocent people. Make me understand."

"I don't have the time, Mr. President, nor do you have the intellectual capacity."

"Wrong answer, doctor. The fact is you tried to wipe out the human race, and for that I sentence you to death."

Dr. Matsushita smiled in defiance, a gesture the President wasn't prepared for and took the bait.

"And what exactly do you find so humorous about your current situation?"

"I'm smiling because I have a two-part failsafe that I've been dying to use."

"What are yo..."

Yamato twisted around, stared straight at Emily, and spoke.

"Michelangelo."

Emily's eyes immediately glazed over. Before anyone realized what had happened she bolted away from Thomas and Laura towards Yamato.

"Em!" Thomas screamed.

Barely two seconds had passed before her hands found Yamato's arm, and when she did the command he had whispered to her, when they'd first arrived, activated. In less than a second she unlocked his mind, giving him full access to his ability that she'd taken from him. Sam and Bill rushed Yamato but he instantly took control of them, and then Thomas as well. Utilizing Sam and Bill as human shields he unleashed Thomas' full telekinetic power on the multitude of armed guards scattered throughout the room.

Thomas, unable to control his actions, stripped the guard's weapons out of their hands before they could react and dropped them in front of Sam and Bill, who in turn picked them up. The guards bodies were then tossed about the room like rag dolls; thrown back and forth to smash into one wall after another, their bones audibly splintering under the forceful impacts.

Sam and Bill, now armed and protecting Yamato, fired on the remaining guards that Thomas hadn't managed to neutralize yet. Blood sprayed the walls and their lifeless bodies hit the floor. The stench of blood, bile and gunpowder filled the room as the carnage concluded.

A mere ten seconds had passed since Yamato had spoken his failsafe word to Emily and Laura, Kim and Julie were left in utter shock. Their children, unfamiliar with such horror and bloodshed, especially at the hands of their own fathers, wouldn't let go of their mother's legs. Sam, Bill and Thomas on the other hand stood there like statues, still under Yamato's control. Dr. Glover cowered on the floor next to Dr. Matsushita, his hands over his face.

The President had watched in fascination, and in revulsion, as Dr. Matsushita used the three men to easily dispatch the guards. When it was over he tried to appear confident and restarted the conversation.

"Impressive, Dr. Matsushita. I don't know how you managed that but you must know that you're not getting out of there."

Yamato smiled again. "Do you play chess, Mr. President?"

"Occassionally. What's that have anythi…"

"I mention it because I saw the moves you were going to make long before you ever made them. I knew you would perceive me as a threat, abilities notwithstanding, and nullify me. The fact is, I allowed it to happen to make you think you had the upper hand. But your hubris got the better of you when you incorrectly decided to meet with me one-on-one."

"I don't understand."

"You don't have to."

"Enough then," the President announced. "What's to stop me from flooding that building with gas?"

"Nothing," Yamato replied. "But I'll be leaving before that could ever happen."

"You're not getting out of there."

"Oh, but I am. You see, I am the least if your worries."

421

The President grinned. "The world already has the cure. There's nothing else you can do."

"Mr. President, the world isn't prepared for what's coming."

The President's grinned faltered. "What are you talking about?"

"You thought my plague was something. Well, it wasn't. It was just the beginning. Now I'm going to make it Hell on Earth."

"Wha…"

"Remember when I told you I had a two-part failsafe? Well, I only used the first part. Here's the second part I whispered in your ear, Mr. President. Poseidon."

On the video monitor the President's face changed to one of pain. He clutched his chest as he began to have a heart attack. His torso twisted and his face contorted as he slid out of his chair and out of view. Some Secret Service agents rushed to his side from off-screen.

"Mr. President! Mr. President. Shit, he's having a heart attack. I need medical to the Oval Office right now! POTUS is down, I repeat POTUS is down!"

"Goodbye, Mr. President. The world will be better off without YOU in it."

Alarm bells started up throughout the facility as Dr. Matsushita, eyes wide, recognized he was in full control.

"And NOW for the final act!"

Yamato slowly swiveled until he and Gavin's eyes met.

"Hello young one. I saved the best for you. I hope the booster I gave you works as I intended it to."

"No!" Laura yelled. "Stay away from my son!"

Yamato ignored her pleas as Stir appeared by Gavin's side, red yes blazing. Stir promptly bounded towards Yamato, his throat in his sights. A moment before Stir would have landed the death blow he disappeared into thin air as Yamato took control of Gavin.

Yamato laughed loudly. "I'll give you props for trying, Gavin."

"Let him go!" Laura yelled.

"I don't think so. The world barely got a taste of what it's like to feel helpless and afraid, just like I did when the bombs dropped all those years ago. I only gave the world the cure so they could hold onto a glimmer of hope. But now, now I get to rip it all away!"

Gavin, under the control of Yamato, formed his portal in the middle of the room.

"Go ahead," Laura yelled. "Go on through!"

Yamato's smile was wicked. "Oh, I know what's on the other side, and now so will the rest of the world. It's time for everyone to die."

Out of the portal's depths a large hand, with talons for fingers, began to emerge. A shadowy head pushed through, its mouth ready to tear into whatever flesh it could get its hands on.

"OH SHIT! RUN!" Laura shrieked as she forced Kim, Julie and their children towards the room's exit.

Within moments the portal's exit overflowed as denizens of the Other Place rushed uncontested into the world.

Visit my website at

http://www.dwneuman.com

If you enjoyed this novel please consider taking a moment and writing a quick review about it (on Amazon). It helps me out more than you know and fuels my motivation!
Of course, word of mouth works wonders too! ;)

Thank you!

And you can look forward to the final book of the series, book ten, entitled
Shadows of the Ever-After
coming soon.

www.ingramcontent.com/pod-product-compliance
Lightning Source LLC
Chambersburg PA
CBHW072336020726
47506CB00004B/896